Wild Horizon

by F. van Wyck Mason

VALLEY FORGE, 1777

PROUD NEW FLAGS

THREE HARBOURS

RIVERS OF GLORY

GOLDEN ADMIRAL

CUTLASS EMPIRE

BLUE HURRICANE

EAGLE IN THE SKY

SILVER LEOPARD

OUR VALIANT FEW

STARS ON THE SEA

THE YOUNG TITAN

THE COLONEL NORTH STORIES

MANILA GALLEON

FIGHTING AMERICANS (*ed.*)

AMERICAN MEN AT ARMS (*ed.*)

WILD HORIZON

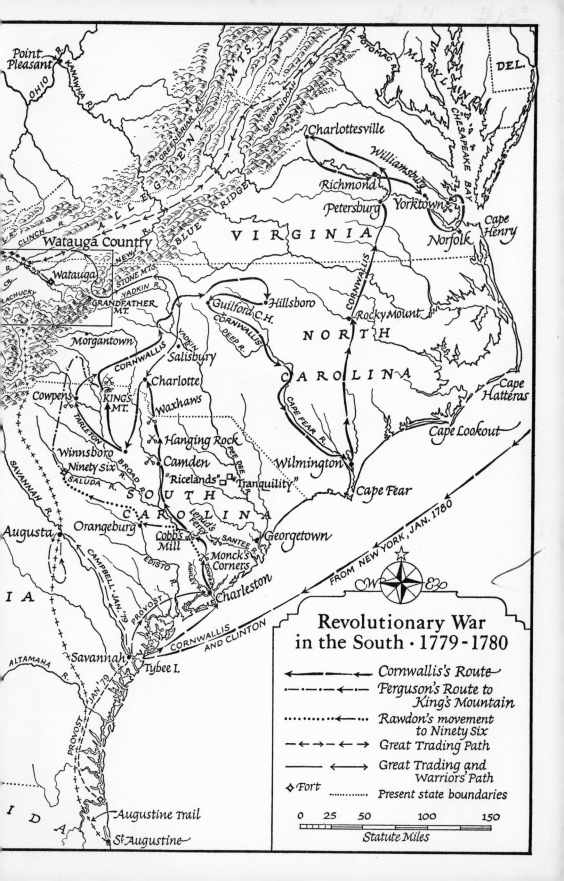

Revolutionary War
in the South · 1779–1780

- ←— ←— Cornwallis's Route
- ─·←·─ Ferguson's Route to King's Mountain
- ···←··· Rawdon's movement to Ninety Six
- ─←─←→ Great Trading Path
- ──←── Great Trading and Warriors' Path
- ◇ Fort
- ·········· Present state boundaries

0 25 50 100 150

Statute Miles

F. van Wyck Mason

F. van Wyck Mason was born in Boston and educated in Europe, and at Berkshire School and Harvard. He served with distinction in both World Wars, and his interest and experience in military matters are reflected in his books. Since he began writing in 1931, Mr. Mason has written over sixty novels, including OUR VALIANT FEW, YOUNG TITAN, EAGLE IN THE SKY and MANILA GALLEON. His books have been translated into fifteen languages, winning him wide recognition as one of our finest historical novelists. His most recent work is AMERICAN MEN AT ARMS, the best of fiction from three wars, which he selected and introduced.

Wild Horizon
by F. van Wyck Mason

Drawings by SAMUEL H. BRYANT

Little, Brown and Company · Boston · Toronto

Published simultaneously in Canada
by Little, Brown & Company (Canada) Limited

PRINTED IN THE UNITED STATES OF AMERICA

For
those fine, understanding friends
Richard and Kay Mann

Foreword

WHEN one lists what generally are considered to be the decisive battles of the American War for Independence only Saratoga and the Siege of Yorktown as a rule are selected. However, recently it has become realized that there was a third battle which, although involving comparatively few troops, nonetheless served as a very definite turning point in the outcome of that protracted and world-changing conflict.

This battle also is important as the decisive engagement of the First Civil War — which was fought as a war within a war — by Americans against Americans. In this case embittered Loyalist Americans who supported the British Crown were pitted against American Patriots who as fiercely and often just as savagely supported the cause of Independence.

The Battle of King's Mountain, fought on October 7, 1780, in which only one British Regular was present, was unique because of the ferocity displayed by both sides.

But for the raw courage of the "Over-mountain Boys," Patriot refugees and frontiersmen already settled in western North Carolina and Virginia, the War for Independence might have ended as many of the best American generals and statesmen for a time expected — with a general retreat of their defeated armies and devoted civilians across the Alleghenies where they intended that still another young Republic should rise, phoenix-like, from the ashes of defeat.

The first part of this story covers efforts made to prepare a reception for this mass of refugees. Much has been written about the dangers and privations suffered considerably later on by emigrants to the West and to the far West, but who ever has heard of the sufferings and inarticulate heroism of the members of two expeditions which struggled out to Kentucky and middle Tennessee during the terrible winter of 1779-1780?

These ill-equipped and largely inexperienced bands of civilians were led respectively by Lieutenant-Colonel James Robertson and Lieutenant-Colonel John Donelson, both renowned frontier fighters. Since space did not permit a description of the tribulations and fate of both expeditions I decided to describe, as well as I could, the adventures and almost incredible hardships suffered by the party which was headed by James Robertson — not that John Donelson's long midwinter voyage down the Holston and Tennessee Rivers was any less colorful or arduous.

Of all the many characters appearing in this volume only a very few are completely imaginary. These include the Valentine and Colcord families, Dr. Samuel Mason, Saul Black Buck and Parthenia Bryant. All the rest bear at least the names of persons who lived and were present at the time and places indicated. Among such characters are Timothy Murphy, the famous sharpshooter of Saratoga; the Tory, George Walker; Major du Buysson and Colonel Armand. Joe Drake, Cash Brooks, Thomas Sharp Spencer, Isaac Bledsoe and other frontiersmen basically are all authentic characters.

A great number of instances and details which might appear to the reader to be products of the author's imagination actually happened, such as the adventures of Jonathan Robertson; the raid on Fairlawn; the punishment of George Walker; and Thomas Sharp Spencer's feats of strength. Needless to say, military engagements and maneuvers are reproduced as accurately as a painstaking and selective research can render them.

I wish herewith to acknowledge the invaluable assistance and coopera- tion of the following scholarly ladies and gentlemen: Mrs. Frank L. Owsley, Director of the Tennessee State Library and Archives; Mrs. Harriette Simpson Arnow of Ann Arbor, Michigan, whose excellent *Seedtime on the Cumberland* was a source of much invaluable incident and detail; Mrs. Clara Mae Brown, Reference Librarian of the Joint University Libraries, Nashville, Tennessee; Mr. Lawrence S. Thompson, Director of Libraries for the University of Kentucky; Mr. Howard L. Applegate, Administrator of Manuscripts, Carnegie Library, Syracuse University, New York; and most especially Miss Katharine Lyford of the Library of the Boston Athenaeum, whose help has been most gen- erous. Finally, my greatest thanks are due to my wife and secretary, Jeanne Hand Mason, for her devoted and untiring efforts in behalf of this volume.

Hampton Head   F. van Wyck Mason
Southampton, Bermuda
May 1, 1966

Contents

PROLOGUE: *September, 1779*   3

BOOK I

The Great Hunting Ground

1. Colonel Sevier's Ill News   11
2. The Point   23
3. The Mauling   29
4. Samuel Mason, M.D.   34
5. Revelations by Firelight, I   38
6. Revelations by Firelight, II   51
7. Dying Moon   55
8. Jonathan Robertson, Aetat Eleven   60
9. The Giant   66
10. Crisis   76
11. Experiment with the Future   80
12. Carpenter's Station   82
13. The Twins   92
14. The Gentle Art of Persuasion   98
15. The Raft   106
16. Bullet in the Back   116
17. Warm Interlude   121
18. The Hostiles   125
19. By the Riverside   128
20. Showdown   132
21. The War Party   141
22. The Surprise   147
23. Break-up   156
24. Dr. Mason's Portfolio, I   161
25. Dr. Mason's Portfolio, II   168
26. Chance Encounter   179
27. Camp Misery   188

BOOK II

No Band of Brothers

1.	Ricelands	199
2.	Sails off Tybee Island	205
3.	Rebel! Rebel!	212
4.	Tory! Tory!	216
5.	Colonel Washington's Headquarters	223
6.	Threatened City	228
7.	Brother-in-Law	242
8.	First of the Green Dragoon	250
9.	Letter to Laura	258
10.	Monck's Corner	263
11.	Fair Lawn, I	270
12.	Fair Lawn, II	280
13.	Flotsam of Defeat	284
14.	Nadir	289
15.	The Fugitives	293
16.	Colonel Armand	299
17.	Last Resort	306

BOOK III

Phoenix Republic

1.	Over the Crest	315
2.	Woods Colt	319
3.	The Movers	325
4.	The Road to Watauga	331
5.	Frail Nemesis	338
6.	Sycamore Shoals, I	343
7.	Sycamore Shoals, II	348
8.	Sycamore Shoals, III	354
9.	Jollification	364
10.	"The Sword of the Lord and of Gideon"	369
11.	King's Mountain	373
12.	Aftermath	384
	EPILOGUE	389

Wild Horizon

September, 1779

SELDOM, decided Lieutenant-Colonel John Sevier, had he more thoroughly appreciated the beauties of such a fine, warm and crystal-clear September day. Riding a few yards in advance of his escort, a file of eight grimy, sunburnt troopers who, because they'd been drawn from various units, were haphazardly equipped and uniformed, the Colonel made the most of this unfamiliar sense of well-being. Opportunity to indulge in such relaxation had been rare during the past four years. Yes. To be able to slack his reins, to ease his long and wiry body in the saddle and allow his dusty black charger to select its own pace in crossing this wide and nearly treeless plain approached sheer bliss. Frankly, the Colonel had had more than his bellyfull of battles, cold, heat, interminable marches and death in all its hideous guises.

The hatchet-faced officer allowed cavernous eyes, dull and red-rimmed by fatigue, to wander over a succession of low, gently rounded foothills rising through a faint blue haze towards the red-bronze and yellow slopes of the Bald Mountains and the Alleghenies which towered beyond them.

"Wagh, ai-yeh!" as a Cherokee would have cried; it sure was finer than silk to have left the ravaged and hate-filled East Coast so far behind and no longer expect to come upon another burnt-out cabin about which buzzards wheeled and squabbled over decomposing bodies or perched hopefully upon trees from which flyblown corpses dangled, limp and pathetic.

Worst of it was, one never could be really sure which side should be held responsible. Such an outrage might just as well have been perpetrated by one of many British-led Tory detachments which vied with bands of equally savage American irregulars in ravaging the back country and murdering without compunction anyone even suspected of favoring the enemy.

John Sevier rubbed weary eyes before again surveying the Alleghenies' eon-softened summits, which suggested a series of gigantic blue-green billows, lying at least another full day's ride farther on.

How wonderfully peaceful was the surrounding countryside! This far west of the theater of war it was most unlikely that even small bands of Tories or Patriotic irregulars would be operating. Beyond a few small and widely scattered settlements there was nothing worth the attention of these white savages.

Of course, on the far side of those haze-blurred mountains lurked many terrors of a different sort; with these he was all too familiar. Well, right now he didn't intend to worry about them. He pulled out and began to suck on a blackened and short-stemmed clay pipe, for all it was cold and didn't taste good, and half listened to the faint jingling of curb chains, the rattle of his sword in the scabbard strapped under his left knee and the rhythmic *creak-creak* of saddle leather.

A bee droned by sleepily. Now and then bevies of brown-and-white bobwhites burst out of the tall, yellowing hay grass and scattered like fragments from an exploding bomb. The voices of his escort sounded faint and, for once, contented. He was tempted to doze, but fought off the inclination.

For all Sevier would have preferred to travel alone on a mission of such critical importance, he reckoned maybe it was wise to have along these leathery, hard-bitten veterans. While the Cherokees were *supposed* to be at peace with the Thirteen Fires, you never could tell when some hothead young chief might get steamed up and set out to avenge the tribe's shattering defeat at Fort Watauga.

The sun's heat beat gently, soothingly through the officer's dusty, threadbare and often mended uniform tunic of dark blue serge with its spotted and stained dull red cuffs and lapel facings. He hated to be seen like this. In normal times, courtly and soft-spoken John Sevier was known to be something of a dandy.

Once this narrow track — pretentiously described as "the Charlotte Pike" — took a southwesterly direction, Sevier sighed, roused himself to study the terrain immediately ahead. The nearest foothills, he saw, were speckled with vivid patches of scarlet, yellow and orange foliage and rose gradually from the meadows he and his party had traversed. The nearest hill, a chimneylike monolith, thrust out of the earth straight up, like a great stone blade. Its base was concealed by a ring of hardwoods dappled by bright autumnal tints.

A tiny dot in the cloudless, golden-blue sky, a huge hawk, wheeling on motionless pinions, whistled, a cry so faint that it seemed to have been let in by a pinhole made in the heavens.

Even while relapsing to his comfortable half-doze, Sevier made note that perhaps a quarter of a mile ahead the Pike disappeared among a clump of scarlet maples flaming about the base of the rock chimney. Idly, he noted that on that tall rock's summit an eagle's nest showed as a crazy tangle of sticks. Long since, the eaglets reared way up there must have spread uncertain wings and flapped away.

The soft, not unmusical obligato played by hoofs upon the dry earth so far increased Sevier's relaxation that his head definitely commenced to nod under a rusty black tricorn. Vaguely, Sevier wondered how long his party would take to cross the mountains. Perhaps two or, more probably, three days. This detail hadn't been able to make good time after some of the troopers' mounts had cast shoes; they'd go lame if ridden at speed over any distance and that wouldn't fit in with his plans at all, at all.

Sleepily, he conjectured about the conditions he'd find among the Watauga settlements — always provided any of them still existed. Nowadays, news trickled across the Alleghenies so slowly and uncertainly that a sudden Indian outbreak might have annihilated those feeble little outposts weeks ago without anybody in the East even hearing about it.

The sharp-faced officer briefly debated halting in order to relight his pipe with the tinder pistol he invariably carried, but ended by dropping his pipe into a side pocket. He then roused sufficiently to glance back at his escort. Judging from the way a pair of troopers were sagging forward in their saddles with forearms crossed over cantles, they must have fallen sound asleep. Others of the bearded or long-unshaven cavalrymen had rendered themselves comfortable by riding sidewise or with one leg hooked over the equipment strapped in front of them. They looked as if all they wanted in life was to dismount, water their horses, fill their canteens and then sleep the clock around.

Sevier calculated that one of the many brooks which came purling and splashing prettily down from the mountains probably would be discovered among those gay, autumn-tinted trees crowding about the rock chimney's base.

After smothering a yawn he called back, "Rouse up, boys! Soon's we reach yonder woods we'll dismount and —"

His sentence remained unfinished, for from the woods ahead burst at least a dozen puffs of smoke instantly followed by as many hard, slamming reports. Musket balls buzzed by like gigantic hornets. Behind Sevier one of his men uttered a piercing yell and fell heavily off his horse. More shots rapped out; then out over the meadow charged a swarm of horsemen, some wearing scarlet tunics, some in Tory green regimentals; others were clad in rough civilian garb. Their screeching yells and whoops beat clearly, menacingly through the warm, still air.

That more of his escort had been hit Sevier knew by screams and agonized cries rising behind him.

Savagely reproaching himself, Sevier bent low in his saddle and spurred hard. How *could* he have allowed himself to get so goddam careless — especially when bearing intelligence of such vital importance as that with which he'd been entrusted? In a cold rage he snatched out both ponderous horse pistols he carried strapped in heavy holsters at either side of his pommel. Over the quickened drumming of his charger's hoofs he only half heard sibilant *zweeps* caused by sabers being jerked free of their scabbards.

A few pistols banged as in an irregular double rank the enemy at an extended gallop pounded forward to ride down the hopelessly disconcerted Americans.

Sevier, guiding his horse with his knees, cocked both pistols and made straight for a purple-faced British officer galloping well out in advance of his men. A good thing this thick-bodied Britisher — a lieutenant by his single epaulet of tarnished silver lace — hadn't possessed sufficient patience to wait in ambush for only a few moments longer. Had he done so, the American detail must have been destroyed in its entirety.

John Sevier's entire consciousness focused itself on the English officer, who also had snatched out horse pistols. The other's bay horse surged straight at him, a large white blaze on its forehead flashing in the warm sunlight. The Colonel extended his right arm to full length, then fired, but was unaware of his pistol's recoil, for the Englishman's flushed, contorted face vanished beyond a sudden blossom of gray smoke; it then reappeared, magically dissolved into a crimson pulp. With a burst of speed, Sevier's charger carried him past the Englishman reeling helplessly in his saddle, on through rotten-smelling clouds of burnt powder.

He sensed, rather than saw, a green-uniformed Tory, who seemed to be all wide-open mouth and bared teeth, closing in with saber upswung. Desperately, Sevier slewed sidewise and just managed to dodge the Tory's whistling slash, then used his second pistol to dispose of the fellow. Again and again his spurs raked his charger's barrel. Must get away! *Must.* MUST! No matter how, he must get to Watauga.

Sevier yearned to drop the pistols, rip out his sword and charge the nearest knot of attackers, but his duty remained to win clear, for all he might be deemed a coward for deserting his men.

Later, the Colonel dimly could recall bowling over a gaunt, black-bearded fellow astride a miserable little bony horse, then caroming violently off a big English trooper who'd raised his blade but wasn't quick enough to use it.

All at once, Sevier burst into the clear and caught an unobstructed view of the woods, then started thundering along the Pike pursued hell-for-leather by a trio of well-mounted British cavalrymen.

BOOK I

The Great Hunting Ground

1. Colonel Sevier's Ill News

FLAT on his belly just beneath the crest of a steep, wooded ridge which afforded a clear, comprehensive view of Fort Patrick Henry lay Moluntha, eagle-featured War Chief of the presently dispersed but still powerful and warlike Shawnee tribe. At the moment Moluntha again was brooding over the treacherous murder of his predecessor, Chief Cornstalk, slain while visiting an American fort under a flag of truce.

Deliberately, the Shawnee's wide-set and vivid jet eyes traveled back and forth over the scene below several times, counted the roofs of shacks, huts and cabins crowded together in disorderly fashion behind an absurdly low palisade of rough-pointed pine logs which, as nearly as the Indian could make out, mounted but a single swivel gun. These dwellings also enjoyed the dubious protection of a small, two-story blockhouse.

Moluntha felt pleased on discovering that only fourteen crudely shingled roofs showed *within* that palisade which could only recently have been erected upon a long, flat and once heavily wooded peninsula. This jutting piece of territory was created by the confluence of the Holston River, deep and fast flowing, and a busy smaller stream known as the South Branch of the Watauga which came tumbling down from the mountains of western North Carolina. While a big black ant boldly explored his wrist, Moluntha made note that the Fort had been situated with a view to protecting a number of primitive boatyards in which flatboats, gundelows and even a large keelboat lay in various degrees of completion.

Yellow birch bushes and sumach which already had begun to take on the scarlet hues of autumn stirred only slightly when the War Chief beckoned Ocondago and Standing Bear to come snaking silently up beside him. The former's face was painted in wide, horizontal red-and black bands; the latter had affected a blue-and-green checkerboard design through which little bright beads of sweat were breaking.

Like their leader, these wiry young braves had taken the precaution of pushing backwards headdresses of frayed and travel-faded eagle feathers tipped in red; customarily, such were worn secured to the scalp lock in an erect position — which instantly would have been spotted by any keen-eyed person down on the peninsula.

Originally, Moluntha's scouting party had numbered five, but one brave carelessly had allowed himself to get tripped amid a vine tangle with the result that he'd been fatally gored by a rutting bull elk. Another warrior had been killed quite as dead by a rattlesnake which had slid under his blanket in search of warmth and had bitten him in the neck when the luckless fellow stirred in his sleep.

Although none of the three Shawnees would have admitted it, they were more than glad to rest for a little while. Even their tough and sinewy backs, buttocks and thighs ached from long hours of guiding bony-backed horses over some of the roughest country any of them had ever traversed. Because their buckskin leggings by now had worn thin and been torn ragged in many places their legs had been cruelly slashed and raked amid the countless cat-briar and blackberry tangles through which they had been forced to follow tough and wily James Robertson and a small party of Long Knives southward, all the way from the Great Falls of the Ohio where Moluntha's hunting party first had cut their trail.

Aside from curiosity as to what these white men were up to, the Shawnees found good reason for tracking Robertson's party so long and patiently clear across Kentucky — they were driving and protecting a sizable herd of uncommonly tall, finely conformed horses!

Long since, the War Chief and his companions had reasoned, accurately enough, that these temptingly handsome and clean-limbed animals must have been acquired by the redoubtable Colonel Robertson somewhere near Kaskaskia, where horses, as everyone knew, had been bred on lands belonging to the Illinois tribe. Thereabouts, the blood of fiery Spanish Barbary stallions ran strongly.

Unfortunately for Moluntha, no opportunity had presented itself — especially since the loss of his two braves — to stampede those desirable mounts now switching flies and grazing peacefully on a little meadow near the palisade. Colonel Robertson, former American agent among the Cherokees, had proved himself too old a hand to get caught off guard — even for a moment.

That was bad enough, but now came this alarming discovery of a new fort erected farther west in Virginia — or was it North Carolina? — than any other. Scowling, Moluntha crushed the ant, which, uncautiously, had decided to nip him, but what drew deeper furrows across his yellow-and-blue-painted forehead was the number of those canvas, bark or brush shelters which stood scattered without any semblance of order upon the peninsula behind the Fort. *Gissa!* For some time sizable parties of immigrants must have been arriving in this Watauga country.

Several groups of obviously new arrivals were unloading pack animals — there was yet no wagon road across the mountains from any direction — or busy pitching stained and weather-beaten tents among stumps left to mark the never-ending retreat of the forest.

Under the eyes of girls and half-grown boys several herds of pigs, furry brown cattle and flocks of gray-white sheep were browsing on or rooting among those giant canes which grew so tall and succulent along the banks of both rivers.

For over an hour the three Shawnees lay statue-still on the ridge making detailed mental drawings of the blockhouse, its armament and the ridiculous palisade surrounding it. Also they noted how best the defenses might be approached and penetrated when the time came — as surely it must.

The incessant loud *thud-thudding* of mauls and hammers and the rasping snarl of whipsaws at work in the boatyards created an unfamiliar and most distasteful racket in the Indians' ears.

That these white men were accompanied by their families and livestock, and had brought along every possession they could transport, was what alarmed Moluntha and his companions most of all. The people below were intending to stay wherever they decided to settle, which, inevitably, must be on land belonging to Indians, for west of the Appalachians there remained no territory legally ceded for permanent white occupation.

While a few Long Hunters might be tolerated and allowed to trap upon tribal hunting grounds for a season, it was known that such lonely characters never had betrayed an urge to clear land, to build cabins or to plant crops; nor would such men wastefully slaughter or frighten away that big game upon which the Indian depended for shelter, food and clothing. But for the tribes to permit immigrant families to settle on their principal hunting grounds would be tantamount to inviting quick ruin.

At length Moluntha tilted his narrow, strongly modeled head towards his sub-chief, Ocondago, and whispered, "How many *Americani* does my brother tally?"

"*Kish-kal-wa!*" Using hand signs, the Shawnee indicated the presence of at least three hundred people, but Standing Bear, hissing like an angry bobcat, indicated his belief that no less than five hundred whites were encamped in and around the blockhouse above which floated the red, white and blue flag of the Thirteen Fires. Although homemade, it was readily identifiable.

Moluntha started to squirm backwards off the ridge crest but checked his move because a horseman had appeared riding at a slow canter. His mount's hoofs were raising small, regularly-spaced puffs of dust along that trail which, for countless generations, war parties had used in crossing the Bald and Stone Mountain Ranges when raiding into southwestern Virginia and the Carolinas.

Soon the Shawnees could see that the rider, though small of frame, sat tall and easy in his saddle. He was wearing a black tricorn hat and a dusty blue uniform coat sporting collar, cuffs, and lapels of dull red. Presently it became apparent that this horseman must have covered a lot of ground since sunup, his bay's flanks were streaked with sweat and its strides were short, holding no hint of springiness.

Beneath the cracked and badly smeared paint applied to his forehead, Moluntha's eyes glittered and his hand closed hard over the ponderous British Tower musket lying beside him. "*Gissa!* He who yonder rides is Nolichucky Jack, himself!"

Standing Bear's vitreous black eyes asked a question.

"He is that same Colonel Sevier who helped to beat us so badly at Point Pleasant on the Great Kanawha."

The Shawnees, of course, had no way of guessing that the travel-stained rider loping along toward the fort was bringing an item of news which ultimately would shape the destinies of several nations — red and white alike.

On nearing the encampment's outer limits, the horseman waved once at a party of shirt-sleeved men engaged in felling timber for the boat builders. These waved back and beckoned, but the uniformed figure kept on until he arrived before the palisade's main gate which, as usual, was standing wide open and quite unguarded.

Frowning, Sevier stiffly dismounted, thinking: By damn! Won't these bloody greenhorns *ever* take care till it's too late?

Looping bridle reins over an arm, he heeled his mount right up to the blockhouse door, then hitched the panting animal to a post before dashing indoors.

Once Nolichucky Jack had disappeared, Moluntha and his braves resumed their cautious retreat from the crest. After they had regained a hollow in which their gaunt and rough-coated mounts stood tethered, the Shawnees re-erected headdresses and otherwise made ready to move out. Their War Chief, however, checked them. "Brothers, from this place we ride together no longer. From what we have seen it is plain that the Long Knives are planning to take away more of our land, but what is of the greatest importance is that *this* time the white men are casting hungry eyes upon the Great Hunting Ground, where, by ancient custom, even warring tribes may hunt in peace.

"Standing Bear, go make peace talk among the chief men of the Chickamauga, then seek out the Moytoy of the Cherokee. Offer them any terms within reason to bring our disputes with them to an end. Warn them of their fate if the Great Hunting Ground is lost to the *Americani.*"

"It shall be as my brother Moluntha commands," Standing Bear assured grimly.

"When these missions have been accomplished you must appear before the Tostenuggi-hlako and the grand Council of the Overhill Creek. Make them understand that if we do not utterly destroy these invaders, then they and their people will perish miserably, for surely, once the *Americani* begin to farm our common Hunting Ground, the buffalo, elk and deer no longer will come in their thousands to seek the salt licks there. They will not come at all! The invaders must be crushed — like this!"

Without making any noise whatever, the War Chief flattened a deerfly feeding on his horse's withers and created a bloody spot on his narrow, pink-brown palm.

Moluntha then faced Ocondago, who was checking his musket's priming. "My brother must ride hard towards the northwest to the lands of the Wyandot, the Miami, the Illinois and the other tribes across the Ohio and warn them that strong parties of settlers soon will trespass upon the Great Hunting Land." Moluntha's wide-set eyes flashed. "Tell their chief men that these invaders *must be destroyed,* but *only* after they have traveled beyond hope of rescue or reinforcement."

Ocondago's battered headdress fluttered briefly and a British officer's silver gorget flashed over his throat when he sprang onto his mount.

While gathering his reins the sub-chief asked softly, "And where will our brother Moluntha ride?"

Before replying, the War Chief lifted a folded blanket which, secured by a broad cincture of elkskin, served him for a saddle, and drew it backwards from his mount's withers, causing hairs on the animal's back to lie smooth, in the direction in which they grew, thus diminishing the danger of galls and saddle sores.

Once Moluntha had mounted he said in a savage undertone, "Moluntha will ride to seek out certain *Englasi* agents." The Shawnee's grim expression relaxed a trifle. "Now that the *Englasi* grow confident that soon they will put out the Thirteen Fires forever, they will gladly furnish the tribes with money, many guns, much powder and other warlike gear. Moreover, they are certain to offer good prices for Yankee scalps."

A small group of men, bearded or merely long unshaven, sat or stood in uncomfortable silence around a grease-stained trestle table made of rough-finished planks. This hurriedly had been set up near the center of that hot, dirt-floored chamber which included Fort Patrick Henry's entire ground floor and was as gloomy as it was sour-smelling because air and sunlight could only enter through a single narrow door and a row of loopholes let into raw, pitch-dripping log walls.

Lieutenant-Colonel James Robertson, occupying a stool near the table's head, had clear, wide-set and strangely penetrating bright blue eyes which roamed ceaselessly from one weathered, hairy face to the next. His dark-brown hair hung shoulder-long but he had clubbed it, neatly using a length of red-dyed rawhide. Robertson's handsome bronzed features were sprinkled by dark-red fly and mosquito bites.

Seated to his right and with both elbows planted on the table crouched that shrewd surveyor and land speculator, full-fleshed and soft-spoken John Donelson. Originally from Virginia but long a resident of North Carolina, Donelson had been one of the very first to settle in the Watauga region. For the present, he, like Robertson, was holding a well-earned lieutenant-colonel's commission.

Others squatting about the board on uncomfortable three-legged stools included Amos Eaton, a seasoned borderer and surveyor; a round-shouldered, sharp-featured fellow named Billy Cocke; Edmund Jennings, a lanky, uncertain-tempered young fellow who appeared much older than his actual twenty-four years. This illusion perhaps was created by the fact that a long and jagged red scar crossed his nose and left cheek; also that he had traveled far with Daniel Boone and had fought beside him many a time. And then there was broad-backed and golden-bearded Fred Stump, who spoke with an almost comically rich German accent.

Other leaders of important immigrant groups stood, arms folded, along the walls; in varying degrees they displayed concern over having been unexpectedly called in from their labors.

In a soft, Virginia-accented voice, James Robertson began to speak. "Sorry to have you sent for, boys, but Colonel Sevier here's just ridden in bearin' some pretty serious tidings. Since he damned near got killed on the way, I reckon you-all had better listen hard to what he's come to say."

"What kind of tidings?" Amos Eaton demanded, using a dirty sleeve to blot a sheen of sweat from his forehead.

Sevier, looking much taller than he really was, swung a balding head towards the speaker and summoned a bleak smile. "I only hope that you fellows ain't going to do like the kings of old and slay me for being the bearer of ill tidings."

"Ill, you say?" rumbled Donelson.

"Yep, and that's putting it mildly."

James Robertson cleared his throat, steadily regarded the spare figure standing erect in dusty, often-patched and badly faded blue-and-red regimentals. "Your meanin', John, is that lately our side ain't been farin' extra well against the King's Armies?"

Sevier's steel-gray eyes made a swift circuit of the dim and crowded room. "Reckon that's about the size of it. By all accounts our people are losing ground, skirmishes and battles up North, down South — everywhere, for that matter."

"Don't tell us dot *verdammt* Prevost has beat us again!" growled middle-aged but still stalwart Fred Stump, who only recently had escaped from a British prison in St. Augustine.

"Yes. Prevost has reinforced the garrison holding Savannah so strongly that our siege of that town most likely will end in a bloody disaster. Charles Town, too, soon will be invested by a powerful force shipped down from New York and New England, and they've brought a whopping big fleet of men-o'-war along to help pound the port into submission."

Sevier sighed, slapping a white crusting of horse sweat from his tunic's skirts. "And that's not all the bad news, either."

"What else is there?" demanded Edmund Jennings, raising shaggy black brows.

"Up North, British and Tory landing parties have been raiding and burning towns and shipyards along the Connecticut shore of Long Island Sound almost at will; so far, we haven't been able to give them any opposition worthy of mention."

A low growl arose from the listeners.

"What'd ye expect of them damn' cowardly Yankees?" demanded Billy Cocke.

"Stow that kind of talk," rasped Amos Eaton. "They've fought hard and suffered plenty. Go on, Colonel."

"Worse still, our patriotical, high-minded and windy Congress is proving itself ever more incompetent to pay, arm, feed or otherwise supply the miserable Continental regiments we still have left in the field. Every day our Continental scrip-money grows more worthless."

"— Und iss dot possible?" rasped the yellow-bearded German.

The shrill whooping of sunburnt and tousle-headed children playing tag on the cramped and uneven "parade ground" just outside beat in through loopholes which also were admitting swarms of fat and loudly buzzing bluebottle flies.

In a gesture expressive of supreme disgust Sevier flung heavily freckled brown hands wide apart. "Now comes the worst part. 'Tis reliably reported that our French friends are growing mighty sick of their alliance with us and are ready to pull out.

"All through the Southern Colonies Tory regiments are being recruited and outfitted to help in capturing Charles Town. Once that town's taken the Loyalists swear they'll burn out or hang every last Patriot they can catch in the Carolinas.

"After that, the British are expected to drive north into Virginia ravaging, killing and plundering. Guess you already know that they've captured and burnt Norfolk and Portsmouth on Chesapeake Bay?"

Sevier's spurs of tarnished brass jingled softly when he took a few turns before the table. He came to a halt confronting James Robertson and John Donelson. "To sum up, at this moment there appears little reason to doubt that the Cause of the United States is doomed."

Sevier lowered his voice. "To many, the most disturbing of all these woes is talk that our Commander-in-Chief, for the first time, no longer appears confident of eventual victory."

Eaton spoke up, "What you're saying is that even Gin'ral Washin'ton figgers we've lost the war?"

The droning of flies sounded absurdly loud before Sevier nodded and said in a somber tone, "I fear so, for barring Divine intervention or a military miracle of some sort, our armies must soon be out-maneuvered and defeated piecemeal or, at best, the remnants will be driven west, away from the seacoast."

"But suppose they surrender?" demanded Billy Cocke in a hollow voice. "What happens then?"

Colonel Sevier's fine features flushed as he almost shouted, "Dammit, man! They don't intend to quit! They've fought too long, and that's the reason why I came here. The Commander-in-Chief and many of our best generals, such as Knox, Greene, Marion, Harry Lee, along with states-men like Tom Jefferson, John Adams, George Mason and Patrick Henry, are determined to continue the fight for liberty —"

"— Along with a lot of smart land speculators, I expect," interpolated a harsh voice from near the doorway.

Using a scarred and tar-stained forefinger, Donelson scratched at a tangle of sand-colored hair, said slowly, "Well, John, granted that our folks won't be able to whip the Britishers and still don't intend to sur-render, what course is left open?"

He in the bedraggled blue-and-red uniform stiffened. "What course is left for our defeated Patriots, you ask? Why, sir, they and their leaders mean to fight on, retiring westwards in such a fashion as will cost the enemy very dear should they attempt a pursuit."

Sevier's voice swelled until it filled the crowded, gloomy little room. "I tell you fellows we've plenty of men left who mean to keep on shooting so long as they've left among 'em a handful of cornmeal, a full powder horn and a bag of bullets.

"The plan is for our people to withdraw behind what His Excellency terms 'the lofty ramparts of the Alleghenies,' there to settle and build a new free nation which can, and will, defy tyranny till hell itself freezes over!"

Robertson looked up, inquired, "Is it your meaning, John, that only armed forces will conduct this retreat?"

The shake of Sevier's sun-darkened head was emphatic. "Hell, no!

Troops and patriotic-minded civilians alike will emigrate westward —
like you already have — taking along their families and as many possessions as they can bring."

Billy Cocke pushed a flat, wide-brimmed brown hat onto the back of
his head, then combed sparse, ginger-hued chin whiskers with his fingers.
"Easy enough said, and a noble thought — 'specially for dealers in soldiers' land warrants — but tell us, Cunnel, where in hell are all these
refugees goin' to settle?" Cocke spat noisily. "How do they expect to be
pertecked from Injuns, fed and otherwise supplied? Hell, them dunder-
heads back East must be crazy. Ain't they got no idee how hard life is in
Lower Kentucky and Middle Tennessee? How goddam easy death's
come by out here?"

"Not yet. The most of 'em, that is," Sevier admitted slowly. "But I
figure that men like you, Jim Robertson, John Donelson, Fred Stump,
the Bledsoes, Evan Shelby and Kasper Mansker can, if you're so minded,
go into the Great Hunting Ground and prepare that fine, rich country to
receive fugitives by clearing land, putting in crops, building shelters, for-
tifying critical points and —"

"— And at the same time," Jennings snapped, scarred features taut,
"the handful of us is expected to fight off swarms of the meanest, cruel-
est savages God ever turned loose in North America! Do you *really* mean
that?"

"Und make no mistake, Colonel," Fred Stump grunted, "der tribes
vill pounce like hungry pant'ers vunce dey t'inks us vhites mean to settle
on der Great Hunting Grount!"

Briefly, Robertson's fingers drummed on the greasy table, then his
level dark brows merged into a single line. He ended by throwing back
his big clean-featured head and looking thoughtfully from face to face.
"Don't know how the rest of you fellers feel about what Colonel Sevier
proposes, but let me say it would appear that we're all in the same boat
— whether we like it or not.

"Now let's suppose that General Washington and the rest change
their minds and decide to give up? Where would that leave us old settlers and the new immigrants 'way out here? You and I know damn' well
the few of us wouldn't last longer'n a snowflake in hell were the British
to rouse and arm the tribes against us."

No one commented, only stared at the gritty floor over which a lost
brown-and-white puppy trotted about sniffing hopefully at various shoes,
boots and moccasins in the hopes of picking up a friendly scent.

At length Robertson shrugged, then turned to Donelson. "John, every-one hereabouts knows we're figurin' on leadin' expeditions out to the Cumberland country come next spring. So, I hear, are Kasper Mansker, Long John Rains and some others."

"That's so. What's your meanin'?"

"Well, if we wait here till spring before settin' out, why, by the time we reach where we aim to go it would be away too late in the season to start clearing land and making crops which could help feed refugees from the East."

"Dot iss so," grunted Fred Stump who, despite several celebrated mili-tary exploits, remained a farmer down to the soles of his clumsy cow-hide boots. Thoughtfully, he picked at a hairy nostril. "Neffer could ve plant crops which would come ripe in time."

Robertson heaved himself erect and looked about the dim and increas-ingly stuffy little room. "That being the truth, I propose that we don't wait for spring but set out for middle Tennessee soon's we can."

At once Cocke stepped forward, thin, parchment-hued features sud-denly suffused. "My God, Jimmy!" he shouted. "You gone stark, staring mad? Or are you funnin' us?"

"You know I'm not!" There was more than a trace of anger in Robert-son's reply.

"Then you must be crazy to think, for even a minute, about movin' a parcel of men, women, children, freight and livestock above eight hun-dred miles through an unmapped wilderness *in the dead of winter!*"

Murmurs of agreement circulated the hot and fly-filled meeting place. Unkempt heads were being shaken with varying degrees of violence.

Colonel John Donelson started up, shiny-smooth, full features gone brick-red. "Might have reckoned, Billy Cocke, you'd talk along those lines." He snorted contempt. "Small wonder folks still talk about 'runnin' like Billy Cocke' did before the Battle of Long Island began." The big, heavily built figure glared about him. "Make no mistake, fellers; to even think on attemptin' such a journey calls for plenty more than an average supply of guts."

Said a gray-haired fellow wearing an old linen hunting shirt, "As I see it, having guts and taking a reckless gamble on our lives, our folks and our property — which is all most of us have left in this world — is two mighty different things."

Colonel Sevier's spurs clinked again as, absently, he snapped flecks of mud from his uniform coat. "Hold on, boys, I don't want you to imagine that I'm inviting an immediate decision. Even after what I've told you, you'd be mad to start off on so damn' dangerous an errand at the half-cock." His leathery, thin lips formed a fleeting smile. "— And I intend no pun."

"That's as may be, suh, but I can give you my decision right now!" burst out a big, raw-boned man who carried a broad ax he'd been using. "Me and my family ain't joining in no winter march."

"Nor me, either," cried another. "I ain't drove my livestock this far to watch 'em starve and freeze in the forest."

Edmund Jennings, tall and lithe-looking in new, fringed white buckskins, spoke up. "They won't, Mister, if yer leader knows his job as well as Jim Robertson does."

Amos Eaton nodded slowly. "Sure, there still are good reasons for delaying till spring — among them the fact that by then we'll have plenty of boats built. And there'll be more of us. Ain't immigrants coming here all the time? By spring we'll have a lot more men ready and able to fight off the savages."

"That's undoubtedly true, Amos," slowly admitted James Robertson, "but what Colonel Sevier's told us still holds true. An we don't have food and shelter ready by the time those people from the East start crossin' the mountains, why, they'll just naturally perish and —" He treated the men lining the walls to a level, penetrating look. "And us, too!"

Fred Stump bit off a chew of tobacco. "So den it seems like ve get kilt no matter vot ve do, hey?"

Sevier quietly pointed out, "You all knew what you were risking when you moved out here." He unslung a pair of pistols which he wore supported by crossbelts of undressed leather. "So, suppose you sleep on the matter, as I suggested, and give me your answer come morning. Right now, I could do with a bait of food — and so could my mount. We've come a far piece in a big hurry."

2. The Point

At daybreak of a bright, crystal-clear morning in mid-October, 1779, Sergeant Daniel Maddox, recently discharged from General Dan Morgan's Regiment of Virginia Rifles, came to quickly, completely awake. If, after three campaigns, a soldier hadn't learned to rouse all in an instant he'd likely have become a casualty of some sort.

In a single, lithe motion Maddox rolled out of the ragged woolen blanket he'd brought along after he'd been mustered out, and leaped to his feet. The tall, copper-haired young fellow spat, then yawned and stretched until his joints and back tendons protested.

Somebody's black-and-tan 'coon dog sniffed curiously while the veteran tugged on light but tough and pliant leggings of snakeskin won at dice from an Iroquois during the Saratoga campaign.

After scratching vigorously under a fringed linen hunting shirt dyed butternut brown he slung on his food pouch, bullet bag and a large brass powder horn bearing the elaborately curling cypher of King George II.

Next he pulled on a wide-brimmed farmer's hat that had been pinned up on one side to support a sprig of hemlock, then stood rubbing a squarish jaw and watching Corporal Tim Murphy, also late of Morgan's Rifles, rake together the few live coals that remained among the ashes of their watchfire.

When a tiny flame wavered into being, Murphy, a dark-complexioned and slightly built but wiry individual, went over to his saddlebags and jerked from them a blackened can in which he would brew the point's morning coffee — which was no coffee at all, only finely cut chunks of potato scorched to a dark brown before being coarse-ground.

Farther on, Colonel James Robertson, tall and powerfully built, was blowing his long, straight nose between his fingers and at the same time relieving himself upon a fallen log. Short-lived twists of steam spiraled up from the puddle thus created.

No doubts lingered in the minds of the two-hundred-odd Long Hunters, frontiersmen, ex-soldiers and former farmers composing this expedition that ruddy and soft-spoken Jim Robertson, who'd first seen the light of day some thirty-seven years earlier in Brunswick County, Virginia, was a born leader and in the very prime of life.

While a woodpecker high in a yellowing hickory tree set up a steady hammering, Robertson tied his breeches' flap back into place. His well-spaced, bright blue eyes then commenced their eternal roving about. Maddox already had noticed that they'd the same peculiar farseeing quality one so often thinks of as characteristic of sailors or plainsmen habitually accustomed to surveying great distances. The leader then pulled out a scarred brass pocket compass and took several bearings among a series of forested ridges rising ahead like a succession of gigantic blue-green rollers.

Fringes decorating a pair of thigh-high Indian leggings asway, Robertson next strode over to a short picket line stretched between sturdy beech trees. First he examined every animal's back for saddle sores, then lifted hoofs looking for loose shoes or bruised fetlocks.

Meanwhile, a bandy-legged, leather-complexioned Long Hunter named Joe Drake, called for Bruce MacLean, a half-breed Scottish-Chickasaw, to help lower an elk's haunch from a sharpened branch.

Robertson's men hardly talked at all while they rolled blankets, slung gear and repacked grease-marked supply baskets made of hickory splints. Meantime, Tim Murphy, as brisk of movement as a squirrel, bent over a big, iron skillet and set about cooking a breakfast of black-eyed beans and bear bacon — which wasn't at all bad when properly smoked.

By the time riding horses and pack animals had been saddled Corporal Murphy called softly — one didn't sing out in the wilderness the way one did in an army camp, "Come along, boys, and get it before I throws it out."

The seven scouts riding as advance guard for the main expedition gathered around to hold out cups whittled out of black cherry or yellow pine.

After gulping his breakfast Dan Maddox went over to the picket line to untie his animals, which consisted of a pair of big, wiry horses of no special breeding he'd bought in Watauga and the bony black jackass he'd ridden all the way out from Lancaster.

Momentarily, the sergeant deliberated whether or not to ease "Ilsa" — that slender, long-barreled rifle he'd fashioned for his personal use just before going off to join the war — into a crude boot of wrinkled and well-greased buckskin. He decided not to stow his weapon on noting that

Tim Murphy wasn't putting away his double-barreled Golcher rifle —
the same with which he'd mortally wounded General Fraser, "Gentleman
Johnny" Burgoyne's most capable general officer. Almost everyone agreed
that the loss of General Fraser during the battle of Freeman's Farm had
done a good deal to cause Burgoyne's subsequent surrender at Saratoga.
Obviously, Tim was going to carry his piece ready for instant use.

In soft, unmistakably Virginian accents Robertson drawled, "Now
while we ain't over-likely to bump into a bunch of hostiles in this neck of
the woods at this time of year, we just *might* meet up with a big party of
Indian hunters on their way home from the Licks —"

"— Or a mess of Iroquois out on a raid," drawled Jennings.

"That's true, so best keep ready for action at short notice." Dwarfed
among the giant trees all about him, Robertson squinted at his small
brass pocket compass.

"All right, boys, mount up. Let's move lively and make the most of
this fine weather."

The point set out along the Trace following buck-toothed Joe Drake
and the thin-faced half-breed Chickasaw called Bruce MacLean.

Thoughtfully, Maddox watched the leather-clad veterans kick their
tackeys — ugly little horses brought up from North Carolina — along
the Kentucky Trace at a slow but distance-consuming jog-trot.

The trail, which in places had been worn by long usage to the depth of
a foot or more, now followed a tortuous course over a seemingly endless
succession of wooded ridges and high foothills watered by brooks, creeks
and pretty little waterfalls. In the valleys many good-sized lakes and
ponds reflected their surroundings or mirrored the sky of vivid azure.

While proceeding downhill at a comfortable four-mile-an-hour shuffle,
the point settled back in their saddles, watching their dogs rove and sniff
about the underbrush. Occasionally, through force of habit, one of the
rough-coated mongrels would cock a leg at a log or rock.

Dan Maddox, riding immediately behind Robertson, again noticed
how evenly the leader's powerful, gray-serge covered body tapered from
wide shoulders down to a flat stomach and youthfully narrow hips, that
his muscular legs encased in Indian leggings, boots and buckskin
breeches dangled almost to the ground.

Always the leader's head kept swinging from side to side as he studied
not only the sun-dappled countryside, aflame here and there with autumnal hues, but also the point's more immediate surroundings.

Upon a blanket roll strapped before him, he balanced "Jenny," a well-used but still handsome rifle decorated with bright brass mountings and a cluster of six-pointed silver stars let into its stock of tiger-striped maple. What with his broad-brimmed, flat-crowned hat which sported a small buck's tail, James Robertson, all in all, presented a powerful and a picturesque figure.

While listening to a pair of gray squirrels sauce the riders from the top of a giant hickory, Sergeant Dan Maddox felt annoyed to find his mind drifting back to that day last summer when, after being mustered out, he'd returned to Lancaster, Pennsylvania, only to find his cabin occupied by a sister-in-law and a bevy of her brats. Silently she'd led him to the graves of Ilsa and the infant she'd died trying to bear. A few blades of tender young hay grass had just begun to sprout on the mounds above them.

The veteran's small, almost round dark-blue eyes filled, so he blinked rapidly a few times and his squarish jaw jutted a little. He then drew a breath so deep that it set a line of thrums that ran across his hunting shirt's breast to swaying, and firmly banished grief from his thoughts. Hell! Wasn't it more worthwhile to conjecture on the fate in store for him in Middle Tennessee — always provided he lived to arrive at the Frenchman's Lick?

Why worry? A good shot and proficient gunsmith like me *ought* to make out — if anybody can.

Whichever way I look I can't help feeling this is the most magnificent country I've ever seen. If only it weren't so damned near empty of people. Makes me feel as little as a cork afloat on the ocean.

A pair of bald eagles wheeling on motionless pinions, high and tiny above the age-softened but still lofty summits of the Cumberland Range, only served to emphasize the scope and grandeur of his surroundings.

Dan bent and crushed a deerfly feeding on his mount's neck and noticed the staccato click and rattle made by iron-shod hoofs among pebbles paving a dry brook's bed.

A mile and a half to the rear of the point — or advance guard — the main body of travelers rode or tramped along in a straggling single file except when the Kentucky Trace, sometimes known as "Boone's Trail," widened briefly and permitted men to travel side by side and speculate about what might happen today.

On reaching the summit of a steep, cedar-covered ridge, Jim Robertson turned in his saddle to cast a long look over his shoulder. Seen at this distance his column suggested a thin, dark cable winding unevenly down the hither slope of a high, heavily forested foothill.

He reckoned he had around two hundred men still with him — only a very few of his followers had lost heart enough to head back to the Watauga country. A good thing that, with one exception, there wasn't a woman or child back there to slow down the expedition's rate of travel. The exception was his eleven-year-old son Jonathan, now riding herd on a small flock of sheep.

That this column should be unencumbered by dependents is just as well, reflected the leader. Long Hunters and timber beasts alike are predicting that this will prove one mighty hard season. Haven't squirrels, woodchucks, bears, 'coons and other hibernating creatures been seen gorging themselves extra fat? For a fact, every pelt I've seen seems unusually thick and glossy.

Well, no use fretting about the weather — we'll just have to take what comes.

While trotting down the ridge's far slope the rangy North Carolinian experienced a pang of conscience — he really had undertaken the easiest part in this dual immigration into Middle Tennessee. He didn't envy John Donelson one little bit his task of floating, in midwinter, more than three hundred men, women and children over a thousand miles from Fort Patrick Henry down the Holston and the Tennessee, transporting also a wide variety of livestock, farm implements, seeds and household furniture.

By noon the column began to pick its way across a stretch of almost impassible country. What rendered progress so extremely difficult here was the fact that, years earlier, a tornado had cut a swath through the forest, toppling huge trees across the Trace to create a succession of windfalls so gigantic that they must be detoured through all but impenetrable forests in which beeches, maples, black walnuts and hickories glowed golden-yellow and sumach and ivy tangles blazed as bright as a Cherokee's war paint.

Maddox learned from gnarled old Joe Drake that the expedition at present was heading for a little settlement on the Duck River known as Whiteley's Station. How far off it was, Joe couldn't say.

Again the Pennsylvanian was impressed by the unrelieved loneliness of this vast region in which signs of human activity were so rare. Why, after passing through the Cumberland Gap, two days back, only a solitary spiral of smoke had been sighted and that in the far distance.

All the same, decided the former soldier, this seeming emptiness must be deceptive, or why should big game continue to prove so 'cute and scarce?

In support of this reasoning the advance party yesterday had come upon a pair of bearded, hard-bitten characters who, clad in dirty buckskins, were waiting quietly beside the Trace. How they'd learned of Jim Robertson's intent to ride this way was a mystery; but there they were, lugging full packs and bulging war bags.

When James Robertson, tall and supple in his buckskin-covered saddle, had ridden up one had called out, "Heyo, Cunnel Jim! We'd admire to go along with you an ye're really intendin' for the Great Huntin' Ground."

Robertson tugged at his long, straight nose a moment. "You afoot?"

"Yep. Injuns stole our hosses last summer along with three packloads of pelts."

"Can you walk fast?"

A foxtail attached to the taller man's cap swayed to his nod. "Sure thing. Me and Tom c'n walk and run the legs off'n a bull elk."

The other said almost shyly, "Take us along, Cunnel, we've plenty of pemmican, powder and bar lead. Swear we wunt cause you a mite o' trouble."

While his mount impatiently switched at swarming deerflies and horseflies, the leader's sharp blue eyes considered these shaggy would-be recruits. Finally he drawled, "How're you named?"

The short applicant, who'd a drooping eyelid, exposed gapped teeth in a brief grin. "Me, I'm Cash Brooks and this here porcupine humper's Tom Gordon. We both been rangin' with Boone, Bo'quet and others for many a blue moon."

"Reckon you'll do. For the present you boys will join the main body when it comes along. Tell Major Phillips I said so." At the same time, Robertson was racking his memory; somewhere he'd heard mention of Cash Brooks, but for the life of him he couldn't recall right now when it had been.

With Caesar, his shaggy, battle-scarred, black-and-tan bear dog trotting sedately behind his bay gelding, Colonel Robertson advanced until he found Sergeant Maddox and his crony, Tim Murphy, riding a couple of hundred yards in advance of the rest of the point.

"Howdy, Cunnel Jim." Out of habit Murphy touched his hat's brim in easy salute.

Using his chin the leader pointed to a pleasant little valley down which the Trace was winding. "I'd like you boys to hurry on ahead and see if you can't come up with some game before it gets frightened off. Try to knock over at least half a dozen head; two hundred men and as many dogs c'n tuck away a powerful lot of meat." His gaze shifted to the rifles they held balanced across their pommels. "I know that's a tall order. Any fool c'n tell game's growing scarcer all the time, but I hear the two of you c'n kill at mighty long range. See you later."

3. *The Mauling*

FOLLOWED by a trio of ugly-looking bear dogs which seemed to have become separated from their masters, the two ex-soldiers cantered ahead until they discovered a game trail which showed fairly fresh tracks and branched off in the direction of a long, park-like meadow the hunters had noticed from the last ridge's crest.

As Robertson had admitted, big game hereabouts *was* scarce and easily alarmed. Time and again they heard the washing *crash* of underbrush made by fleeing animals even before their species could be identified.

It was unfortunate that certain of these flight noises were not caused by game but by a small party of well-mounted and lynx-eyed Shawnees who, for the past two days, had been scouting the numbers, composition and progress of James Robertson's column.

By following a buffalo track, the Indians made very little noise as they galloped off to the northwest to rejoin their leader.

The better part of three hours was required by the meat hunters and their dogs to start and shoot four fat cow elk and a big, white-tailed buck deer — all of which had had to be killed at not less than a hundred yards' range.

Dan Maddox felt particularly pleased over his last shot — a difficult one of nearly two hundred yards' distance — Ilsa *had* remained accurate despite having been rebored which had had to be done because he'd used his weapon so often during service with "The Old Wagoner," as Dan Morgan's men long ago had nicknamed him.

At the first possible moment the meat hunters cut the throats of their quarry, for even in cool weather like this, un-blooded meat could spoil in surprisingly short order.

Watched by a big brown mongrel, Maddox sank onto his heels and drew his long knife — which was really a carving knife of beautifully tempered Sheffield steel — across the buck's still quivering windpipe. He stood up and watched streams of steamy scarlet arterial blood form a glistening puddle which presently overflowed and went meandering off among fallen leaves, weeds and grass roots. The dogs then advanced and lapped eagerly.

"Reckon that'll about do for now," Tim remarked while tamping down a fresh powder charge and ball — buckshot in this meadow country wouldn't carry far enough.

From his war bag Maddox pulled a strip of white cloth which he tied to a branch high enough above the fallen buck to attract the attention of skinners who, leading pack horses, should soon appear to butcher the carcasses and fetch in the meat.

While slipping his bloodstained knife back into its sheath Tim Murphy shook his head. "B' God, Dan, don't know why cuttin' throats makes me feel so randy, but I've sure got to find me a playsome wench else I'll spoil my britches some night. Ain't bedded a girl in a month, which is uncommon hard on a full-blooded young buck like me."

"My Gawd, Tim, must you always be dreaming of a 'fidgety fork'?"

"Reckon so," grinned the rifleman while swinging up into his saddle. "I'm told my balls are small so I work 'em extra hard to prove they're just as good as big ones."

Resting Ilsa across his saddle bow, Dan Maddox kicked his rough-coated gelding and led off through the sweet-smelling and sun-dappled forest. "Guess we better kill two more beasts." His head swung sharply. "See yonder? There're fresh elk droppin's on that track leadin' downwards."

Murphy took the lead, kept his dark, bullet-shaped head swinging in steady arcs until he reined in abruptly and bent over to peer at the ground. "Look there," he invited softly.

Maddox saw a broken arrow which, fletched with dark-red turkey feathers, lay on a carpeting of bronze oak leaves. One thing was certain. That shaft couldn't have lain there long; the break's jagged ends shone a bright yellow-white. Moreover, a few blades of live grass remained bent under the arrow's slight weight!

After checking primings and drawing back their hammers to half-cock, the meat hunters commenced, much more slowly, to follow this game trail marked by the fresh spoor of elk and now of *unshod horses!* Which, certainly, couldn't have been made by animals belonging to the expedition.

Hum. These tracks must have been made not very long ago. Pretty soon the trail led to a fair-sized spring where crystal-clear water bubbled from beneath a pile of moss-grown boulders to flow, shimmering, over a streak of yellow sand.

Then, on mucky black earth surrounding the spring, the meat hunters recognized several more or less clearly defined footprints made by moccasins — not shoes or boots. Fervently the meat hunters began to wish they had with them a Long Hunter like Joe Drake, Cash Brooks or Edmund Jennings. Most likely, any of them could have told, after having examined that broken arrow and having studied these prints, to which tribe the Indians were likely to belong and what they were up to.

After riding around the spring's circumference the meat hunters agreed that a party of Indians numbering perhaps a dozen must have drunk and watered their horses here.

Both were sufficiently experienced to realize that this handful of savages had kept on moving and probably had no reinforcements nearby, so the point, not to mention the main column, stood in no immediate danger. They watered their horses and washed blood from their gear before drinking from small cherrywood dippers attached to the ties on their war bags — small canvas or deerskin haversacks carried slung over one shoulder. Somehow, the spring's icy water didn't taste sweet; knowledge that an unknown number of savages were in the vicinity rendered it flat.

Scarcely had they remounted than a sudden excited clamor arose from beyond an alder thicket about which one of the bear hounds had been nosing after lapping to wash down the blood he'd consumed. Instantly, the other two dogs raised a terrific tumult and raced off among the trees while the meat hunters reined in sharply and stared at one another in lively uncertainty. What had alarmed the dogs? A fox, a panther, or were there Indians hiding among the sun-speckled underbrush? Dogs, they knew, hated the very smell of Indians — probably because the redmen greased themselves with bear fat and never washed.

At length Tim Murphy grunted, "Don't think it's Injuns — dogs are actin' too bold and noisy." He loosened his rawhide reins and rode slowly forward, the double-barreled rifle's stock halfway to his shoulder.

Tim looked relieved. "By damn! Trust them fool bone-destroyers to chance on fresh bear tracks."

"With Injuns about, and all that racket, I reckon our hunt's about over," Maddox grunted. "So let's go kill the critter. Most of the fellows favor bear over venison."

Once the hunters had urged their unwilling mounts into a little clearing carpeted with bright-leaved huckleberry bushes they saw the dogs circling about and then rushing in to snarl about the base of a dead and peeling linden tree. On its lower branches a pair of fuzzy, comical-looking black bear cubs had taken refuge and were whining shrilly while keeping furry round ears pressed flat against their heads.

When he saw what was up, Murphy swung off, tied his horse to a tree, then strode forward a few yards before again raising the Golcher. Two flat, cracking reports sounded in quick succession and the dogs' yelping rose to a crescendo when the cubs came tumbling earthwards and made two dull thuds among bushes beneath the weathered old tree.

Beset by snarling hounds, one cub struggled to rise but collapsed with a dog's teeth in its throat. The other black-brown body stirred not at all despite savage worrying.

Without comment, Maddox dismounted and, with bridle looped over one arm, snatched up a stick and began to beat off the dogs. "Good eye. Got 'em both center line."

"Aw, hell! They was easy. Now if only I'd have such luck with women I'd —"

A deep-throated roar caused both hunters to whirl about barely in time to see a huge sow bear come humping, red-eyed, out of a sumach thicket, saber-like claws flashing and long teeth a-gleam.

Murphy for once had neglected to reload so dropped the Golcher and went for his sheath knife — too late. The raging animal already was upon him, rearing and lashing out. Tim leaped nimbly back and succeeded in avoiding the bear's first swipes. There wasn't much Maddox could do at that point for his horse had shied so violently that it tore loose its reins and plunged away, throwing him off balance and spinning him half about.

The sow now shuffled forward with deceptive speed and launched another savage blow at Murphy's reeling figure.

The gunsmith instantly recovered, spraddled legs and whipped Ilsa to his shoulder fast — too fast — because the weapon went off a split second before he was ready.

Beyond a rolling blossom of gray-white smoke Murphy screamed shrilly, again and yet again; there followed snarling growls and wild threshing noises amid the underbrush. Snatching his tomahawk out of its frog, Maddox charged through whirling, bitter-smelling fumes, then pulled up, all standing. From the way the bear was charging blindly about in semi-circles and knocking down sturdy young trees Dan sensed he'd been lucky enough to have driven his bullet into the brute's head.

Presently one of the bear's blind rushes carried her off to one side and into a stand of golden-leafed poplars. There, after hugging and snapping at a clump of saplings, the sow all at once sagged to the ground as if suddenly overcome by sleep and lay, muzzle down.

When Dan had reloaded he advanced cautiously and saw that the beast's tongue had slipped out between its jaws, that blood was spurting in such furious torrents from the nostrils and mouth he could be pretty sure that the animal must be dead or nearly so. All the same, he sunk his tomahawk's blade deep into the brute's brain before running over to kneel beside his friend.

"You hurt bad?"

Tim Murphy blinked, then stared dazedly upwards, black eyes wide and unfocused. His small, wedge-shaped features looked pasty like a piece of badly cured doeskin rather than their usual bronze-red. "Wha-a'?" His voice barely was audible.

"How bad you hurt?"

Murphy's eyes rolled and he drew a slow, shuddering breath. "Dunno. Ain't checked — Guess — ain't no worse off than — after Brandywine, but — reckon I'm in for — session — who's that sawbones in — main column?"

"Mason, Sam Mason. They say he's knowledgeable. Take it easy, Tim — where d'you hurt most?"

"Can't feel much — left side." Tim managed the ghost of a grin. "Lucky — critter missed my balls —"

Maddox forced a grin. "There'd sure be a lot of wenches sleep easier if that bear hadn't." Frowning, he estimated Tim's hurts with the sureness of one who had helped many a wounded man.

After slitting the linen hunting shirt's crimson-soaked left sleeve he uncovered a deep, ragged double gash running from Tim's shoulder clear down to his elbow. While the wound was torn and wide, at first glance it didn't appear to be too deep, although dark venous blood and plasma were coursing freely from it.

Maddox contrived a tourniquet out of a stick and a length cut from the long rawhide thong he carried looped over his left shoulder when in the field. He tried to look unconcerned although he knew that such a clawing would prove hard to heal because bears were partial to eating carrion of any description.

Next, the rifleman took a precaution which — as every veteran knew — was the best possible treatment under the circumstances; he opened his breeches and urinated thoroughly upon the wound and soaked the wad of moss he secured in place using Tim's and his own sweaty neckerchiefs. Nobody ever had explained why, more often than not, this procedure would keep a wound fairly sweet and open till a physician could dress it.

4. Samuel Mason, M.D.

THE sun had begun to set behind strata of sickly, yellow-gray clouds when the main column straggled onto and spread out over an old beaver fly Colonel Robertson had selected for tonight's bivouac.

Doctor Samuel Grineau Mason, Harvard College, Class of 1771, felt pleased that this open place had been chosen. Followed by an awkward young man, he rode to the meadow's far side and there prepared to camp in comparative seclusion. Because of what had happened not long ago, the doctor hated the sensation of being hemmed in.

Carefully, he unloaded first a battered black medicine chest, a flat wooden map case, then heavy saddle bags containing a slender supply of surgical instruments, clysters and a couple of sturdy bone saws all wrapped in oilskins.

All over the meadow sounded a jingle of harness and trampling caused by nearly a thousand hoofs of all sorts. Soon these sounds became lost in the *ta-chunk!* of hatchets and axes cutting firewood and boughs for bedding.

The spare, square-shouldered physician seated himself on a tussock and, using his thumb, tested the edges of scalpels removed from a scuffed leather wallet. Pretty soon, he knew, the first of this day's crop of injuries would start showing up. Impatiently, he looked about for his apprentice, Josh Freedly, a tall, weedy youth of nineteen with the alert, beady eyes of a chipmunk, carrot-hued hair and absolutely colorless eyelashes. Right now he was busy off-loading a small, lop-eared jackass which carried the bulk of his master's camping equipment.

Sure enough, a lean, sad-looking fellow with straddled eyes drew near. He was supporting a bleeding hand slung to a belt. "Hey, Doc, damn' ornery mule bit me a while back. It hurts some. Kin you fix me up?"

"I'll be ready for you in a minute," the doctor told him. "Sit down and rest your feet."

Narrowing small, dark-brown eyes, Mason continued to unpack. On a fairly clean cloth he laid out a few curved surgical needles, bandages, some ligatures of varying length and a bag of pledgets made of fine-picked tow. Next he opened his medicine chest; he never knew what he might be called upon to treat — anything from a sprained ankle to an ax cut, a bellyache, a burn, a fever or even a flare-up of syphilis. Almost always he could count on having to dress some old or half-healed wound which had reopened.

Watched by the man with the bitten hand, Josh shambled up, slopping water out of a battered copper pot which he set down beside the beginnings of a fire.

"Heard the word, Doc?"

"No. What's the rumor this time?"

"Some of our advance party have come acrost fresh Injun sign." Josh was proud to use real frontier terms, but all the same he glanced anxiously about the darkening meadow. "Colonel's ordered outposts set tonight. Hope to God them savages ain't fixin' to assault us."

Stiff and sore as he was from this long day in a most uncomfortable saddle, the doctor chuckled, "An they do, Josh, that carrot thatch of yours will be the first scalp they'll go for."

Josh's pale gray eyes rounded themselves. "Really, Doc? Why for?"

"Old woodsmen among us say that the savages fancy an off-colored scalp above all others. Better stay close to camp tonight. Now pass me a blanket. No, you numbskull, not the one with burrs stuck all over it."

Tonight Sam Mason was lucky; outside of his jackass-bitten patient he'd only had to smear sulphur-and-goose-grease over the foot of a man who'd got it scalded when a stewpot had overturned unexpectedly, and then he'd had to employ forceps to yank a mess of porcupine quills out of a big ex-farmer's leg. During the process the yokel had howled like a moonstruck hound.

Darkness had descended before Dan Maddox walked up to the physician's fire, leading a short-legged and disreputable-looking tackey. On it Corporal Tim Murphy sat, all bunched over and groaning softly.

"Howdy, Doc," Maddox greeted. "Got time for one more?"

"Surely, but I wish you'd come in when the light was better."

Maddox and Josh eased the hurt man out of the saddle. "Sorry we couldn't get here sooner, Doc, but we were a long ways off when Tim, who's always been a lady's man, lost an argument with a she-bear."

"True love always demands a price — so they say." Mason's features, broad-jawed beneath a thin, hawklike nose, gradually tightened while he examined the lacerated arm. Supported by a crude sling, it slowly wept dark-red tears, caused a faint *spat-spat* upon fallen leaves.

"You hurt, too?"

"No. Tim hogged the entertainment."

Murphy's forehead grew shiny with sweat and he was shaking all over by the time his companion had helped him over to a pile of packs over which Josh had spread the blanket.

Shadowy figures wandered over from nearby fires to learn what was taking place, but, for the most part, the travelers kept attention on cooking or rolled up in their blankets and went to sleep.

During the last hour Tim's arm had swelled considerably and he'd bled freely whenever the tourniquet had been loosed for a little while, but the mauled limb hadn't yet turned that ominous plum-red which Samuel Mason, M.D., always hated to see.

As he stripped off a long-skirted coat of rusty-black, the doctor called over his shoulder, "Josh! Fetch plenty of pitch-pine splinters, and you, Maddox, stir the fire under that pot. I'll need a lot of hot water pretty soon."

Doctor Mason's stained red waistcoat glowed in the firelight while from his saddle bags he jerked a thick plug of leather, scarred and indented by the spasmodic clenching of many teeth.

Tim recognized a surgeon's gag the moment he saw it and shook his handsomely homely head. "Keep that for the next feller, Doc. I won't be needin' it — honest. Didn't yell when the sawbones sewed up my leg after Brandywine."

"As you please," Mason said while selecting needles and damp sutures of split deer sinew. "Josh, give this man a swallow of Medford rum. I'll save the laudanum for later."

By now a considerable group of rough-clad, tobacco-chewing immigrants, veteran frontiersmen and greenhorns alike, had been attracted by those flaring pine splinters which Josh had distributed among the onlookers with instructions to "hold these high and steady." Now they crowded around the impromptu operating couch, creating the pool of smoky yellow. Nor was it idle curiosity which drew all of them; here, a fellow might acquire a bit of knowledge which sometime might come in handy if he got hurt when off in the woods by himself.

A silence fell in which the faint crackle of the flares sounded sharp and crisp. Using a swab of tow, the doctor began to wipe the long wounds free of flesh particles, clotting blood and urine. "Good thing you are old soldiers and had the sense to piss on such a wound. Now, Maddox, do you grab his good arm and hold hard. Josh, pin down his feet. Lock your teeth, Murphy, I'm about to hurt you."

After deftly snipping away loose little tatters of flesh and skin, Samuel Mason removed a threaded needle from his waistcoat's lapel and went to work.

"Uh-h-h! Uh-h-h!" gasped the patient; he gurgled several times but made no other sounds, only squeezed his eyes so tight shut that tears began to slide over his quivering cheeks.

"Keerist!" muttered a gnarled old man. "He's the brave one. I'd have squalled like a stuck shoat long before this."

After quickly knotting nearly a dozen sutures the physician applied unguent-smeared pledgets which he held in place by means of loosely wound bandages. Finally Doctor Mason straightened, eyes smarting from the flares' smoke, said, "You're fortunate, young fellow, that those claws only scored the main muscle and severed some nerves and blood vessels — no arteries. If you're lucky, and there's no dirt or poison off the claws in there, you should be able to do light work in, well, maybe a fortnight. Here, take another swig of Medford."

Sweating hard, Murphy, helped by Maddox, struggled to sit up.

"None of that!" snapped the doctor, wiping hands on a piece of rag. "You'll stay here for tonight and keep that arm quiet."

Murphy blinked several times, summoned the caricature of a grin. "Thanks, Doc. Someday soon I hope maybe to do *you* a favor. Meantime, in my bag there's a silver-mounted pocket pistol I took off'n a

Hessian officer who didn't need it anymore. I mean for you to have it; it's real pretty and don't weigh hardly anything."

The doctor shook his powerfully modeled, dark-red head. "Thanks, Murphy, but I'm not accepting compensation of any sort till we reach the Frenchman's Lick."

"My God, why not?" someone asked.

"I don't want anybody to figure he's going to get better care than the next man on account of what he might give me. Is that clear?"

A bony, one-eyed fellow in a shapeless linsey-woolsey shirt and ragged duroy breeches burst out laughing. "Wall, dog bite my butt! I campaigned plenty 'round Noo York and I never heard no *real* sawbones talk like that. They all had an awful itchy palm."

The audience soon drifted away, some to go on guard duty, others to look after mounts and livestock. Still others, dog-tired, sought their blankets; quite a few immigrants now were traveling on foot and carrying all their possessions on their back.

5. *Revelations by Firelight, I*

DR. MASON's straight, faintly quizzical brows merged as he strapped shut and then locked his medicine chest. "Maddox, you'll find an extra blanket in that roll. Spread it over the patient so he doesn't wake up. He'll start suffering from chills before long. Another thing, you'd better make sure he gets an easy-gaited nag tomorrow — provided he's fit to ride."

Sergeant Maddox paused to look curiously at the physician. "Say, sir, do you know that you talk like some Britishers I've heard? Even if you don't act like them."

"How so, Sergeant? Er — you still are one?" he asked quickly.

"No, but a lot of people keep on calling me 'Sergeant,' so I let 'em 'cause I served out my enlistment and got an honorable discharge along with a soldier's land grant warrant in place of pay-money. It calls for five hundred acres somewhere on public land west of the mountains." Maddox nodded to himself. "That surprised me, sir, 'cause folks in the Army claim the Congress has got so stingy they'll try down a mouse for its fat. You're not English-born then?"

Methodically, the surgeon wiped blood from his curved needle on a patch of linen, then restored it to his wallet of surgical instruments. "Small wonder you might think so," said he easily. "You see, I was born in Boston and have studied in England."

Maddox paused after rubbing down his and Murphy's mount. "Reckon you must have spent considerable time there."

"Why?"

"When I first heard you speak I really mistook you for a born-and-bred Britisher."

By the uncertain firelight Morgan's former sergeant noted a flush spread slowly out over the physician's rather prominent cheeks. "Unfortunately, others have fallen into the same error." Quickly, he continued, "Was it you and Murphy who found Indian sign this afternoon?"

"Yep. We saw the fairly fresh tracks made by maybe a dozen Injuns."

The doctor peered through pungent-smelling wood smoke. "Does Colonel Robertson think we are in danger of attack?"

"Don't think so, but all the same he's posted sentries." Maddox cast an anxious look at the patient before sinking onto his heels beside the fire.

"Edmund Jennings and Cash Brooks followed the trail for a good distance. When they came back they said 'tis likely a Shawnee huntin' party on their way to hunt 'round salt licks farther west — numbers 'round ten — twelve men. They and the Colonel believe these savages don't yet suspect we're in their neighborhood."

"Hope they're correct; I'd hate to see us get hit while we're all strung out like we've been."

"The Colonel keeps saying he don't expect real trouble till after we've crossed the Duck River."

"When will that be?" Mason opened his map case, glanced inside, then shut it again.

"Two, maybe three days' travel, depending on the weather."

In precise, clipped accents the physician then demanded, "And just where lies this 'Great Hunting Ground' we're heading for?"

Before replying Maddox went over to his friend and, finding him asleep, gently pulled a horse blanket up to his chin. "Don't know — Ain't ever ranged that far west, but Colonel Robertson has, lots of times, and so have Ed Jennings, Joe Drake, Cash Brooks and maybe a half-dozen other timber beasts we've among us."

"And what do they say?" The doctor was paying close attention.

"Well, they say it lies well south of the Ohio River and east of the

Mississippi inside a great bend made by the Tennessee River. Daresay that's a heap of territory."

"So it would seem. Sergeant, I trust you are not expected to report for duty with the advance guard in the morning."

"When the Colonel heard Tim was hurt he told Joe and Cash to ride in our space."

"Good. Then you'd better spend the night here and help care for your friend."

"I'd admire to do that, sir." The tall, red-haired Pennsylvanian then leaned his long rifle handy-like against a tree. Automatically, he peered up to see what the weather portended — was relieved to glimpse a multitude of stars through the treetops. Wolves hunting along a nearby ridge raised a chorus of eerie, mournful cries.

"Well, Doc, to go back to this Great Huntin' Ground you asked about — if the Long Hunters ain't been lyin' 'tis a great, forested basin — mostly flat but laced by hills and low mountains. Former farmers amongst 'em claim most of the land there's about the richest they've ever seen anywhere and, best of all, it's studded with sulphur springs and salt licks."

"Exactly what is a 'salt lick'?"

Maddox began to rock gently on his heels, like an Indian, to keep blood circulating in his legs and so avoid cramps. "Joe Drake says it's any place where rock salt, which was formed by an old, old sea one hell of a long time ago, shoves up through the earth.

"Almost every kind of animal —" he grinned briefly — "includin' men, crave it; they swear that deer, elk, buffalo, bears, lions, wolves, foxes and even porcupines will travel hundreds of miles just to lick that salt. Maybe that's so, maybe not." When Maddox shrugged, a dark spot on the right shoulder of his hunting shirt indicated where his sergeant's green-worsted shoulder-knot once had rested.

"Why not?"

"Sometimes a body can't readily credit some of Joe's yarns; for example, he vows that sometimes them buffaloes travel so thick that a nimble feller can walk clear across a ravine on their backs."

On a nearby mountain a bull elk began to bell hoarse defiance; it promptly was answered from not one but from three different directions, since this time of year was what the Indians called "the Rutting Moon." Farther away, a woods bison began to bellow as if the urge to couple on this crisp autumn was spreading. Next, a panther raised its deep, throat-tearing screech, which woke up drowsing horses and set them to sidling about and jerking at their halter shanks.

"Queer. This wilderness seems so quiet by day," Mason remarked, pulling out a battered pipe. "Please, Sergeant, tell me more about this so-called Great Hunting Country."

Maddox paused to scratch under his armpit where a louse had gone seriously to work. "All the Long Hunters claim that for time out o' mind the place has been a sort of 'neutral ground' on which the members of any tribe can hunt in peace — guess there must be enough game there for everyone. Yep. They allow as how Cherokees, Creeks, Shawnees, Chicka-maugas, Iroquois and even Catawbas who come all the way up from Georgia hunt side by side sometimes. Joe says he's never heard of a regu-lar treaty between the tribes but 'tis a fact that nations which may be scrappin' elsewhere will leave each other alone while on the Huntin' Ground."

Mason's small eyes narrowed and his lips formed a soundless whistle which expelled his pipe's smoke. "So this is to be our Promised Land?"

"Yep, looks like it. Say, Doc, should I wake Tim up and feed him? He ain't swallowed a mouthful since sunup. He'll need strength, won't he?"

"He will and plenty of it, but right now it's better for him to sleep as long as he can — that arm's going to pain like hell when he comes to."

Now and then a horse coughed or squealed when nipped by some short-tempered neighbor. Mules and jackasses, being more intelligent, began to lie down, caused soft crackles in the underbrush.

Dr. Mason peered across the flames. "Tell me, Maddox, isn't 'the Frenchman's Lick' on the Cumberland where we're supposed to rendez-vous with Colonel Donelson's boat expedition?"

"That's the idea. You see, Doc, Robertson's people are supposed to travel fast and arrive yonder in time to ready things for those folks who'll be travelin' by water along with their families."

"You've a family?"

Maddox's mouth tightened. "No. Not any more."

"Then why are you here?"

"Well, sir, me and some other time-expired soldiers came along be-cause we aim to reach this new country early and take up our land war-rants on the choicest land we c'n find."

Deliberately, Mason tapped the dottle from his pipe. "How do you think the Indians are going to react when they find half a thousand whites invading their Great Hunting Country?"

Maddox grunted and dug at his teeth with a black-nailed forefinger. "If I was a redskin I'd fight like a stack of black cats to keep 'em out. Old buckskins amongst us are certain-sure the Creeks, Chickasaws, Shawnees, Miamis and the rest will try to wipe us out."

"I've heard it said that the Transylvania Company has bought rights from the Cherokees to settle there. Is that true?"

"Dunno, 'cause the other tribes claim the Cherokees had no right to sell the common huntin' ground. They hold that it doesn't belong to the Cherokees more than to any other tribe."

A row of coarse thrums or long fringes decorating Maddox's chest stirred as he shifted his position.

"You c'n bet your hat that we're going to get attacked, so the main question is — where, when and how?" With calloused fingers the Pennsylvanian picked a coal from the fire, relit his pipe. "Howsumever, I reckon life in the wilderness never was meant to be easy or long, if a fellow don't act mighty careful *all the time.*"

A brief and mirthless laugh escaped Dr. Mason. "One could observe, Sergeant, that you're considerable of a philosopher. I hope you'll forgive my inquiring what prompted you to accompany an expedition which, by your own admission, seems headed for disaster? Please don't reply unless you feel so inclined. I won't be offended."

After casting still another glance at Murphy's small, blanket-shrouded outline, Maddox picked up Ilsa before settling back against a pack saddle. The fire picked out various bits of brass on the rifle's mountings. "I don't mind — provided *you* tell *me* why a smart, eddicated sawbones like you is willing to risk his scalp in a wilderness he knows nothin' about."

Once Samuel Mason, M.D., had checked ex-Corporal Tim Murphy's condition — he had begun to snore loudly — he seated himself, elbow-on-knees, on his medicine chest, and for once yielded to impulse. In wry amusement at himself he wondered why he was choosing a hard-eyed ex-soldier for a confidant. Possibly it was because Maddox was obviously intelligent, spoke softly and never bragged or cursed without cause. Besides, he used reasonably good English, which was a relief to hear amid all this frontier jargon. Most likely it was because Maddox looked a man squarely in the eye when talking to him.

Feeling somehow less lonely than he had for a long time, the physician groped in a saddlebag beside him until he found a flat and often-dented silver flask. From it he poured tots of a fine French brandy into two little silver cups screwed neatly over the container's mouth — normally, he employed these for measuring out medicine.

Maddox offered no comment when his big left hand that bore a wide dull-red scar across its back engulfed the tiny cup. On sniffing its contents he smiled almost shyly. "This, sir, is rare, fine stuff, much too good for a common soldier."

"Allow me to be the judge of that, Sergeant," Mason said and drew gently on his pipe, aware that while he felt comfortably tired he wasn't sleepy at all.

Maddox was deciding that likely he and this red-haired New Englander with the hawk's nose and well-bred features might become real good friends for all he talked disturbingly much like an Englishman.

Why did Dr. Mason so often gaze off into space as if looking for something he knew he wouldn't find? What did he write during moments of leisure in a notebook that never seemed to leave his person? Sometimes he made hasty sketches of the terrain traversed by Robertson's men. Was he making a map? Plenty of men were, including the Colonel. Such would bring a stiff price back East where maps of any description plotting unknown territory were in urgent demand. Suddenly he became aware that the physician had begun to speak.

"I presume, friend Maddox, you've already noted that to certain of our company I present something of an enigma?"

"Well, sir, I don't know just what you mean by that five shillin' word, but if you mean you've got some of our people guessin', you're dead right."

"Well, I know some people rate me a queer duck, which is partially my own fault and that of my parents."

"You ain't to be blamed for what your folks did." Then he added hastily, "Whatever it was."

The bowl of Mason's charred pipe glowed rose-red as he drew a deep puff and chuckled softly. "I'm not a bastard, if that's your implication. My family has lived in and around Boston since 1660, when old Sampson, our first ancestor, who'd been a colonel in Cromwell's Ironsides, was forced to flee for his life following the Restoration.

"I'll spare you further genealogy save to state that my father served in the Ancient and Honorable Company of Artillery when it went to the Siege of Louisburg back in '45. Incidentally, the Provincials captured that great fortress by themselves without help from the British Regular Army, which sent not a single soldier to the siege. That's a fact worthy of remembrance in these grim times."

Dan Maddox scratched absently under his shoulder-length, dark-red hair, then cocked an eyebrow. "Am I wrong or wasn't there another siege — later on?"

"That's quite so, Sergeant. General Wolfe took the same fortress back in '59 after His Majesty's Government restored Louisburg to the King of France." Doctor Mason took a small sip, then rolled the cognac over his tongue before continuing. "Know something else? Plenty of people believe that the seeds of this present war were sown when the British Government gave Louisburg back to the French without the least 'by your leave' to the Provincials who'd taken the place and, in so doing, discovered that, by acting in unison, they could accomplish a great deal without British assistance."

"Why'd the Yankees want to take that fort so bad?"

"Needed to rid their shipping of attacks by French privateers and pirates who nested in Louisburg, for one thing. Then there was a much greater danger: for over a century the French, working out of Louisburg, had roused, equipped and led countless Indian raids deep into New England."

Against a sudden blast of cold air sweeping down from the mountains the physician turned up the collar of a muddied gray riding cloak. "Shouldn't wonder but you're trying to understand what the First Siege of Louisburg has to do with my being here? Well, here's the reason. It was there that my father met Adrienne Grineau, who was the daughter of a Swiss mercenary officer taken during the Siege of '45."

The speaker hunched forward, and with small, dark eyes intent upon the coals, commenced to speak more rapidly. "Since my mother was Protestant, pretty and, for a female, well educated, my respected sire married her and brought his bride back to Boston." Mason laughed softly.

"They got on well enough and it may be that they deeply loved one another, although it seems strange that two persons of utterly contrasting temperaments could have got along so well for so long."

Maddox nodded, took a sip of cognac, then glanced at Murphy, who seemed to be sleeping quietly.

"Once Father returned from the Siege he bought into a shipping firm doing business with the West Indies — horses, lumber and salted fish for rum and molasses. He prospered. A year later I was born — my parents' only child."

Only when the doctor paused did Dan become aware that an almost comically varied chorus of snores was rising in various directions.

Dr. Mason resumed, "Don't know if you'll understand this, friend Maddox, but I'll try to explain. Even when quite young I began to realize I had become a battleground for conflicting ideas. On one side there stood my father. He was insensitive, honest to the nth degree and a strict, though just, disciplinarian.

"To relieve these dour qualities he'd a fine, dry sense of humor which came to the surface on unexpected occasions. Always a good provider, Cap'n Edwin, as his associates called him, nevertheless required that any outlay of cash, no matter how small, be justified."

For all he couldn't understand half of what this sawbones was saying Maddox listened with a genuine attention.

"What were your Pa's political views?" he queried just to keep this strange conversation on the move.

"He wasn't interested in politics, but when this confounded war broke out, he bought shares in a big privateer and sailed on her as supercargo."

"How'd he make out?" Dan had heard considerable talk about fortunes made through privateering.

"I'll tell you about that later. Let me try to keep this absurd dissertation in chronological order." The physician suddenly got up and, cloak swaying, began to pace back and forth past the shadowy, blanketed figure of Josh, who long ago had curled up on the ground and was enjoying deep if uncomfortable slumber.

"It took time for me to discover that being an only child is no bargain. My mother was a busy, gay finch of a woman, but her will on certain subjects was quite as inflexible as my father's. One such subject was the matter of my education. My father felt it unnecessary that my mother should instruct me in French along with a smattering of Swiss-German. He declared that, after graduation from Boston Latin School, a year's apprenticeship in accounting and bookkeeping was about all his son required by way of schooling before he started to work in Wheelock & Mason's counting house."

On glancing across the fire he realized that Sergeant Maddox's round, dark-blue eyes were almost disturbingly intent and fixed unwaveringly upon himself. What was the fellow making of all this?

"Sergeant, am I boring you?"

"Hell, no." The Pennsylvanian grinned and locked hands behind his head. "Tell me, sir, when the trouble began in Boston where did your Pa stand?"

"Why do you ask?"

Dan blinked slowly — like a cat dozing in front of a hearth. "It's because I — well, somewheres back in the Watauga settlements I heard tell you've Tory connections. Not that I or any sensible man believe such rumors," he added quickly.

Harsh lines formed around the doctor's mouth, added years to his appearance. "That is shrewd of you. Too many fool stories circulate and cause all manner of needless grief and trouble." His voice deepened. "Allow me to assure you, here and now, neither I nor any member of my family have ever held the least sympathy for the Royalist cause."

Deliberately, the sergeant's narrow, reddish head inclined. "I'll take yer word on that — sir."

"Then, by your leave, I will continue. After I had graduated from Boston Latin it was as if a bomb had burst in our home when my mother calmly informed my father that she had enrolled me in Harvard College. Father — as I've forgotten to state — was a firm Methodist and flew into one of his rare rages; he declared that no son of his would attend an institution so largely supported and directed by the Church of England. Why, roared the old man, 'twas nearly as bad as sending him to a Roman Catholic seminary!"

Samuel Grineau Mason, M.D., tossed twigs onto the coals; they blazed up to illumine his cleanly delineated and lightly pock-marked features. He then attempted to pet a sad-eyed dog which, diffidently, had approached the flames in search of warmth and companionship.

Suddenly the physician's grim expression relaxed. "Who'd you suppose won the argument over Harvard College?"

"Your Pa?"

"Wrong. 'Twas my little birdlike mother."

"I'd admired to have watched that set-to," Maddox admitted, settling farther against a back rest of saddles. "Must ha' been kind of like a bitty banty hen standin' up to a turkey gobbler."

"You've a rare gift for similes, Sergeant," smiled the physician. "In any case I went to Harvard College, where I earned a bachelor's degree — *cum laude*."

The barking of a fox filled a brief silence before Samuel Mason went on. "I was about to work for my father's firm when I became friendly with a surgeon on duty with the garrison in Boston. He invited me one day to watch him operate. Well, Sergeant, I became fascinated with the practice of medicine. Possibly I felt so strongly about it because, to me, it seemed this regimental surgeon's methods and those of his fellows were too brutal, too unskilled, too disinterested in the individual patient. You understand why I felt impelled to become a doctor?"

"Yep. From what I've heard and seen around field hospitals it's a wonder any wounded ever pulled through; most of 'em didn't, either. 'Twas a shinin' wonder poor Tim ever survived that bayonet wound he took in his leg at Brandywine. Well, what did you do?"

"I got over to England as supercargo on one of my Father's vessels armed with a small bequest from an aged aunt which made it possible for me to study at St. Thomas's Hospital. There I studied and worked under the famous Dr. Potts for awhile. After that, I progressed to St. Bartholomew's, where I became interested in a growing, but still unfashionable, branch of medicine called surgery."

Maddox caught the familiar word "surgery" and sat up. "You mean cutting, like the barber-surgeons?"

"Just that, except that in England surgeons for a good while had departed from association with barbers." Only nearby snores and the occasional snuffling of a sick horse now broke the chill stillness. Mason continued quietly, "I attended the lectures of Mr. John Hunter — amazing in depth and boldness."

" 'Mister'?" Maddox grunted.

"Yes, you see surgeons abroad always are called 'Mister' unless, of course, they've already earned an M.D. For that reason I am entitled to be addressed 'Doctor.' But be that as it may, I might still be practicing surgery in London except for mounting troubles with the Crown in Boston. First, there was the burning of the *Gaspée*, which was followed by the Tea Party and finally the so-called Boston Massacre.

"When my father ordered me to come I was glad to obey, but by that time passages to New England were almost impossible to book."

The physician stooped to warm broad, short-fingered hands over the coals while the stray dog yipped softly and twitched limbs in pursuit of a dream rabbit.

He fixed his eyes on the Pennsylvanian's face as if seeking to record the least reaction to what he was about to say. "So it came about, friend Maddox, that, in my haste to return home, I committed a grievous, though quite unconscious, error."

" 'Error'? I don't catch your meanin', sir. What sort of a mistake did you make?"

"In order to gain the quickest possible transportation across the Atlantic I signed on as contract surgeon for a detachment destined to reinforce the 52nd Foot then on duty in Boston."

The sergeant's lean features tightened. Maybe there *had* been something in that rumor? "D'you mean to tell me that you've really served in the King's Army?"

Doctor Mason's voice became as incisive as one of his scalpels. "No! You misunderstand. I never have accepted a King's Commission and I never will!" He hoped he sounded convincing. "I merely signed on as a temporary civilian employee of the British Army who contracted to attend troops on their way to Boston. I took no oath of allegiance to the Crown, nor for that matter was I ever invited to."

The speaker's voice now sank so low that Maddox was forced to lean well forward. "It was most unfortunate that the transport docked on the very same day that fighting took place in Lexington and Concord. Even more disastrous was the fact that the black civilian coat I'd expected to wear ashore was stolen. The day being a cold one I was constrained to borrow a tunic from a young ensign with whom I'd made friends and so I came ashore in my hometown wearing a British officer's scarlet jacket!"

Maddox said carefully, "That sure was a damned unchancey happenstance."

"Of course I was seen, and although I removed that tunic the instant I reached home, word already had spread that I was serving the enemy."

Maddox, trying to make up his mind what to think, tossed more wood on the fire and by its light watched Doctor Mason's hands slowly clench and unclench.

"For all I made a sworn deposition and the officer in command of the reinforcements certified in writing that my contract as a civilian surgeon had expired with termination of the voyage, a suspicion that I entertained Loyalist sentiments spread so effectively that threatening inscriptions were chalked on the walls of our house. Although I made repeated efforts to enroll among the Sons of Liberty, my friends deserted me and my applications were summarily rejected."

With an angry jerk Dr. Mason tilted back his head and the little silver cup flashed as he drained the last of his cognac.

"Naturally the fact that I'd spent the past four years in England and admitted having made some friends there didn't help to quash the most extravagant rumors."

The physician shrugged. "Following that battle on Breed's Hill life became almost intolerable. Although I tried to get out of Boston several times I failed, so was forced to linger inside the British lines all that winter.

"My poor mother and I became outcasts. No one would have anything to do with us save to sell us the necessities of life at exorbitant prices."

The physician drew a slow, shuddering breath which he expelled in an explosive whirling cloud of vapor. "You'll not be overly surprised to learn that, during the late winter of 1776, lion-hearted little Mother perished of hunger and a congestion of the lungs induced by the complete lack of heating in our home.

"Damn' hard lines," Maddox muttered. "And after that?"

"As you know, *our* troops —" the doctor injected a note of defiance into the possessive and stared hard into the gunsmith's slightly oblique eyes, "invested Boston so successfully that scarcely a month after my mother died, General Gage was ordered to evacuate his troops to Halifax.

"Just before the British departed, a party of high-ranking officers who were drinking in a public house were heard to lay bets that, after having been so scurvily treated by his countrymen, Dr. Sam Mason would accept a commission and accompany them to Canada.

"Although I at once and categorically refused this offer I was arrested on the very day that General Washington's troops entered the town and was thrown in jail for a Tory.

"If I'd imagined that previously I'd suffered injustice I was soon disillusioned," continued Mason bitterly. "I was haled before a drumhead court-martial presided over by a drunken assistant provost marshal who, when I offered depositions attesting my loyalty to the American cause, ripped them to shreds unread. Then he roared, 'Send this damned Kinglover to where he can do us no more mischief!' "

It came to Maddox that if his companion weren't telling the truth then he must be a very skilled liar. In the Army he'd encountered not a few of them. Hum. Rumor had it that the British were clever about planting spies. Where could one be more useful than on an expedition such as this? The King's generals certainly needed to know how best to pursue beaten Patriot forces.

The doctor, in dull monotones, then described his confinement in Newgate, a prison improvised from a worn-out lead mine at Simsbury, Connecticut, in the lightless depths of which convicted or merely suspected Tories were imprisoned without trial. In that ghastly living tomb, some sixty feet below the earth's surface, faint daylight sometimes was visible for maybe an hour, but water, seeping from the cavern's roof, never ceased its *drip-dripping*. In the course of time, stated the physician, this dripping drove many prisoners insane. In Simsbury Prison the motionless, chill air would penetrate to the marrow of a prisoner's bones and bleach his skin a lifeless, fish-belly white.

"I spent over a year in that hell-hole before I escaped."

Despite himself, the Pennsylvanian was impressed, queried, "How come you got away?"

"By shamming to be a corpse, which wasn't difficult because I'd almost become one," the doctor explained. "Fortunately, when my 'remains' were brought to the surface it was late in the day and the grave diggers too drunk or lazy to attend to their business straight away so I was left in a shed among the real cadavers to wait for morning. During the night I managed to creep off into the woods. Maybe the burial detail failed to count the dead so failed to notice my absence; anyhow there was no pursuit.

"For months, under false names, I wandered among the backwoods of New Hampshire and Connecticut treating the sick and regaining my strength. Finally I felt sufficiently recovered to venture into Hartford, where I communicated with a classmate, one of the very few who'd refused to believe me a Tory. It was thanks to his generosity I was able to assume the identity of a physician who'd been lost at sea and so purchase a stock of drugs and a set of instruments.

"I then felt emboldened to offer my services to the Continental Army and was accepted. I was attending wounds after the battle of Monmouth when I was recognized and forced to run for my life." Harsh tones returned to Mason's voice. "After that, I dared not remain in the East so worked my way westward to Fort Patrick Henry where, of course, I heard about Colonels Robertson and Donelson's expeditions."

Mason pulled out his silver flask and offered it to Maddox, who, finding it nearly empty, resisted temptation and merely wetted his lips.

"I've told Colonel Robertson my story — most of it, that is — which he professes to credit. Maybe he really does, but I've the notion I'm only here because he sorely needs the presence of a trained physician."

"Why d'you think that, sir?"

"Because he asked so few questions." Mason laughed. "In a way, I flatter myself to believing that I'm more valuable to him than almost anyone else we have with us. Except for —"

Maddox pushed his rifleman's broad-brimmed hat onto the back of his head and yawned. "Except for what?"

"A first-class gunsmith like you. In this most imperfect world it would appear that capable killers are far more in demand than capable healers."

6. *Revelations by Firelight, II*

HIGHLIGHTS glinted across former Sergeant Maddox's high cheekbones when he inclined his dark-red head and smothered a yawn; at the same time he began roughly to pat the black-and-brown stray hound which finally had come over to lie beside him.

"Ain't no doubt but that you're damn' handy with your dosin' and your knives, sir," Maddox began in his strong, low-pitched voice. "Well, 'thout braggin', I could say that, in my own way, I'm just about as handy. Me, I c'n work and put together as fine a rifle-gun as any slab-sided Dutchman you'll find makin' arms around Lancaster, Reading or Allentown — I ain't lyin'. Anybody in those parts can tell you the same.

"Me, I been makin' and repairin' firearms of all sorts ever since I stood knee-high to a grasshopper and was apprenticed by my uncle to Jake Deckerd, the master armorer. Now, sir, sometimes you'll hear old Jake called 'Deckard,' 'Deckart,' 'Deckheart' or 'Dickert,' and some other ways, too, but 'Deckerd' is the way he really spelt his name. I know. I've stamped it on too damn' many red-hot gun barrels and locks ever to forget the true spellin'." He cocked a heavy brow. "You've heard tell of Deckerd?"

The doctor sighed and pushed his feet in often patched and otherwise worn riding boots across fallen leaves towards the coals. "Of course. The name is known everywhere in America. You were born in Lancaster?"

"No. My Uncle Hank once told me my Pa and Ma hailed from somewhere near to Philadelphia; said they traveled with a party of Moravians and Mennonites to homestead on the frontier which then was near Lancaster.

"At first, Pa tried to farm, but he got nowheres because he'd been a blacksmith back East, so he took to huntin' for our livin'. Then when game got scarce on account of so many settlements was springin' up, he took up blacksmithin' again. Didn't he, old girl?" Maddox reached out, gently lowered his rifle onto his lap and stroked its stock a moment before he reloaded a charred corncob pipe. "So I guess it's only natural, sir, that I should enjoy workin' iron, specially —"

The sergeant broke off, then jumped to his feet and looked sharply about, for, across the meadow, a number of dogs had commenced a furious barking.

By the dozen, shaggy, shadowy figures roused up and, grabbing arms, immediately sought cover behind the nearest tree. Indians?

" 'Tain't nothin' — this time," Dan said after a pause. "Only a few elk or maybe buffalo over there. Listen and you c'n hear 'em snapping twigs and branches. Critters can't see well in darkness and blunder about considerable."

Maddox spat softly then reseated himself. "I must ha' been a tadpole of about nine or ten when a scourge of real bad smallpox swept our countryside. Pa and Ma and my little brother all took it and died in short order. Since I'd no other kin left, Uncle Hank, a bachelor who made his bread at carpenterin' and doin' a little surveyin', took me in. Uncle was grouchy and pretty hard to get on with but I reckon I owe him a lot 'cause he licked me into learnin' how to read, spell and, best of all, to figger fairly well." Meditatively, Maddox patted his backside. "Whenever I couldn't answer up pert and correct on a lesson he'd set me to learn Uncle Hank would frale me plenty fervent. Fact. Then, when I was 'round fifteen years old, he decided to go back East but, before leavin', he apprenticed me to Jacob Deckerd.

"Well, sir, I was just about clear of my apprenticeship when tidings reached Lancaster that a rebellion had been started up in Boston 'gainst the British tyrants.

"Next, we got word of the skirmishes fought around Lexington and Concord and then about a great bloody battle which was fought on a place called Bunker's (or Breed's) Hill. Our people didn't worry much over the war — it bein' Yankee troubles — till New York, New Hampshire and then some other Colonies — I still don't mind which ones — raised militia and voted to fight against the King's men.

"Soon as Independence was proclaimed the heft of our men and older boys marched off to 'fight for Freedom,' so they said, but I reckon they just wanted excitement and to find out how a big war was fought."

Maddox sucked hard on his pipe. "Of course I pined to leave right away before the fighting ended and the Britishers got driven out of America with their tails between their legs."

The doctor chuckled. "So you went early?"

"No, sir. Old man Deckerd wouldn't allow it on account of most of his best artificers had gone off; besides, he claimed he needed more time to make me into a full-fledged gunsmith. So I sweated over the forges and rifling tables till word came that Gen'ral Washington had got licked real bad at a place in New York called Long Island and that another of our armies had been smashed to pieces 'way up in Canada.

"Around then a feller rode into Lancaster sayin' that the King's generals were plottin' to divide our Colonies into two parts."

"— Which was true enough," grunted Samuel Mason. "Burgoyne was to march south from Canada while Sir Henry Clinton was to drive north up the Hudson and meet him; thus they would split the Colonies apart and fatally weaken them."

"Well, that same feller who brought this news told about a brand-new regiment bein' raised by an old Injun fighter name of Morgan. His first name was Dan'l, same's mine.

"This regiment, says he, was bein' recruited from expert hunters and frontiersmen. Only real crack shots bringin' their own weapons need apply. Well, sir, I liked the sound so I packed a blanket roll, stored my tools with old Deckerd, shouldered Ilsa here —" he dropped his gaze to the wickedly graceful six-foot rifle resting across his lap — "and set out for Winchester there to enroll with Morgan's Virginia Rifle Regiment for two years' service." Dan peered across the fire, "Say, Doc, sure I ain't agein' you with all this chin-music?"

"Not in the least," Mason assured quickly. "While I was — well, with our troops — I heard all the while about how Morgan's sharpshooters raised holy hell with the Hessians and British Regulars at Freeman's Farm and Bemis Heights and then again at Monmouth and Briar Creek. Please go on."

"Well, by the time I got to Winchester, Morgan's Rifles was almost filled up with Long Hunters, Injun fighters and a lot of picked marksmen who'd been sent in from near every regiment in the Patriot armies.

"Like I said, we were expected to fetch along our own weepons, molds, repair tools and bar lead. Yep. Ilsa was plenty admired, weren't you, sweetheart?" Using a hard palm he began to buff the rifle's gleaming brass patch pocket which, neatly let flush into a stock of bird's-eye maple, contained tallow used to grease patches so that a charge could be rammed home quickly and easily; all too often a man's life might depend upon the speed with which he could reload his piece. Everyone knew that.

"There were plenty of hard cases in our ranks, the sort who bragged like hell but could show plenty of nicks in their knife handles and a lot of scalps. Colonel Dan never questioned about where a man's scalps came from — so long as they didn't look like hair off'n a woman or a child.

"Well, sir, 'Old Wagoner' — we called Dan Morgan so on account of he'd been in the freightin' business for a long while — used us hard, mighty hard, but he never did waste time tryin' to teach us to parade pretty — like the French or the British. All he minded was whether we'd show up in good shape where we were supposed to go on time, and whether we wasted powder by missin' too many Redcoats.

"The Long Knives 'mongst us especially were tickled with Dan'l Morgan's notions about how to fight the enemy."

Mason's small, intense eyes bored through the dim firelight. "Just what is a 'Long Knife'?"

"He's a frontiersman who's collected two or more scalps — or says he has. Course to start with, I was green as spring grass and had a pretty rough time till I twice dropped a runnin' deer at near on two hundred yards.

"After that the boys acted more friendly — 'specially Tim Murphy who was champion marksman of the regiment. That I could mend almost any piece that wasn't really wore out helped a lot, too.

"Yep. Believe it or not, Doc, Ilsa's accounted for near as many Redcoats as Tim Murphy's Kitty — which is that double gun over there; 'tis the same he used at Freeman's Farm to mortally wound a famous Scotch Gen'ral named Fraser. Hit him at over three hundred paces.

"Bein' a friend, he says he could have turned the same trick with Ilsa."

"Why Ilsa? Isn't that an unusual name for a rifle?"

Harsh lines deepened upon the gunsmith's leathery features. "Ilsa was the very first rifle I built that I could really brag on — so I named her after Ilsa Bauer, the Lancaster girl I married first time I came back on furlough.

"Her Pa, George Bauer, was and is a champion gunsmith — near as good as old Jake Deckerd himself."

Mason's level dark brows lifted a trifle. "So you're a married man? Odd, I'd never have thought of you as such."

Maddox's hands suddenly closed over the long rifle, whereupon the hound beside him lifted his head and briefly thumped his tail on the ground. "I ain't; happened Ilsa perished tryin' to have our first child. Folks said the baby was big, a real buster. Reckon Ilsa must have been built too slim in the chamber to handle such a big bullet. Little feller died, too."

"Sorry, Sergeant. I shouldn't have asked. How long ago did this misfortune occur?"

Dan Maddox began slowly to beat his fists together then turned and looked off into the gloom. "Three months, two weeks and four days ago. Reckon you'll deem me soft, but after they died I didn't crave to linger 'round Lancaster so I was more than pleasured about then to hear from my old friend Tim Murphy. A month later he rode into town carryin' Kitty and his soldier's land grant warrant. Like me, he was seekin' for a place to use it to advantage.

"Well, just about then someone came in from the Watauga settlements, said an expedition was startin' soon to take up free land along the Cumberland River, so I got out my own warrant, packed up my gunsmithin' tools and sold my cabin for the price of that there mule and the horses you've seen."

Sergeant Maddox got to his feet. "So, there you are, sir. Maybe, like you, I stand in need of a fresh start in life. Wonder what kind of country we'll find around the Frenchman's Lick — an we live to behold it."

7. *Dying Moon*

DYING MOON, a sub-chief of the Shawnee tribe, was unusual in that he was disfigured by a harelip. Since most Indian children born with obvious flaws were quickly exposed, he had cleverly minimized his handicap through the use of sign language whenever possible. He also possessed boundless energy and considerable intelligence.

While trotting along with the twin tips of buffalo horns that rose from his headdress jabbing rhythmically at the late afternoon sky, Dying Moon felt pleased with himself; the detailed completeness of his report on Gitchi-Mokoman's — Robertson's — expedition should earn him considerable praise from Moluntha.

Over a mantle of wolfskin he cast a quick glance backwards and saw that broad-chested Shel-towie, hatchet-faced Blue Dog and the six perpetually alert and lean-limbed braves rode closed up as they followed him along an old buffalo road which roughly paralleled the Kentucky Trace.

Yes. His medicine today had been good in that those tough-looking meat hunters hadn't sighted his party but had continued on their butchering expedition, apparently quite unalarmed.

Moluntha should be interested and possibly excited to learn that an expedition numbering well over two hundred white men right now were heading towards the Ohio; also that they had brought no families along. Their rate of travel was slowed only by livestock, which included a pleasingly large herd of fine-looking horses.

He decided, come nightfall, to detach Shel-towie and a few strong, well-mounted braves so that they could continue to watch the column while he and the rest of his following rode in search of Moluntha.

Twice, the Shawnees encountered small groups of buffalo plodding leisurely southward; they promptly detoured these great, bearded, stupid-looking brown-and-black beasts which appeared so placid but generally weren't, especially during this, the rutting season, when any grown bull would charge in blind rage at any movement.

Dying Moon decided to spend this night in a deep hollow where, with two steep ridges separating him from the invaders, he felt it safe to kindle a small fire. After all, he and his followers hadn't tasted warm food in two days — only pemmican or greasy jerked bear meat.

Tiny yellow flames had just appeared when Shel-towie, who had climbed a nearby mound to cast a final look about, suddenly came bounding downhill and began hurriedly to kick dirt over the fire.

Blue Dog, always hot-tempered, rasped a curse, "*Gissa! Sassagouns!*" and jerked out his skinning knife; barely in time, he checked himself, because Shel-towie urgently was pointing to that mound he'd quitted in such a hurry. At once Dying Moon and the rest grabbed their mounts' heads and forced them earthwards to prevent a betraying whicker.

Dying Moon's twisted lip lifted but he said nothing; only his narrow, dark eyes asked questions. The Shawnees gathered in a tight circle, head-dresses and gun muzzles outlined in sharp silhouette against a flaming sunset.

What Shel-towie had glimpsed was a party of whites going into camp on a deer run which, judging from the slope of the land, probably soon would join with the Kentucky Trace.

He had counted, Shel-towie stated in a hoarse whisper, six grown men, three women and three papoose in that group which had halted near a small salt spring ringed with the dull white bones and skulls of hundreds of animals which had been attracted there.

Dying Moon's broad, yellow-and-red-painted features lighted and his deformed lip twitched, exposed big yellow teeth in a mirthless grin. *Wagh!* So there were only six men yonder? *Wagh!* This was good. His party numbered nine, all of them seasoned warriors. Five were armed with fairly new British muskets while two others carried ancient firelocks of dubious dependability. Best of all, reported Shel-towie, these travelers had seemed pathetically unwary — had taken no precautions whatever against surprise.

There was no need for consultation — everyone knew what was to be done in these circumstances; one warrior would be left to guard the horses while the rest, silent, dark and sinuous as so many rattlesnakes, would encircle the camp. Then, on a screaming blast from Dying Moon's turkey's-wing-bone whistle, they would whoop, rise out of the under-brush and shoot down as many men of the party as possible. After that the braves would rush in joyously to stab or tomahawk the survivors.

The Shawnees were forced to delay their enveloping movement for a time because, over yonder, someone had fired a shot. The Indians soon discovered that one of the immigrants, obviously a pitiful greenhorn, had gone out to shoot something for supper. He came striding into camp proudly holding up a huge turkey which, as he declared — much too loudly — had been so danged fat that its breast had split on striking the ground.

The other men cursed and warned him to shut up. Grown a trifle more vigilant, perhaps because of the recent racket, the travelers set about hobbling horses and otherwise preparing for the night — always keeping their weapons within easy reach.

Then another unexpected incident occurred. These people had

brought with them a small, dun-colored cow which carried a deep-toned bell slung about its neck. The creature on being released promptly nosed off through the underbrush seeking an open patch where grass might be growing. When the beast came wandering up to Shel-towie's hiding place he sprang and split the stray's forehead with a vicious swing of his war hatchet. The cow's knees immediately buckled; then, uttering a soft, gurgling grunt, it collapsed, shuddering, amid a bed of sweet-smelling ferns.

Shel-towie paused just long enough to make certain that no one in the immigrants' camp had noticed that the cow bell had ceased to ring, then he cut loose the bell and began to ring it gently while trotting deeper into the woods.

Dying Moon, who had seen what was taking place, signaled to the brave on his other side to sit tight in anticipation of what was bound to happen. For several minutes the Shawnees remained crouched in the shadowy undergrowth motionless as so many "freezing" rabbits and were just about as impossible to distinguish.

These men, Dying Moon decided, were incredibly unobservant. Five minutes passed before anyone noticed that the cow bell's *tunk-tunk!* now sounded only faintly through the gloom.

A shock-haired fellow wearing a duroy shirt suddenly cried, "Hey! That damn' fool cow of mine's strayed off a piece." He jumped up and, without pausing to catch up his gun, set off in pursuit of the bell's *tunk-tunk.*

He died a moment or two later as quickly and easily as his cow. The Shawnee lingered just long enough to rip off the scalp any which way, then loped back to resume his place in the invisible ring.

When Dying Moon finally sounded a piercing blast of his whistle and raised the scalp-yell enough light remained to permit reasonably accurate shooting, with the result that two of the immigrants crumpled and died instantly while the remaining three dropped heavily onto the ground. Throat-tearing screams of sheer terror rang through the forest.

Dying Moon thought that he and his men had shot surprisingly well, having dropped five out of five targets. It turned out, however, that he was being over-optimistic, for when he and his braves came rushing in to finish the affair three of the fallen figures reared up onto their knees and let fly with deer loads — four buckshot to each charge.

The effect was deadly. Dying Moon, with a ball through his throat, forgot his dream of triumph, dropped his smoking musket and staggered crazily about for a long moment before he fell. As a result of that blast, four of the Shawnees either fell dead or got so badly hurt that they could only screech and limp about clutching dripping limbs. The rest of the attackers had almost completed their rush when a skinny, wild-eyed old woman stood out from behind a tree and fired a load of bird shot at short range which caught Blue Dog squarely in the stomach and nearly blew him in two.

Dreadful sounds ensued when the three women, hopelessly hampered by long skirts, tried to get away. Like hungry panthers the amazed and furious Shawnees leaped onto their backs and with blades briefly gleaming, rode them to the ground.

Shrill shrieks from the children lasted only very briefly.

The whole affair came abruptly to an end — within two minutes from the moment Dying Moon had sounded his whistle. To Shel-towie it seemed incredible that such a handful of inexperienced immigrants should have caused so much of a loss. Dying Moon, Blue Dog and two others lay sprawled among the white men's gear, dead as dead could be; two others had been seriously, if not fatally, hit.

Gradually, it sank in on Shel-towie, who never had been overly bright or quick-thinking, that now he was leader of this scouting party. *Yowp!* His situation appeared both bewildering and critical. Too bad that Dying Moon, now lying slumped on his side amid a widening dark puddle, never had deigned to confide in him. What should be done?

The new leader wasn't at all sure, so he consulted the surviving braves. Some thought one thing, others offered different ideas. Finally it was agreed that the dead and wounded should be carried to wherever Moluntha might be and a report given about Gitchi-Mokoman's expedition. Fervently, Shel-towie prayed that this not inconsiderable loot consisting of several salable scalps, six guns and over two dozen horses, plus a generous supply of powder, shot and other useful equipment would soften the great War Chief's wrath over having lost four experienced warriors — one of the wounded having already died.

In the end Shel-towie decided to take one sound man along and continue, warily, to scout the column. The rest — conducting the dead, the wounded and the plunder — must try to find a Shawnee village which was presumed to exist about three sleeps to the northeast.

It turned out that Moluntha was to lose two more of his followers for, the day after Shel-towie had split his command, a party of wolf-lean Cayuga Iroquois on their way to the Great Hunting Ground were delighted to have a little band of plunder-laden Shawnees ride blindly into a hastily contrived ambush.

⌒

8. *Jonathan Robertson, Aetat Eleven*

ONLY eleven sheep now ran in the flock Colonel Robertson had entrusted to his eleven-year-old son, Jonathan. Descended from a strain brought from the Highlands of Scotland to the mountains of North Carolina, these long-legged, sturdy and dirty-white beasts with black faces had proved able to thrive under the most rugged conditions.

Patriarch of this precious flock was "Old Scratch," aptly named for the Devil by Jonathan after a particularly trying day during which that evil-tempered and wily old ram again and again had proved just as stubborn, strong-minded and persistent as his herder.

As a rule livestock traveled near the long column's rear, led by Colonel Jim's herd of horses. Some of these, bought earlier in the year near Kaskaskia, revealed Arab-Spanish blood through proudly arched necks, short-coupled conformation and flowing manes and tails. But not too many of Robertson's horses suggested such distinguished lineage; the majority were undersized, tough, cold-bred Carolina tackeys, brutes designed through survival to live on next to nothing and to die hard.

Care and protection of this invaluable herd — which represented most of the colonel's current capital — had been entrusted to Mark and John Robertson, two of Jonathan's several uncles; both were in their mid-twenties and were powerful and energetic.

Jonathan much preferred Uncle John who, broad-shouldered, fair-haired and with clear blue eyes, suggested his much older brother both in build and temperament. Uncle Mark, on the other hand, was wiry, slightly built and dark of hair and complexion. Mark seldom spoke unless he had to, but everyone respected his undoubted ability; there was mighty little woodcraft he'd missed acquiring from "Uncle" Daniel Boone, that great authority on various kinds of Indians and the savage tricks peculiar to each tribe.

Just behind the horse herd plodded about two dozen cattle, all sharp-horned, furry and nearly as scary and nimble as deer. After these trotted a sounder of smart but ill-tempered swine; mostly, they were ridge-backed and brown-black in color.

Once he'd gulped breakfast, Jonathan secured his scant gear for the day's travel before saddling a runty little horse Pa had presented on his last birthday.

Subdued cursing and shouts came from the woods together with a noisy crashing of branches caused by men riding about to sort out and round up various kinds of livestock.

Horses, presently, were tied head-to-tail, but the other animals were kept on the trail through a liberal use of voices, sticks and switches.

On this bright October morning Jonathan felt finer than fine while gathering reins and watching the dipping and darting flight of a yellow hammer. Criminently! This sort of life sure beat hanging 'round the Fort and having book-learning rammed, willy-nilly, down his throat. Pridefully, he shook out long yellow linen fringes decorating a black-dyed hunting shirt Ma tearfully had bestowed just before he'd left the Fort.

Although, short of torture, he'd never have admitted it, Jonathan kind of wished Ma and the other kids had come along with him and Pa instead of waiting for Colonel Donelson's boat expedition to commence its long and dangerous journey down the Holston and the mighty Tennessee. Nobody seemed to know just how far they'd have to travel or through what sort ot country. Likely, Donelson's people would see plenty of wild Indians and meet with all kinds of adventures before reaching the Cumberland's mouth. Too bad this journey so far hadn't proved even halfway exciting.

While riding into the woods he congratulated himself: Well, so far I ain't lost but one measly old ewe, so mebbe Pa figures I'm earning my salt and ain't too sorry he's brung me along. Who could have guessed a wolf would dare sneak so near to camp without some dog taking notice? Yep. If it weren't for that dratted Old Scratch this here job would be a tight cinch.

He reached out and broke off a long, tough sapling which he'd use to whack straying sheep back onto the Trace and trimmed it with a short, razor-sharp sheath knife which was his most prized possession next to a saddle pistol so ancient that it had to be held together by windings of copper wire.

He found most of the sheep browsing peacefully on a patch of burnt-

over ground near the lip of a ravine and, for a wonder, Old Scratch was
feeding in their midst! Criminently! When the order came to get moving it shouldn't prove any trick at all to get his flock in place and traveling right on time.

Despite Old Scratch's air of innocence Jonathan thought to detect an
all-too-familiar wicked gleam in the tough old buck's amber-and-black
eyes. He had just driven his last ewe onto the trampled and manure-
sprinkled Trace when the ram gave a buck-jump and went tearing off
towards the ravine.

One of the rear guard laughed and yelled, "Go get him, Sonny! I'll
mind these blattin' fools for ye."

Ducking and whipped by branches, Jonathan set his little horse to
slipping and sliding down the slope. He kept hollering shrilly, "Come
back, you blasted ijit! Come back here!"

Old Scratch paid not the least attention, only vanished into a clump
of juniper bushes. A moment later Jonathan was hard put to keep from
tackling an incline so precipitous that he and his horse might well have
been killed had they attempted to slide down it.

Spouting words that would have astonished and pained his Ma to hear
him use, Jonathan reined aside and at the same time lifted a short lasso
from his pommel — he'd found plenty of use for it before now. Hurriedly he tied his mount to a tree before plunging downwards amid a
rattling torrent of small stones to where Old Scratch was browsing as if
he'd never entertained a wicked thought in all his life.

"C'm here, you mean old cuss!" Jonathan panted and ran forward
shaking out his noose for a quick cast. For all the ram seemed willing to
be captured the boy remained wary; sure enough, just as he prepared to
throw, Old Scratch suddenly lowered massive yellow-brown horns and
charged.

By now the boy had learned to be pretty spry on his feet but this time
he wasn't quick enough; Old Scratch connected with a mighty butt that
lifted the lad clean off his feet, propelled him a good two yards through
the air and made him lose his wide-brimmed hat in which he'd tucked a
hawk's-wing plume in imitation of Edmund Jennings's eagle feather.

Twice more Old Scatch rushed but failed to hit his target; on the
buck's fourth try Jonathan succeeded in flipping the noose over the cul-
prit's curling horns.

By the time Jonathan returned to the Trace towing Old Scratch, still
violently uncooperative, the rear guard had disappeared, and only extin-

guished cook fires, rough bough beds, gnawed tree trunks and a scattering of worn-out equipment indicated that an expedition had passed this way.

Half-strangled, the ram finally condescended to travel at a slow trot. Even so, Jonathan overtook the rear guard considerably sooner than he'd anticipated and at once realized that something must have gone wrong, for his two uncles, Major Todd and Edmund Jennings were standing behind trees with rifles ready and eyes mighty busy with their surroundings.

Just before daybreak Cash Brooks had roused and sought Colonel Robertson, whom he found rolling out of a blanket. Hunkering down he muttered, "Mebbe I'm loony, Jim, but jist after sundown yester eve I fancied hearin' a bit of shootin' and whoopin' somewheres 'way off 'mongst them hills yonder. You notice it?"

Robertson yawned cavernously, shook his big, handsome head. "No, Cash. Likely what you heard was the crackle of an old tree fallin' and the cry of wolves runnin' game. Like you know, at a distance such can sound mighty like people hollerin'."

Cash rubbed white bristles standing out all over his chin. "Yep. I know, but one reason my Ma's favorite son is still wearin' his hair is on account of when he ain't sure about something he allus goes and takes a look."

Robertson knuckled his eyes. "Generally I do, too, so suppose you and Joe Drake take a quick look-see, but mind you don't ride too far. We need to cover a lot of ground; this fine weather ain't going to last much longer."

Moving at a cautious trot, Drake and his companion soon came onto a well-used game trail which they followed till they came upon the clearing about which the bodies of several whites lay scattered among the underbrush and old animal bones.

Once the column had been alerted James Robertson and the point made a quick but perceptive survey and through long experience deduced, accurately enough, what had taken place, how and why.

"Well, Cunnel," demanded Drake, "what d'you make of this?"

"The hostiles numbered about ten, but all the same they got hurt pretty bad by only five of our people — always provided none have been carried off prisoner."

After circling the place Joe Drake decided that the murderers, who

apparently must have been scouting the expedition, had split up; two
Indians riding south as if to continue watching the column, while the
rest, four or five warriors, had carried off their dead, wounded and loot
and a possible prisoner or two to the northeast.

"What's your notion, Cash?" Drake wanted to know.

"Why, 'tis 'bout the same as yours, Joe," grunted the Long Hunter
while studying forms only partially concealed beneath the torn and
bloodied remains of garments. "These poor devils, three or four families
of 'em, must ha' been makin' for the Trace on their way to Whiteley's
or mebbe Harrod's Station. From the style their scalps bin lifted looks
like some Piankasaws or Miamis bin at work."

Hard-eyed, Sergeant Maddox was all for an immediate pursuit.
"Please, Colonel, let's ride; those brutes can't have gone very far — not
leading pack horses."

Firmly, Robertson shook his head. "I'd sure like to, but now we've
plenty to worry about on our own account; these people were none of
ours."

Over the loud buzzing of clouds of flies the Colonel said quietly,
"While we may be travelin' in a hurry we can't leave Christian bodies to
feed the ravens and wild beasts. Couple of you ride and fetch men with
spades."

Dan was amazed to recognize so few evidences of disgust or outrage
written on the hard, whiskered faces about him. By God, these people
seemed to accept this tragedy as unemotionally as if it had been some
natural phenomenon like sunrise or sunset!

The only person who appeared to be at all shaken was Samuel Mason,
M.D. His long, strong face turned taut then pallid beneath its weather-
ing while he went through the formality of making certain that not even
the faintest spark of life lingered in any of these horribly disfigured
corpses.

Once he'd done his duty, the physician pulled out a frayed black notebook and in it noted the sex and apparent age of the deceased; since
nothing remained to identify the dead, he gave each corpse a number.

Turning aside, he scribbled:

*Trail this party was following would seem to originate in Va. Crosses
the mts. somewhere NE or ENE of here. Since party included women,
children and livestock, route followed cannot be overly difficult. Should
be identified and studied.*

On the Kentucky Trace Mark Robertson wheeled his mount, rode up to Jonathan and said in a flat voice, "Young'un, all along you been wantin' to find out what wild Indians are like, so come along. Tom will tend those fool sheep."

While uncle and nephew turned onto the game trail the rest of the column moved on; everyone, even poor, semi-conscious Tim Murphy, was aware that winter lay just around the corner.

To his last hour Jonathan was never to forget his sensations when he rode his furry little horse into a hollow and found a party of hot and red-faced men in galluses and shirt sleeves hurriedly patting down grave mounds. They must have been working hard, for the only bodies visible were those of a shriveled, yellow-faced old woman and a boy only a little younger than himself.

A savage twist flattening his small, lean-lipped mouth, Uncle Mark directed, "Look yonder, Bub."

The dead boy's meager body lay stiff and naked save for a pair of ragged homespun breeches. His fingers and toes were oddly rigid, spread like talons. He'd had plenty of freckles and his light gray eyes peered at the morning sky sadly, wonderingly — as if he hadn't realized what was happening to him. Ugh! The place where his hair had grown showed as a sickening circle of reddish-white bone upon which a peppering of blue-bottle flies had settled and were crawling busily about.

For all Jonathan already had killed, gutted and skinned many a wild creature and once had beheld the corpse of a man who'd accidentally shot himself, he became aware of bitter bile surging from his stomach, up into his throat and mouth. Lordy! He felt the ground shift under him. Sure, he'd heard plenty of talk about scalping, but this! *This!*

He became aware of Uncle Mark's toneless voice grating, "Aye. Take a good, hard look, boy, and *always* remember that this lad perished because his folks didn't have guards posted nor could they have scouted around this place worth a thin damn before they made camp."

Jonathan, angry all at once, felt prompted to retort that he hadn't noticed any such precautions being taken by the expedition. But, wise for his years, Jim Robertson's son kept quiet.

9. *The Giant*

FOR two days slow, cold autumn rain falling from a slate-gray sky, dripped and piddled endlessly from evergreens and bare-branched hardwoods. Eventually, the silver-gray downpour turned into a brief but severe sleet storm which encased the land in a crystalline, icy sheath, caused beasts to lower their heads and stung men's faces until they hardly could see through red and badly swollen eyelids.

Hard on the heels of this ice storm followed a fall of light, dry snow barely thick enough to cover the ground and etch tree trunks in stark silhouette.

Through this miserable varying weather Colonel Robertson's column plodded sullenly along, shivering and often drenched to the skin.

Evidences of hard travel now increased: packs, saddles and other kinds of harness constantly had to be re-stitched or replaced whenever opportunity offered. More and more horses fell sick and several died, with the result that men who previously had been mounted now were forced, unless they could borrow a ride, to tramp doggedly along on foot. Strangely enough, the cattle, mules, pigs and Jonathan's sheep — still undiminished in number — seemed far less prone to fall sick.

At the same time, an epidemic of colds and rheumy sore throat spread among the weary immigrants.

Not a few men on foot begged permission to ride the Spanish stock or pack animals already overburdened. Such a concession usually was denied unless Doctor Mason approved. Permission seldom was granted even though many boots were beginning to disintegrate. Such unfortunates were forced to improvise moccasins out of canvas or to bind their footgear together with strips of cloth.

The expedition pressed on towards Harrod's Station with Dr. Mason so overworked that Josh Freedly began to wonder how long his master could keep going.

With regard to Corporal Murphy's recovery the physician's manner remained outwardly confident, although he felt deeply concerned. For a couple of days after the rifleman's mauling it seemed that his gashes were going to heal without complications, but then his arm suddenly grew discolored and began to swell with alarming speed; soon threads of incredibly foul-smelling greenish pus commenced to ooze from between stitches and fouled dressings faster than they could be replaced.

When this happened Mason ordered a litter to be contrived from a canvas dodger supported by side bars of lodge-pole pine and strips of ragged tarpaulin. Suspended between two old mules, led by Josh, the patient traveled in reasonable comfort.

Once more on point duty, Dan Maddox rode beside Cash Brooks, who because of the bedraggled fur cap and cape he was wearing, suggested nothing more than a huge old raccoon improbably bestriding a horse. For some time now the Trace had followed the Green River's east bank. Swollen by recent rains, the Green caused a soft roaring which swelled into a furious tumult whenever its current entered a rapids.

This morning Colonel Robertson had ordered Maddox and Brooks to ride well ahead of the point in order to locate and examine a pair of fords reported to exist in the vicinity and to decide which would offer the most practicable crossing.

One glance at the upper ford's wild water flinging clouds of mist and spray high over a formidable barrier of boulders convinced the scouts that they'd better ride on downstream until they came upon the alternative — Uguhu, or Hunting Owl ford.

Without conversation, Maddox and Cash started southwards, dogged by a trio of muddy, burr-stuck and hungry-looking bear hounds.

All at once Cash reined in and bent low in his saddle before pointing at the snow-covered ground. "See that?"

Clearly and recently imprinted in the snow was a line made by several moccasined feet which had emerged from the deep forest to follow the Kentucky Trace.

Breath vapors shifting about their heads, both scouts bent low, studied the tracks at which the dogs had begun to sniff with mounting interest.

Maddox raised a quizzical brow. "Well, Cash, what're you thinking?"

"Ain't nothin' to get yer sweat started. Only four Injuns went this way — mebbe a hour back. Likely they've been out huntin' or followin' trap lines."

"How can you tell?"

"Prints ain't deep or close together, which means they ain't tired or carryin' heavy packs like they were travelin' far."

Preceded by the dogs, the riders had followed the tracks only a short distance when Cash again jerked on his reins and turned, a puzzled look on his weatherbeaten features. "Look! What in hell can have scared them redskins so bad they quit the Trace in so big a hurry?"

"How can you tell they got frightened?"

Cash looked pained. "Dan'l! Dan'l! Be you blind as a bat? Take note o' the great, long strides each man's suddenly taking!"

"I do now. *Somethin'* sure scared the eternal whey out of 'em. Look! They've busted through the underbrush like a rutting moose."

"Still cain't figger what scared them redskins so bad," Cash mumbled after they'd returned to the Trace and he'd bitten off a generous chew of "nigger's heel." "You might think they'd come on old Chitokaka himself."

"Who's 'Chitokaka'?"

"The Injuns' top-dog devil."

The scouts dismounted and, with the Green's monotonous roaring filling their ears, started along the trail.

Maddox straightened so suddenly that his horse shied. "God above! What — what made *those?*" Entering the Trace from the direction of the river and sharply imprinted upon the snow was a line of impossibly huge human footprints!

Cash knuckled granulated, red-rimmed eyes, then shook his head as if to clear it. "Je-sus! They *cain't* be real. No human man can own such goddam tremenjus feet."

Incredulous, Maddox studied a particularly clear impression and estimated it to measure around *twenty* inches in length by *nine* in width! Further, he noted that these tracks had been left by someone wearing shoe-pacs, or hard-soled moccasins.

Remounting, they cocked rifles and, after waving the bear dogs forward, started at a slow walk to follow these incredible footprints. In fact, they took so much time about it that, before long, Colonel Robertson, Joe Drake and others of the point trotted into sight.

Bright blue eyes gone hard and narrow, Robertson growled, "What in hell ails you boys? Trees grow faster than you been movin'. You should have found Uguhu Crossin' an hour since."

Maddox indicated one of the huge footprints. "My God, sir, ain't you noticed *those* tracks?"

The Colonel burst into laughter louder than the river's roaring. "My God! So *that's* what's been holdin' up you stupid bug-tits?"

Dan Maddox flushed under his fringe of short, dull red whiskers. "But, but sir! Look at the *size* of them tracks!"

Joe Drake rode up, exposed gapped, amber-hued teeth in a cavernous grin. "My Gawd, Maddox, you ain't seein' no miracle. Them's only Tom Spencer's footprints."

Cash, coldly furious, snarled, "Who's Tom Spencer?"

"Onliest feller I ever see, or hear tell of, who c'n leave tracks the size of bear paw snowshoes!"

Drake turned to the Colonel. "Say, Jim, 'pears to me like Tom's camp oughter to be somewheres close by."

"That could be. I'll take a look and talk with him. Rest of you — except you, Joe, move on and damn' well find that ford. We'll catch up."

Robertson followed Spencer's trail until it turned off the Trace, and penetrated an alder thicket and then headed towards a grove of towering sycamores, the scabrous trunks of which showed an unhealthy greenish-white in the weak sunshine. Over the tops of these huge trees lingered a thin, blue-gray stratum of wood smoke.

Joe said to his chief, "What say I ride in first? Tom knows me, so he won't likely shoot first and talk later like he gen'rally does. And can that man shoot! I've seen him shoot the balls off'n a squirrel atop of the tallest hickory you ever *did* see."

He cupped hands and called softly, "Heyo! Tom, you thar?"

Presently Thomas Spencer materialized from a clump of junipers. He lowered a long rifle and halted, his vast brown-clad body effectively framed against the snowy background. Maddox found it very easy to credit that the man yonder stood six-feet-nine in his shoe-pacs and that he must weigh well over four hundred pounds. Surely, his shoulders measured a full yard across.

Large steel-gray eyes busy with his visitors Spencer raised a massive arm above a broad-brimmed hat and made the universal peace sign — palm out, fingers straight.

"Heyo, Joe! What're you doin' in these parts?" he boomed in a low-pitched, deliberate voice.

The old Long Hunter's gaunt, Indian-like features relaxed before he pursed leathery lips and squirted an arc of tobacco juice through a broken front tooth. "Why, Tom, we seen yer hoof prints on the Trace so I reckoned I'd bring these fellers over for a little visit."

The giant nodded, then blew his nose between his fingers; obviously he was suffering from a heavy cold. He swung forward moving almost gracefully, his long and tawny hair bobbing gently. When he drew near, Robertson glimpsed golden glints in the depth of a curly, brown beard.

"Well, Joe," greeted Spencer, "surprised to see that mangy scalp of yours still in place. Who's that with ye?"

"Meet Colonel Jim Robertson." When Joe swung lightly off his horse the leader followed suit, then advanced covertly studying this mountainous figure clad in stained and well-worn buckskins. Solemnly, they shook hands all around.

Colonel Robertson led forward his mount to grip Spencer's enormous hand. Smiling he said, "Well, I'm sure tickled to meet the famous Tom Spencer. I've heard so many tales about you I figured you must be at least half a legend."

The giant's clear gray eyes twinkled. "Well, I ain't no legend, and won't be till I forget someday to look in the right direction."

The two, each impressive in his own fashion, remained a long moment frankly taking each other's measure.

Robertson looped his bridle reins over an elbow. "You camped nearby?"

"In the next hollow, Cunnel," drawled Spencer, shouldering his rifle. "Come over and sit a spell. I'm sure starved for news. I ain't laid eyes on a white face in nigh on two months."

The brim of Robertson's floppy farmer's hat dipped to a brief nod. "Be glad to, but I can tarry only a short while. My main body will be comin' up soon and I aim to get us all across the Green 'fore dark." Then the straight-backed leader turned, dwarfed by the giant trees all around him, and followed the giant over a low wooded ridge to a flat clearing dominated by a vast sycamore.

A single comprehensive glance about this open space suggested that Tom Spencer must have been camping here for a considerable length of time, for around the massive tree all firewood had been cut; the clearing was strewn with the scorched and broken bones of deer, elk and turkey; bushes had been trampled flat; water-smoothed stones forming a crude fireplace had become blackened and heat-cracked through long use; from a pole slung between forked boughs dangled a few iron traps and snares; a rough lean-to sheltered several bales of what appeared to be beaver, mink, wildcat and other valuable pelts while a number of raw skins were stretched on willow frames.

Robertson was puzzled, for nowhere within the clearing was there evidence of a cabin, shack or wigwam.

The huge man coughed, cleared his throat with a tearing hawk, then spat. "I see ye're lookin' for my shelter, eh, Cunnel? Well, it's over yonder." When Spencer inclined his tawny-maned head towards the giant sycamore a chance ray of sunlight pierced his curly light-brown beard and revealed a spattering of bluish powder marks ingrained upon his left cheek.

Robertson blinked. "I see no human habitation."

"You might," Spencer chuckled, "were you to circle the tree. On its far side you'd see the entrance."

"Entrance?"

"Yep. That tree's hollow a good space up from the ground, which makes the best wind-and-weather-proof wigwam a man can find."

A grin spread over Spencer's rather flat face. "I'll admit that sometimes it seems just a mite cramped in there for a little feller like me, but, what the hell? I didn't have to bother felling trees and all I have to do is to sling a deerskin over a frame to make a door. So, Cunnel, I live snug, warm and dry."

Robertson fetched his thigh a resounding smack. "Say, Tom, ain't I heard you spent a whole winter like this near Castalian Springs?"

The giant chuckled deep in his throat. "Sure 'nough. That was durin' the winter o' '76-'77, and so I'll do anytime I c'n find me the right tree." He coughed rackingly, then wiped his short, ruddy nose on his sleeve and peered steadily into Robertson's eyes. "Well, Cunnel, reckon you're not here just to pass the time o' day?"

"Of course I'm not. I want you to join my party and come with me to the Frenchman's Lick. I've heard you're extra well acquainted with that part of the country. True?"

Solemnly, the gigantic yellow-brown head inclined under his disreputable brown felt hat. "Sure am. It's a choice country, best I ever seen — exceptin' for —"

"Exceptin' for what?"

"That Injuns hunt all over that country. There's hundreds, maybe thousands of redskins from all the tribes rangin' that ground all year." Spencer frowned at his huge feet. "I was damn' lucky, Cunnel, to quit the Cumberland Valley that spring with a few packloads of pelts and my hair in place. I'm not the one to tempt my luck too far."

"Nobody but a fool would doubt that," Robertson admitted, deep-set blue eyes narrowed. "All the same, what d'you say about comin' along with me?"

Deliberately, the giant scratched at a tangle of tawny-brown hair. "Well now, I don't know really how to answer. I might agree to go along with you, and then again, I mightn't."

Robertson went over to ease his mount's girth, a precaution he took whenever opportunity offered.

"Suppose I ask first why you mightn't?"

Spencer looked him square in the face, spoke slowly. "There's too damn' many mean Injuns out there for a man's health. They're not gentle playmates at best, but they'll surely go into a rip-snortin' rage an you try homesteadin' their Big Huntin' Ground. Fer another thing, you're headin' for Cumberland Valley at the wrong time o' year and, if I guess right, your party is strung out along the Trace — has to move pretty much in single file." The trapper's enormous shoulders rose in a slow shrug that wrinkled his grimy shirt. "You know as well as I, Cunnel, that even a small war party hitting hard from either flank could cost you dear. Such an attack could cut you up so's you couldn't keep on."

"Don't think I'm not aware of that," Robertson said. "But, unless the Indians have changed their ways considerably, there's not too much risk at this time of year once the real cold weather has set in. Another thing stands in my favor — I've only picked men and fine shots along; no women or children. Besides, as near as I know, the tribes don't even know we're here or where we're headed."

Spencer snuffled and spat onto snow marred by his vast shoe-pacs. "How many men you got along?"

"Near two hundred, more'n half of 'em mounted. So far, I've been lucky; haven't lost a man from ambush, sickness or stragglin'."

"Now that shines, Cunnel. Stragglin' is the curse of most parties."

While his horse, dragging its bridle, ambled over to nose at some tufts of dead grass Robertson spoke briefly about Colonel Donelson's water-borne party, described the route his colleague proposed to follow: Once he'd loaded his immigrants into scows, canoes, river boats and anything else that would float, he'd descend the Holston River until it joined with the Tennessee, then follow the latter around the Great Bend and, if lucky, eventually would reach the Mississippi. After that, he explained that Donelson intended to struggle up the Ohio to the Cumberland's mouth and then ascend that river to a high bluff near the Frenchman's Lick where, despite all manner of perils, Timothy de Monbreun's trading post had stood for a long time.

"Um. Sounds like it ain't no Sunday School picnic Donelson's settin' out on. Say, Cunnel, when d'you people figger to reach old Monbreun's cavern?"

" 'Round the middle of December; got to get there in time to throw together some shelters for the party. Then we start clearing land and killing and smoking game to feed Donelson's people."

Aware of this shaggy giant's interest, Robertson tried to play upon his curiosity. "After that I mean to forward a hand-picked detachment from Monbreun's across Tennessee to the bottom of the Great Bend. There they'll try to intercept Donelson's expedition and tell 'em that everything's all right at the Frenchman's Lick. Then they can abandon their boats and save a lot of time by cutting across the Hunting Country."

During the Colonel's succinct discourse Spencer's leonine head swung to face muffled noises from the river's bank. "Your people?"

"Yep. That'll be the main body." Robertson got up, weather-tinted features taut. "Well, Tom, how about it? I sure could profit from your advice and experience."

Gradually, Spencer's high, reddish-brown forehead furrowed itself. "Cunnel, I'll make a deal with you. I'll come along *provided* you listen to me if I speak up when I think it's necessary."

"Sure will."

"Also I'll need transportation for the pelts I've taken. I've nary a horse 'cause, come spring, I figgered on buildin' a canoe and paddling my furs to market."

"We've a deal." Robertson held out his hand. "How many pack animals will you need?"

"Two big critters or three small ones." Spencer heaved himself to his feet. "Get back to your boys, Cunnel. By the time the horses show up I'll be ready. Now let me get busy."

Followed by his dogs, Spencer made for the lean-to protecting his pelts.

The rear guard had just pulled up to wait for Spencer when the giant appeared with a huge, horse-sized pack riding his shoulders and bulging haversacks slung over either hip.

Immediately in his wake young Jonathan herded along a pair of pack horses. The boy was grinning like a horse collar, pleased to be even briefly freed of Old Scratch and the rest of the sheep.

Criminently! Wouldn't he have a deal to brag about to the other lads when the two expeditions became united?

Most of the men gawked in astonishment when Tom Spencer's huge figure loomed into sight. A few old timber beasts however greeted the giant with affectionately obscene remarks. In no time, wild yarns concerning Spencer's feats of strength and endurance traveled along the plodding column which was advancing at its best speed; with the afternoon so far advanced everyone wanted to get across the swollen Green while plenty of light remained.

Shortly after Tom Spencer had joined the column it slowed, then ceased to advance; the Trace became clogged by tangles of tired men and animals. Some of the immigrants brushed snow from logs and flat rocks, then, easing off their burdens, plunked themselves down to enjoy a breather.

After a while the word was passed back that a wind-felled oak was blocking the Trace at a point where the track passed between two almost vertical walls of rock. Apparently there was no way of passing except laboriously to chop through the two-foot-thick trunk.

"Damn!" grunted a gaunt, sad-faced fellow as he sank onto his heels and fell to sucking morosely on an empty clay pipe. " 'Twill take easy a hour to cut the damn' thing through."

"Maybe there's another way," mildly remarked Spencer. "Let me through, boys, and you, Bub," he paused, towering above Jonathan Robertson, " 'bide here and keep an eye on my property till I get back."

Huge pack bobbing, the giant shouldered forward along the line of men and muddied, slowly steaming pack animals.

Spitting and hawking because of his cold, Spencer soon arrived at the van where Colonel Robertson and the advance guard stood looking almighty disgusted and watching a pair of long-haired axmen strip off their gear.

Joe Drake was growling, "Reckon we'll have to bivouac this side o' the Green tonight if Uguhu Crossin' ain't a heap nearer than I think it is."

"Begins to look like it," admitted the Colonel. "You axmen don't hesitate to sing out the minute you feel tired. Heyo! What you doin' up here, Tom?"

Spencer came shoving through the crowd as effortlessly as a bull moose through an alder thicket. "Reckon maybe I can lend a hand." He slipped off his huge pack and stood studying the barrier. Um. This big oak in falling had managed to jam its trunk between sharp rocks rising sheer on either side of the Trace. Resting on pointed stone crotches, it suggested a Cyclopean customs barrier.

Thus far the axmen had accomplished little beyond trimming away minor branches and hacking off some bark.

"What's the trouble, boys?" Spencer observed.

Said one angrily, "This here oak's been dead a long time; 'tis seasoned harder'n a mother-in-law's heart!"

"Reckon that's *one* reason I ain't never married," Spencer said mildly and, after wiping his runny nose on his sleeve, strode over the chip-littered snow. "Suppose some of you fellers lop off the rest of the branches you can reach; others had better crawl over the trunk and hew off those on the far side."

Axmen, already red-faced and sweating, fell to work so furiously that, as Cash Brooks put it, they made a racket like a flock of giant woodpeckers gone crazy. Surprisingly soon a yellow-bearded fellow panted from atop the log, "All right, Mister, she's all yourn."

"Keep an eye on these." Spencer passed his rifle to Cash Brooks, also his belt with its dangling tomahawk and a big knife in a fringed sheath. Next, the tawny-haired giant spat on his hands and told the axmen to get out of his way.

Cash Brooks muttered, "By damn! If he figgers he c'n heave that log aside he's coon-cub crazy!"

Spencer heard and a grin spread over his heavy, powder-marked features. "Maybe I can't; had this goddam cold on me for over a week."

After shaking long brown hair onto his back, he squirmed his prodigious feet through mud and snow down to hard footing, then locked arms as thick as a small man's legs about the trunk. He gave a tentative heave, but the obstacle only quivered and bits of black bark broke off among the imprisoning rocks. Spencer grunted, then straightened in order to work his moccasins still deeper into the ground.

He'll never do it, James Robertson told himself. That tree must weigh a hundred stone — easy.

A penetrating silence descended when Spencer's massive arms once more encircled the oak. Then, hunching knees under the trunk, he drew a deep breath and commenced, very slowly, to heave upwards. His mighty legs quivered and muscles began to stand out in ridges along his reddening neck and to bunch themselves under his tight-fitting hunting shirt.

Gasps and small, incredulous cries arose from the witnesses when, a fraction of an inch at a time, the mangled trunk commenced to rise. The onlookers' cries swelled while Spencer, face purpling, lifted the tree level with his chest, then with his shoulders. Everyone could hear the giant's back tendons crackle when he raised the tree until its trunk was high enough to clear the cleft of rock in which it had lain. With breath bursting through his lips in steaming, explosive puffs, Spencer shoved his burden in a semi-circle until it cleared the Trace.

Eyes popping, Spencer gradually removed his support, then stepped clear, gasping, "Reckon you c'n go ahead."

While yells, shouts and whistles made the dark forest resound, the giant unconcernedly started to re-sling his gear.

10. Crisis

Samuel Grineau Mason, M.D., was occupied in sewing up a long gash gouged across a good horse's withers by a flying ax head when, just after the dangerously swift-running Green River had been crossed, Joe Drake trotted up to the physician, his wrinkled, butternut-hued features anxious and spangled with sweat. "Hi, Doc," he panted. "Come quick! Tim Murphy's runnin' a fever that'd melt a stone and has gone clear out o' his haid."

Mason frowned and nodded, then knotted some final stitches before tucking his bloodied needle, suture and all, into his lapel. Grabbing up his instrument case, he started running across the bivouac after Drake. Josh pelted along behind his master, hugging the medicine chest.

Instants before Dr. Mason pushed through a circle of hard-eyed immigrants, standing in silence about the crude litter, he'd recognized the distinctive sickish-sweet reek of gangrene.

Dan Maddox, crouched by the litter's head, was finding trouble in restraining Murphy's spasmodic struggles. Said he, "I'm feared you've come too late, Doc. Tim's fair burnin' and he can't swallow water without choking."

It was as well that Colonel Robertson had ordered this day's halt — ostensibly to rest foot-weary men and animals and to allow harness and all manner of equipment to be mended.

The sun still stood sufficiently high to send rays of bright, steady light lancing through the tops of this seemingly endless virgin forest.

Once the physician had tested Murphy's narrow forehead his mouth compressed itself into a straight, colorless line, for the injured arm had turned purple-red and had swelled out of all proportion. Over his shoulder he called for a pot of hot water to be brought from the nearest cook fire.

"Tim's poorly, ain't he, sir?" the gunsmith wanted to know.

"Yes. His condition is grave — to say the least." Mason straightened, small, dark-brown eyes gleaming, and spoke crisply, "I'm going to need a lot of light, so you fellows stand well back. Also, I'm going to need some fine white wheat flour, so find enough — I don't care where — to make a couple loaves of bread."

The shaggy onlookers stared, then glanced curiously at one another. That the Doc had been sorely overworked they knew, but for him suddenly to run off his rocker like this!

"*White* flour?" repeated a gangling, freckle-faced youth.

"That's what I said!" Mason snapped, "and I'll also need a cup of vinegar and a clean bowl." Meanwhile, he slipped off his rusty-black jacket and, apparently lost in thought, began to roll up sweat-stained sleeves.

A dozen men hurried away, broad hats flapping, coontails a-sway and lugging their weapons any which way.

"Josh! Fetch that bottle of French wine I've been saving." High, smooth forehead furrowed in concentration, the physician then added a cup of cider vinegar to two cups of Burgundy mixed in a tin pannikin. After adding a cup of hot water, he set the mixture to heat over a low fire. Once the utensil began to give off little tendrils of steam he sank onto his knees beside the litter.

Using crisp, English-inflected accents, he directed Maddox to hold steady the patient's head.

"Aye, sir. But what are you fixin' to do?"

"I'm about to attempt a treatment I once heard of in London." He shrugged faintly. "Of course, there's no guarantee it will work in Murphy's case, but, since your friend certainly will die if he continues like this, I feel justified in going ahead."

From the instrument bag Josh had fetched the physician removed scalpels, two pairs of broad-jawed retractors, a good-sized sponge and a number of swabs of raw cotton.

"You," he flung at a wide-eyed spectator, "no matter how the patient squirms or jerks steady the wounded arm. Cash, you hold down his feet. Drake, pinion his good arm."

Watched by a circle of onlookers, Mason sliced through a shapeless mass of horrible-smelling bandages until the shiny, purplish-crimson flesh of Tim's upper arm became exposed. Previously applied split-deer-sinew sutures had all but become lost to sight beneath the swollen and fearfully taut skin.

Over his shoulder the doctor snarled at onlookers who had edged closer. "Stand back, you bloody fools, and turn aside unless you want to risk your eyesight. When one lances a wound like this, pus sometimes spurts a long way."

Mason selected a heavy scalpel and turned his head an instant after making a quick incision. As he'd predicted, a jet of incredibly foul-smelling matter squirted high and far while Tim shrieked like some luckless wretch at an Indian torture stake.

"Easy, Tim, easy on!" Mason soothed while his assistants struggled to restrain the rifleman's spasmodic writhing. He coudn't tell whether the patient either heard or understood him, but he continued all the same. "Now, Tim, most surgeons would amputate your arm right now, but I'm going to try to save it."

This time the leather gag was forced between the gasping, gurgling patient's big, yellowish teeth and tied into place.

"Now," the physician began to speak as if he were lecturing a class at Surgeon's Hall rather than a gathering of rough and generally illiterate woodsmen, "while my assistant uses these retractors to keep the aperture as far open as possible I will employ this number two surgical knife to excise — cut away, that is — such fungus flesh as can be reached without risking the rupture of important blood vessels." The tall young physician then bent and quickly began to cut away shreds of putrescent flesh.

Murphy's small and wiry body commenced a series of convulsive heaves; his congested and bloodshot eyes rolled wildly about their sockets. The men restraining Murphy did an excellent job.

"Next," Mason's clipped, precise voice penetrated the awed and silent crowd, "we press out whatever gleety matter — pus to you — remains in the wound. Then, because the two main gashes lie so close together, I will remove the partition, thus laying the gashes into a single wound."

A hungry jackass, somewhere off in the forest, commenced to bray just as Sam Mason dipped his sponge into steaming hot water and commenced to swab out the single wound. Tim then fainted dead away, ceased to struggle and lay limp.

Mason heard a voice in the background mutter, "By God, they was right!"

"Who was right about what?" someone wanted to know.

"Them as wrote, 'He that sinneth before his Maker, let him fall into the hands of the physicians.' "

"Shut up!" snarled Drake over his shoulder. "Else I'll pin yer ears back. The Doc's doin' fine."

Mason passed a wrist over his sweat-brightened forehead, selected a fresh sponge, then said in even tones, "Had I some *balsam traumatic* I would use it, but since I haven't, I will make do with this mixture."

He called for the pannikin of heated wine and vinegar, and when Josh, pallid, piggy gray eyes round, brought it, the physician soaked his sponge in the mixture.

"Now you, Maddox, watch carefully how I do this because this procedure must be repeated every hour for perhaps the next twenty-four hours, possibly longer. I cannot perform this service myself since other patients need my services, too. Now give me your undivided attention."

Holding his slowly steaming sponge just a few inches above the wound, Samuel Mason, M.D., squeezed it gently to allow dark, red-brown drops to fall a few at a time into the wound until the cavity was filled. "You must allow these drippings to remain for near ten minutes, then wipe out the wound and cover it with a dressing."

Maddox drawled, "Damn' good thing Tim ain't awake. That slop must burn like hell's own fire!"

"It will burn worse than that," Mason smiled thinly, "but it's worthwhile if this poor devil keeps his arm."

"He'd better," muttered Joe Drake through his ragged, drooping mustaches. "One-armed men don't last extry long in country like we're headin' for."

After winding a strip of clean white flannel loosely over Tim's arm, Mason strode over to cleanse bloodied hands with sand in a nearby runlet. While drying them on his breeches the physician demanded sharply, "Where's that white flour I sent for?"

"Nobody's brought any," someone volunteered. "Say, why's a little measure of white flour so all-fired important?"

Mason's small and intense brown eyes hardened. "That's no concern of yours! I *must* have some right away — and yeast and milk — there surely must be one fresh cow in that herd behind us. Meantime, some of you rig an oven that'll bake bread which just *may* save the poor fellow's life."

Joe Drake rasped at the onlookers, "The Devil take you useless bugtits! *I* ain't goin' to stand around an see the finest rifle shot in North Americky die for the want of wheat flour!" Fringes on his hunting shirt a-sway, the veteran Long Hunter parted the onlookers and began to range about the smoke-veiled bivouac.

By the time the surgeon for the second time had started to drip hot wine and vinegar into the unconscious rifleman's wound, Drake returned accompanied by a wizened little man half his size. "Ben here 'lows he's got a bit of white flour — but only a bit — and he wun't give it away lest he gits a few bites for hisself on 'count of his teeth is gone so bad he can't chaw no pone nor biscuit."

The small, shriveled man held out a canvas bag protected from dampness inside an oiled deer's bladder. "Oughter be sufficient for three middlin' loaves; ye c'n have it all, provided I c'n have one for myself."

He beckoned forward a bittern-thin companion wearing a filthy Dutch blanket coat. "Charley here's got a bottle of yeast which he's kept workin'."

"Thank you."

"Doc, ye're sure welcome," Charley said, "but I'd be grateful if ye'd tell us why're so all-fired set on bakin' a mess of white bread."

"In due course I intend to make a poultice," Mason explained.

"What d'ye mean by 'in due course'?"

"I shan't use this bread till it grows moldy."

The wizened man's red-rimmed gray eyes rounded themselves. "You surely ain't going to feed this pore feller on moldy bread?"

Slowly, Sam Mason shook his head. He was very, very weary — worried, too. "No. As I said, as soon as the bread turns moldy I mean to make a poultice of it. I've heard there's nothing like such to draw poisons out of a suppurating wound."

11. Experiment with the Future

BEFORE his expedition next day resumed its progress towards Carpenter's Station, Colonel Robertson issued orders that a handful of men should remain behind to care for Tim Murphy.

This decision was the result of a brief talk with Samuel Mason, M.D., who'd stated flatly, "To move Murphy at this time would ensure his death, for all his fever has abated for the time being."

"Good. Murphy's too valuable to lose. How's his arm?"

The physician's shoulders lifted under his rusty black coat. "It would win no prizes, but, as I've said, Tim's temperature *is* lower. What he needs is to be kept quiet for another day or two and grant me time to try a dressing I'm preparing."

Robertson gathered his reins, then started his mount towards the Trace. "Very well, I'll leave four men behind to help you. You've permission to keep Murphy where he is for two days. After that, you'll have to promise to move him and catch up with the rest of us as quick as you can." The bold blue eyes narrowed briefly. "Can't spare your services any longer for the sake of a sick man — or risk the lives of four healthy men. You can keep Ed Jennings, Maddox and Josh with you."

The white bread baked by the wizened little man turned out to be surprisingly palatable. He accepted his loaf and departed masticating it joyfully between his blackened stumps of teeth. Dr. Mason, however, sliced the remaining loaves into thick slabs which he stuffed into a rotten hollow log.

Joe Drake, Josh and Maddox watched the New Englander. Finally Drake grunted, "You really mean for this fine bread to spoil?"

Mason summoned a wry grin. "That is true; as I told you earlier, I intend to attempt a rare treatment which may save your friend's arm."

Not until late in the afternoon of the day Robertson's column had moved on did the first fibers of sage-green mold begin to appear like a gossamer beard on some of the bread.

Mason muttered more to himself than to his assistants, "Wish to God I could recall exactly how such a poultice is prepared and applied. Question: should the bread be crumbled and rendered into a thick paste, or should slices showing the most mold be bound, whole, over the wound?" After a moment's deliberation he elected the second method.

Tim's fever-parched lips formed a tremulous, pallid smile. "Go ahead, Doc, whatever you decide is all right with me. I don't feel near so feverish as I did."

"Thank you for your confidence. Now brace yourself because it's going to hurt a lot whilst I remove the old dressings."

The men who'd been left behind crowded about and were incredulous, because now the terribly lacerated flesh didn't appear anywhere near as angry-looking as before. Somehow, that slow dripping of warm wine and vinegar into the gash had modified those deadly hues previously visible in the long, evil-smelling wound.

Breathing a prayer, Sam Mason placed several greenish-white slices of bread over the wound, then, despite Murphy's gasps and half-stifled groans, bound the applications lightly in place with a flannel bandage.

Drawled Joe while biting off a chew, "In my time I've heered of plenty queer notions 'bout physicking, but this one sure beats 'em hollow. Expect that mess to do Tim some real good?"

A hard laugh escaped the physician. "Now isn't that a damn' fool question? Why else would I attempt this technique? Tomorrow should tell whether or not Tim stands a chance of keeping his arm. Right now, I'm so hungry I could eat a horse and chase its driver."

12. *Carpenter's Station*

LONG before a scout came riding back with news that another expedition was encamped about Carpenter's Station, James Robertson had known about it. Why else should several smoke columns be rising above the forest? Even on a peaceful mission, Indians never would have lit so many fires close together.

Taking along Cash Brooks and his brown-and-black bear dog, Bassoon, Robertson trotted forward to join the point.

"Heyo, Cunnel!" someone sang out. "Any news from Maddox and Murphy?"

Robertson turned in the saddle, shook his head. "Never a peep. Still, I expect they'll be along directly."

This was a small lie. To Major Phillips, his saturnine second-in-command, he muttered, "If all had gone well, Doctor Mason and his men would have joined the main party by now. Maddox is still enough of a soldier to carry out orders and Mason knows how badly he's needed."

Cash Brooks resettled his broad hat and sprayed a stone ten feet away with tobacco juice. "Cunnel, s'pose me 'n Tom Spencer an' a couple of fellers backtrack a ways? Likely the Doc's party has met with trouble."

Robertson's voice was incisive. "No. If Mason's party *has* come to grief then we'll have lost only a few good men. But were I to send back a search party, why, I'd risk doubling our loss. Sorry, I ain't prepared to gamble."

The point continued to push on along the Green River's west bank, anxious to come upon the fortified station not long ago established by a tough old frontiersman named Charley Carpenter. For some obscure reason, here in Kentucky, such civilian outposts — no matter how weak or small — had come to be known as "stations."

Robertson readily could visualize what Carpenter's Station would be like; a pair of small, square two-story log houses — each built with a slight overhang to its upper floor and connected with each other by two palisades of roughly pointed logs. One of these curtain-walls likely would be pierced by a small gate flanked by firing platforms.

The courtyard thus created might enclose perhaps a quarter-acre of bare ground on which travelers and settlers could take refuge when the Shawnees and Piankashaws or some lesser tribe threw away their peace pipes and replaced them with red-shafted tomahawks.

Joe Drake rode up beside the messenger from Carpenter's who was a sad-faced, slightly cross-eyed fellow with a gray-streaked beard and wearing a ratty clump of turkey-cock feathers stuck, Indian fashion, into the back of a round cap of fox fur.

"Say, friend, anybody at the Station 'side from Carpenter's folks?"

"Yep. Party of settlers from New River in Virginny came in yesterday. 'Tis led by an old-timer called John Rains — and a loud-mouth windbag name of Valentine." The cross-eyed man snorted. "How them two ever got together I'll never figger out, 'cept that Rains knows this here country, while the Squire, or 'Major' Valentine — as he calls himself — must be carrying plenty of hard money in his saddle bags —" the speaker snickered, "or maybe he's got it hid 'neath his girls' petticuts."

"Then Rains has got females along?" Drake demanded.

"Yep. Four wives, two girls and eight children, two of which is useful, half-grown boys." The scout winked. "Man! Wait till you lay eyes on the Valentine girl-twins; they're pert and handsome as a pair o' speckled pups."

Drake's expression relaxed. "Be they old enough?"

"Sure. Must be all of seventeen. And willing, too — well, one of 'em sure looks like it."

Joe's yellowed teeth glinted in the depths of his gray beard; he thought,

Tim Murphy better hear about this! He'll get better real quick so's to get to them fillies quicker 'n a flash lest their Pa kills him first — always provided the poor feller's still alive and kicking.

Even before Robertson and the point pulled up on the edge of an open space cleared amid tall oaks, walnuts and hickories, most of them were deciding that Charley Carpenter hadn't picked a particularly good site. For one thing, the Station had been built in the center of an area dominated on three sides by high, heavily wooded ridges, and unless a spring was flowing behind these palisades, Carpenter's place was much too far from the river to prevent its garrison from growing thirsty during a prolonged attack.

Carpenter's Station turned out to be pretty much as Robertson had anticipated: a pair of plain two-story stronghouses connected by crude palisades of pointed pine logs.

Robertson asked of the cross-eyed man, "Which way is Rains headed?"

"For Harrod's — if it's still there after the Hair Buyer's doin's last year."

"It's still there, friend," Robertson said. "George Rogers Clark and some Virginia troops took Vincennes last winter."

"Yes. I know about that. Saw Colonel Rogers there a few months ago."

Robertson's sharp, bright blue eyes considered this fellow in fraying homespuns. "Who's along with Rains?"

"Why, lemme think; there's an old Big Knife named Bledsoe."

"— Ike or Abe?" interjected Joe Drake, busy re-securing a blanket roll bound over his pommel.

"Ike. Know him?"

"Sure. I know 'Whisperin' Ike.' Back in '69 him, me and Cash Brooks with Johnny Rains ranged about considerable 'mongst the Licks. Yep. We traveled over most of Kentucky."

From the small, smoke-veiled encampment outside the Station came John Rains limping on a leg which once had been broken and not set correctly. Rains was as dark-skinned as any Catawba and, like them, wore his hair in twin braids. A few yards behind Rains strode a thick-bodied individual wearing a bleached, almost white, buckskin hunting shirt and Indian leggings. Ike Bledsoe had a small, round head and enormously long arms.

"How are ye, ye ornery old wampus cat?" called Drake.

"Fit to swaller ye whole 'thout butterin' them hairy ears of yourn," the other yelled back.

In an unabashed display of affection Joe leaped off his horse and fell to bear-hugging Bledsoe.

Meanwhile, James Robertson shook hands warmly with John Rains, who, bronzed, Indianlike features impassive, said, "Come along, Cunnel, want you to meet Chuck Carpenter. He owns this station."

To Robertson it was a fine thing to see and hear children again — mostly sunburned and clad in thick linsey-woolsey or homespun garments. As they drew near the little fort a number of significant facts became evident: for instance, a couple of spinning wheels stood in plain sight, and two pairs of heavy cart wheels, tired with iron, rested against convenient trees.

Robertson grinned inwardly. Imagine John Donelson's expression when his party arrived and found wagons already rumbling around the Frenchman's Lick! Of course, these settlers also must have brought along farming tools such as spades, mattocks, pitchforks, rakes and hoes. Above all he was delighted to see a portable anvil at work just outside the station's gate, for, by now, his expedition's mounts had broken or lost so many horseshoes that a lot of the riders were forced to travel on foot lest their beasts go lame.

With poorly concealed satisfaction Robertson spotted a small herd of rack-ribbed brown cows and some scrawny pigs browsing or foraging along the edge of the woods under the guard of a pair of youths. Hmm! For the most part this stock looked to be undersized and piss-poor creatures, but, by God, they sure enough could become a welcome addition to the new settlement's starting stock.

Back in Watauga, last summer, it had been planned that Colonel Donelson's waterborne expedition should fetch out most of the livestock, heavy utensils, such as wheels and the like, along with the families of several men at present following the Trace — his own included. Briefly, the leader wondered how Charlotte, his wife, and Jonathan's sisters and brothers were making out. Yes. 'Twould be a tall feather in Jim Robertson's cap were Donelson's party to arrive at the Frenchman's Lick and discover a full-fledged settlement already established on the Bluff.

Other members of the point also were pleased by the homely sight of a family's laundry hung out on bushes to dry and by the sound of soft, feminine voices and the excited yells of children.

Even unusually silent Major Phillips, when he appeared at the head of the dangerously strung-out main body, allowed it was mighty fine to watch a flock of red-brown hens and a couple of splendidly lecherous roosters scratching, chasing insects and otherwise making the most of this unseasonably warm November day.

The open curiosity of Carpenter's and Rains's people achieved its highest pitch when, to the excited yelping of dogs, the foremost immigrants rode out of the high forest which, for days, had kept the sun from solidly striking the ground.

Among Rains's people stood a tall, stoop-shouldered fellow who'd a new scar flaming across his left cheek. Beside him was a handsome, straight-backed young woman whose brown hair was worn tightly skinned back into a neat bun. Clinging to her hand was a little boy who resembled his father so much it was ridiculous.

The couple were ex-militiaman Andrew Dickinson and Peggy, his capable-appearing wife. They were present today in Carpenter's Station chiefly because, last July, British, Hessian and Loyalist troops under General Ben Garth and his Tory second-in-command, General William Tryon, had attacked, burned and thoroughly looted the thriving and, to them, pestiferous little port of Norwalk, Connecticut.

When the British forces had pulled out they'd left Dickinson's boatyard a seething mass of flames along with a salt works, two churches, one hundred thirty dwellings — Andrew's among them — eighty-seven barns, twenty-two stores, seventeen shops, four mills and five vessels.

In idle curiosity the Connecticuter viewed the haphazard arrival of Robertson's main body. He paid these shaggy, dusty fellows no real attention until he watched Dr. Samuel Mason's black-clad figure come riding out of the forest and into the clearing. Peggy then heard Andy's jaw shut with a sharp *click!* and watched him shade his eyes against the sun to get a better look at that somber, well-set-up figure.

Peggy Dickinson cast her husband a quick sidewise glance. "What's wrong, Andy?"

"Don't know yet, but do you mark that tall, red-haired feller with the hawk's nose?"

"The one wearing a broad-brimmed black hat?"

"Yes."

"What about him?"

Dickinson's hand crept up to stroke a long, forceful-looking jaw. "I'm pretty near certain I've seen that man before."

"When?"

"Not too long ago. That's what bothers me."

"If you could remember where it was, maybe that would help?"

"No, I can't." Dickinson used fingers to erase wrinkles from his forehead. "Yes, Peg, I *know* I've beheld that face before."

"Is the recollection pleasant or unpleasant?"

"Unpleasant, seems to me."

"Maybe you're mistook."

"Could be, but I hardly think so. Maybe I'll remember when I inquire amongst his fellows."

Behind the hurriedly dropped and plentifully mildewed flaps of the only sizable tent in the clearing, the twin daughters of Virginius Virgil Valentine, Esquire, began to comb long, honey-hued tresses — Rosemary for the first, Choice for the third time that day.

"Mercy, Rosie! Aren't you going to change to a prettier gown?"

"No. Why?"

"Might be a good-looking man among the strangers." Choice's voice sounded muffled beneath the blue lawn dress she was lowering over her head; then her fingers hurriedly secured a series of small bows of yellow velvet fastening its front.

Rosemary wavered, but decided that no matter what she did she'd still look pretty untidy, so why bother to unlash her clothes chest?

"No. I'll go as I am. Probably won't be a single fellow out there worth the bother."

Choice sniffed, then her large, dark-brown and velvet-soft eyes sought her twin. "Darling, will you lend me your blue grosgrain hair ribbon?"

Knowing by experience that she'd probably never see it again, Rosemary shook her bright blonde head.

"Oh, please! You know you hardly ever wear it. Besides, I promise to take extra good care of it."

Rosemary's wide, dark-red mouth firmed itself as she bent over, her small-boned figure gilded by sunlight beating through the travel-stained canvas, to peer through the rear flaps at the dust-clouded clearing. "Sorry, poppet, but you'll have to make do with that black ribbon you borrowed just before we set out on this horrible journey. I'm going to need the blue one myself."

Still fluffing her hair, Choice wrinkled a pert little nose. "All right, *be* a meanie! What do you see?"

"About what I expected. A lot of men, all dirty, ragged and coarse."

Choice came over to join her sister in surveying the new arrivals. "You're right. If there's one man of substance or gentility among 'em, well, I'll be switched — and worse than Papa does it."

Their mother's petulant voice penetrated the canvas partition dividing the tent into two compartments. "Why bother primping for a parcel of timber beasts and assorted scalawags?"

At that moment the tent's front flap was swung apart as an orotund voice boomed, "Not so fast, my love. Not so fast! I have just been in conversation with Colonel Robertson, who leads these new arrivals. Damme, if he ain't a man of parts. And in more ways than one, I'd say. Ha! ha! ha!"

"Mr. Valentine!" Agnes Valentine squeaked in shrill indignation. "Pray do not lower yourself to a level with the coarse manner of our fellow immigrants."

"Tush, woman, and hold your tongue. Mr. Rains informs me this fellow's a Virginian of birth and breeding, much respected in high places. He is also a famed explorer of this infernal wilderness. Moreover, for a long time he served as agent among the Cherokee Indians; handled 'em in masterful fashion. Besides, he holds a bona fide colonel's commission. How does that sound to you young ladies?"

Choice's contralto voice affected a mincing tone. "La, Papa, I shall do my best to earn the Colonel's favorable opinion — of our family. Is he married?"

"Don't yet know, but there's no doubt he's influential out here."

Choice finished tying saucy little bows to either side of her softly oval face, then called, "Please, Papa, I must straightaway breathe fresh air or die; I'm fair stifling."

"Very well, you have leave to go out."

Before going out onto the dung-strewn clearing, the girl thrust stout but not ungainly traveling brogues into those same wooden-soled pattens which ages ago, it seemed, had protected her feet from mud puddles on the streets of Bethlehem, Pennsylvania.

She hadn't taken two steps before her father called out, "Wait, you little fool! We will greet Colonel Robertson as a well-mannered family, or my name ain't Virginius Valentine."

From a certain slurring of Papa's enunciation Rosemary deduced that he must several times have referred to a certain stone jug mislabeled "vinegar."

Agnes Valentine's thin voice snapped, "For pity's sake, Mr. Valentine, do lower your voice! I'll be ready the minute I tie on another petticut. You, Choice, keep your eyes lowered and mind your tongue. Since we've been forced to join a new community I want no idle gossip concerning *my* daughters. Sally, you lazy blackamoor, get out my second-best bonnet."

Choice called, "Ma, can I have the loan of your Spanish comb?"

" 'Mother,' you baggage! How many times must I remind you not to talk like these common half-savages? No, you mayn't have the comb. You're much too young."

When the Valentine family emerged from their tent, straight of back and with noses slightly elevated, Robertson's whiskery crew gaped and stared. Mark Robertson, who hated all Easterners, sang out, "My Gawd! Some goddam Royal Gov'nor must be holdin' a levee somewheres near!" Almost everyone else, however, gazed in grudging respect at the little group — the first and only examples most of them had ever beheld of what, dimly, was known as "quality."

Eyes demurely downcast and full skirts a-sway, the girls, so amazingly identical, squelched along after their parents' disproportionate figures.

Squire Valentine stood nearly six feet tall and looked almost imposing in a liberally braided and brass-buttoned tunic of blue and buff. Pinned to a well-brushed black tricorn was that soiled red-and-white cockade which indicated his rank as major in the "Pottstown Fencibles" — a Pennsylvania militia organization of which neither John Rains nor anyone else previously had heard.

The "Squire," as Valentine insisted upon being addressed when he didn't choose to be dignified with his military title, possessed very broad shoulders which might once have been powerful but now sagged under disfiguring layers of fat. He was wearing well-cut brown breeches but his jack boots were so muddy that spurs protuding from their heels had degenerated into shapeless excrescences. His roseate nose was long and straight and covered with dark hairs while his ears were both erect and pointed, so, all in all, Major Valentine strongly suggested a raffish dog fox.

Agnes Valentine, on the other hand, was as tiny and as quick-moving as a wren — a bird she otherwise resembled in that she had beady, black little eyes and a pointed beak of a nose.

The Valentine family discovered Colonel Robertson sitting with his boots off before a fireplace and chatting easily with Rains and Charles Carpenter while he sipped at a beaker of rum and water. This, the host's only downstairs room, was where he and his numerous family lived, cooked and ate. To go to bed they had to clamber up a crude ladder to a chilly loft where a number of shapeless bough beds were revealed by light filtering through a series of crudely shuttered loopholes.

Squire Valentine tramped forward, plump wide hand outstretched, booming, "Ah there, Colonel! Pleased to find you taking your ease. As I've just informed my family here, 'tis a vast pleasure to make the acquaintance of another gentleman amid this benighted wilderness."

James Robertson got to his feet as the three ladies filed in and, standing in stocking feet, offered a neat bow. "That's kindly spoken, sir, but 'tis an undeserved compliment. Before long you will encounter many gentlemen in this 'benighted wilderness' who, though they may appear a trifle unpolished in speech and manner nevertheless are truly gentlemen."

Imperceptibly, Robertson's attention shifted from the faintly absurd figure gripping his hand to the petite young blondes hesitating behind their father. By God, they certainly were as delicate-looking and as prettily alike as two fresh blossoms on a flowering wild cherry.

Mrs. Valentine acknowledged the tall Virginian's bow with a brief curtsy, then rather diffidently declared herself vastly pleased to meet this raw-boned and weatherbeaten but still somehow impressive individual.

"My daughters, sir." Valentine waved them forward to curtsy in their turn and then retire behind their mother.

Once Rains and Carpenter, bearded, sweating and malodorous, had been presented, along with Major Todd Phillips, who came tramping in, there ensued considerable talk and speculation about the progress of the war back East.

With pompous gravity, Squire Valentine presently informed the company that he was emigrating westwards because he foresaw with certainty that the Patriot cause was doomed, French help or no French help, and that, within a few months, there wouldn't be a single American army left in the field.

"No, gentlemen," rumbled the big-bellied man in the militia coat, "we can't possibly win. Everything militates against us — ruined economy and finances, shortages of men and warlike materials indicate a complete British victory within six months — or eight at the outside."

Valentine made a wide gesture and summoned a lugubrious expression. "And that, my friends, is why I decided to abandon a flourishing estate in Bethlehem to hazard life and — ahem, fortune — in order to assist in founding a free new nation in this magnificent Territory of Kentucky. Eh, John?"

John Rains's hairy and prominent Adam's apple worked several times as if he were swallowing hard. He jerked a nod but said nothing.

Once the family had entered Carpenter's stronghouse, Rosemary, venturing to raise her eyes, decided that this Colonel Robertson, for all his frontier garb and dirty hands and unshaven face, was one of the most impressive persons she'd encountered during her sixteen and a half years — including a good many elegantly dressed and smooth-mannered officers encountered in Bethlehem and Philadelphia.

Choice immediately became intrigued by the quiet reserve of straight-backed and dark-browed Major Phillips, whose powerful profile at once reminded her of an engraving she'd once seen of Caesar Augustus — or had it been Julius Caesar?

Three-legged stools were dragged forward to accommodate the ladies before lantern-jawed Charles Carpenter produced a stone jug of throat-searing Monongahela whisky and some wooden noggins. Everybody was eager to exchange scraps of news about how George Rogers Clark and his little force nowadays were faring up in Vincennes and whether the British were going to succeed in bribing the Chickasaws.

Rains predicted that next spring the Miamis and Cherokees surely would send out their red sticks. Voices rose once Carpenter's whisky had begun to "spread out." Squire Valentine's big voice dominated the general babble.

From the doorway someone called in clear, ringing tones, "Greetings, gentlemen!"

With cup immobilized halfway to his lips Colonel Robertson wheeled to face the entrance and almost voiced his vast relief on recognizing Sam Mason, M.D., who strode in looking haggard but neatly shaven and wearing a taut smile. Rosemary Valentine cast him a quick glance, thinking she'd never beheld finer or sadder dark eyes than those of this tall young man in rusty black.

Robertson took the physician's hand between both of his. "Glad you're safe. How's Murphy?"

Mason replied in the abruptly quiet room, "We're all here, sir. Murphy still has both arms."

"Good. I began to worry a little when you didn't catch up a couple of days back."

Major Phillips queried, "How's Tim Murphy?"

"As I've said, he's mending well." The physician's thorn-torn fingers drummed against the noggin he'd been given. "What that moldy bread did for his festering arm was nothing short of miraculous. But seeing is believing, so —" Mason called over his shoulder, "Maddox! Bring in Murphy, will you?"

Everyone crowding in the smelly little room turned to face the doorway and watched Maddox enter with one arm supporting the Rifleman of Saratoga. The famous sharpshooter looked gaunt, but his dark eyes were bright and his color looked good. He grinned broadly and pointed proudly to his hurt arm now riding in a moss-padded sling.

Robertson said quietly, "Glad to have you back in one piece!"

Murphy reddened. "Thank ye, Colonel. Reckon I'll not tangle with no more bears for a while — she-bears least of all."

"Bet that'll be the only she-critters he'll avoid," grunted Joe Drake, then turned to greet Dan Maddox but checked himself because the gunsmith, having just caught sight of Mistress Rosemary Valentine, was staring across the room with a foolish grin spreading all over his face.

———— ◡ ————

13. The Twins

To allow time for weighing a mighty serious problem that just had arisen, Colonel Robertson decreed a full day's halt at Carpenter's Station.

Shock-haired Jonathan Robertson was feeling extra pleased with life. During the three weeks that had elapsed since the expedition had pulled out from Watauga he still had lost but one sheep from the herd under his protection and nobody really could blame him for that.

Jon — as he generally was called — drove his charges into a rude pen along with the Rains people's stock, then sought out Dr. Mason's tent and built his bough bed as near to it as he could. Quite a while ago he'd figured out that by watching the Doc he might learn something about doctoring which might come in handy if he ever got to fight Indians or go off lone trapping by himself.

Besides, Pa held that a man couldn't learn too much about anything which might serve to keep him alive and his hair in place.

Keeping one eye on a mean buckskin stallion tethered apart, Jon used his knife to hack off spruce tips for a bed. Criminently! How long before Pa would let him smoke a pipe like a grown-up? Once he'd tried chewing tobacco, but Pa had caught him red-handed and had fraled him so fervently with a stout hickory switch that he'd no intention of repeating the experiment.

By now he, like the rest of the expedition, knew just how many people composed John Rains's party, which included Rains, his wife and four children: George, aged sixteen, Dwight a year younger, and two daughters twelve and five years. They'd along with them two steers, nineteen cows and seventeen horses of varying value. Then there was the Dickinson family and Squire Valentine, Agnes, his wife, and their pretty sixteen-year-old twins, Rosemary and Choice. They'd brought no livestock other than riding and pack horses — the Valentine ladies all rode sidesaddle, to the envy of the other womenfolk who rode astride with men's pants concealing their nether parts under a wide skirt. The Valentines owned Black Sally — the only slave in Rains's party — and had hired two brawny young men to help them travel.

Only two other families had come out from New River — a couple of newlyweds, Jared Barker, a Connecticuter, and his wife, Emily, who was so obviously pregnant that the other women on hearing the date of the marriage counted on their fingers and whispered that a shotgun probably had figured in their nuptials. Finally, there were the Mackenzies, dour, stand-offish folk of Scottish descent who kept pretty much to themselves: Angus, Meg and their two children; Hamish, twelve, and Betrag, a long-legged eleven.

There were also three single men on their way to Harrod's Station who thought it safer to travel in Rains's company.

Around Carpenter's clearing people were mending gear, washing clothes or drifting from one fire to the next to exchange gossip with the newcomers. Horses whickered and cattle lowed and bellowed; the expedition's dogs sniffed strangers in intimate canine fashion and, on occasion, got into brief but noisy fights.

Bursts of song and raucous laughter suggested that on either side of the raw palisade jugs were being up-ended.

Once Rains's party heard that a sick man was among the newcomers most of the women hurried over to Dr. Mason's tent.

One gap-toothed bony female whispered, "Now, Doc, don't pay no heed to anybody else, just listen to me. An you want this poor young fellow to heal real quick, here's what to do. First bleed him of a pint; next dig up a quart of fish-worms and wash 'em clean; then put a pound of hog's lard in a pot and stew them worms for around a hour. After that, you strain the mess through a filter and then add half-pint turpentine and half-pint of whisky which ye'll simmer for near two hours. 'Twill then be fit fer use."

Although barely able to keep a straight face, Mason queried gravely, "And then what must be done?"

"Just flush out the wound with my recipe and you'll see how the proud flesh will slough off and get healthy-like quicker'n a flash. Never fails."

"I'm sure you are absolutely right and I thank you, ma'am," Mason stated in perfect seriousness. "Do you mind if I share this precious panacea with certain colleagues in London?"

The instant he'd said "London" Sam Mason knew he'd made a mistake.

"What was that you said about 'London'?" snapped a short bony fellow. "What've you to do with that tyrants' nest?"

Several men standing nearby turned to stare, Jared Barker especially.

"Nowadays nothing," Mason averred hastily. "Absolutely nothing! You see, before the war I, well — used to exchange medical information with certain doctors well known over there."

The little woman who'd given him the prescription narrowed beady black eyes. "You've lived in England!"

"I studied there for a brief while," Mason stated calmly. "My home is in Boston. I returned there before the war began." Disregarding the curious onlookers, he turned to his patient. "Well, Tim, how'd you like to try this kind lady's medicine?"

"I'd admire to," grinned the rifleman, "provided ye leave out everythin' 'cept the whisky."

Tim drawled at Maddox, busy splicing a broken patch pocket cover, "Dan, you and the Doc have saved my life — no doubt about it — but I've the feelin' all yer trouble will go fer nothin' if," he fetched a windy sigh and his eyes rolled to the treetops, "you don't tell the Valentine twins that I'm about to go into a decline and only they can pull me free of it."

Sam Mason overheard, turned from setting his bag of medicines in order and grinned over his shoulder. "Murphy, about the only thing that can pull you into a decline is a span of oxen." Then he laughed briefly. "Go ahead, Dan, and fetch the girls — if their mother will let them come. I suspect Tim won't rest easy till he lays eyes on a pretty girl long enough to find out whether his — er — spirits still can rise."

Rifle shouldered, Dan presently made his way past a paddock contrived of ropes strung between trees in which Robertson's best horses stood switching flies and nibbling rich green canes freshly brought up from the river's banks.

Soldiering and adventuring in the wilderness were fine most of the time, all the same a fellow on occasion did come to miss such homely sounds as the lowing of a cow, the cackle of hens and the high-pitched voices of women and children.

Despite himself, Dan found himself recalling Lancaster and those two new mounds of earth at the back of a log chapel the Lutherans had put up — Ilsa and her Pa had belonged to that denomination.

The sun soon would set, so the children were lugging dripping water buckets up from the stream, women and girls were preparing supper while the men, for the most part, split firewood or drowsed on bough beds near the fires. Some of the younger fellows were horsing about and wrestling within a circle of shouting onlookers and, off to one side, towering Tom Spencer and that sinewy Big Knife called Ike Bledsoe were settling a bet by hurling tomahawks at a stump target. Judging by their bursts of loud laughter and occasionally uncertain movements, they must have tested some jug's small end more than once.

Dan Maddox, treading light as a two-year buck courting a doe, reconnoitered Squire Valentine's tent till he'd made sure that the feminine members of the family were enjoying this fine sunset by sewing outside the tied-back flaps.

The twin Dan took to be Rosemary sat with small head bent over hickory needles with which she was knitting what appeared to be a muffler. Choice, dark-red lips pursed in concentration, was mending a bright green taffety petticoat. Separating her daughters sat waspish little Mrs. Valentine. Her needle flashed steadily while she darned a clumsy worsted stocking from a pile squirming across her aproned lap. Just behind the Valentine ladies crouched Sally, an ancient Negress who sucked noisily on a black-brown corncob pipe clenched between nearly toothless jaws. A yellow-and-red turban twisted about her nearly white hair showed brightly in the sunset's ruddy glare.

Squire Valentine wasn't on hand, but his big voice could be heard booming on the far side of low palisades intended to protect Carpenter's Station.

Dan hesitated, crumpling his hat's broad brim between powerful, well-shaped hands. "A rare fine evenin', ladies, for this time of year."

Although Rosemary kept on knitting as if he hadn't spoken, Choice and her mother glanced up to note this tall and well-proportioned young man with dark-red hair and strong bronzed features. Somehow, despite his rough clothing, he didn't at all suggest the ordinary frontiersman. For instance, this handsome fellow didn't grin foolishly, hang his head or scrape at the ground with his toe when addressing well-bred ladies.

In a flat, weary voice Agnes Valentine said, "I presume it *is* fine, young man. If you've come in search of Major Valentine I expect you'll find him in the fort."

"No, ma'am. 'Tis your daughters — and you," he added with belated tact, "I've to speak to." Why wouldn't Rosemary look up from her knitting?

Mrs. Valentine's tiny bright black eyes quite brazenly explored him from the ground up. "Before I ask your mission perhaps you'd better tell me who and what you are?"

A smile slowly parted Choice's full, dark-red lips. "La, sir, from the way you bear yourself *I'd* hazard that you've been a big, brave soldier."

"Fie!" hissed the girl's mother. "How dare you talk so bold?"

Rosemany still would not look up even when he explained in a deep, deliberate voice, "Ma'am, yer daughter's right. I'm Dan Maddox, for two years a sergeant in Gen'ral Morgan's Regiment of Virginia Rifles. But I don't know how big or brave I was."

Finally Rosemary's small blonde head slowly raised itself until he became aware of large and lovely dark-brown eyes showing in sharp contrast with her smooth and pale-pink complexion. "Indeed, sir? Is that the famous General Daniel Morgan whose men did so well at Saratoga and in other battles?"

Dan's uneven but fairly white teeth flashed. "Yes, ma'am. 'The Old Wagoner,' as we called him on account of he was a freighter before the war, is a rare fine general."

Mrs. Valentine resumed darning. "Now that your identity seems to have been established, young man, just why have you made bold to address us?"

Maddox quit throttling his hat's brim and advanced a few steps with the sunset picking out a series of well-polished brass mountings banding Ilsa's five-foot octagonal barrel. "Why, ma'am, I've come concernin' my friend, Tim Murphy, who mortally wounded General Fraser at nigh on three hundred yards' range."

"I presume that is commendable," sniffed Agnes Valentine. "But what has that feat got to do with me and my daughters?"

Dan swallowed on nothing, kept his eyes on Rosemary for all that Choice had begun to smile at him as bold as brass.

"Well, ma'am, you see, Tim got himself clawed by a bear on our way here — pretty bad, too. I was wonderin' if maybe you ladies mightn't consent to come over by Doc Mason's tent and help us 'tend to him? For all he's gettin' better Tim's still pretty damn' — excuse me, ladies — pretty weak and uncomfortable."

Choice jumped to her feet, frilled petticoats daintily a-flutter. "Why — why I'd be happy to! That is, I mean, *we'd* be pleased to 'tend a Patriot who's killed a Redcoat general!"

"Choice! Don't be so pert! I declare someday I'll — I'll —" Mrs. Valentine broke off and commenced to stuff her mending into a little bag. "Well, perhaps we'll go see what can be done for your friend."

Without appearing to, Maddox found — or thought he had — an easy way of distinguishing the twins — at least for the moment. The one called Rosemary had her hair plaited into a single heavy braid worn before her left shoulder, while her sister's equally gleaming locks were plaited from the middle of her scalp into two pigtails.

"Tim — we all will be mighty grateful, ma'am." Then he discovered another means of telling Rosemary from Choice; Rosemary's full crimson mouth, although of identical shape, seemed just a shade wider than her twin's and her upper lip looked to be a bit longer.

"Well, they're coming — or said they would," Dan told the sharpshooter. "Be here 'fore long."

"B'God, Dan, I'll never forget this. I was about ready to trade my good arm for just a whiff of woman-smell. Ain't gone this long 'thout my greens since I begun to use a razor."

14. The Gentle Art of Persuasion

FOR Colonel Robertson to escape from Squire Valentine's verbosity without injuring that gentleman's sensibilities called for resourcefulness, but he managed to do so by summoning a rueful smile and pointedly shaking the last drops from a whisky flask they'd been sharing.

" 'Tis been a rare pleasure, sir, for me to converse once more with a real gentleman," boomed the big-paunched figure; he then departed breathing noisily and moving a trifle unsteadily toward his tent.

Jim Robertson found it wonderfully restful just to sit under the stars beside the Green with only his dog, Bassoon, for company. For a while he allowed his mind to remain blank and listened to chuckling gurgles caused by the Green's current hurrying over or around exposed stones. Whew! It sure was fine to be shut for a while of Squire Valentine's loud and overbearing voice.

Presently, two quietly treading figures appeared: one was John Rains, who by starlight might well have been mistaken for a Mohawk sachem what with his straight black hair and thin hawk's nose. The other proved to be soft-spoken and usually laconic Ike Bledsoe, who so much resembled Rains that frequently they were mistaken for brothers for all that they were in no degree related.

Rains slipped his dully gleaming long knife from its sheath, then caught up a dead twig and, settling onto his heels, commenced to whittle an Indian "prayer stick" — later on it would prove handy in raising a flame among dying coals.

Foxes had commenced to bark across the river when at last the old Long Hunter spoke. "Well, Jim, what'd you make of my genteel partner?"

Robertson paused in stroking Bassoon's scarred head and grunted, "My God, John, whatever drove you to join shares with such a windy jaybird? Damned if he don't talk longer and louder'n any drunken Choctaw. And what's he doing in those silly regimentals? Bet he'd soil his pants if anybody was to shoot even close to him."

By the light of the waning moon John Rains shook his dark and narrow head. "I'll grant you Valentine's noisy and bone-lazy to boot, but all the same I've the notion that the fellow's no coward and, gen'rally, Jim, I ain't mistook 'bout that quality in a man."

"Even so, why'd you team up with him?"

Thoughtfully, John Rains started cutting another ruff of splinters around his prayer stick. "Ever heard about a useful thing called 'money'? Well, he has some — plenty, I'd say, whilst *I* ain't seen a pound — hard money — in above a year."

Ike Bledsoe added in his low, deceptively tired-sounding voice, " 'Nother thing; the four young bucks travelin' with us have gone coon-cub-crazy over them Valentine girls. Those raunchy rascals would never have joined us 'thout such a bait."

Rains nodded. "He's right, Jim, and I've been expectin' trouble in that direction — luckily, it ain't happened so far."

For a while no one spoke. Across the river some large animal began crashing about and breaking branches with the careless arrogance of a rutting bull elk or bison. Briefly Bassoon pricked shaggy ears but then sighed and resumed dozing by his master's side.

At length Colonel Robertson queried almost casually, "Tell me, John, are you dead-set on takin' your folks to Harrod's place?"

"Yep. Why not?"

"Look, John, you've ranged all 'round the Frenchman's Lick and must know that the Bluff is a far better location for a settlement than Harrod's."

"Why?" Ike grunted.

"Why, the land's wonderfully rich around there."

Rains nodded, said carefully, "That's sure 'nough so, but I ain't forgotten that Harrod's lies in Kentucky and don't occupy none of the Great Huntin' Country. I figure the savages won't bother us much if we settle close by Harrod's."

"No tellin' about that," Robertson remarked quietly. "But that far into Kentucky you're going to be awfully lonesome and spread out mighty thin for a long time to come." He straightened, looked Rains in the face. "Now, John, suppose you were to come along with me to Middle Tennessee and settle along in the Cumberland River Valley — then you'd find plenty of neighbors within easy reach within a few months' time."

"Maybe so, maybe not. What makes you so sure we'd have plenty of neighbors in that there bloody wilderness?"

Robertson began to speak quickly, earnestly. "Here's the reason. What with the war going so poorly back East people already have started flockin' westwards. Most of 'em want to start over, damn' well out of reach of the Crown. Amos Eaton, Kasper Mansker, Jim Freeland and the Buchanans all are headed west that way right now and leading sizable parties — or ought to be.

"Then there's something else." When Robertson bent forward long thrums dangling in a double row across the breast of his hunting shirt swayed lazily. "Expect by now you and Ike have heard that John Donelson's leadin' over three hundred people west by water?"

"Which way he going?" Ike wanted to know.

"Down the Holston to the Tennessee — where he'll join up with a party headed by a Captain Blackmore, who's built a fort up on the Clinch River."

"Are they on the way?"

Robertson hesitated. "Ought to be; I've no way of knowing for sure." Smoothly, he hurried on, "So, come next summer there ought to be around six–seven hundred people settled or settling along the Cumberland Valley."

Bledsoe snickered. "All that many?"

"I figure so. At least that many." All three men glanced when, silent as a cloud, a great horned owl drifted low over their heads. "Yes, boys, come next spring plenty of solid immigrants will be crossin' the mountains which is why Donelson, I and the rest of us are headin' for Middle Tennessee right now."

Rains cocked a shaggy, black brow. "Sure you ain't funnin' us, Jim, when you tell of six–seven hundert people seekin' the Great Huntin' Ground this time of year?"

Robertson knew when to backtrack. "All right, John, maybe I have exaggerated our numbers maybe by a quarter, but all the same, we're due for plenty of reinforcements."

"Who for example?"

"Why, as I just said, Kasper Mansker, who first discovered those big licks along the Cumberland. Besides him, I'm expectin' a big party from South Carolina to be led by the Buchanan brothers, Alex and John, and a fellow called Jim Mulherrin."

"How many will they bring with 'em?"

"Wish I knew for sure, but it stands to reason they won't try comin' out without bringin' along a lot of seasoned frontiersmen." He sensed that Rains was wavering, so hurried on. "Suppose you've heard that, right now, Sir Henry Clinton is assembling a powerful British army to be commanded by a general name of Cornwallis. His orders are to crush and overrun Georgia and the Carolinas and then Virginia. By next summer there'll be plenty of our folks desperate to get away from the coast."

For a space John Rains lay settled against a tree, craggy Iroquois-like features impassive. Absently, Ike Bledsoe explored the front of his hunting shirt in pursuit of an especially nimble louse.

Robertson waited a while, then inquired briskly, "Well, John, what d'you say? Will you keep on for Harrod's or come along with me?"

A soft sigh escaped Rains. "Dunno. Right now I feel kind of like the feller who knew two pretty gals and could ha' wed either of 'em, but he couldn't decide which he wanted the most. Well, I'm in the same kind of a bind; both Harrod's and the Frenchman's Lick have a lot to recommend 'em."

"It's a hard choice, friend Rains, that much I'll admit." Robertson leaned forward, elbows on leather-covered knees. "And I, too, have had to make a tough decision today."

"How's that?"

"I've been wonderin' how much your families and livestock might slow me up." He arose, slapped twigs and leaves from his seat. Bassoon got up, too, yawned and stretched. "We're behind time already, so we'll have to set a brisk pace if we're to reach the Cumberland before winter really closes in."

Bledsoe asked in a husky whisper, "What'll you do if you find we slow you too much?"

Robertson stared out over the hurrying, white-flecked river. "Well, Ike, I reckon I'd just have to push on and leave you people to follow the best way you can."

Rains adjusted a coonskin cap. "Which, in this great empty country ain't a over-comfortin' prospect."

"No, it's not. But that may not happen and, at any rate, you'd be no worse off than if you were to keep on for Harrod's by yourself."

Because he was suffering from a touch of the "rheumatiz," Bledsoe arose stiffly, like an old horse on a frosty morning, then said, "Robertson makes sense."

Rains heaved a deep sigh, then held out a hand. "That's so. Reckon we'll trail along."

John Rains's people greeted his decision to join forces with enthusiasm but Robertson's party heard of it with sharply varying reactions.

"Hell's roarin' bells!" rasped Cash Brooks. "Ain't we goin' to find plenty trouble 'thout gettin' our balls froze off or our skelps lifted? Ever try carryin' a passel of females and their brats 'crost a sizable stream? 'Cause they can't swim or wade they have to get rafted over, which will waste time we can't nowise afford at this time of year."

A stubby red-faced fellow wearing a wildcat-skin cap spat savagely. "Jesus, boys, know what his joining us will mean? A feller no longer can just step off the trail and squat when he feels like it."

Morosely, Tom Spencer inclined his massive head. "Bet you two number one buckskins to three Rains's folks will begin to lag after the first day, lest they rid themselves of most of the freight they've got along."

Although he pretty much agreed with what these men were saying, Samuel Mason, M.D., kept quiet. It might be helpful to have some females around; they could help with the sick or disabled — always provided they themselves didn't become patients.

Concerning the usefulness of the Valentine girls Mason entertained strong doubts; so soft-handed and prettily pink, they didn't appear to have done a real day's work in their whole lives. They seemed so utterly, pathetically dependent upon the old Negress, Sally, for everything of a practical nature. Sally was the only servant — slave or free — present in Carpenter's Station, except for Julius, Colonel Robertson's personal attendant, a burly silent Negro who, in fact, discharged very few menial duties. Mostly, Julius made himself useful by herding horses, hunting or standing guard just like any free man.

In the seclusion of the Valentines' wall tent, Virginius confided, "Agnes, my dear, this joining of our forces presents for me a rare opportunity, although being a mere female, you mayn't have perceived that fact."

Agnes Valentine continued folding an East India shawl. "How so, Major?"

"My love, this merger may mean that soon your spouse again will command a respectable body of troops."

" 'Again?' " Mrs. Valentine couldn't restrain a momentary plucking at the corners of her thin, pale-lipped mouth.

"Aye. What's your meaning, ma'am?"

Laying the shawl in its chest, she said quietly, "You are a very convincing talker, Major Valentine, but what prompts you to imagine that hard-bitten fighters like this lot will entrust their safety to an amateur who hasn't ever sniffed the smoke of battle?"

Far from taking offense, Valentine chuckled, arched bushy black brows. "They will, all the same, my pet. These uneducated rustic block-heads have yet to learn that more battles are won with words than by the use of bullets and scalping knives."

"That may hold true in the East," conceded Agnes Valentine, "but I've a strong notion that things will prove different in this Godforsaken wilderness."

As if Providence had set its seal of approval upon this union of the parties the weather for the next two days remained ideal, clear with a bright sun and gentle wind that stung a man's ears only a little.

Next day it was decided that, from now on, the expedition would have a strong advance guard composed of Ike Bledsoe, Tom Spencer, Cash Brooks, Joe Drake and others familiar with this vast, hilly and forest-shrouded country. John Rains would be in command.

Reluctantly but wisely, Robertson assumed the less exciting but very responsible duty of seeing that the main body kept advancing at its best possible speed.

To Squire Valentine's chagrin he was given a minor post — second-in-command of Major Todd Phillips's rear guard composed of veteran fron-tiersmen and old soldiers like Dan Maddox and Tim Murphy.

The latter had so far recovered that he now was able to sit an easy-gaited horse with his famous rifle slung in a crude buckskin boot rigged under his left knee.

Now that November had entered its first week no one was much sur-prised when, as they left Carpenter's Station, the sky assumed ominous silver-gray and black hues and the wind began to nip ever more keenly.

If Colonel James Robertson felt concern that no less than six pack ani-mals were required to transport the Valentines' property, he offered no objection, only pointed out they would have to keep pace or get left be-hind — a possibility which didn't please the leader for, secretly, and to-gether with a good many others, he enjoyed watching the two girls riding along gracefully sitting their sidesaddles and bending brightly kerchiefed heads under low branches. Full brown serge skirts were designed to con-ceal the eye-catching contours of the twins' shapely legs but somehow these often failed in their mission, for whenever the girls prepared to dismount, knots of shaggy, weatherbeaten men — by no means all of them unmarried — hurried to assist in hopes of leering at a well-turned ankle or even of obtaining a not-soon-to-be-forgotten glimpse of a dainty calf.

During the labored advance towards Pittman's Station, lying some eighty miles to the southwest, it was inevitable that a good many brooks, creeks and streams would have to be crossed. Fortunately, old-timers with the advance guard generally knew of fords sufficiently shallow to permit the livestock and pack animals to be driven across, belly-deep, in the hurrying, icy current. Nevertheless, mounted immigrants generally got their legs and bottoms wet while travelers on foot got soaked clear up to their armpits. Sometimes these unfortunates found no opportunity of drying themselves in a hurry so were forced to tramp along with lips gone blue and teeth chattering.

On the third day after quitting Pittman's feeble little settlement the weather grew considerably colder and, to make matters worse, a light but all-penetrating rain set in and slanted down hour after hour. Because there wasn't any wind, trees, bushes, men and animals became silver-sheathed by particles which stung eyelids and exposed skin like millions of invisable midges.

Shortly after noon the main body was forced to halt when they found the advance guard had stopped, all bunched up, before a sizable, slate-gray river roaring in white fury over a stone-studded ford which, according to Ike Bledsoe, was known as Mad Bear Crossing.

"Why 'Mad Bear?' " Jonathan wanted to know.

"A few years back, a feller got slain here by a bear that'd just raided a bee tree and had been driven crazy by stings," Bledsoe told him.

"That's sure one hell of a current out there," opined John Rains, fingering his bristle-covered jaw. "Must ha' rained hard as hell somewheres up country."

No one disagreed, since the little river already had begun to overflow its low banks.

Looking about, Jonathan could spy rabbits, skunks, foxes and other non-climbing small animals crouched disconsolately on logs, hummocks and big, moss-covered rocks.

For a half-mile back from Mad Bear Creek men and their livestock collected in knots and cursed this relentless downpour which was turning into rattling, biting sleet. Drovers permitted their charges to wander off the Trace to feed half-heartedly on frosty clumps of dead weeds and ferns.

At the river's edge Rains, Robertson and Phillips reluctantly decided that, because of the river's dangerously swollen condition and the ever-increasing iciness of the weather, serious results would ensue if everybody got completely soaked; some of the women and young folk might readily die of such exposure.

Commented Major Phillips, wiping a pellucid drop from the tip of a knife-sharp nose, "Reckon the only thing is to build a raft."

"Aye, but that's easier said than done." Wrinkles already furrowing John Rains's brow deepened while he scanned the current rushing wildly southwards to lose itself in the Green. "But even so —"

"But even so, what — ?" demanded Robertson in a rare burst of impatience.

"But how're we goin' to keep a raft from bein' carried off downstream? Poling alone won't prevent that."

Tom Spencer pushed to the shoreline with drops of frozen water glittering like silver beads strung along the rim of his broad hat. "Ye're right, John, ain't no earthly use tryin' to pole a raft across that stream and back 'thout its driftin' so far downstream with every crossin' that the people couldn't keep abreast."

His large steel-gray eyes narrowed themselves, then he eased off his enormous pack. "Party I was along of a few years back got in the same fix we're in — only we was worse off 'cause there was a big war party somewhere behind us just hankerin' to lift our hair."

Still in the saddle, Robertson flailed arms to warm himself. "Well?"

The giant Virginian grinned. "Show you, Jim, if you'll just pass the word for the boys to start buildin' a raft of straight logs not less'n a foot and a half acrost their center. Cut 'em twenty, no, thirty foot long. Meantime, anybody who owns a length of stout rope is to fetch it here straightaway."

Rains's weathered features relaxed with comprehension. "I get it. You'll have 'em knotted into two long lines."

"Yep, and use the weaker lengths to lash the raft together."

The necessary orders having been given, Robertson studied the furiously leaping water, then drawled, "Reckon I understand your intention, Tom."

"And that is?"

"You'll hitch long, stout ropes to each end of the raft and, by snubbing them around trees on either shore, control the raft between banks."

Spencer grinned in the depths of his beard. "That's correct, Cunnel. Always did claim us Virginians are smart above the rest."

Ike Bledsoe spat and juice sketched a brown spatter design across the frosty ground. "How about the livestock?"

Rains spoke up. "They'll be towed and swum over on leads."

"What about pigs?" inquired a wistful-looking little man who'd "farmer" written all over him. "I got ten along. S'pose you know swine can't swim very far — too apt to cut their own throats with their front trotters."

"Reckon those critters of yours ain't all that fat," Rains grunted, "but since they'll be damn' valuable where we're going, guess they rate a free ride when the time comes."

"That raft's sure a 'cute idea, Spencer," drawled Bledsoe, "but suppose you tell a stupid dumblock like me just how you aim first to land a leadin' rope on yonder shore?"

Spencer winked. "Reckon it'll just naturally have to be swum over, lest you fellers figger out a better way — and I sure hope you can."

Robertson looked dubious. The hurrying, gray-white creek was becoming dotted by a good many drifting snags; sharp rocks showing here and there were growing shiny with sleet which now was falling harder. "Think you can make it?"

"Dunno, but it's worth the try," rumbled the giant. "Depends on how far I can wade before I hit the deep water in the main channel. Feller can get numbed-stiff pretty quick swimmin' in water like that."

15. *The Raft*

It having proved impossible to complete a satisfactory raft before darkness fell, the miserable settlers belatedly made camp any which way amid semi-darkness.

Never before, decided Choice Valentine, had she felt anywhere near so miserable, untidy and disgusted as on the next morning. How many days had she been wearing these same damp, shapeless and now smelly garments? Of course, there'd been no opportunity for her or any other woman to change clothing. Anyhow, to have done so wouldn't have been practical; on the march everyone's garments got soaked, ripped and dirty in no time at all.

The Valentine family had spent the night huddled close together under a tarpaulin which, carelessly rigged, had permitted cold rain to *drip-drip* onto them as they shivered under half-soaked blankets.

Papa had snuffled and snored intermittently throughout the night except when he roused in order to gulp from one of several earthenware jugs of "vinegar."

Once his wife had demanded, "Are you ill, Mr. Valentine?"

"No," he'd grunted over the endless delicate pattering of sleet against the tarpaulin. "I'm just takin' a draught of — er — preventative. It kind of warms a man up."

"Wouldn't it warm a girl up, too?" Choice suggested. "Please, Papa, can't I have a little? I'm so awful cold I — I fear I'll take my death."

"And so do I," Rosemary announced through chattering teeth.

Instantly, Agnes Valentine's acid voice rang out. "That will do! No well-bred lady ever touches hard liquor, no matter what the excuse."

"Mamma is right," belched the Squire. "Now, girls, go back to sleep."

Choice sighed, "Wish to Heaven I could. Can you, Rosie?"

"I just don't care anymore," sniffled her sister, putting arms about her. "Oh dear, oh dear! Why did Papa have to fetch us along on this dreadful journey? Oh-h! Now water's trickling down my back and I'm growing so chilled I fear I'll die. Hug me tight, dear."

By the time dawn broke, gray and cheerless, Agnes Valentine and the twins had taken colds varying in degree. The old Negress Sally, however, appeared to be immune; Squire Valentine hazarded that perhaps this was because of the snuff the slave woman kept taking.

While scanty breakfasts were being prepared word was passed along the column that, on this frigid morning, Tom Spencer had added another feat to the legend of his prowess. After stripping to his pants he'd tied a bundle of clothes onto his head, had knotted a slender rope's end about his middle, and had waded boldly into the raging current until forced to swim across white water marking the creek's main channel. Naked as a fledgling bird, Spencer then had endured the freezing wind to kindle a fire with a tinder pistol brought over in a waterproof bag.

Once he'd dressed and got his fire really going Tom pulled across a heavier line which he'd then anchored to a sturdy tree. Once this had been done half a dozen hardy Long Knives had pulled themselves along the submerged rope to arrive on the far shore blue-lipped and with their sodden buckskins clinging as if modeled to their bodies. Once they'd partially thawed themselves at the giant's fire, they'd set about kindling more blazes since it stood to reason that even folks crossing on the raft-ferry couldn't avoid getting pretty wet in places.

Although it wasn't visible, the sun must have been well up before the raft made its first spray-drenched crossing, watched by wide-eyed immigrants who didn't like the way the ungainly craft kept swinging and tugging at the lead line that was hauling it across. So awkwardly did the raft maneuver that water often boiled over its unplanked surface or spurted up between the logs to drench passengers and render a poler's footing dangerously slippery.

Each time the raft made a crossing its progress was further impeded by wild-eyed horses, sheep, mules and cattle being towed along, willy-nilly, at the bight of long reins or halter shanks. It proved difficult enough to haul or drive these unwilling animals into the frigid water, but to usefully employ a pole between rearing, threshing bodies proved almost impossible.

Midday found nearly two-thirds of the expedition dripping and shivering on Mad Bear Creek's far shore. The Valentine party and another family of Rains's following were fortunate in having to await their turn for a long while; by then the ferry gangs had grown experienced.

Just before her family started to cross a stretch of trampled mud speckled with broken shale ice towards the ferry-raft, Choice suffered a cramp in her bowels so agonizing that she knew, come what might, she simply couldn't any longer postpone a "visit to the bushes." She knew she should have yielded to this embarrassing need much earlier, but she hadn't done so because with such an icy wind snapping at her exposed private parts it was certain to prove a dreadful ordeal. In fact, not a few of the women and older girls all along had suffered from self-induced costiveness because of their reluctance to "seek the bushes."

In the depths of a willow thicket Choice could hear voices — including Papa's — angrily calling for her to hurry and take her place on the waiting raft, but for the life of her, she couldn't bring herself to call out. As a result cold and weary Major Phillips, in charge of loading the raft, yelled to the pole men, "Don't tarry longer. Shove off! She can cross later on."

"Count on Choice to complicate things unnecessarily," growled the

Squire, then added softly and with relish, "Silly little fool's earned herself another smart switching the first chance I get."

The balance of the Valentine family crouched, huddled together on baggage piled near the clumsy raft's center. Water licking up between hastily aligned logs nipped at their ankles and they felt inclined to agree that this time the head of the family had a real cause for chastisement.

They forgot about the missing girl once the raft commenced to leap and plunge under them.

Choice, on returning pink-faced and self-conscious to the river's edge, found a group of men squatting about a fire and cooking a brace of half-plucked partridges on broiling sticks.

In no great hurry either to face her furious parents or to board the ferry-raft on the next trip, she walked boldly up to the fire.

"My! Don't they look good!" she commented, then treated each of the whiskery, muffled men to a slow look that made them jump to their feet.

Color rushed into Tim Murphy's thin and long-unshaven cheeks. "These birds ain't done yet but ye'll be welcome to a few chaws once they are."

"Thank you. I'll stand here till I get warmed up a bit." Risking a knowing grin, she turned her wind-nipped backside to the heat. Thankfully, Choice accepted the piggin of bitter but steaming-hot acorn coffee which Dan Maddox held up to her.

Once the birds were at least partially cooked Tim slipped his arm out of its sling and vied with his companions in offering this pretty, bedraggled young thing some tidbits.

Tim sank onto his heels beside a stump serving Choice as a seat, said in a low voice, "By grabs, I'm sure pleasured you got left behind."

"Why, whatever for, sir?"

He wiped greasy lips on the back of a thorn-raked hand. "Why, Sissy, you light up these damn cold woods like — like a sunbeam."

Dan, overhearing, used his teeth to tear off some shreds of breast meat. "Pity her sister ain't here, too."

"What's yer meanin'?" flared Tim.

"Why," laughed Dan, "then we could peel off our shirts and warm up in all that there sunlight you talk about."

Choice and her companions lingered around the cook fire, quite content to watch group after group of immigrants advance by fits and starts towards Mad Bear Creek, whose dull roaring was growing steadily louder.

Finally, Major Phillips appeared, cold and angry. "What the hell's been keeping you men?"

"We're detailed to the rear guard, sir," Dan explained.

"That may be so, but the Colonel's been calling for you, Maddox, and Cash and Murphy."

Maddox immediately got up, slapped wet leaves from his seat, then picked up his pack and rifle. "In that case, boys, reckon we'd better get moving and ye'd better come with us, Sissy."

Before long the raft was loaded again with some hog-tied pigs that kept shrieking outrage over being piled among baggage near the ferry's center.

To leave their arms free, Tim, Dan and Cash strapped their rifles, muzzle-down, between their shoulders, then heaped war bags and belts on the baggage, where Choice sat with skirts hitched high to keep them free of water that kept spurting up between the logs.

She watched the pulling gang on the far shore take up the rope and brace themselves while the crew steadying the raft from behind spat on their hands and also made ready. Along with the four regular polers who would bring the raft back for another trip, Cash and Dan prepared to use long, hastily-trimmed saplings.

Although at this point Mad Bear Creek was only about eighty yards across, its current had grown so powerful and noisy that it was hard to hear a mournful blast sounded on a conch-shell bugle from across the stream. Jerking and bucking, the raft commenced to move out following the pull rope which, by now, had chewed a series of pale rings out of the bark on a snubbing tree on the far bank.

Meanwhile, the gang on the east bank strained at the line attached to the ferry's after end in order to steady the raft during the crossing and also prevent its being swept away downstream — which no amount of hard poling could have prevented.

Tim's bad arm still wasn't well enough to permit his handling a pole, so he did what he could by encouraging Choice and using a cudgel to keep the terrified pigs under control.

Cash and Dan, legs braced wide apart, drove poles into the rocky bottom and pushed with all their strength when the ferry began to heave and plunge so violently that it appeared ready to disintegrate.

Choice, cowering on the baggage with her cloak's hood flapping wildly about her head, wished most of all that these wretched struggling pigs would stop their terrified squalling. When water began to rise inches deep over logs beneath her feet she became scared by the abrupt awareness that, on this freezing afternoon, she might perish.

A lantern-jawed fellow in charge of the raft kept yelling back to the tail-rope crew, "Haul harder! Goddam it, you're allowing too much slack!"

Dan, bending to his pole, began to wish he'd thought to unsling Ilsa with the rest of his gear; right now his rifle seemed to weigh a ton and its muzzle kept slamming into the backs of his legs and causing them to buckle again and again.

The raft was halfway across Mad Bear Creek when a large, uprooted tree suddenly appeared in the boiling current and neatly severed the ferry's lead rope. At once the raft slewed so violently as to hurl a pair of the regular pole men into the water along with some of the pigs.

Choice tried to shriek but couldn't — she was too terrified.

"Christ A'mighty!" Cash Brooks gasped when, his pole having been wrenched away, he fell flat on his back. The raft yawed and then started to swing on its stern line back towards the east bank.

The sudden increase of pressure on the tail-rope was enough to rip that line from the grip of the men on the east bank. Freed, the raft went plunging and spinning crazily downstream.

At this moment Dan's pole snapped, sent him lurching up to his knees in frothing water.

Uncontrollable now, the raft began to revolve and speed towards a rapids roaring downstream. Maddox groped for one of those ropes which bound the raft together, then with a free hand gripped one of Choice's ankles. Tim, all white eyes, streaming hair and gaping mouth, got the idea and seized the other while the last pigs followed the baggage overboard.

The raft began to rear and plunge like a cruelly spurred horse and the air became filled with sheets of icy blinding spray until the ungainly craft struck a reef with so violent an impact that the ferry captain and his remaining pole man fell into the foaming water.

Mad Bear Creek suddenly narrowed between walls of rock, causing its current to accelerate and carry the raft inexorably towards the rapids — a smother of leaping, twisting white water.

Numbed by fear, Choice tried to pray, but couldn't find the right words — unlike Rosemary, she'd never been very attentive to such matters.

Bitterly, she told herself that what was about to happen wasn't fair; so far, she'd not had very much fun out of life. Without actually formulating the thought, she resolved that should she survive this ordeal she'd never again deny herself a joyous moment, no matter what people said or did.

By the time the raft had bumped and reeled through the rapids it had been swept clear of freight; many of the logs comprising it had snapped their lashings and broken clean away or were being towed harmfully along by their bindings.

Several times Choice would have been swept overboard but for Maddox's iron grip on her ankle. Presently so much water began buffeting her face that she began to choke and her ears were deafened by the creek's booming, rushing tumult.

Time and again the raft collided with snags or struck rocks with such violence that its last bindings snapped and the people aboard suddenly were hurled into the icy, churning current.

Choice managed to hook an arm over a big log and was whirled away, babbling incoherently. "Know — I — wanton — vain. I — too young to die — not for a while. Don't wrinkle — pink gown — No, Ben — Papa might —"

To Choice, only semi-conscious, it seemed that she had become immersed in flame clear over her head; she'd no realization that intense cold, not heat, was causing such agony. Her last sensation before losing consciousness was of something tugging savagely at her hair.

When, dazedly, she began to recover her senses, she heard a barely audible voice mumble, "Reckon she — dead?"

"Hell, no! Look, Dan, her tits are beginnin' to stir a little. Here, lend a hand, let's drain some o' the creek outen her."

Then Choice felt herself held upside down by the ankles so that her streaming skirt and triple petticoats fell and muffled her head while she retched quantities of water out of her lungs.

Finally someone remarked, "Well, Cash, can't be much more water left in her. Help ease her down."

"All right, but I hate to do it," said someone else. "Ain't likely I'll soon view another such a pretty white arse."

"To hell with this biddy's arse! Where's Tim?"

"Saw him come ashore below us."

She recognized Dan Maddox's voice when he said, "You sure?"

"Yep. Spied him crawlin' up the bank on hands and knees."

"Say, where's your war bag?"

"Same as yours — in the river — bullet mold, bar lead, picker — everythin'. Now ain't that *hell?*"

Gradually, Choice's head cleared till she knew that she lay prone on evil-smelling mud which felt, as Papa would have put it, "colder than Christian charity with a deficit."

Once again the girl lost consciousness until on coming to she became aware that Tim Murphy was rubbing hard at the back of her neck. She rallied, then sneezed and lay peering hazily up into the rifleman's sunken, almost jet eyes and wedge-shaped face.

"Uh — thank you," she whispered through stiff and colorless lips. "I — much hurt?"

"Naw, Sissy, you're kind of bruised here and there but there's nothin' broken we can see. Now that the boys have drained you, you'll be right as rain, but you sure were plumb waterlogged when you got pulled ashore."

Chiefly to get rid of water which kept running out of her hair and into her eyes Choice turned sidewise and peered about while wringing it out. "Cold," she whispered. "I — awful cold."

"So are we all." Dan Maddox's deep voice came from somewhere beyond her range of vision. "But we'll soon thaw out once I get this goddamn' lock fixed and a fire goin'."

Choice felt content to lie where she was, even if sleet continued pitilessly to sting her; it was just as if a million needle-footed spiders were running over every inch of her exposed skin.

Tim bent and in an undertone suggested, "Maybe I'd better rub circulation into yer legs — wouldn't want you to get frostbite."

Not altogether sure that she wanted to protest, Choice nodded, and felt his palms begin to chafe under her sodden underpinnings all the way up her thighs. Presently, when friction began to restore warmth to her lower body, she sighed.

"Oh-h. That's wonderful — don't stop."

Maddox, however, called out sharply, "Leave off, Tim, you've had fun enough. Go collect dead grass."

"Found some tol'able dry punk," Cash Brooks's gruff voice announced. "And plenty of dead branches on yonder pine. How you doin', Missy? 'Pears like ye're less peaked-lookin'."

"Why, thank you, I'm feeling ever so much better."

Choice sat up but didn't recognize Cash Brooks at first. His gray-black hair and beard now dangled in eldritch festoons over knobby, almost fleshless shoulders to which his filthy buckskin shirt clung with tenacious fidelity. Slowly, Cash revealed the black stumps of his few remaining teeth in a loose grin.

The gunsmith stooped and slid hands beneath Choice's armpits, easily heaved her to a standing position. "Once you recover your balance, Sissy, you'd better start walking about till yer blood really gets to movin'."

Meanwhile, Cash, sheltering beneath a thick hemlock, filled his rifle's pan with dry punk; after drying the pale-brown flint imprisoned between the cock's jaws, he pulled the trigger. A brilliant stream of sparks streaked down the frizzen into the pan which customarily would have contained priming powder.

She watched Cash's whiskery cheeks round themselves again and again as he blew until the faint, acrid smell of fire began to eddy about. For the first time since she'd left Bethlehem — dear, safe, comfortable Bethlehem — she welcomed the eye-stinging reek of woodsmoke.

Once the fire began to crackle — regardless of possibly dangerous consequences — the four survivors huddled about it and presently became aware that they still were alive only because the last units of the raft, while breaking up, had been carried into a backwater on Mad Bear Creek's west bank. At present they were crouching on a short, tree-covered peninsula which marked the confluence of the creek with the much larger Green River. Had their raft been carried only a few hundred feet farther south it must then have drifted out into the Green where, undoubtedly, its passengers would quickly have perished.

Maddox, pressing as close to the blaze as possible, asked abruptly, "Anyone still got his powder horn?"

Cash Brooks said, "Yep. And I don't know why. Howsumever, the feed plug's fell out and so my powder's soaked wet as fresh cow turds. Don't make no difference, though, 'cause my bullet bag and mold are chasin' each other somewheres along the creek bottom. And so's my war ax."

Quickly the realization sank in on Maddox that, like the others, he not only had lost his bullets and gun-mending gear but also his war bag and tomahawk, not to mention other "possibles."

Since the castaways had lost their hand axes and between them there remained only Dan's skinning knife, they were forced to break off dead branches to keep their fire going amid a tangle of driftwood heaped in wild confusion among big boulders.

"Don't like buildin' a big blaze," Maddox complained through chattering teeth. "But otherwise we're likely to freeze before morning."

Cash nodded. "Yep, that's a fact. Anyhow, we're lucky the wind's blowing hard downstream so mebbe the light and smoke won't warn anybody we're here with our pants down."

Once they'd got an efficient fire glowing the men started to dry their footgear. Bronzed by soaring flames, Choice unconcernedly removed and then wrung out stockings of coarse gray wool before toasting sizable but well-formed feet. She would have felt a sight better had she not lost both shoes.

"How long before dark?" Tim queried, extending skinned and blistered hands to the leaping flames.

"Maybe half an hour," Maddox told him, then stood up and flailed his arms. "God send it don't get any colder or come on to snow. Christ! In my whole life I've never been so damn' close to freezing stiff."

Cash meanwhile had begun to dance awkwardly about, the long, gapped fringes on his shirt and leggings grotesquely a-sway.

"I'm hungry," Choice announced in a dull voice. "Isn't there anything to eat?"

"No, Sissy," Tim said, "and there ain't nothin' to be done about it now."

The old Long Hunter quit leaping about and scanned the darkening woods. "Don't spy no slippery elm or white oak bark we could gnaw on but there's a tangle of raspberry bushes yonder. Can we find some dead leaves in it reckon I could brew us some 'Liberty' tea. In a fix like this, anything hot in yer gut kind of helps."

Tim nodded. "Now that's a shining idee, old feller, but how're we goin' to heat water?"

Cash held out a slowly dripping copper powder flask. "Maybe this will do, though I hate like hell to spoil it. If we can cut off its top it will serve."

Since no tomahawks remained, Dan was forced to risk ruining the party's only knife for all it had an unusually heavy blade. Employing a rock, the gunsmith soon amputated a brass teat-valve through which powder normally was fed into a rifle.

"Don't look like it'll hold much," Maddox admitted, "but it'll serve to heat around a pint."

Cash nodded, then retied his hunting shirt's throat laces. "Murph, you been banged about pretty bad; you bide here and get this thing a-boilin', and you, Missy, go pick all the raspberry leaves ye can find. Me and Dan will scout around and rig some twitch-ups, do we come across a rabbit trot."

They found one just before it got really dark and fine, dry little snow-flakes started to sift down through naked treetops. They also came across something else of deep significance.

Maddox was whittling a trigger for a snare when Cash hissed, "Listen a spell, then come here quick and quiet as you can."

~

16.   Bullet in the Back

WHEN Dan Maddox cautiously pushed through a tangle of briars he found Cash bent over a sprawled human body. Both Maddox and Cash saw at once, though the light was fading fast, that this pale-haired corpse had been shot through the back at the level of his kidneys; several trails of dark-brown blood had meandered over a short-skirted deerskin hunting shirt while gouts also had splashed the backs of his leggings. These last immediately attracted Brooks's attention; they had been cut, he observed softly, in the Huron style; therefore the dead man's leggings must have originated somewhere north of the Ohio.

Barely visible amid deepening darkness, the sunken eyes of both men met when the fact sank in that this unknown had on him no powder horn, ax or knife.

Maddox whispered, "Was he one of Rains's?"

"Naw. Ain't laid eyes on a yellow head like that in a 'coon's age."

"How long's he been dead?"

"I figger by the state of the gore 'round that bullet hole he likely got shot early this mornin'."

Balanced on his heels, Cash again studied the sleet-silvered corpse, then reached out to finger a stiff strand of pallid hair. "What beats me, Dan'l, is why whoever jumped this feller didn't foller and lift his skelp. Let's turn him over."

When they'd done so Dan brushed snow from the corpse's tallow-hued face and revealed a short and curly blond beard of rather fine hair;

the glazed and staring eyes were of a very light shade of blue. Otherwise, the victim appeared to be about thirty years of age; he was short, lightly built and lay on the snow with dirty, stubby fingers crooked as if he'd been seeking to cling to life.

Fumbling about the corpse's breast pockets Dan Maddox was delighted to discover a flint and steel, a frayed plug of tobacco, a small brass crucifix and a few copper coins.

"What's them?"

"French pennies — *sous*, they call 'em. Burgoyne's Britishers brought quite a few down from Canada with 'em." Dan blinked through the gloom. "What d'ye make over findin' him like this?"

"I'd say he got jumped just when he was wakin' up."

"Sounds reasonable. What happened then?"

"Well, I'd say this Frenchy must ha' been out trappin' by himself and got shot by some lone Injun who'd spotted his camp."

Maddox touched the corpse with the soggy toe of a moccasin.

"Seems likely this feller only found time to hurl his war hatchet and maybe cripple his enemy."

"— And then?"

"Not bein' sure whether his attacker really *was* alone he didn't wait to find out, only took to his heels and ran like hell till he couldn't travel no farther."

A sudden faint crackle in the underbrush caused both men to whirl about, miserably conscious of their helplessness.

"By damn!" snarled Cash. "And us 'thout ary a charge of powder!"

Maddox's heartbeat faltered. The beautiful, deadly-appearing rifles they carried were less useful than a pair of stout quarter-staffs. All the same, both men leaped behind trees and cocked their weapons.

Boldy, the gunsmith called, "Come out of there and keep yer hands up high!" Then in rudimentary Iroquois he added, "*Ai-yeh! Kocu Ketellunsi* — Hi, there! What is your name?"

There came no reply in that tangle of honeysuckle and grapevines from which the noise had come.

Cash yelled, "*Gissa, m'majewelan!* You must be an ugly woman who fears to show herself."

More faint crackling noises made Dan mad; for a seasoned campaigner to get snared like a recruit on his first scout was absurd! Especially so because he hadn't been careless or used poor judgment.

Slowly, the former sergeant eased Ilsa from his shoulder and leaned the

rifle against the tree behind which he was hiding. Next he slipped his skinning knife out of its rawhide sheath. From the corner of his eye he could
see Cash getting set, shifting his weight onto the balls of his feet for a
quick spring when out into the open moved a sizable, rough-coated dog!

The black-and-white beast advanced uncertainly, sniffed at the dead
trapper's body and then peered warily about.

Maddox whistled, then said, "Steady, Mister Dog. We didn't do in
yer master."

The animal wheeled and bared its teeth.

"We ain't Injuns neither," Cash informed. Likely this was the dead
man's hunting dog, one who enjoyed tangling with a redskin in preference
to anything else.

Wiry and high-shouldered, the dog kept growling until Cash rasped,
"*Tais-toi, imbécile!*"

Surprisingly, the dog stopped snarling, lowered his hackles and then
cocked furry ears; but he wouldn't let either man come near.

"What did you say to that critter?"

"I only told him to stop his fuss, so it stands to reason this deader, sure
'nuff, was a Frenchy."

Since by now complete dark had fallen, it simply wasn't possible to
bury the corpse, so they heaved the rigid figure into the fork of a tree just
high enough to prevent bears or wolves from reaching it.

While making their way back to Mad Bear Creek they noticed that the
big black-and-white dog sniffed continually of the wind which now came
beating out of the northeast.

"What ails the critter?" muttered Dan.

"Dunno. Acts like he smells Injuns nearby. Hope to Jesus he's mistook."

For all that Tim Murphy's injured arm again had begun to ache like a
bad tooth he accomplished several chores while the other two men were
absent. For one thing he collected a pile of sere brown rushes. Had he
been a mite stronger he'd have broken off evergreen boughs to build a
single big bed — but he wasn't, so armfuls of reeds would have to do. All
the same, it would be pretty bad passing this frigid night with no blankets, no lean-to, no food and no weapons to speak of: pity this Valentine
girl was so useless and lacking in spirit. Any wench raised along the frontier would have busied herself collecting firewood or building a proper

fireplace; all this young female did was to hug the fire, sniveling and complaining about how hungry and cold she was.

Finally, Tim mumbled with a taut smile, "I sure can't feed you, but maybe I can warm you up again."

When he came slipping silently out of the darkness Dan Maddox wasn't much surprised to find the girl huddled before the now roaring fire beside Tim Murphy who held an arm draped about her shoulders. All the same, Choice was shivering and her full, clearly limned lips remained lavender-tinted. That she'd lost her shoes, thought Dan, was most unfortunate; to get so delicate a female shod again wasn't going to prove easy. But she'd have to be; in this sort of weather she couldn't travel any distance on stockinged feet.

The gunsmith beckoned Tim out of earshot, told him about finding the corpse and repeated Cash's theory about how the stranger had met his death.

"— That's his dog in the underbrush. He'll come in closer once the wolves start cryin'."

Tim looked grave. "So he didn't have a bit of powder on him?"

"Never a bit."

"Too bad, because like always," he tapped his broad belt, "I've got some emergency balls stowed in here. Does anything make you think we may get jumped before daylight?"

"No, but all the same, tonight we'll stand guard by turns."

When the two returned to the fire Choice was plaiting her abundant pale hair into a single heavy braid although its tangled locks included bits of twigs, grass and leaves.

Tim went over to feed the fire from the driftwood piled around them. "Come across any rabbit trots?" he asked Cash.

"Yep. Plenty of 'em and fresh droppings, too. Ought to catch some afore long."

Smooth features tinted red-gold by the firelight, Choice batted long black lashes in Maddox's direction. "Please, sir, I'm so hungry my stomach hurts and rumbles. When can I have something to eat?"

"Ain't none of us feels exactly gorged, Missy, so you can quit yer bellyaching. It don't help none," growled Cash.

The girl got to her feet to settle her braid, whereupon the hollow-cheeked men more or less openly enjoyed the vision of well-developed breasts lifting under a blouse of fine lawn.

Choice made a transparent effort to appear cheerful. "Mercy! I'm *that* scratched and bruised and sore, but I do want to thank all of you gentlemen for having saved my life." Her gaze lingered on Dan Maddox. "I wish I might reward you more suitably but, if you please, I — well, I'd like to give each of you a kiss. Will that serve?"

Tim chuckled. "Better'n fine gold! Suppose, Sissy, you buss t'others first and save yer best for me?"

When Murphy's arms finally fell away Choice said brightly, "I fear I've not been reared to make myself useful in the wilderness, but if you'll be patient and instruct me, I'll attempt the best I can."

In the deepening gloom a wolf's howl, infinitely eerie and ominous and not very far off, arose in the forest crowding in on Mad Bear Creek.

As expected, the dead Frenchman's dog moved in and finally made bold to sit on the edge of the firelight with unblinking eyes glowing green-gold.

"Well," Cash drawled, "the brute ain't been extry friendly, yet he ought to warn us if hostiles try to close in. Hi! What's that?"

The dog had leaped to its feet bristling, and all three men froze momentarily before catching up sticks of driftwood; Maddox got his knife out in a hurry. Choice emitted a quavering moan of fear when shrill, agonized shrieks commenced to sound in the woods.

Immediately, Cash hurried over to pat Choice's shoulder. "Don't carry on so, Sissy. That there's only a rabbit which has got itself foul-snared."

Accompanied by the always wary dog which inevitably had been named "Frenchy," the men cautiously entered the woods and were overjoyed to discover that two of the springs, rigged from bent saplings and nooses fashioned from lengths of that rawhide line which Cash habitually carried looped over his left shoulder, held rabbits. One, suspended by a hind leg, struggled and squealed, but the other had strangled quickly and quietly.

The castaways' luck continued fair — for another trap held a half-grown turkey which had been following a rabbit path through dense underbrush.

17. Warm Interlude

CHOICE and her companions, although bruised and apprehensive, sank into the death-like sleep of near exhaustion. By turns the men kept watch and at intervals replenished a fire smoking at the head of that communal bed which proved uncomfortable, no matter how they twisted and turned beneath an easily dispersed covering of dead rushes and reeds which offered only a miserably inadequate substitute for blankets.

Fortunately the sleet quit early in the night and then the wind began to lessen, so, by huddling together, spoon-fashion, the sleepers achieved a measure of repose. The unbroken howls of nearby wolves kept the dog, Frenchy, close by the fire.

When Cash roused him, Maddox awoke, feeling considerably refreshed, to view a bright and cloudless dawn etching in detailed silhouette treetops across Mad Bear Creek. He stretched, hawked and spat, then heaved himself stiffly erect, leaving Choice and the ex-rifleman clasped in each other's arms — and very sound asleep.

At first Dan was prompted to awaken them, but Tim looked too peaked, and by now he knew that Choice Valentine wouldn't be of any use, so he decided to let them stay asleep.

Neither man spoke till they'd attended to their natural needs, an example gravely copied by Frenchy upon a piece of driftwood.

Finally Cash cleared his throat. "Dunno what you think, Dan'l, but to me it 'pears like it mightn't be a bad idee to backtrack a while along that Frog Eater's trail; mebbe we could find his campin' place and mebbe come across some powder and shot and other possibles."

Maddox's coppery head inclined. "Let's do that. If that Frenchman really was jumped by a lone savage who he hurt so bad that the Injun couldn't follow, then his gear still ought to be there."

Before setting out the two brewed raspberry tea in the mutilated powder flask, then gnawed a few shreds of flesh from rabbit carcasses warmed over the coals.

Maddox, looking mightily unkempt, picked up his rifle and paused, small dark-blue eyes narrowed, above the sleeping pair. Even though the girl's honey-blonde hair suggested what sailors would call a "mare's nest" and her clothes remained smeared with mud, Choice Valentine offered a surprisingly stimulating vision as she slept pressed close to the Sharp-shooter of Saratoga. Hum. This female, with lips parted just enough to reveal the ends of small white teeth, *might* have seen less than seventeen summers, but already she surely had everything a grown woman could hope for — and in the right places. To his mild resentment he was fleetingly reminded of his dead wife; she, too, though bigger boned, had been short in stature, blonde and finely proportioned.

Just before he and Maddox set out Cash gave Tim a light kick on the rump, whereat the rifleman came awake all in an instant and snatched up his useless gun. "Hey — wha'?"

Dan shook his head. "Go on sleepin' like that, Tim, and you'll never reach the Frenchman's Lick."

Tim yawned cavernously, then sat up knuckling black and almost round eyes. "What's afoot?"

"Don't know yet," grinned Maddox, "but it seems like a fine day for it."

This was no exaggeration; the sun had commenced to peer over a distant hilltop and sketch delicate crystalline patterns among clumps of sleet-silvered underbrush.

"Now listen; Cash and I are going to try backtrackin' and see if we can find the dead man's camp; considerin' that hole in his back it shouldn't lie too far away. Meantime, I want you to keep a sharp lookout; perhaps some of our people will come lookin' for us though I don't think it's likely. They'll think we've been catfish food long since."

Cash rubbed his balding scalp. "Now, Murph, better get cracking and 'tend the snares; then fix up some kind of lean-to." He shot a glance at Choice, whose gray-stockinged feet protruded from muddied, ill-adjusted petticoats with toes curled against the cold. "After that see if you can figure out some way to get Sissy shod."

He pointed to woodsmoke which, clinging close to the creek's surface, lazily drifted downstream. "That's risky, but I guess there's no help for it — she'd freeze. But if any red bastards smell it and start nosing about, get into the woods and hide."

On being whistled in, the big black-and-white dog appeared a trifle less mistrustful and followed readily once Maddox and his companion set out to find that spot where they'd come across the Frenchman's corpse.

As he worked, Tim locked his teeth and tried to ignore darts of searing, eye-watering pain which, upon occasion, shot the length of his tender arm. Of course, he'd several times strained it badly yesterday. At length he gave in and contrived a sling out of a wild grapevine; all the same, it throbbed like an ulcerated molar when he lifted the turkey's half-consumed carcass from a sharpened bough on which it had been impaled out of Frenchy's reach. Selecting a broiling stick used last night, he set the bird to warming.

Twice he stiffened to subtle sounds in the woods but relaxed in concluding that these had been caused by a deer or some equally harmless creature.

When he'd gnawed a charred drumstick clean he felt very much better. Yep, this promised to be really a fine day; the sun's rays were warming his back and soothing his bad arm. Already, sleet had begun to melt and drip and splash off the trees onto the snow-covered ground.

Once he'd washed his face and hands, the rifleman returned to consider the sleeping girl. Little scratches and streaks of charcoal and grease from last night's supper marred the girl's pink and delicate heart-shaped features, but even all tousled and grubby like this Choice looked prettier than a speckled pup. Blood started pumping into his loins.

In what sort of mood would she awaken? Would she try to act hoity-toity, or would she simply rejoice that she still was alive? He decided to find out, so stooped and gently ran his fingers down her back, then over her upturned buttocks. Whew! A goose-down bolster couldn't have felt any softer!

A pleased grin widened over the rifleman's grimy features when, little by little, he eased a hand under her skirts, but she didn't even stir until his rough fingertips were experiencing the warmth and incredible smoothness of her thigh. Finally, Choice sighed, then slowly rolled over onto her back and sleepily batted dark-fringed eyelids.

"Hi, Sissy! You want somethin' to eat?"

Her clear, dark eyes stared blankly upwards. "Wha —?"

Reluctantly getting to his feet, Tim said, a bit sheepishly, "Best to rouse up. I've got some vittles heatin'."

The girl smiled faintly, then blinked at the rangy figure which seemed to blot out most of the brilliantly blue sky. Choice yawned, then sat up and began to pick bits of debris from her hair.

"What have you got to eat?"

Grinning, he offered her a chunk of the turkey on a strip of birchbark. "This — and some raspberry tea. Sorry, there ain't no salt or even hickory-ash pepper."

All at once her intense brown-black eyes rounded themselves. "Mercy! Where are our companions?"

Tim said gravely, "Gone off."

"Gone off? Why — why, have they deserted us?"

"'Tain't nothin' like that. They've only gone to seek the Frenchman's camp and maybe bring in some powder and shot."

"Oh, dear! I only hope they'll return soon. They understand the wilderness — and what to do about this pickle we're in."

Choice took a sip of the raspberry tea before she commenced briskly to rub her feet.

"How do they feel?"

"Bruised and numb."

"Put 'em nearer the fire, Sissy, and they'll soon warm up. Mine did."

"But you're wearing moccasins." Slowly, Choice's dark-red lips assumed a pathetic curve. "I don't know how I'll manage without shoes of some sort."

Despite her obvious hint Tim turned away. "I'd lend you mine 'cept they'd be away too great. Besides there's a lot of work to be done afore the boys return."

"But — but, Tim, what *am* I to do? I can't go about like this. Really I can't."

The wide bed crackled softly when Tim sat down beside her. "That's correct and I just been doin' some hard thinking on that subject and maybe I've hit on a good idee."

"What is it?"

More than ever Tim wished he weren't smelling so all-fired high and looked less unshaven and otherwise disreputable.

" 'Tis a pity I've just forgot. But maybe, Sissy, if you was to buss me real nice — heartier than you did yestereve — I might remember."

To his considerable surprise Choice Valentine didn't appear in the least offended. "You mean you know how to make me some footgear?"

"I will, if I have to, but it mayn't be necessary." Tim's dark, deep-set eyes were glinting below heavy but ruler-straight brows. "Well, how about a memory lesson?"

Choice's long black lashes fluttered down, became outlined against her grimy cheeks. Then she pursed lips and tilted her face upwards.

For all his heart had begun to hammer, the rifleman was much too experienced to rush matters, so he kept his lips together when they kissed. He didn't even attempt to pass an arm around her. Apparently his restraint was appreciated, for this slim little creature appeared in no hurry to break away.

Said she demurely while using the back of a hand to rub lips scored by bristles, "Now what about those shoes?"

Fighting an almost overpowering impulse to stay where he was, Tim got up. "That was a beauty of a kiss, so I'll go look into the matter whilst you tidy up a bit."

Softly, she demanded, "Why, where are you going?"

"Into the woods. I'll soon return, so don't you fret."

"Oh, no, no! Please! Don't leave me alone."

He patted her cheek, added seriously, "Don't fear, Sissy, I ain't goin' far so just neat up and keep the fire goin'."

It proved easy to follow Cash and Dan's footprints, clearly sketched in snow that was beginning to melt, so he experienced no trouble in locating the Frenchman's corpse. Around the base of the tree supporting the body he noticed the tracks of a good many wolves whose blunt claws had scored futile furrows along its bark.

He slipped his arm out of its sling and, after trying it once or twice, decided it would serve to help him lower that rigid figure whose glazed blue eyes stared fixedly downwards, as if in reproach.

18. The Hostiles

WARILY, Maddox and Brooks followed the dead man's faint tracks and at times were guided by congealed spots of blood shed by the Frenchman during his flight.

Before long it became all but impossible to make out the trail, for the rising sun had commenced to thaw the ground's covering.

Several times Cash, employing a mixture of frontier French and various Indian languages, attempted to encourage the dog to trail, but accomplished nothing. Whenever the bareheaded men halted, the furry black-and-white dog sank onto his haunches, cocked pointed ears and lolled his tongue while casting suspicious and uncomprehending glances at his new masters.

Before long only a few patches of fast-melting snow remained to silver the forest's floor; finally, no amount of patient circling enabled the trackers to follow the line of blood splashes.

Cursing softly, Dan Maddox halted, used a forefinger to scrape sweat from his forehead and then eased Ilsa into the crook of his arm. "Onliest thing left for us is to try to find the course a sore-wounded man likely would follow — where the going's easiest, of course."

Cash nodded, also cursing for fear that, with slushy snow soaking his moccasins, he might contract a case of "foot scald," one of the most dreaded crippling diseases known in the wilderness.

While following a line of least resistance over slopes covered by bushes and vine tangles, they saw a lot of wolf tracks and the spoor of several bobcats and panthers but sighted no useful game beyond a few turkeys, partridges and a half-grown deer which Frenchy pursued energetically but unsuccessfully. The big dog returned after a while looking disgusted, as if he couldn't comprehend why no one had fired to furnish him and themselves with a meal.

At length Maddox halted. "Cash, it's plain we're wastin' our time just roamin' about like this; had we found the right course we'd have discovered his camp by this time. With such a great hole in him he couldn't have traveled any farther."

Cash broke off a twig of sassafras bush and fell to chewing it. "That's so, but I don't cotton to the idea of not makin' *sure* there weren't other redskins along when that Frog Eater got jumped." He cocked a grizzled brow the color of a wolverine's pelt.

Dan hesitated while a huge and glossy black squirrel sauced him from the top of a towering hickory. "You got any idea which way the Kentucky Trace heads after it crosses Mad Bear Creek?"

"No. All depends which way the country runs — it might even lead north for a while, away from us. Reckon you're thinking we oughter strike cross-country till we cut the Trace somewhere?"

"Why not?"

"Because around here lies some of the meanest country *I've* ever seen — it's full of creeks and swamps, tempest-felled trees and deep ravines."

"If that's so, I expect we'd better try to rejoin the column by workin' our way upstream to the Crossin'. You got any idea how far we got carried down the creek?"

"Naw. I was that rattled I ain't the least notion; maybe 'twas seven miles — maybe more."

Soaked and miserable amid the woods' icy *drip-drip*, the men agreed that, since they'd come ashore where Mad Bear emptied into the Green, they might as well return to camp along the latter stream's northern shore; there was always the faint possibility that they might find some kind of derelict. Canoes, dugouts, pirogues, even small scows were well known to go adrift mysteriously and sometimes to wind up, waterlogged, in some backwater or stranded on a sandbar.

Now that he knew his new masters were heading back to their bivouac, the dog commenced to range farther afield and probe tangles of cat briars and wild grape. When rabbits bounced off into the underbrush, their cotton-white tails flashing like miniature deer flags, Frenchy started yipping. Cash cursed him in a variety of Indian languages but the mongrel refused either to come in or to keep quiet.

They were nearing the tip of that heavily forested point upon which the castaways had landed when Cash halted abruptly, raised a hand in warning. Then, lifting his battered nose, he sniffed like a good bird dog testing the wind for a bevy of bobwhites. "Smoke!" he muttered. "By damn, we must be closer to camp than I'd figgered."

Evergreen growing on the apex of the peninsula permitted Maddox and his companion to scout a narrow stony beach littered with tangled mounds of dryki, heaps of dead canes and jagged shards of drift ice and so obtain a clear view of the confluence of the Mad Bear with the Green. A flock of sheldrake appeared, flashed by, headed downstream, but neither man noticed them. What held their attention was the presence of bluish-gray smoke that was drifting over the Green's tan-colored current!

"My God!" burst out the gunsmith. "Tim's gone crazy to use green wood like this!"

The old Long Hunter caught his breath sharply, *"Look yonder!"*

A canoe had appeared on the Green, apparently headed for the Creek's mouth. From the cautious way its four occupants hugged the river's shore they must, long since, have sighted that fateful stratum of smoke.

The scouts faded skillfully backwards and disappeared in the underbrush.

Off the mouth of Mad Bear Creek the Indians quit paddling for a short while and just drifted on the current. Maddox had begun to hope for the best when their paddles again began to dip and flash in the sunshine, driving the canoe towards that same peninsula on which he and Cash were concealed.

Cash whispered, "Let's make tracks for the Trace; they'll soon jump Murphy and the girl; ain't no use our gettin' scragged into the bargain."

Maddox's lank, coppery hair swayed in negation. "Do as you please but I'm goin' to try to warn Tim."

"All right. We'll have it yer way, ye bloody ijit."

The two ran ducking under branches, slipping on mossy rocks and circling windfalls, unaware that, at the bivouac, a far from unpleasant interlude was being concluded.

19. By the Riverside

As soon as Corporal Tim Murphy's leather-covered back became lost to sight amid frosty underbrush, Choice Valentine indulged in some distinctly unladylike scratching at various intimate parts of her anatomy, for like everyone else, she'd acquired vermin. Until now her lice had been chilled into inaction, but, warmed, they were making up for lost time. As best she could, Choice picked the seams of her garments, a proceeding which required so much time that the fire burned dangerously low. Hurriedly, the girl tossed the handiest sticks onto the coals — ignorant that they were of green wood.

Glory! This was such a rare fine day it became almost possible to forget yesterday's miseries. Suddenly she flung wide her slender arms, lifted her face to the sun, laughed out loud and executed a few dance steps.

Choice then stripped off her blouse the better to wash at a little pool where, as she'd recently been taught, she scrubbed herself with fine sand, but winced when the gritty substance encountered various scratches and bruises. Characteristically, Choice was giving never a thought to the anxiety her family must be suffering. She only knew that she was feeling uncommonly joyous, perhaps because Tim Murphy, despite bristle-covered cheeks and leather-hard lips, surely knew plenty about kissing a girl. Of course, the rifleman was no part of a gentleman, but right now that didn't matter a bit.

Brief as his caress had been, she'd been far more excited by it than by the best of Tommy Burnett's puerile efforts. For a moment she wondered what had become of poor dear Tommy. Did he still cherish memories of that esctatic, experimental afternoon in the loft of Papa's carriage house — the only one in the village of Bethlehem, Pennsylvania?

Smiling, Choice watched a dense column of grayish smoke begin to twist away from the fire. In dreamy detail she relived what had taken place on that unique occasion; her halfhearted struggles in arms which she'd pretended were stronger than they actually had been. After all, Tommy had only just turned seventeen and had been growing too fast. After a deal of awkward kissing, fumbling at her clothing and tumbling about, she'd suddenly experienced a pang of sharp yet somehow delicious pain.

Yes, poor pimpled Tommy had been pretty maladroit, but then she guessed that she must have been just as green — so green in fact that she hadn't taken care to obliterate certain stains the presence of which she couldn't satisfactorily explain to her mother. As a result, Papa, grinning strangely, had applied a strap to her bare bottom and other tender regions with such vigor that she'd struggled and squealed like a shoat stuck under a gate. Even now she remained proud that even when her buttocks had become crisscrossed by fiery, bleeding welts she'd refused to betray her seducer's name.

"Curse you for a fine, foolish baggage!" Papa had panted when, purple-faced, he'd dumped her whimpering and tear-bathed onto his study floor. "An this spark of yours, whoever he is, goes about bragging that he's taken yer maidenhead, by God, you'll die a whore unless you can trick some lout without fortune or breeding into marrying you."

How relieved poor Mamma had been when, in due course, it became evident that, for all her folly, she wasn't with child!

Even now, she still couldn't be sure whether her seduction had played a part in Papa's abrupt decision to buy land shares from the Transylvania Company and then move west.

To still recurring hunger pangs Choice drank a lot of water and soon felt better, especially with the sun's increasing heat which sent warmth flowing into her breasts and thighs as she sat beside the Creek trying to untangle her long, honey-hued hair.

At the same time she renewed a vow that she would prove Papa wrong about her future; she'd *never marry* an unimportant, ignorant or coarse-bred fellow. While watching the current boil over a big snag she determined to bide her time. Didn't it stand to reason that plenty of promising young men soon would be crossing the Alleghenies to a land where the hand of any female, no matter how plain or poor, would be at a premium?

Choice also reached another decision; that near-escape from death yesterday proved that, in this country, nobody could be certain they'd be alive tomorrow. Therefore, a lively young girl should waste no opportunity to enjoy life to its fullest.

Once she'd plaited her hair and had scraped as much mud from her clothing as she could, Choice tossed more sticks on the fire before settling onto the bed of rushes in order to resume her hunt for vermin.

In the process she was forced to raise her underpinnings so high that she exposed shapely, pinkish-white legs almost to her hips. Faugh! Her limbs scarcely looked their best in shapeless gray woolen stockings gartered by strips of rawhide.

So silently did Tim Murphy return to the bivouac that, at a flicker of his shadow, she looked up and gasped. When she saw the rifleman he was standing not a yard away, grinning broadly at her déshabille.

Tim's small, black eyes were shining and his uneven, old ivory-tinted teeth peered through a slack smile. His good arm supported his rifle while over the other he was carrying a dingy buckskin shirt and a pair of ankle-high moccasins decorated with a few strands of blue-and-yellow beadwork.

God A'mighty! Choice certainly was *something* to look at as blushing bright as a poppy she tugged at her skirts. She looked so fresh and young that he, too, went brick-red.

"Sorry to scare you like that, Sissy, but I ain't seen a girl so — nigh so pretty and soft-lookin' in time out of mind."

She smiled brightly. "Mercy, what a start you gave me!"

Tim advanced holding out the moccasins. "How d'you like the look of these?"

"They look wonderful! Wherever did you find them?" she asked, and after arising in a single graceful movement, hurriedly smoothed out her skirts.

The rifleman chuckled. "Off of that Frenchman the boys found dead in the woods yestereve. But if these moccasins won't fit reckon Cash knows how to fashion a pair out o' this here leather shirt which looks like it's smoke-tanned. Hi! What ails you?"

The girl's huge, dark-fringed eyes had rounded themselves. "You — you mean you took these things off a *dead* man?"

"Sure." Tim stepped closer, filling his eyes with her disordered loveliness. "He weren't able to make me a present of 'em, so what's the odds?"

He motioned to the couch. "Iffen you'll sit we can try these for size."

Lips compressed, Choice hesitated, then nervously complied, all the while hoping that the moccasins *would* fit for, already, she'd noted that small, round hole situated midway down the shirt's back.

Tim squatted onto his heels and tried to keep his hands steady whenever he looked up into the delicate oval of her face. Small, good-natured crinkles spread from the corners of his little round eyes when he began to brush the sole of a stocking free of grit and leaves and discovered that Choice's feet, although long and narrow, were by no means diminutive, so the moccasins proved to be only a trifle large. Yep. Given a little judicious re-stitching, the Frenchman's footgear would do fine.

Once he'd eased on the other moccasin Tim shifted to sit at the girl's side. She had begun to work her toes, all the while emitting small exclamations of satisfaction.

"Since these things seem to do," he announced softly, " 'twill be easy to fashion a vest for you o' his shirt."

Somehow no longer appalled at the prospect of wearing a dead man's garments, Choice laughed. "Oh, Tim, how *can* I thank you?"

"Why, that's easy," he informed in a husky undertone. "Suppose you give me a hearty buss?"

Choice not only nodded but turned sidewise to face him. Once he had her inside his arms she fetched a shuddering sigh and at the same time placed a palm between his shoulder blades and pressed her lithe, young body against him as hard as she could. Following a series of lingering kisses which rasped harshly, excitingly on her lips and cheeks, he eased her backwards upon the couch, quivering and with eyes half closed.

To the rifleman's astonished delight she failed to hamper his practiced exploration of her garments — only responded with timid readiness to his boldness.

Spent and short of breath, Tim only emerged from ecstasy when a faint crashing noise sounded in the woods. He sprang to his feet and at the same time sought to secure his belt.

"Criminently!" he gulped. "What the hell was that? The boys can't have come back *this* soon!"

Still dewy-cheeked and with lambent eyes Choice Valentine managed to straighten her skirt an instant before Dan Maddox came loping into sight with Cash Brooks a yard or two behind.

"You 'tarnal fool!" Cash wheezed. "Why the hell did you have to chuck green wood on the fire? Injuns close by!"

Amazed at the man's fury, Tim recoiled. "I didn't, so help me God! Sissy must ha' done so whilst I was away. Injuns you said?"

"Damn' right. Four damn' big bucks."

Cash cut in. "Now everybody listen. If them redskins got useful firearms we're most likely done for, but, if they ain't, let's try to make 'em believe our guns is workin' and grab our chance to jump 'em if they start to act mean."

"You just give the sign," Maddox said.

Cash glowered, "Now remember this, you goddam greenhorns! There ain't nothin' gets a redskin madder or meaner'n that if he gets the idee a man's weak or afraid of him. So don't anybody act the least bit scared, no matter what happens!"

20. *Showdown*

Four Indians in shaggy winter robes appeared climbing lightly over tangles of driftwood cast up on the creek's bank. After them slunk a large and shifty-eyed yellow dog at which Frenchy immediately commenced to hurl rasping threats and growls.

The white party watched with their guns held just as if they weren't completely useless. When the dark-faced apparitions were about fifty yards off Cash called, "*Woopan-a-cheen!* — We are well met!"

None of the savages replied; only kept on advancing, walking stiff-legged and on the balls of their feet like dogs getting ready to fight. The three white men, therefore, moved closer together while Choice got to her feet still clutching a piece of driftwood she'd been about to place on the fire.

When less than thirty feet away the Indians at last halted, but still said nothing. Frenchy, meanwhile, bristled his back hairs and bounded, snarling, to attack the strange dog, whereat the latter emitted a few half-hearted growls then dashed off into the underbrush. Neither the Indians nor Maddox's party paid the least attention, only stared fixedly on one another; all stood poised for instant action.

Choice, vaguely aware of an unfamiliar but delicious glow in her loins, peered in frank curiosity at these lean, evil-looking savages which were the first wild Indians she'd ever beheld, suddenly felt chilled and repelled by a certain reptilian glitter in their vitreous black eyes.

"What tribe are they?" Maddox demanded in a casual undertone.

"Piankashaws by their looks," Cash said.

"Must ha' been in a scrap lately," Tim commented. Fresh blood was saturating a rag loosely bound about one Indian's shoulder and another was limping from a gash on his upper thigh.

All three white men were infinitely relieved to note that these intruders carried only one firearm among them — a rusty, old musket — although two others wore powder horns slung over mangy fur mantles.

"Copy me," Cash hissed, while slowly advancing his rifle butt foremost — the armed frontiersman's peace sign.

Tim's heart began to thud faster when he saw how big and tough-looking these savages were. The Piankashaw leader stood tallest of the lot and had shrewd black eyes that narrowed when, carelessly, he returned the peace sign then continued to advance with a brief mantle of otter pelts gently swaying.

Attached to the back of his head he was wearing a *gus-to-weh*, a sort of headdress composed of four heavy, red-tipped feathers which, having been set in a metal stem, revolved erratically like the arms of a miniature windmill. The leader's broad and brutal-appearing features retained only a few streaks of red and black paint; he carried a few arrows stuck into a quiver made out of a spotted dog's skin and in his left hand he carried a short but powerful hunting bow. His principal weapon, however, was a ponderous *casse-tête* or war club, the rounded head of which was studded with sharp iron points that gleamed evilly in the sunlight.

A pace behind the Piankashaw leader stalked a young warrior who wore a dirty bandage twisted around his left forearm. What immediately attracted Maddox's attention was that a big powder horn was slatting heavily against this Indian's right hip; so the only weapons he carried were a long-shafted tomahawk and a skinning knife.

Although the third Indian, who was bowlegged and afflicted by a ferocious squint, carried the party's only firearm — an ancient Charleville smoothbore — he had no powder horn. Tim quickly noticed that the Charleville was lacking the cover to its priming pan, so this particularly unattractive savage, in reality, was armed only with a thick-bladed tomahawk.

The fourth savage was lithe and lighter-complexioned than his companions. His head was shaven except for a stiff blue-black crest roached in the Creek fashion. Because of a cut across his thigh which had splashed his deerskin leggings, he limped a little. He, too, wore a powder horn, but carried only a slender spear tipped with a fine, probably French-made, steel point.

When the visitors halted with expressionless jet eyes flickering about, Cash demanded first in Shawnee, then in Cherokee and finally in Creek, "Who are you, O my brothers?"

The tall Indian flung back his head, then in an arrogant gesture slapped his chest. "Me Orenda, Piankashaw half-chief." He pointed with the bandaged shoulder. "Him Big Jack."

Next, Orenda indicated the young, pale-skinned warrior. "Him Tskili." The bowlegged warrior apparently was called Blue Jay.

"Who wounded your friends?" Cash demanded, so abruptly that Orenda was startled into saying, "One sun gone we hunt, got surprised by Shawnee war party. They many, we few. We lose," he held up a hand, fingers spread, "men, much furs, guns."

Cash listened and at the same time tried to foresee what the Piankashaws might do; certainly, they must be wondering right now why three frontiersmen carrying fine-looking rifles should have allowed a superior number of strange Indians to march into their camp unchallenged. How long before they caught on to the truth of the situation?

Choice Valentine, standing a little apart, felt increasingly uneasy over the intent way Tskili stared at her pale yellow hair. Ugh! How dirty, greasy and dreadfully smelly these savages were! More than anything they reminded her of dangerous wild beasts.

Following a brief conversation carried on in Creek supplemented by considerable use of sign language, Cash informed, "Like this feller Orenda said, he and his people was huntin' close by the Kentucky Trace when they bumped into a swarm of Shawnees busy trackin' a big party of whites — our people, of course."

"How many Shawnee were there?" Tim asked without removing his gaze from Big Jack, who he was pretty sure understood a deal more English than he was letting on.

"He didn't let on beyond sayin' 'twas a big bunch, which might mean anything from ten to fifty — Injuns always talk big about their enemy's numbers — 'specially when they get licked."

Orenda pointed to Maddox's rifle, then held out a hand as if he wished to examine Ilsa. Something in the Piankashaw's expression lent the former sergeant a split second's warning before Orenda whirled up his *casse tête* and sprang. Maddox leaped sidewise and won time to bring Ilsa's heavy octagonal barrel crashing down on the Piankashaw's *gus-to-weh*. Although partially stunned, the half-chief lurched aside and raised his club again so swiftly that Maddox only had opportunity to jab at Orenda's solar plexus with his weapon's muzzle. Missing his mark, the gunsmith nevertheless maintained momentum so successfully that he was able to drive his shoulders into the Indian's middle, knock out his wind and sent the half-chief sprawling onto the leaf-covered ground. Maddox pounced. While grappling he succeeded in jerking Orenda's skinning knife out of its sheath and driving it between the Piankashaw's ribs.

They rolled over and over with the Piankashaw attempting to shorten his grip on his *casse-tête* sufficiently to job it against the white man's head. Maddox, meanwhile, kept turning the knife in the wound until Orenda went limp and began to cough up torrents of blood.

Tim also was mighty occupied, for at the same instant Orenda made his move, Big Jack freed his war hatchet, screeched *"Kish-kal-wa!"* and charged. In order to win room to use his rifle's butt, Tim sprang backwards but tripped on a stone and went staggering hopelessly off-balance.

As in the grip of a vivid nightmare Murphy glimpsed the Piankashaw's tomahawk flashing downwards bright as an embodied sunbeam. He was bracing to meet the bite of its blade when suddenly it veered aside; Choice had flung her billet of firewood with such astonishing accuracy that it struck Big Jack on the side of his head and sent him reeling aside. Tim instantly whirled up his rifle and brained Big Jack with its brass-heeled butt.

Far more experienced and alert than his companions, Cash disposed of the bowlegged Indian through a lightning throw which sank his knife deep into the base of Blue Jay's throat. Dropping his ancient musket, the Piankashaw spun sidewise with bright arterial blood spurting from between his fingers as, futilely, he struggled to check the flow from his severed windpipe.

Tskili, the pale-skinned young Indian, apparently had no stomach for this fight; when his companions attacked he wheeled and raced for the woods with Frenchy snarling and snapping at his heels.

The encounter came to an end so suddenly that, for a long instant, the whites remained immobile, panting and incredulous of the situation.

Maddox recovered first and bent to snatch Orenda's war hatchet from its sling. He beckoned Cash. "Come along. That runner may be tryin' to reach their canoe! Tim, take care of Sissy and plunder these fellows."

Without even pausing to charge their rifles from the captured powder horn, the two bounded off like hard-chased bucks, hurdling trash littering the creek's shore. Cash panted, "Hi, Dan, you got blood runnin' down yer back."

"That devil's club must ha' grazed the back o' my neck when I dove at him. Nothin' to fret about."

All the time maintaining a sharp outlook for the cowardly Indian, they ran out on that cedar-shrouded point where the Piankashaws had put in. A moment later they spied the canoe, sheathed with elm bark and clumsily contrived but apparently unharmed, drawn up on a narrow, stony beach. They halted, gasping and fingering their war hatchets, surveyed their surroundings but had no sight or sound of the fugitive. They began to wish now that they'd lingered at the scene of the fight long enough to load their rifles from the bowlegged warrior's powder horn.

Tim, meanwhile, anxiously examined his double-barreled rifle's stock and was unspeakably relieved to discover that its curly maple wood hadn't suffered a crack resulting from that terrific blow with which he'd felled his assailant. This was luck, for while a damaged gunlock might be mended in the wilderness, it was almost impossible to replace a broken stock once one left the settlements behind.

Aware now that his arm was sending out searing darts of pain the rifleman growled, "Damn' if I understand why this bugger didn't get me."

"I can," Choice announced while staring in morbid fascination at Blue Jay's still feebly stirring body.

"You can? How?"

"Because I flung a piece of wood at the savage which hit him on the head."

Tim gaped. "You — you — *what?*"

"Just what I said." The girl passed a quivering hand over her eyes. "When I saw you in trouble I, well, I threw a piece of firewood at him as hard as I could." She uttered a breathless little giggle. "I — I guess we were just plain lucky; I could just as readily have hit you."

Tim's gaunt and long-unshaven features relaxed. "Well, I'll be dipped in sh — er, damned. What made you act so quick?" He looked straight into her eyes. "Was it because of — of what we did — a while ago?"

Choice flushed and lowered her gaze. "No, I guess I'd have acted the same if either of the others had stood in such danger."

"Oh!" Tim felt suddenly deflated, but quickly recaptured his self-respect; after all, he'd had her, and the others hadn't — not yet. He went over and patted her shoulder. "Tell you something, Sissy — you got more courage than any female I've ever heard *tell* of!" He slid an arm about her, pulled her close, then chucked her under the chin. "So that being that, and since we've had a romp together, what say we get married soon's we c'n find a preacher?"

Choice giggled as she slipped free, then stood with head tilted to one side looking at him. Finally she wrinkled her pert little nose and commenced to laugh, softly at first, then louder and in the end, hysterically. "Now, sir, I vow that's the tenderest proposal of marriage," she mimicked him, "I ever hear *tell* of."

Tim burst out laughing, then patted her on the buttocks. "Mebbe so. I'll admit I ain't no part of a courtier; the main point is, will you?"

He fully expected that Choice would rush into his embrace; instead, she retreated another step and stood there with a puzzled look in her lovely dark eyes. "I vow I'm vastly flattered by your offer, Mr. Murphy, but now is hardly the time to consider so grave a matter." Her manner changed. "And now that we've been deserted again, what is to be done first?"

Angrily, he became aware that this disheveled, smudge-faced chit of a girl was actually turning him down! Smothering an exasperated curse, the rifleman strode off stiffly to detach Blue Jay's powder horn.

His scowl relaxed when he shook it. "By grabs, Sissy, this damn' thing's near full." He tilted a trickle of coarse black powder down his famous rifle's barrels. "All right, Kitty, drink yer fill, sweetheart. Won't ever let you go hungry again for so long."

After he had spilled and smoothed a priming charge into the Golcher's twin pans and had snapped shut their covers, he extracted a pair of the four musket balls from an emergency pocket stitched to his belt. To have his beloved weapon undamaged and useful once more sent a heartening wave of confidence surging through him.

Gruffly he snapped, "Sissy, go pull the cape off'n that feller Dan killed and wear it, lice or no lice." He was fast losing his anger, so added in a kindlier tone, "Guess you'd better lash that knife of his 'round yer mid-dle. Since you can heave a piece of wood so brisk you can likely learn to fling a knife true — which can serve you well out here."

They then systematically stripped naked all three twisted, bloodied and evil-smelling corpses lying so flat among the trampled and frost-killed weeds.

Once Tim had selected a war hatchet that suited him, they piled the other weapons and gear near the water's edge.

Just about then Cash Brooks appeared. His small, red-rimmed eyes lit when he saw Tim hold up the powder horn. "Good thing we got us some powder again, but what'll we do for balls?"

"Here's two," Tim held out the small blue-gray spheres. "Always keep a few spares in my belt."

Cash reloaded, then casually surveyed the dead Indians. "We was pretty damn' lucky this little rookus turned out like it did. Eh, Sissy?"

"That's right, Mr. Brooks," Choice smiled while settling Orenda's cape about her shoulders. "What do we do now?"

"We'll go to their canoe, where Dan and me figger to make camp; 'twill get dark too soon to risk paddlin' in fast water. Besides, looks like we're in for another spell of weather."

Tim was preparing to shoulder a bundle of captured gear when Cash exposed yellow-black, gapped teeth in a grin. "Hold on, son, ain't you forgettin' a leetle matter that needs attendin' to?"

"Such as — ?"

"— This," Cash chuckled, went over to Blue Jay's body, knelt on the dead brave's chest and jerked his knife free from the Piankashaw's neck muscles.

He paused, then called, "Sissy, you go down by the creek whilst Tim and me tally *coups*."

Choice hesitated. "What are *coups?*"

"Scalps worth hard money, can we ever lay 'em out before a pay-master."

Choice didn't move, only stood where she was for a space and kept her gaze on the racing waters of Mad Bear Creek, until an irresistible compulsion made her turn in time to see the grizzled Long Hunter make a precise incision in the dull bronze skin above one of the half-chief's ears. In helpless fascination she followed the blood-dimmed blade's course until it had completed a circle below the Piankashaw's hairline. Next, the frontiersman worked his knife's point well up under the skin and, jiggling it all the while, repeated the circle. "Me," he announced without looking up, "whenever I've the time, I always trouble to lift the full scalp."

"Why?" Tim demanded.

"An a man knows how, he later on c'n cut *three* scalps out of the one so clever they'll fool all but the smartest of hair buyers."

"You've done this how many times?"

"Dunno fer sure; I've lost count. It'll be twenty at the least." He spat onto the blood-splashed leaves, said quietly, "Wonder how many more I'll take 'fore someone lifts mine — not that he'd be gettin' much — I'm balding pretty fast."

To the girl's surprise she failed either to feel faint or throw up when Cash, after driving his knife into the ground, knelt on Orenda's shoulders and wound fingers of both hands into the dead warrior's coarse, blue-black hair. Then his bony shoulders hunched and he gave a sudden tug which detached the scalp and exposed the pinkish-white cranium beneath.

Cash got to his feet, snapped his trophy several times to rid it of loose blood. "Well, Sissy, for all yer soft looks I allow ye're as tough as any squaw of yer age." He chuckled. "Well, be that as it may, you've seen how it orter be done; some fellers can be real butchers about takin' a *coup*."

Choice turned aside, pale and shuddering. "How awful — how dreadful."

"Shore 'tis. But it's more awful when it happens to Number One. And, by the bye, you'd better take damn' good care of that honey-colored mop you wear. Injuns are mighty partial to off-colors like yours. Didn't you note how that young warrior who ran off was droolin' at the sight of you?"

"Y-yes, I did, but I didn't understand." A sharp icy shiver suddenly ran the length of Choice's spine. Dear God! Could this be an omen of some sort?

Unconcernedly, the Long Hunter retrieved his knife, drawled, "Tim, suppose you take the scalp of that brave you slew whilst I lift the other. Think you c'n do it?"

"Maybe. Till now I ain't been fightin' that kind of war." Tim swallowed on nothing. "But I suppose the time's come to make a start."

"That's right. Now, Sissy, just you lug some of this plunder along the shore to the canoe. Tim'll bring the rest."

The rifleman barely had reached that cove where the canoe had been drawn up than Cash arrived. Among other burdens he was carrying a human forearm.

Maddox called out sharply, "My God! What's *that* for?"

"Good dog food. Frenchy ain't ate hearty of late. 'Sides it'll remind him to act fierce towards Injuns."

The three Easterners soon were treated to another look at the way of existence in Kentucky, for shortly after the Piankashaws' possessions had been divided and some rashers of greasy bear bacon found in Tskili's war bag had been cooked in a hurry, Cash arose on bowed legs and, checking his priming, whistled in Frenchy.

Maddox also got to his feet, elevated a quizzical bronze brow. "What you fixin' to do?"

"Go and find that there Injun who took to his heels. I've the notion he don't fancy bein' all alone out there." His grizzled features formed a fleeting grin. "Me, I don't fancy traveling far with less'n a horn of powder 'mongst the three of us — and he's got one."

Tim also stood up, wincing because of his bad arm. "Suppose me and Dan come along?"

"Naw. I figger I c'n — well — talk to that young savage more persuasive-like by myself."

Dan nodded. "Have it your way. Meantime, I'll try to fashion some head coverings out of a fur cape; we're surely goin' to need some kind of protection when the weather turns bitter — which I figger it will before long."

Although he pretended otherwise, Tim was quite satisfied to linger beside the canoe; he still was feeling hungrier than a bitch wolf with pups and wanted to cook another chunk of bear meat.

About half an hour after Cash had disappeared among the trees, those remaining on the creek's bank heard a furious barking in the distance followed by a faint report.

Not long afterwards the veteran Long Hunter reappeared, red-rimmed eyes shining bright as fresh-run musket balls. He had slung on another powder horn and was carrying a fresh scalp that was sketching a trail of bright red drops on the dead leaves in his wake.

"What happened?" Tim wanted to know.

"Oh, real polite-like, I invited our friend to come in for a powwow." Cash squirted tobacco juice and hung his *coup* on a bush. "He agreed, but when he got close I didn't fancy the way he'd parted his hair — so I let him have it 'twixt the eyes."

Choice uttered a gasp. "You — you mean you murdered that Indian in cold blood while he was trying to surrender!"

Maddox rasped, long features stiffened so that a knot of muscle stood out on his jaw, "By God! You're no better than a stinkin' savage."

Cash glared, snarled, "Stow that missionary crap! Play your way, Maddox, and in these here parts I'll go on playing mine. Lay you ten buckskins to one I'll live to bury you, if there's enough left to make it worthwhile." He tossed the young Indian's possessions onto the canoe's bottom, then suddenly grinned a snaggle-toothed grin. "Now, let's see what sort of headpiece ye've fashioned fer me."

21. The War Party

As soon as there was light enough to see what they were doing, the castaways broke camp and found that Maddox had been right about a change of weather. During the night the temperature had dropped considerably and successive squadrons of ragged, lead-hued clouds charged by so low that they appeared ready to trip over the claw-like tops of the taller trees.

Everyone hated leaving the campfire's heat — Frenchy especially; the big, rough-coated dog had to be caught and lifted, growling, into the canoe but once there he quieted at once and sat peering interestedly over the thwarts.

Long before they shoved off, Maddox and his companions were mighty glad they were wearing shapeless fur caps. Choice felt embarrassed but oddly stimulated to be wearing the murdered Frenchman's breeches. She'd donned them after consenting for Tim to slit her gray woolen skirt and three petticoats halfway up in front, which as he explained gravely, would permit her the almost unhampered use of her legs. In a cap of spotted lynx skin, the Piankashaw leader's otter-fur cape and wearing crude mittens cut out of the same garment, the girl made a comic yet somehow appealing figure.

To the gunsmith it proved of interest to observe how, gradually but steadily, Choice Valentine was adapting herself to hardships. For instance, she didn't complain nearly so often nor act so helpless and pathetic. Yes, the way she'd behaved when Cash had fed Frenchy on that Indian's arm had been an indication. No shrilling of disgust, no quaking or vomiting — just a dispassionate, stony-eyed acceptance of an unpleasant necessity tinged with something like curiosity.

Since they'd been cast away her pointed features had thinned considerably, but her great, dark-brown, round eyes shone as brilliantly as ever, while her soft and full lips actually seemed to have assumed a brighter hue.

Small, dry and sharp-edged snowflakes began to sift down lazily, lightly at first, but soon it began to snow in earnest and the wind to pick up. By the time the paddlers had driven their craft around still another bend, they had hard work to recognize the crossing place.

Because of the freezing weather countless little rivulets and brooks had become iced up and congealed so today the Mad Bear was running by no means as angrily as it had two days earlier. Nevertheless, the current remained extremely swift, and soon the men's shoulders ached from unaccustomed plying of heavy, shapeless paddles. Sure enough, the landing did lie ahead; a number of pale, horizontal stripes gouged out of tree trunks by the ferry's snubbing ropes showed faintly through rolling veils of powder-fine snow. But nobody could be seen moving about and, worse still, nowhere was smoke visible.

By the time the canoe's prow grated over the landing's gravelly beach an icy wind was whooping and roaring through the treetops and lashing Mad Bear Creek's surface into a white fury.

Only by shielding their eyes were the men able to range for a short distance about the landing to discover nothing significant beyond the wolf-scattered bones of a cow and, lying deserted beside the trail, a pair of those stout wagon wheels Colonel Jim had so admired. Thus far, this new storm hadn't yet had time to obliterate frozen footprints and the droppings of various animals converging upon the Trace. Soon these would vanish beneath a soft, crystalline carpet which was thickening with almost incredible speed.

Tim's heavy black brows were turning white as those of an old man when he yelled over the rushing wind, "Well, boys, and what do we do now?"

Turning his back to the blast, the gunsmith shouted between mittened hands, "We've no choice but to try to overtake them."

Vaguely, Choice dabbed flakes from long, dark eyelashes. "When did our people move on?"

"Sometime yesterday," Cash speculated. "Must ha' figgered we was drownded — so didn't tarry."

To contrive packs proved easy, there was so little useful loot to be taken along, but before they set out Cash insisted that the canoe be hauled into a dense thicket, turned upside down, and hidden under a pile of brush. "Ye never can tell when such a craft will come in handy."

They had followed the Trace only a short while before they glimpsed their first wolves. Almost invisible, the beasts were ghosting along between tree trunks and, although Frenchy several times raised a racket and offered battle, a good many of the great, gray-black beasts continued to slink along to either side of the Trace.

"What if I plug one?" Tim ventured during a brief halt after an especially difficult stretch of ground. "Would it maybe scare the rest off?"

"Naw. 'Twould accomplish nothing. Them goddam brutes won't close in till it gets dark or unless we get into trouble. Main worry is not to lose the Trace. God help us if we stray."

Because of ever-deepening snow, the footing became so difficult and treacherous that it became necessary to halt and cut walking sticks to steady the little party's half-blind and floundering progress.

At length Choice struggled up alongside Maddox and panted through almost smothering hard-driven flakes, "Can't carry — musket — longer. Too heavy. I — weary."

"Drop it." Maddox put out an arm to steady the girl against a series of extra-violent gusts. "Can't fix — no tools." All the same, he hated to abandon the ancient Charleville because the musket's pan cover could be repaired without too much difficulty and a useful firearm of any description was worth plenty out here.

Although it seemed impossible, the blizzard increased in intensity, transformed the forest into a dim and confusing icy limbo in which leafless branches flailed like scourges and evergreens swayed and bent as if executing a demoniac minuet while the threshing of their lower boughs often swept the ground bare.

All at once the convoying wolves ran ahead as if to block the party's progress but soon the real reason became apparent; a swarm of snow-plastered wolves were tearing, ripping and slashing over a fallen horse.

When the predators proved dangerously reluctant to leave their feast,

Cash slipped off his lock's cover and yelled, "All right, boys. Reckon we'd best touch 'em up 'fore they get real excited and turn on us."

The men had shouldered their pieces and were trying to see through the hard-driven snow when a curious thing happened; several wolves could be seen pointing muzzles towards the invisible sky as if to test the wind, then, like as many embodied phantoms, they vanished into the silvery tumult.

Maddox chafed ice-fringed eyelids. "Wha' the hell!"

Cash shook snow from his cape. "Must ha' scented some deers or bufflers somewheres."

Maddox, with clumsy, stiffened fingers, uncocked Ilsa before painstakingly replacing the rough-and-ready lock cover he'd fashioned out of a Piankashaw legging. With chagrin, the three men recognized the half-devoured horse to be one of Robertson's fine Spanish-Arabian mares; apparently, after having suffered a broken leg, it had had its throat cut.

Cash wasted no time over futile regrets. "Better keep moving. This tempest's worsening — don't catch up 'fore dark we'll end up wolf bait."

Heads bent into the frigid blast they trudged on, slipping and gasping, with Cash leading and Maddox bringing up the rear. By now snow was falling so hard a footprint became invisible almost as soon as it was made.

Choice surprised them all because she didn't lag — only plodded on, a small, shapeless figure grown white as Lot's wife.

They had covered possibly half a mile more when Cash again halted and stiffly raised a mittened hand. Once the four grotesquely shrouded figures came together the old Long Hunter yelled over the wind, "Something's wrong!"

"What — you mean?"

"If them wolves was running game — have heard 'em wailing. You heard 'em?"

Nobody had heard any howling.

"Mebbe wind's too great — but something's queer."

Before starting on, Maddox and his companions pulled their caps so low they could hardly see and at the same time hitched snow-thickened mantles up over their noses; nevertheless, ice particles formed at once on their nostril hairs.

Cash began to flounder along so far in advance that, on occasion, his bent figure became lost to sight. It was after one of these eclipses they found him studying a partially sheltered stretch of ground. There, still clearly distinguishable, moccasined footprints only recently had entered upon the Trace from a northerly direction; some of these already were filling up, but a caprice of the drifting snow had left a frightening number recognizable.

Several facts slowly penetrated Dan Maddox's semi-numbed intellect: one, a powerful band of Indians must be tracking the expedition; two, since these redskins without exception appeared to be on foot, it stood to reason that they could not be very far away; three, this lot of savages must be traveling between the castaways and the main body. Last but most important, was the rear guard in any way aware of this danger closing in upon them?

With Frenchy hovering closer than ever before, the party paused in the lee of a huge, overhanging rock.

Slowly, Cash thumbed snow from badly swollen and streaming red eyes. "They'll be the same bevy of Shawnees what jumped those Pianka-shaws."

"How many are there?" Tim wanted to know while flailing his arms.

"Hard to tell with the ground like 'tis, but I'll hazard they'll number 'round forty. Yep. Those wolves must ha' scented them redskins — that's why they ran off."

Although Choice was feeling increasingly weak and hopeless she kept quiet, ineffectually attempted with a forefinger to hook out snow which had sifted inside the mantle around her neck. Lordy! Perhaps mercifully, her feet seemed to have lost the sense of feeling and, mittens or no mittens, her hands were growing numb. Dully, she resolved that, come the first opportunity, she would hack a strip of fur from her cape to sling in a diaper-like band to protect her privates, which now were paining like fury. Strange, like other girls, she had always believed that a man's trousers must be warmer than a number of petticoats, but by now she was learning that this just wasn't true and bitterly regretted having allowed Tim to slit her underpinnings.

The men at once agreed that the only thing to do was cautiously to scout the Shawnee party in hopes of getting near enough to see how many they numbered and, more important, what condition they were in.

From the presence of many discernible footprints it became inescapable that these Shawnees could not be very far off; although ravenously hungry and aware of mounting fatigue, Maddox forced himself to ponder a vital question. Were these Indians slowing down because of the hard going or because they now found themselves close enough to attack the column at will? The latter explanation seemed the more acceptable, for in such frightful weather Robertson's attenuated column could only have been crawling along.

The blizzard continued to blow harder than ever; sometimes it seemed impossible to catch's one's breath without inhaling and being smothered by incredibly fine snow. On occasion it became impossible to see anything beyond an arm's length.

Only the dog appeared unaffected, although his coat long since had changed color so completely that, more than anything else, Frenchy now resembled a misshapen, pink-tongued white wolf.

Cash again halted, lifted his nose clear of his muffler and drew several quick breaths, then nodded in what must have been satisfaction. "Smoke! Means the redskins have halted and are making camp. That'll be because our folks must have stopped up ahead. Besides, it'll grow dark 'fore long."

Again Tim queried, "What do we do now?"

Cash rested his rifle against a tree in order to rub snow hard over cheekbones that were turning a dangerous pinkish-gray. Said he, "Tim, you and Sissy better hole up in some sheltered spot whilst me and Dan try to circle the savages and alarm the rear guard."

The gunsmith shook his head so hard a shower of flakes fell from his furry cap. "No! They'll surely die before we can come back and find them."

Cash squinted. "So will all the rest of our people an we don't bring warning in time."

"True enough. So you go on ahead. We'll follow your trail as long's we can."

"Naw. You'd lose it in no time. Besides, two men's going will double the chances of reaching our people."

"No. We'll all go — or only you." Maddox's sunken, dark-blue eyes, fringed in white, sought Tim. "Think you and Sissy can keep on a while longer?"

The rifleman managed a stiff smile. "Sure 'nough. 'Twould be a mortal sin to let such a warm armful freeze to death. Pass me yer pack, Sissy; best hang onto my belt when you tire."

22. The Surprise

HAD it not been for the accumulated experience of Colonel Robertson, Tom Spencer, Edmund Jennings and Joe Drake and several others who had traveled the Kentucky Trace before — a few of them more than once — the expedition must have lost its way with probably disastrous results. As it was, the numbed and discouraged immigrants struggled on through waist- or even shoulder-high drifts forever forming and shifting at the storm's whim. The pitiless sting of sharp particles forced men on occasion to peep through their fingers as they floundered along.

To keep them from straying off to an icy death they led animals and guided one another at rope ends. The women all rode hunched so far over in their saddles they saw nothing of their surroundings. They clasped their smallest children, bundled into shapelessness, before them while the older youngsters clung flat, like frightened squirrels, to the loads on pack horses that blundered slowly along with low hanging heads.

At length visibility worsened until the point was forced to slow down so much that, eventually, it formed no more than a forward element of the main body.

Never in her previously secure and comfortable existence had Rosemary Valentine felt more despondent than while she rode along tugging at the lead rope of a pack horse carrying two men crippled by frostbitten feet.

Although growing more and more hopeless, Rosemary nonetheless guessed herself luckier than her twin who now must be lying, stiff and lifeless, somewhere at the bottom of Mad Bear Creek. She guessed she'd never get over that awful sensation of helplessness she'd suffered while watching the wildly plunging and spray-smothered raft disappear.

What a pity that plainly handsome, capable and soft-spoken Dan Maddox also had had to lose his life, along with raffish Tim Murphy and that Long Hunter whose name she'd never learned.

Drearily the girl thought, maybe Choice is the lucky one after all. At least she won't die by inches from hunger, cold and exhaustion. Mechanically, Rosemary bent to avoid a half-seen branch, then made efforts to rearrange her traveling cape's hood into warmer folds.

The way Papa was reacting to this dreadful experience had proved a pleasant as well as unexpected surprise. Continually his big-bellied, broad-shouldered figure could be seen plowing through drifts and snow clouds, now helping a fallen man to his feet, now beating a lagging pack horse to a faster pace, then herding some storm-blinded cow or mule back onto the Trace.

Poor Mamma! When glimpsed through this hateful, freezing haze she looked small as a doll, as with muffled head weakly lolling, she rode behind and clung to Black Sally in a pitiful attempt to find a measure of shelter and support.

Only out of sheer necessity did Colonel Robertson order an early halt in the depths of a ravine in which a heavy stand of larch, pines and dense clumps of laurel and juniper seemed to offer a little protection from the shrieking wind which, as John Rains growled, "sure's been honed on the North Pole."

Jonathan, especially, felt happy when the order was passed back to make camp. He set about building still another low little shelter out of evergreen boughs. Once it had been thrown together he considered Old Scatch, who was collecting his ewes into a tight circle suggesting a small, slow-moving snowdrift. Nowadays, the boy had begun to admire, even to feel kindly towards that perverse patriarch. Hadn't he on several occasions charged timber wolves sufficiently hungry to reconnoiter the camp's outer rim? Once he'd actually succeeded in butting one of the gray terrors so hard that the brute was sent flying and howling back into the brush.

Since the blizzard set in Jonathan's task had grown easier for, like all the stock, his sheep remained so terrified by what appeared to be a swarm of marauders that they didn't stray and kept near the Trace. Most of them now were so thin and poor from hunger that they were glad to lie down whenever they could.

Jonathan sure appreciated nowadays that Ma — veteran as she was of life on the frontier — had outfitted him wisely and well. A long, blue-and-white woolen scarf she'd been knitting all summer was proving especially useful; it could serve as a belly band, a shawl, a foot warmer at night, or as a warm ear covering whenever he needed to tie down his cap.

When would this pesky storm leave off? Most of the old-timers were claiming that a blizzard like this could be expected to last three days. Criminently! What a prospect! — to endure another day like the last two.

With flakes whirling endlessly about his head he tugged two sheep, which came willingly enough, into his shelter and made them lie down, despite reproachful looks from Old Scratch.Then he went over to thaw a strip of smoked buffalo hump over a campfire flaring recklessly nearby.

When he got back to his shelter, which resembled a rough cone lying on its side, Old Scratch was still on his feet and peering stolidly through miniature cyclones of snow that, in rapid succession, were racing down the ravine without offering any sign of a let-up; darkness already was setting in, hours ahead of time.

Before squirming in between the ewes, which had gone to sleep, he took care to follow Uncle John's advice and smeared bacon grease over his ears, lips and eyelids and rubbed hard at the tip of his snub nose. Then he pulled up his blanket and covered his face with that blessed muffler.

Soon the sheeps' bodily warmth began to penetrate and lessen the aching cold of his lean, hard body; if conditions grew no worse he reckoned he'd make out. Briefly he wondered who, if anyone, might be standing guard in weather like this and, for the first time, was glad he was too young to be entrusted with such a responsibility.

Jonathan dozed off but soon was awakened by a sustained barking of the rear guard's dogs. Their clamor was so fierce he guessed something must be wrong. When a shift in the wind brought the distorted sound of shouts and yells he roused up, pulled his ancient pistol out of a protective bag of greased leather.

Figuring he could safely leave Old Scratch on guard, Jonathan pulled down an oversized fox-fur cap, then wound the precious muffler high and tight about his face before setting out for a wind-flattened fire about which were gathering a ring of snow-covered figures.

"What's up?" he yelled at his Uncle John.

"Look who's just come in."

To the lad's delight he recognized through smoke-like clouds of snow the familiar figures of Dan Maddox and Tim Murphy. Then, looming just beyond them, he made out Cash Brooks and what appeared to be a slight young fellow. So they hadn't "drownded"? Criminently! Ed Jennings had been right when he'd said that if anybody could pull the raft's people through Cash could do it. "He's just too ornery to die."

The moment he learned that a sizable band of Shawnees probably was closing in Robertson summoned his principal subordinates. While wood smoke and stinging snow beat at their whiskery, weather-gnawed faces the leaders swiftly reached a decision.

With first light John Rains, Squire Valentine and Major Phillips, guided by Edmund Jennings, would lead the main body at the best possible pace towards that not-too-well-identified spot on the far side of the Barrens where Kasper Mansker was supposed to be building a station.

To cross the Barrens, an enormous expanse of rolling and sparsely wooded prairies on which big game ran scarce even during the best of seasons, wasn't going to be easy. Everyone knew that. Feed for the stock would be hard to find since canes and grasses grew only around ponds and along creek bottoms.

At dawn the rear guard, augmented by every experienced frontiersman and expert shot in the expedition, would turn back in an attempt to surprise the Shawnee encampment.

"What beats me," complained Ike Bledsoe, "is why all these redskins is trailin' us. This time of year they shouldn't be about in any number."

Joe Drake's shaggy head ducked in agreement. "Beats me, too. No savages ought to be found any distance from their villages."

Sour-faced Mark Robertson blew his nose between grimy fingers, growled, "Reckon we're just unlucky. These Shawnees probably were on their way home from huntin' when they cut our trail and then bumped into those Piankashaws Cash spoke of. Because the Piankashaws were so few the Shawnees likely believed they must be followin' only a small party of immigrants."

Jonathan listened to all that was being said until, his breath quickening, he made up his mind that come what might he would go along and take part in the attack. Of course Pa would belt the living whey out of him once he found out about it; Pa took any form of disobedience mighty seriously.

With his breath vapor torn away the instant it passed his lips, Jonathan entered into negotiations with one of the Rains party's younger immigrants, a lad named Abner, who had almost colorless hair and eyelashes. "Listen, Ab, I'm goin' off for a little while first thing tomorrow morning. I want you to mind my sheep whilst I'm gone."

Abner banged one booted foot against its fellow, then knuckled frost-engendered tears from piggy blue eyes. "Why in Tophet should I? I hate sheep."

"Aw, come on, Abner. They won't cause you to fret. Once the people start moving they'll keep to the trail and won't stray. Snow's too deep."

"Naw. I got enough trouble lookin' out for Ma's cow and keepin' from gettin' froze stiff."

"If you mind 'em I'll give you that spare pair of mittens I got."

"Naw. They're worn out and full of holes. I seen 'em."

"Well, how 'bout a nice warm sock my Ma knitted?"

"One sock?"

"Yep. I lost its mate, but you could make a muffler out of it."

"Naw."

Jonathan drew a deep breath, then in desperation made a final offer. "Suppose I — I was to give you this here fine cuttoe knife? She's of good English steel and honed so sharp she'll cut you if you even look hard at her."

The other boy's colorless lashes batted judiciously. "Well, mebbe, if she'll be mine for keeps, and ye won't ask to take her back."

"Naw. She'll be yours for keeps. Honest Injun." The assurance cost him an effort, but he just had to be free to take part in the surprise.

Since it still would be dark when the settlers set out, he felt sure he'd not be noticed with a storm like this raging; all he had to do was just mingle among the raiders. Suppose, suppose he actually got to slay an Injun all by himself! At the possibility his heart began to hammer so hard he feared Abner might hear it. Then a cheering thought forced a stiff grin to his lips. All redskins carried a knife, so if he got him a Shawnee, he'd be right back where he'd been before bargaining with this snot-nosed Abner.

When dawn finally became more than a presentiment it appeared that the blizzard hadn't abated, not in the least; its biting blasts smote faces like clenched fists and hurled such endless clouds of snow that they all but blinded a man.

Colonel Robertson therefore delayed setting out until his attacking force had consumed whatever food they could come across and had made a final check of their firearms.

Only Jonathan was glad of such weather; amid this whirling tumult his slight, snow-shrouded figure should prove almost impossible to identify.

As the augmented rear guard was moving out, floundering and cursing their lack of snowshoes, the wind abated briefly, just enough to permit a man to make out a companion struggling along at a distance of ten or even fifteen feet.

Glad that he'd kept his old pistol's lock wound in a length of greasy rag and that he'd begged, borrowed or stolen half a dozen paper cartridges and a supply of assorted musket balls, Jonathan decided it might be wise if he worked his way out on the attacking force's right flank as far as possible. He'd seen both of his uncles moving off to the left. Pa, of course, was commanding the center.

Because Tom Spencer's huge outline was easy to identify, the boy kept close behind him, especially while traversing a piece of extra-difficult terrain like a deep ravine in which the snow was piled deep enough to close over the boy's fox-fur cap.

Once the advancing line regained level ground it bent and curved; gaps were created as individuals were delayed in coping with various sorts of obstacles; for the attackers to keep even approximately in line-abreast became impossible. How long the right flank struggled after Tom Spencer through dense thickets and between an endless succession of great, snow-coated tree trunks Jonathan, now sweating and breathless, hadn't the least idea.

At length the boy's strength started to give out and at the same time he began to conjecture what might happen to him if those painted devils were alert and prepared to charge the immigrants' thin and irregular skirmish line.

He quit wondering when, somewhere away off to his left, a muffled *boom!* successfully penetrated the wind's noise. A few faint yells followed, then the boy heard a ragged fusillade that sounded dull — like sticks beating on a wet drumhead.

Copying Tom Spencer and everybody else in sight, Jonathan immediately sought shelter behind a big tree; he lingered there, waist-deep, strained desperately to see through the baffling, ghostly-white atmosphere.

Suddenly the giant bellowed, "Come on!" and leaped from behind his tree with rifle held at the ready and a war hatchet swinging from a thong looped over his wrist. Spencer dove through a drift so forcefully that snow spurted from his powerfully driven knees like waves from a ship's prow.

Panting wildly, Jonathan struggled to keep his place at the far end of a line of swaying, half-seen dark figures. Quite close at hand someone's musket roared and, turning, he glimpsed ragged wisps of gunsmoke being whipped away from the musket of a chunky, black-bearded fellow who whooped and started forward after yanking out a foot-long carving knife. The sight reminded him that once he fired his pistol he'd be helpless as a blind kitten until he got a chance to reload.

Men began humping forward through the drifts; experienced Indian fighters like Tom Spencer, who hadn't fired yet, were carrying their weapons as high above their heads as they could in case they tripped.

Jonathan's stiff and uncertain fingers were stripping the rag from his pistol when, through the shifting, whirling storm, he suddenly made out the dark outlines of several figures plunging towards him.

Spencer halted, shouldered his piece and, at thirty yards' range, dropped a fur-swathed Shawnee just as he straightened from bending under a low-sweeping hemlock bough; the stricken Indian fell forward and vanished completely beneath the snow. Since he didn't struggle at all, he must have been instantly killed.

Reasoning that if he stuck close to Spencer he probably wouldn't get hurt, the boy continued to follow him.

A scattering of shots sounded in the distance, then through veiling snow clouds Jonathan made out a tall, narrow-shouldered Indian coming straight at him from a frozen tangle of bushes. Using both hands he was raising his wire-trapped weapon and trying to sight when a disconcerting thing happened. The Shawnee suddenly flung arms skywards with a jerk that sent his tomahawk flying, then half turned and fell with brown limbs threshing spasmodically beneath the powdery snow.

The boy felt outraged. Why did someone else have to go and shoot his particular brave? He had started to look around for another target when one of several bear dogs which had been slinking along behind the skirmish line ran across the backs of his legs; he tripped and fell, half choked, under a snow bank.

The boy scrambled to his feet still clutching the pistol, but because there were guns going off all around him, he forgot to find out whether or not his priming had got wet or had sifted out of the pan.

Somebody shouted, "Look out!"

An Indian who, seen through flying flakes, loomed even bigger than Tom Spencer, was charging towards him and raising a screeching scalp yell.

To his surprise, Jonathan was able to keep his head; gripping the pistol in both hands he pointed at the center of the Shawnee's snow-spattered hunting shirt but when he pulled the trigger only a dry *click!* resulted. Panic-stricken, he yanked back the trigger and squeezed a second time, but the weapon remained obstinately silent as the Indian continued to close in with red-and-black-streaked features contorted into a deadly grimace.

Jonathan knew he was going to be killed. What a great fool he'd been in trying to play the man! Throat convulsively constricting, he tried to spring aside, but his foot caught on some invisible object and he fell sprawling into deep snow.

He braced for the tomahawk's impact, saw it rise, miles above him it seemed, but then unaccountably it wavered aside. That same dog which just had tripped him had left off worrying the Indian killed by Spencer to spring and drive his fangs deep into the Indian's thigh. The force of his charge knocked the Shawnee off his feet so that man and dog rolled over and over in the snow, but the latter hung on to his enemy.

Jonathan swayed to his feet, then clubbed his cumbersome pistol and hovered above the struggling figures waiting for a chance to bring the weapon down on the Indian's head, but somehow the Shawnee got a fresh grip on his tomahawk, beat off his attacker and succeeded in rising to his knees.

Snarling like all of Cerberus' heads at once, Bassoon then grabbed the savage's shoulder, offering Jonathan an opportunity to strike that swiveling black head.

For all the blow was a shrewd one, it still wasn't sufficiently powerful to knock out the Shawnee. Jonathan, therefore, was forced to hit several times more before his enemy finally went limp and sank forward, half-buried in a drift.

Too bewildered to know what he should do next, the boy swayed above his enemy only partially aware that Pa's bear dog now had the Indian by the throat and had driven his fangs into it so deep that bright blood was beginning to spray the tumbled snow.

Gradually, it dawned on Jonathan that, because of this, it wouldn't be necessary for him to cut the redskin's throat — which was just as well; he wasn't too sure he could have managed that.

Finally Bassoon let go, then, after licking blood from dripping jaws, stood guard over his victim while Jonathan deliberated making an attempt to scalp the dying Shawnee. The boy ended by seizing the brave's tomahawk and preempting his skinning knife, which appeared to be a lot longer and heavier in the blade than the one he'd traded away.

As an afterthought he slung the redskin's war bag over one shoulder before whistling in Bassoon. Still shaking all over, he set out to catch up with the skirmish line.

On the way he took a good look at his surroundings and vowed that once the fighting was over he'd come back and lift that there scalp. It would make a fine trophy to show and to brag on; besides, such a hank of greasy black hair had a cash value which would go far towards the purchase of the fine rifle he was yearning for.

Nevertheless, Jonathan somehow never found time to return and take his *coup.*

For a brief interval none of the men standing with backs turned to the blizzard could believe that the attack had been so completely and overwhelmingly successful. Once the attackers had rendezvoused in the Shawnee bivouac laughing and talking sixty to the minute in their relief, a tally was taken which revealed that not one white man had been killed and that only two had suffered wounds so minor that they weren't even partially incapacitated.

Everybody felt especially fine when a dozen-odd snow-flecked, red-and-black scalps were held up for inspection; moreover, if various claims were to be credited, nearly as many more *coups* lay concealed by the tumbling, ever-shifting snow.

Most of the Shawnees, it appeared, had died when Robertson's central party abruptly had charged, *whoop-whooping,* out of the blizzard to catch their enemies completely unaware; the savages either were lying rolled in their blankets still asleep or numbly were preparing food.

For a while the victors lingered to warm themselves around Indian fires or to seek scraps of cooked foods, after which they set about collecting weapons, warm garments and other useful gear.

Retribution overtook Jonathan shortly after he'd swaggered up to Pa to tell him that a Shawnee was lying dead in a gully somewhere off to the right.

Pa's lips tightened ominously. "How d'you know that?"

" 'Cause I — that is, me and Bassoon killed him."

"Tell me about it — and give me a strict account."

Encouraged, the boy told the exact truth, hoping that maybe Pa wasn't going to whale him after all.

"Don't you think, Pa, I've earned a real gun?"

"No. You didn't kill that buck. But for my dog you'd be nothing but a sad memory right now, and just what the hell d'you mean by sneakin' off and desertin' your sheep?"

Recognizing a hard gleam in his father's piercing blue eyes, the boy hurriedly explained how he'd hired Abner to mind the flock.

James Robertson said in a certain soft voice which invariably meant serious trouble, "You'd no right to do that without permission, Jon; were everyone to disobey like you have, this expedition'd not get very far. Come here!"

Although the Colonel was hollow-eyed with worry and fatigue, he nevertheless gave Jonathan a beating such as the lad never before had experienced — or would ever again risk suffering.

Characteristically, Jonathan endured the savage punishment without making a sound and sobbed softly only when he was back with Old Scratch and the ewes, but after a little while, he didn't feel so miserable with the realization that, in addition to his crazy old pistol, he now owned a dandy, red-shafted tomahawk with a keen blade of fine French steel. Yep, he judged the weapon to weigh near two pounds. As an added relief to his pain he discovered that the Shawnee's war bag was made of smoke-tanned elkskin, which old-timers claimed was uncommon durable and, better still, almost waterproof. This leather sure would come in handy when his boots finally came apart — which they were threatening to do at any time. Further, the haversack contained several interesting items: a whetstone, a length of iron file, a few pots of face paint, a hunk of sunflower-seed bread and a greasy chunk of smoked buffalo tongue.

The most prized of his new possessions, nevertheless, was the redskin's knife, which boasted a concave blade nearly ten inches long. By now he'd realized that its handle was cleverly weighted, which should make it easy to throw with considerable accuracy. While stroking the new knife's fringed sheath, decorated by broken but still impressive designs done in blue-and-red beadwork, Jonathan somehow forgot all about his smarting backside.

23. Break-up

As if eager to atone for its previous viciousness the blizzard abruptly came to an end around noon of the same day that the Shawnees had been beaten and, so everybody hoped, dispersed beyond hope of re-union. It was amazing how quickly the expedition's spirits revived once snow ceased to fall and the razor-edged wind died out. They felt better still when the sun appeared, clear and bright; but it cast little warmth.

Colonel Robertson ordered a real camp made when he realized that even the hardiest veterans seemed ready to drop from exhaustion. Besides, most of the animals had grown so thin and weak that many must have perished had an attempt been made to keep them moving.

In slow succession tents went up along the bottom of a well-wooded valley along which the livestock was herded to browse beside a frozen creek where patches of dead grass had been exposed by some whim of the wind.

Everyone agreed, even if they didn't say so, that it was mighty comforting to watch dozens of smoke pillars begin to rise once more. When the temperature commenced slowly but perceptibly to climb, stinking, damp and nearly worn-out garments were removed and spread over bushes and dead limbs to dry.

Men skilled in the art demonstrated ways of constructing oval-shaped snowshoes of the "bear-paw" type which were ugly but very useful in wooded country.

Although very few people seemed aware of the fact, this was the first occasion since quitting Carpenter's Station that all members of the combined expeditions had camped together, there being no point or rear guard bivouacked apart.

Thus it came about that the ex-militiaman, Andrew Dickinson, who until now had been riding point, caught sight of Dr. Mason for the first time since Carpenter's. Immediately, he beat his brain trying to recollect when and where he'd previously seen the physician — if, indeed, he ever had. To tell the truth, the Connecticuter had been far too occupied with fighting the elements and in obtaining food for his wife and child to rack his memory before this.

Shortly after sunset James Robertson sent out messengers to summon all leaders and heads of families to attend a general conference, with the result that, before long, nearly fifty gaunt, filthy and bone-weary men collected to stand knee-deep in snow about a huge, soaring bonfire.

Once most of the leaders had appeared, Robertson, standing unbelievably straight in a shaggy bearskin coat, began to speak in a low but surprisingly effective voice. He began by praising them one and all not only for having successfully surprised the Shawnees but even more for their dogged endurance, their ingenuity in solving unforeseen difficulties and especially for their readiness to help one another. With firelight gilding his scraggly, dark-brown beard, the Colonel concluded: "— And don't you think I ain't proud, almighty proud to be leading men the like of you!"

Towering in the background Tom Spencer boomed, "And, by damn, you're all right too! I claim ye're all wool and a yard wide and I'll lick anybody dasts gainsay me!"

Flushing under a mask of grime and grease, Robertson was forced to wave his arms several times to quiet prolonged shouting. "Thank you, boys. I'm sure pleased by your expression of confidence — which, while it's mighty gratifying, butters us no parsnips; so suppose we get down to brass tacks.

"By now, I figure we've covered about two-thirds of the distance from Carpenter's to the Ohio and have overcome a lot of dangers, so I think you ought to know now that —" with a born leader's sense of timing he paused, then raised his voice to dominate the bonfire's furious crackling — "that we've accomplished all this *without losing a single human life!*"

Dark-browed Major Phillips rubbed his thin Roman nose, grunted, "Damned if I realized that before!"

Tim Murphy suddenly felt inspired to jump and crack his heels as he had not since Freeman's Farm, yelling, "E-e-e-yah! Colonel Jim's a shining, ring-tailed wonder!"

Bellowed Squire Valentine, who obviously had been dipping wholeheartedly into his ebbing supply of "vinegar," "Hear! Hear! Tim Murphy, your praish not only ish picturesque but also a gross unner — undershtatmen'!"

Once applause had died away Robertson continued, "Since you all are feelin' so fine you'd best get braced for some bad news. This afternoon Rains, Phillips and I made a survey and found that we now have left only two days' full rations for ourselves while many of our animals are about ready to die of starvation."

His sunken but still piercing light-blue eyes slowly surveyed the assembly. "Therefore, I'll put it bluntly. Right away, we *must* supplement our food stores and find forage. Big game hereabouts is scarce at this season and is like to grow scarcer once we start to cross the Barrens.

"Unfortunately, a big expedition like this can't move fast, 'specially since Doc Mason, here, reports many crippling cases of frostbite."

Samuel Mason, M.D., sensed, rather than saw, many fatigue-ringed eyes swinging in his direction. One pair especially attracted his attention; they belonged to a tall, cadaverous-looking individual wearing a battered, brown tricorn tied down by a ragged red scarf. Something about the intensity of this fellow's regard proved oddly disquieting.

Had this angular, bony fellow, along with certain others, been taking an undue interest in the sketches he'd made of difficult mountain passes and important fords? As a rule, he'd been successful in diverting unwelcome curiosity by remarking that he was only an amateur cartographer making the most of an opportunity to map this hitherto uncharted wilderness. Back East, he assured them, people were ready to pay plenty for even the most rough-and-ready of maps.

One after another, the leaders had their say, but, while their opinions varied considerably, never a one suggested turning back.

Eventually, the principal men agreed on the impossibility of finding sufficient food and fodder for a single, numerous column, so the morrow would be devoted to splitting the expedition into two divisions.

A small, fast-moving force led by Colonel Robertson was to include only physically fit and experienced men who were to ride the strongest horses; they were intended to scout the country around the present campsite for a full day in order to make certain that the Shawnees hadn't somehow got together and were preparing to dog the expedition in hopes of cutting off hunting parties or herdsmen driving stock in search of feeding grounds.

Further, it was decided that, if no evidences of pursuit were discovered, Robertson's party would, at its best speed, strike straight across the Barrens for the Ohio River, then hasten to reach the Cumberland's mouth.

With any luck, this hand-picked party should arrive at the Frenchman's Bluff far enough ahead of the other division, in plenty of time to start the construction of a blockhouse, a few cabins and possibly to gather corn which, hopefully, James Robertson and some others had planted there the preceding spring.

The "slow" division, which was to be led by Major Phillips, John Rains and Squire Valentine, would be guided around the rim of the bleak and inhospitable Barrens by Tom Spencer, Ed Jennings, Joe Drake and other Long Hunters of equal experience. These veterans had decided to follow a system of southwesterly trending creeks and rivers along which they should find patches of woodlands where it was hoped big game would be wintering.

The Phillips party, accordingly, would be forced to follow a circuitous route which might prolong their tortuous journey by a hundred miles or more; however, the fact remained inescapable that, by ranging over widely separated areas, hunters would double their chances of supplying the two parties.

The "slow" division, it was decided, would include John Rains's original group plus Robertson's sick, disabled and hopelessly inefficient members. It would take along all livestock — including the Colonel's priceless Spanish-Arab horses.

Naturally, Jonathan was outraged at the prospect of being separated from Pa and his uncles. Although he begged and pleaded, the Colonel remained patient but adamant. "No, Jon. Where my command is going 'twill be hard enough to feed our mounts and, son, at this time of year none of us aim to try crossin' the Barrens on foot."

Jonathan had to admit, albeit reluctantly, that Pa was right. Only yesterday he'd lost another ewe which, on the point of starvation, had nibbled dark-green ivy showing above the snow. Shortly afterwards the poor animal had died in convulsions leaving only Old Scratch and five rack-ribbed and dull-eyed ewes to worry about.

When the "slow" division set out early next day it was pathetic to notice how many simple but essential possessions had had to be abandoned; here a spinning wheel, there a butter churn hard-worn through long usage, or perhaps a grindstone lay half-buried under the gleaming, eye-torturing snow.

Although the second and last pair of wagon wheels also had had to be left behind, their owner took care to hang them high in a tall tree so that they could be readily seen when he returned for them — always provided he remained alive at the end of this appalling winter.

By employing a shameless blend of guile and common sense, Tim Murphy succeeded in making sure that he and Maddox would be assigned to Phillips's division, ostensibly to shoot meat but really because he was determined to remain near Choice, and Maddox seemed more than a little taken with Rosemary.

For all Choice continued to be sweet-talking and complaisant most of the time, she remained steadfast in refusals to pledge him her hand. This was hard to understand, especially after they'd coupled furtively in some secluded spot.

The gunsmith was only too pleased to stay with his old companion. Why was it that Rosemary so often reminded him of pleasures he'd enjoyed when a married man? Why was it that, whenever she smiled at him, he seemed to feel a touch as of warm and gentle hands on his brow?

Perhaps it was because, so often, there was a shine of quiet laughter in the depths of this blonde girl's glowing dark-brown eyes.

On the top of a hillock Colonel Robertson sat slumped on his horse and soberly watched the "slow" division set out behind a semi-circular screen of scouts on snowshoes who, for the most part, were floundering awkwardly along. This was easy to understand; most of them were un-accustomed to the use of such contrivances. Long before sundown these inexperienced fellows would suffer agonies from cramp; most men needed a week to accustom their leg muscles to such unusual stresses.

Suddenly seized by an unaccountable premonition of disaster, he watched the long, thin line of dots wind out over a vast and almost treeless, white plain. Would he ever meet those people again? Maybe. But it seemed unlikely; their guides, he knew, were none too certain of the terrain — especially in wintertime, when a great many landmarks were either disguised or had become completely invisible. Um. Would troops and immigrants coming from the East next year ever be able to comprehend what those people out there were risking and suffering for their sake? He doubted it.

24. Dr. Mason's Portfolio, I

HAWK-FACED Major Phillips and skinny, stoop-shouldered John Rains were more than pleased when, on the third day after parting with James Robertson, they encountered a noisy little river which ran so fast that it wasn't altogether frozen over; better still, through some whim of the great three days' blizzard, much less than an average depth of snow had been deposited in a shallow valley through which this stream spiraled towards the featureless, dreary and icy expanse of the Barrens.

Their division also had been fortunate in that hunters, snowshoeing well in advance of the column, had chanced upon a small band of elk comfortably and conveniently yarded up on a flat, willow-covered island on which reeds, canes and other grasses grew in abundance.

By dint of expert stalking and marksmanship, Tom Spencer, Maddox and Murphy and two other good shots killed four of the beasts outright and so seriously wounded a fifth that it proved no trick at all to drive the cripple into a deep drift and there finish it off as it lay in panting help-lessness.

After shapeless, crimson hunks of meat had been equally distributed and then cooked as quickly as possible, the immigrants spontaneously commenced their first jubilation since quitting Carpenter's Station.

After a fife, a fiddle and a guitar began to play, gaunt and sunken-eyed people wearing blankets or shaggy fur robes began to caper about, in-venting grotesque dance steps which at the same time served to warm them up. Later, songs and ballads nostalgic of home rose to challenge the eerie wails of the ever-present wolves.

Major Todd Phillips kept an eye on a fine marrowbone beginning to brown and char among the coals while his long, blue-black jaws worked steadily on a half-cooked rib. He was losing some of his taut anxiety when somebody touched his shoulder. Looking up he recognized loom-ing above him that refugee from Connecticut called Andrew Dickinson. His flat and narrow mouth was liberally smeared with grease and streaked with elk's blood.

"Please, sir, will you come with me for a minute? There's need to inform you and some others about something important."

The major in obvious reluctance licked fingers then heaved himself erect. "How important? What's this about?"

"Well, sir, I can't tell you here, but I think it's something you leaders certainly ought to know about."

The Connecticuter led the way to a small fire flickering behind a high heap of dunnage. Virginius Valentine and bow-legged John Rains were already waiting there. Now that the contents of his "vinegar" jugs had all but been exhausted, Virginius Valentine was beginning to suggest a leaner and somewhat younger version of that boisterous, perpetually flushed and bay-bellied snob Phillips first had encountered, and had im-mediately disliked, at Carpenter's Station.

Phillips directed irritably, "Speak up, Dickinson! I've still a lot to see about before I turn in, and though I'm dog-tired, I'll listen."

Rains's bulky, mittened hand hooked thumbs over his belt. "Bet you are. Still, I reckon maybe you'd better hear Dickinson repeat what he's already told us."

"Go ahead, Dickinson, but mind you don't waste words."

The gangling Connecticuter, after casting a quick look about at people still singing around their fires, stepped closer. "Major, I'd like your opin-ion of Dr. Mason."

"What do you mean by that?"

The immigrant's thin, weatherbeaten features contracted. "Well, sir, what d'you make of him?"

Because it was growing colder all the time, Phillips shrugged a watch coat higher over his shoulders, then looked Dickinson straight in the eye. "All right. I'll admit that, to start with, I didn't much like him."

"Why not?" Valentine put in, looking unusually grave.

"Why, Squire, I reckon 'twas mostly because I didn't fancy the way he talked and acted; it was too damn' British-like to suit me."

The Connecticuter's muffled, bony and whiskery face thrust itself forward through the gloom as, in a hoarse undertone, he demanded, "Was there anything else?"

"No. What the devil are you driving at, man?"

"Well, sir, as I've just confessed to these gentlemen, from the moment I first clapped eyes on Dr. Mason I've been racking my memory to recall where and when I'd seen him before; finally, just a little while ago, I suddenly remembered."

Phillips coughed and set a cloud of breath vapor spiraling violently away. "How come?"

"We were eating out of the same pot when I heard him mention Norwalk."

"Where's Norwalk?"

"It's a little port on the Connecticut side of Long Island Sound. That's where I used to own a boatyard."

"What has Norwalk to do with the doctor?"

"Well, sir, you probably haven't heard that, last summer, a British squadron transported a strong body of English, Hessian and Tory troops which, led by that damn' Loyalist ex-Governor William Tryon and a general called Garth, raided and ravaged at will along the Connecticut shore. New Haven, New London, Fairfield and Norwalk all were attacked and, sir, what the enemy did — the Loyalists especially — won't bear repeating."

Over the hiss and snap of a nearby fire, Valentine urged, "Go on. Let Andy tell what took place in Norwalk."

Dickinson's shaggy brows lowered themselves while his voice assumed a harsh, grating quality, "Well, sir, being a corporal in the militia I was called out as soon as the alarm bells rang. 'Fore God, we did the best we could but didn't accomplish much because there were only about fifty of us against near half a thousand trained troops. All the same, we fought from house to house till we ran out of powder and had to surrender.

"After we'd been disarmed some Lobsterbacks marched us to our Common and kept us under close guard there while the town was being set afire. Buildings had begun to burn all around us when a band of Tories fetched in some more prisoners and among them —" Dickinson paused and looked hard at Phillips — "I could almost swear I saw Sam Mason! He was wearing a Massachusetts Continental officer's coat."

Abruptly, Todd Phillips fought down grinding fatigue, rasped, "So he was a fellow prisoner? What's so terrible about that?"

Andrew Dickinson spat onto the snow, said bitterly, "Well, sir, the doctor *may* have been taken prisoner, too, but he sure wasn't treated like the rest of us. Not one little bit!"

"— And what d'you mean by that?"

"If you'll just listen, sir, I'll try to explain." The Connecticuter began to speak more rapidly. "When the Lobsterbacks set fire to the fine houses 'round our Common a few were spared — for the accommodation of their officers, I presume. Be that as it may, come sundown, I and the rest of the prisoners were fallen in and started down to the waterfront. It so happened that they halted us for a moment outside Abel Thorne's dwelling and so close that I could look inside and clearly see what was going on."

"Well, what did you see?"

Dickinson's voice rang out, flat and angry. "There was Mason drinking and chaffing with some British officers and some others wearing Tory green. Well, sir, the doctor was being treated like no prisoner I have ever seen or heard of when our guards marched us on.

"Guess, right now, I'd be rotting aboard some prison hulk in Wallabout Bay if a burning home hadn't suddenly collapsed and filled the street with smoke, flaming brands and rubble. When the guards scattered for a minute, some of us took to our heels and ran. We won clear because there really wasn't much of a pursuit; most of the enemy were too busy getting drunk or looting to chase through the smoke after a few dirty fellows wearing civilian clothes."

The major straightened, then strained to peer through the starlight. "This is a mighty serious accusation you're making; are you *absolutely positive* that Doc Mason is the man you saw hobnobbing with enemy officers?"

Dickinson heaved a deep sigh, then dropped his gaze. "I wish I could say so, certain-sure, sir, but please to remember I'd been fighting for a long time and was worried sick over my family and the burning of my boatyard. Besides, I was awful tired and hungry so, well, I'll admit I just *might* have been mistaken; that's what bothers me."

"A pity it didn't bother you before!" rasped Phillips, his sensitive, dark features suddenly grim. "Just what the hell d'you mean by making such grave charges when you're not dead-sure?"

He had started to turn away when John Rains made a detaining gesture. "Hold on a minute, Todd."

"Why should I?"

"Because several people say Mason keeps adding to a sort of folder full of notes and drawings he's made."

"That's interesting." Valentine's round, red face momentarily became misted by his own breath. "Hasn't anybody found out what he's doing?"

"No, not that I know of."

Phillips, feeling ineffably weary and yearning to roll up for the night, spoke sharply, "I think you're barking up the wrong tree. Probably, like some others, the doctor's only gathering material for a sketch map. There's nothing suspicious about that."

"Not unless Dickinson's story is true," Valentine said. "But I admit we'd have to examine that portfolio pretty carefully before deciding whether or not the sort of information Mason has collected is either significant or dangerous to our Cause."

Rains growled, "Then we damn' well better take a good look at those papers. If the feller's a spy, the sooner we hang him the better. As for me —"

"— Now hold on, John, hold on!" Valentine broke in. "Let's not go off at half-cock. You'd better realize that Sam Mason's a very valuable and respected member of this expedition; plenty of our people owe him their lives."

"On the other hand," Dickinson pointed out, "if he *is* a traitor, uncounted thousands of Americans very likely will lose theirs. Just suppose I'm right and the doctor *is* collecting information about our route to guide an enemy army next year?"

Phillips spoke crisply. "That's worth thinking on. Right now, only one thing seems at all clear; this matter must be dealt with promptly."

Rains's coonskin cap inclined several times. "That's a fact. Me, I don't aim to ride with no traitor alongside, so I say let's take a look at his folder and make sure about him right away."

"It won't be easy to lay hands on it," Phillips said. "I'm told he always keeps his papers in a locked medicine chest."

Virginius Valentine held up a mittened hand. "I may be over-optimistic, gentlemen, but I believe I've a possible solution to our difficulty."

"Then for God's sake speak up."

"I will. I presume you all are aware that my daughter Rosemary for a long time has been assisting the doctor?" The Pennsylvanian's large and still fleshy features formed a fleeting smile. "Aside from that, I've reason to think that she is commencing to entertain what the poets term 'tender sentiments' towards her mentor. She is familiar with Mason's routine and on occasion is entrusted with the key to the medicine chest in question.

"Now, gentlemen, I may be able to persuade her 'tis her patriotic duty to abstract the portfolio long enough for us to examine it and decide whether it contains information of suspicious nature."

"Very well," Phillips said, "see what you can accomplish and let me know in time. I want to see those papers, myself."

On returning to his tent the Squire soon manufactured a pretext to take Rosemary aside, but, although he broached the matter with considerable skill, his daughter flared right up.

"Papa! I'll do no such thing! Sam Mason is the finest, truest and most patriotic gentleman I've ever known in my life!"

"— In almost seventeen years, my dear." Valentine assumed a patient, wheedling manner. "Pray consider my request in this light; if Dr. Mason is what you deem him, a Patriot, you can prove it beyond a shadow of a doubt by fetching me that folder. Now, my poppet, you and I have always understood each other uncommon well; I'm confident you —"

Somber eyes flashing, Rosemary began to tremble in outrage. "No! Never! I — I think you're dreadful, all of you! The very idea of harking to a talebearer who admits he really isn't sure about who he thinks he saw!" The girl's softly rounded chin set itself. "I *will not* betray Sam Mason and what's more I'm going to put him on his guard."

Squire Valentine rapped out a genteel curse, then glowered so fiercely that Rosemary took a backward step before he could seize her wrists and shake her so hard that her head swam. "Be still, you silly ninny! Should you dare even dream of warning him I'll surely make you rue the day you were born."

The girl's lips writhed briefly, bared her teeth in a grimace of pain.

"Oh-h! Please, Papa, please don't hurt me so. I can't bear it. Yes. I'll swear to keep quiet, but, no matter what you do to me, *I will not* steal that folder!"

"Very well, but you'll keep a still tongue and don't go acting as if anything out of the way has taken place out here."

Whatever his failings, Virginius Valentine never had been one to become easily diverted from his course once he had decided upon it. A little later he beckoned Choice out into the brilliant starlight and demanded, quite casually, after commenting on the beauty of the night, "How much do you like Dr. Mason?"

Choice became almost painfully demure. "Why, Papa, you don't think he —"

"I think nothing. Just answer my question, girl!"

"Oh, I like him very well, Papa. Outside of you and Colonel Robertson, he's the only *real* gentleman among us."

"— And how well does he fancy you?"

"While he's kind and polite to me and amusing in that dry way of his, I'm still well aware that he vastly prefers Rosie to me."

After lighting his pipe the Squire puffed hard while staring unseeingly over the chill and smoke-wreathed encampment. "Once I've explained, my dear, what I have on my mind, I'll tell you what I expect of you. An you oblige me I — well, I'm sure I can find a certain handsome gold bracelet which might become you."

Choice's black-lashed eyes rounded themselves, then she tilted her head to one side in a curious little mannerism which invariably had proved pleasing to the opposite sex. She stepped closer to her father's ample outline. "What is it you want me to do?"

Once he had explained in detail, her father added, "I don't care how you go about it but that portfolio must be examined no later than tomorrow if even for a few moments, so you must devise a way to — er — borrow it."

She raised eyes to glance at his face, parted her lips in a slow, inscrutable smile. "Dearest Papa, you may rest assured that I'll do my very best — provided you're not funning me about that bracelet!"

25. *Dr. Mason's Portfolio, II*

THANKFUL for even a two-day halt like this, Virginius Valentine's daughters unlashed bundles in which they hoped to find some reasonably fresh clothing. While sorting out their possessions they could hear their mother on the other side of the tent's partition petulantly ordering Black Sally to prepare some supper for her owners.

"I expect this will have to serve," Rosemary announced, holding up a clean but wrinkled and utterly shapeless woolen shirt. "I declare, Choice, I'm so sick of being cold and having to go about in dirty, smelly garments I could wail. Do you think we'll *ever* again enjoy privacy, pretty clothes and a hot bath?"

Choice, a taut smile on her dirty, grease-streaked features, continued to peel off thick, often-mended worsted stockings in which several new holes had appeared. "Dream on, dear sister, there's no harm in that. But, seriously, I reckon we'll somehow survive this freezing nightmare an we don't encounter another winter storm like that last one."

Rosemary's stiff and dirty fingers awkwardly untied a set of tie-strings securing her blouse, then after momentarily stripping to the waist and pulling on a fresh undervest, she heaved a sigh and donned the wrinkled shirt.

"Of course, we must expect more blizzards but maybe this mild weather will last a few days longer."

She broke off because someone began to scratch at the tent's flap and a small boy's voice shrilled, "Please, Miss Rosemary, you inside?"

"Yes. Who are you and what do you want?"

"I'm Tommy Dickinson."

"What do you want, Tommy?"

"Ma's been took awful sick of a fever."

"Then why don't you find Dr. Mason?"

"I did, but he's too busy fixin' up Mr. Brodhead's busted arm to listen."

"Come in, Tommy," she invited now that her shirt was secured. A tousled yellow head almost engulfed by a huge worsted stocking cap appeared between the flaps. "Which is your tent?"

"It's next to the last one at the back end of the camp, ma'am." Tommy's button-eyes roved briefly over the tent's disorder.

"What seems to be ailing her?"

"Like I said, ma'am, she's got a fever so hard she claims she's fair burnin' up."

"Then run and tell your mother I will come along directly."

An anxious look on her heart-shaped face, Choice watched her twin secure a thick shawl about her and then hook on a traveling cloak. When she reached for the wildcat-skin cap she usually wore, Choice said sweetly, "Suppose you take my marten-fur hat? 'Tis warmer and a lot prettier."

Laughing, Rosemary donned her sister's headpiece. "You really are a puzzle! What earthly difference does it make what I wear so long as it's warm?"

No sooner had the weatherbeaten flaps dropped into place than Choice ripped off her shirt and as quickly donned the spotted blue blouse just discarded by her sister.

As quickly as she could, the girl then re-plaited her pale hair into a single braid, all the while emitting disgusted noises over its lank and greasy quality.

Finally, she tied over her head a red-and-blue-striped scarf belonging to her twin before she hurried to the Brodheads' tent where the Dickinson lad had reported Dr. Mason to be at work. When she entered it was to find him stitching up an ugly wound caused by a compound fracture of the upper arm.

The physician cast the girl a quick glance over his shoulder. "You're just in time, Rosemary; help bandage the patient."

"I fear I can't linger, Sam." Choice attempted to reproduce those small differences in inflection which distinguished her voice from Rosemary's. "The Dickinson woman is so bad with a fever that I must go to her at once."

"She's very sick?"

"Her boy said so. What should I do?"

"Prepare a mild decoction of chinchona, you know, the Jesuits' bark, and administer it."

"But you keep the medicine chest locked."

The physician plunged bloodied hands into a bucket of pinkish hot water, then dried them hurriedly on the seat of his trousers before delving into a pocket and fishing out a key. "You know where the chinchona is kept. Use it sparingly; I'm in short supply and God alone knows when or where I can find more."

Smiling pleasantly to those who greeted her, Choice, for all her heart had begun to pound like an Indian's dance drum, forced herself to proceed at a quick but natural pace to the physician's tent; once there she hastily went to work.

Scarcely ten minutes passed before the girl entered Major Phillips's tent and found it crowded by the presence of her father, Dickinson and John Rains — all anxiously waiting.

Briefly savoring this moment of importance, Choice pulled a worn, black-bound portfolio from beneath her shawl and gave it to Major Phillips. "Here, sir, but I must return it very soon — there's no telling how much longer the doctor will tarry where he is."

Once Phillips had jerked undone the folder's tie strings the other men crowded about to peer over his shoulder like so many naughty schoolboys reading a forbidden book.

Hurriedly Todd Phillips riffled through dozens of sheets bearing remarkably well-done sketches and pages inscribed with long listings of compass bearings and elevations, angles of incline; also included were descriptions of springs, the depth and location of fords and even the kinds of militarily useful timber to be found at various points along the route.

Only a small part of the portfolio's contents had been examined when Tommy Dickinson ran up panting, "Sir! Sir! Doc's packin' his tools and gettin' ready to leave Mr. Brodhead!"

Choice gasped, "Oh dear! Please, sir, I must run!"

"Of course. We've seen enough. It's all-important that this folder should be returned to its place at once," snapped Phillips, wide-set eyes hard and brilliant.

This time the girl had no choice but to risk attracting attention, so ran like a frightened doe, slipping and stumbling across the camp. Gasping for breath, she got the chest unlocked and barely had thrust the portfolio inside when Mason stumped in and, after putting down his bag of instruments, began to kick his boots against each other to rid them of clinging snow.

Releasing the throat hooks to a triple-caped gray riding cloak, the physician yawned and blinked; his vision being still dazed by snow-glare. "From the fact you're back so soon, Rosemary, I gather the Dickinson woman couldn't have been nearly so sick as you were told."

Leaving the key in the lock, Choice got lightly to her feet, then began to retie her headscarf so nervously that he queried sharply, "What's the matter with you?"

"Nothing, Sam. Really, I'm quite all right."

"No, you're not! I know you too well. Something *has* upset you. What is it, girl?"

She summoned an uncertain smile, then, skillfully mimicking Rosemary's slightly throatier enunciation, said, "Well then, I *am* worried — you're exhausting yourself — working too hard. Won't you try to get more rest — if only for my sake? You look ever so much handsomer when you're not all tuckered out!"

Surprised and pleased, the physician laughed, at the same time wondering why he hadn't noticed previously this warm allure in Rosemary Valentine.

"For your sake, I will try to reform," he smiled. "Oh, by the bye," he remarked, chafing chilled fingers, "I presume you've discovered that I had the Jesuits' bark in my bag all the time; only discovered it after you'd gone out. How absentminded can I grow?"

Choice struggled to keep her voice steady. "So *that's* why I couldn't find it."

Quinine bottle in his hand, Mason bent, lifted the chest's lid, then straightened as if he'd been jabbed by a bayonet. In icy tones he rasped, "My folio is untied! What have you been doing with my private papers?"

She ran over to press herself against him, babbling, "Why, why — Sam, dear — I didn't mean to disturb them. Really I didn't! They — they must somehow have got disarranged while I was s-seeking the b-bark."

"Don't lie to me! You know very well I always keep these papers at the very bottom of this chest!" A pulse began visibly to throb on Mason's temples while he riffled through his folio. "Suppose you explain why these sheets aren't in the order I keep them?"

The girl's smooth and pulpy lips began to quiver. "Oh, Sam, please don't look at me like this. Please! I swear I didn't mean any harm; it's only that so often I've watched you working on those papers and I, well, I've been wondering what they were about."

Small, well-separated gray-blue eyes narrowing, the physician stood over her with hands slowly working by his sides. "Why would you do something so very unlike you?"

Choice ducked her face behind her hands and stammered, "I — I don't know. Forgive me, Sam, won't you please forgive me? I shall d-die if you d-don't."

"Very well. This time I will overlook the matter." He relaxed and removed his cloak, but then Choice made a serious mistake. "I'm sorry I've upset you so. Do those papers contain — something which should be kept secret?"

He glared at her, then said stiffly, "That's absolutely no concern of yours!" Kneeling, he turned the key in the lock. "Now please go, Rosemary; I've no further need of your services, however able."

She managed to fill her eyes while darting over to fling arms about his neck. "Oh, oh, Sam, don't look, don't speak like that! Can't you understand that we females are naturally born curious?" She tried to kiss his mouth, but he jerked aside.

"Please leave."

"Oh, Sam, you're breaking my heart! Please recall how often I — I've helped you — worked all hours without complaint. That's true, isn't it?"

"That is true," he admitted, voice cold and indifferent. "So when I recover my temper I'll probably call on you again."

Counterfeiting a convincing series of sobs, Choice squelched out into the melting snow only to sight Rosemary plodding towards her on her way back from Mrs. Dickinson, so she merged among shadows cast by a pair of sagging tents.

Once her twin had passed by, Choice scurried to Major Phillips's quarters and blurted out a breathless account of what had happened.

"By damn! Now we've got to act fast!" growled Rains. "Else that bloody spy may try to give us the slip!"

Dickinson, too, was for immediate action, but Valentine only fingered long bristles standing out all over his plump and dimpled chin. "For my part, gentlemen, I believe that we've seen sufficient evidence to act upon, but, just to make sure, let us observe the good doctor's reactions when friend Dickinson tells about what he saw in Norwalk."

"— Or *thinks* he saw," corrected the Major. Obviously, he didn't know what to believe.

Nearing Dr. Mason's tent, Rosemary Valentine realized that she was at once relieved and puzzled. Why had Mrs. Dickinson pretended to be so sick when, in fact, she was suffering from only a slight sniffle and had had no temperature whatsoever? If there hadn't been any real need to send for help, why had she been sent for?

Long accustomed to free access to the physician's tent, Rosemary parted its flaps and stepped inside, a bright smile curving her dark-red lips. "I'm really annoyed, Sam! Mrs. Dickinson wasn't seriously ill at all, so I —"

At his furious expression her smile faded. "Why, Sam, what's gone wrong? You didn't lose Mr. Brodhead?"

The doctor's reddish brows joined in a single, ruler-straight line. "How dare you return here unbidden!"

Rosemary could only gape. "Why, Sam! Why are you so angry? What have I done wrong?"

"You know cursed well, you prying little sneak! How dared you to riffle my private papers?"

The girl's eyes became concentric rings of utter bewilderment. "What are you talking about? I — I've only just now come from the Dickinsons' tent!"

Fixedly, he stared at her, then barked, "Dare you deny that you sought me where I was operating and asked for the key to yonder chest?"

The girl began to grow frightened: this wasn't Sam Mason, but a dangerous stranger who was towering above her. "You must have gone mad —"

"How have you the temerity to —" Mason took a step towards her, but was halted by the abrupt realization that this girl cowering before him was wearing a dark-red scarf whereas she whom he'd just dismissed had been wearing one of dingy blue-and-red stripes.

Perplexedly, his hand crept up to rub his forehead. "Stab me if I know what to think! I was sure 'twas you I just now caught exploring my chest, but I now realize it must have been that precious twin of yours I surprised. She's fixed her hair like yours and was wearing a cap of yours."

"Whatever was Choice doing?"

"She was replacing my — my travel notes in the chest."

"What a stupid, ill-bred thing to do! I'm so — so ashamed of her. But, Sam, why would she want —"

As if to answer the query trampling feet and harsh voices approached the tent. An instant later a group of grim-faced men burst in led by Squire Valentine. Todd Phillips, Andrew Dickinson and knotty John Rains, limping as usual, appeared in rapid succession.

Major Phillips wasted no time, spoke in curt sentences, meanwhile resting a hand on the brass-mounted butt of a pistol stuck into his belt.

Leanly handsome features set in an expression of contempt, Samuel Mason, M.D., drew himself to full height — he'd seen men look at him like this before. "Well, what can I do for you?"

"That, sir, remains to be seen," snapped Phillips.

"I fail to grasp your meaning."

"Thanks to Squire Valentine's daughter," Phillips continued after casting Rosemary a penetrating look as she hovered among shadows behind Sam Mason, "we've had a look at maps, sketches, engineering field notes made by you and kept locked in your chest."

More and more voices, sharp in inquiry and disputation, could be heard increasing outside.

Mason's squarish chin rose as he demanded in a cold and, unfortunately, supercilious tone, "Just what did you expect to find?"

The major's thin, leather-hued lips tightened. "Not what we did. We think you had better explain your purpose in making such careful and expert recordings —"

" 'Expert'?"

"Yes. Since I once served as a sapper I'm able to appreciate your undeniable skill." His voice rose. "We demand to know why you feel moved to collect such information."

Mason cleared his throat. "I resent this illegal and unjustified interrogation, but, since you seem so insistent, I'll have you know that I was directed by General Knox, at whose headquarters I was serving as a military surgeon, to pretend to return to civil life. Then I was instructed to make my way to Watauga with the express purpose of joining Colonel Robertson's expedition. After I had received considerable instruction from various sapper officers I was ordered to prepare a description of the route followed."

Gradually, the physician became aware of hostile eyes boring through gloom in this crowded little tent reeking of wet wool, sour leather and bodies long unwashed.

Phillips made an impatient gesture. "Were you told to select the possible siting of batteries and list tactically important knolls, hills and ridges?"

"I was."

Dickinson broke in excitedly, "That's likely so, but for *whose benefit* are you preparing this information?"

The physician's tone now became that of tolerant contempt. "For the Continental Army's Chief of Artillery. Who else?"

A sneer distorted the Connecticuter's bony, brutally scarred features. "It's about that we intend to find out. Your information can't possibly be intended for the eyes of Sir Henry Clinton, General Prevost or possibly that bloody Tory, Patrick Ferguson."

The physician stepped forward with fist balled but halted and recovered himself when Phillips jerked out his pistol. "You're not only an incredibly stupid fool, Dickinson, but a complete swine! Had you not so many friends on hand I'd be pleased to ram those outrageous implications down your miserable throat!"

"To hell with you, you damned Tory! Just try and do that!"

Dickinson struggled forward, but Phillips and Rains restrained him while Valentine's booming, self-assured voice roared, "Hold on! It's only fair that the doctor should speak; he's got a right to try to convince us he's telling the truth."

"He is!" suddenly shrilled Rosemary. "I *know* he is! He's no Tory!"

"Be still, you foolish chit!" snapped her father. "Well, sir?"

Painfully aware that the next few moments might be decisive, Samuel Mason spoke almost wearily. "If any of you can understand the term, I give you my word of honor that I am here only in obedience to orders issued by the Commander-in-Chief's own headquarters."

Still gripped by Rains and Phillips, the Connecticuter suddenly ceased to recall the awful readiness with which his boatyard had flamed; his home overflowing with men in foreign uniforms; the jangle of breaking glass and the crackle of precious household furniture being smashed.

"Let me go," Dickinson wheezed. "I — I've got a hold on myself." When restraining hands fell away he passed his palm before his eyes as if to erase memories. "Now suppose you all listen and make note as to how the doctor answers some questions about what I saw happen with my own eyes."

The black-clad physician also relaxed. "Go ahead, but make sure you tell them *only* what you actually saw."

"Do you deny that you were in Norwalk when the British raided the port last July?"

Following an almost imperceptible hesitation, Mason replied steadily, "I will not deny that I was present and in American uniform."

"What were you doing in Norwalk?" Major Phillips wanted to know.

"I chanced to be passing through that place while journeying to join the sapper regiment with which I was to receive map-making instruction."

"You really were taken prisoner?" Valentine prompted.

"Exactly so. Suspecting nothing, I rode into an ambush."

Dickinson stated rather than asked, "At that time you were wearing a Continental officer's uniform — blue with red facings?"

"Quite so."

Dickinson's voice rang out harsh as an eagle's scream. "In that case, why did I personally observe you inside Abel Thorne's house drinking and laughing with British and Tory officers as if you were among good friends?"

Minute beads of sweat suddenly broke out on the physician's badly chapped forehead. "I can explain that. It chanced that some of the British officers you say you saw had known me during the Siege of Boston. Being trapped in the town and unable to escape, I was required to doctor not a few of them and their families as well. However, I treated them no better than I attended any Patriot who required my services." He made a short, impatient gesture indicative of hopelessness. "I presume it's too much to ask you to believe that my meeting such officers in Norwalk was purely a grievous mischance."

" 'Grievous mischance'!" Rains made a flatulent noise. "My arse! Don't the Doc talk pretty?"

"He better talk prettier still," said Dickinson, "and explain how come he was turned loose even while the British were marching the rest of us prisoners and lugging plunder down to their ships! I tell you," he almost screamed, "I saw this man standing right here being escorted inland by Hessians in tall brass hats!"

Throat muscles tightening, Samuel Mason scanned the hairy, weather-gnawed faces ringing him in and attempted to detect even a vestige of sympathy and belief. Finding nothing of the sort he drew himself up, said in a steady voice, "Very well, I had hoped it would not be necessary to strain your credulity by mentioning a fact which, doubtless, will further prejudice you against me."

"Speak up!" prompted a hoarse voice from the tent's entrance. "We'll hear ye out, Doc. Ye've always been good to us!"

"Very well. Here is precisely what happened, so listen with attention. The British, somehow, had learned about my mission over the mountains — our headquarters, alas, swarms with spies and traitors —"

"You sure should know!" Rains snapped; after all, it wasn't he who had recruited this damned, over-educated fellow.

"General Tryon offered me immediate release on one condition: that I furnish British headquarters with the identical information I was about to collect for General Knox. Since I couldn't carry out my mission were I thrown into a British jail," he looked slowly about him, "and since the enemy had no way of *forcing* me to furnish them with correct findings, I pretended to accede to Tryon's offer."

" 'Pretended'! Hell!" Phillips suddenly raised his voice. "How can you expect us to believe you?"

"Why not?"

"Because in Boston you already have been accused, tried, convicted and imprisoned on the charge of being a Loyalist sympathizer!"

Acid welled into Mason's throat. "Where did you hear that?"

"Oh, don't pretend to look astonished. Your friend, Dan Maddox, meaning to help you, of course, got a bit drunk one night and told me and Jim Robertson what you'd confided to him."

Aware that a group standing outside the tent had greatly increased and had been listening to everything being said, the major almost shouted, "That, Doctor, settles any doubt in my mind about where your true allegiance lies!"

"— As if there's ever been any doubt about that!" snarled Dickinson.

Phillips's manner changed and he used brisk, military tones, "Some of you tie up the prisoner and keep him under close guard while we decide what's to be done with him."

After a while Todd Phillips reappeared. Features set in grim lines, he pushed his way before Samuel Mason's tent, where the physician now stood with hands lashed behind him.

The major raised both arms above his head and yelled for silence. "Keep quiet! Now listen, all of you. After discussing the evidence presented against Samuel Mason, a committee of heads of families has deliberated and has found him guilty beyond reasonable doubt of treasonable deeds and intent." Phillips paused, mechanically wetted his lips, and went over to confront the prisoner. "Ordinarily, we would string you up without delay — but, because you have so long been devoted to your duty and have treated all comers with equal skill, well, we have — we have voted to let you off easy."

Samuel Mason re-experienced the old sickening sensation of helplessness in the face of outrageous injustice. By now he'd learned the futility of impassioned appeals and protests at such a moment, so, quietly, he demanded, "And what do my grateful former patients mean by the term 'easy'?"

Squire Valentine told him in an almost sorrowful tone, "You'll be allowed to keep your horse and some blankets. You will be given a sound gun and a reasonable amount of ammunition and food; then you will be escorted to the edge of camp and shot if you try to turn back. Where you go when you leave us is strictly up to you."

Luke Brodhead shoved to the front of the crowd, his hurt arm cradled in a ragged sling. Angrily, he yelled, "You call *that* lettin' the Doc off easy? You know damn' well he's no part of a woodsman; he can't last two days in the wilderness, so whyn't you heroes be truly merciful and string the poor devil up and put him out of his misery in a hurry?"

Tim Murphy, who with Dan Maddox had just returned from a hunting expedition, pushed forward, shaking his fist and fairly chattering with rage."By God, any you bastards thinks I'm goin' to stand aside and watch the man who saved my arm and life get driven out to freeze and starve — no matter what he's been accused of — is moon-struck crazy! You can bet the Doc's goin' to outlive the most of you damned yellow-bellies 'cause where he goes, I'm goin' too."

Dan Maddox, deadly lights playing in his sunken eyes, stepped up to the prisoner and jerked undone his bindings. Then he unslung his rifle and stood, alert and ready, beside the accused. Murphy did the same.

Maddox then snapped, "You're acting like addled fools! You've got no *real* proof Sam Mason's a Tory or that he may be lyin' about his mission. Long while ago he told me the truth about what happened to him up in Boston; I credited his story then, and by the Eternal, I always will!"

"You can think as you please, Maddox," snarled Rains, "but I'm damned if I'll allow you two to go along with Mason; this party can't afford to lose a pair of first-rate hunters!"

The gunsmith stalked over to tower above the black-bearded leader. Said he savagely, "Make sense, Rains! You know you can't *force* Tim and me to find game or to shoot straight. You'll have plenty of other good shots left; you're going to have to get along 'thout us."

26. *Chance Encounter*

SINCE neither Dr. Mason nor either of the ex-soldiers had even so much as glimpsed a map of this bleak and winter-bound country — if, indeed, any existed — frequent consultations were held regarding the route and direction to be taken.

Right at the start, all three had agreed that nothing would be gained by attempting to find Colonel Robertson's division: first, Dr. Mason certainly would find it difficult, if not impossible, to offer a plausible explanation as to how and why he and his companions had become separated from Phillips's party; second, there was no certainty that Robertson could be found on this vast, rolling and nearly treeless prairie; third, the weather, although it continued clear and bright, daily was growing colder. Probably the mercury in that little Fahrenheit thermometer still reposing in Mason's medicine chest would have shown the temperature as only a few degrees above the zero mark.

For five days the three successfully forced their way through or rode around drifts lying along the course of a frozen creek which seemed to run in the right direction — towards the southeast. The voyagers spoke seldom and then only when necessary.

Sam Mason remained the most taciturn of all and would only brighten up a little after supper had been cooked and eaten. It was as if he were lost again in bitter hopelessness; no doubt he was wondering what would happen to his portfolio. The best he could hope for was that, eventually, his information would be forwarded to some American authority — always provided that the "slow" division ever reached its destination.

The three "Ishmaelites" — as Mason with wry humor had nicknamed the little party — thus far had made out reasonably well, chiefly because Maddox and Murphy had taken along all their scanty possessions and had demanded their share of food from the meager common stores.

Although they'd not yet located any yarded deer or buffalo, they had discovered a number of dense thickets along the riverside in which rabbits, grouse, partridges and even a few turkeys had elected to winter.

Towards the end of a week's traveling a series of brief but savage blizzards lashed the Barrens and forced a three-day halt in the scant shelter of a deep gully.

Masked by whirling snow, Maddox dropped an armful of wood on the fire before stolidly winding another spare blanket about him before he sat down and drawled, "Wonder how Jim Robertson and the boys are makin' out in this?"

Tim brushed off snow crusting an improvised hood. "No fear but that old timber beast will pull the most of his people through — which I won't say about them dunderheaded fools, Rains and Phillips. Their critters was lookin' piss-poor when we pulled out. Glad we got out when we'd the chance."

Under an enormous bearskin cap Mason's head inclined wearily. "I'm saddest of all over what will happen to anybody who gets hurt or falls sick."

"How well can your feller Josh and Miss Rosemary tend to 'em?" Maddox asked, turning his back more squarely to the wind.

"They've got my medicines and instruments and they'll do their best, of course, but they can't accomplish much. Oh, *damn* those fools! Why wouldn't they believe me? This is all so unnecessary!"

Tim spat into the blaze. "Sure is. Only God's grace will save the lot of 'em from windin' up deader than Mother O'Leary's hen when she was stuffed with onions!"

When the storm blew itself out the next day the "Ishmaelites," hollow-eyed and with faces turned the color of scorched beef steaks, started on but traveled on snowshoes to spare their starving and stark-coated mounts.

Although Maddox had halved and then had quartered the daily ration, the common food supply became all but exhausted. Enviously, the men watched their horses feed on rare patches of frosty blue grass. When nothing at all remained, they tightened their belts, gnawed on leather straps and swallowed quantities of sassafras tea which, while it warmed them briefly, didn't go far towards relieving their griping hunger pangs.

One afternoon during a halt to rally their energy all three men heard the distinctive *crack! crack!* of rifles being fired somewhere beyond a low, snow-covered ridge that presented a glittering barrier in the near distance. Cautious reconnaissance disclosed a pair of tiny black figures snowshoeing towards a fallen animal; the distance was too great to make sure what it was they'd just shot.

"They whites?" Mason mumbled through a breath-frosted muffler.

"Must be," Maddox told him. "No redskin would be crazy enough to go huntin' in weather like this. Besides, those shots sounded good and loud."

"What do you mean by that?"

"Injuns can't afford to use a deal of powder so, as a rule, they don't charge their weapons so heavy."

Maddox, as most experienced on the frontier, told Mason to stay and guard the horses against some hungry predator which might attempt an easy meal. "Besides," muttered the gunsmith, "those fellows out there ain't goin' to be so wary of two men as they would be of three."

Maddox was careful to raise a long "hallo-o" before he and Murphy showshoed over the skyline. Both of the distant hunters ceased to bend over their quarry and, snatching up guns, flung themselves flat behind the fallen animal.

Repeatedly making the peace sign, Tim and Maddox advanced until they were able to make out fur caps barely showing above the dead buffalo's snow-smeared bulk and two pair of eyes squinting behind gleaming iron rings made by rifle muzzles.

"Hey there!" sang out one of the hunters. "Keep them rifles pointed up and halt where you stand!"

When they had complied the other stranger called, "Who are ye?"

"Me, I'm Dan'l Maddox and this here half-pint is Tim Murphy."

"You fellers from Robertson's?"

Dan thought quickly while shouldering Ilsa in a gesture intended to be reassuring. "That's correct."

"How come you're wanderin' 'round?"

"We were out huntin' meat for him when a blizzard cut us off. We've looked around a lot, but we ain't seen any sign of him."

"Then ye're lost?"

"That's the way 'tis and there's no 'tiser," grinned Tim. "We're damn' well lost and powerful hungry, too. All three of us."

The taller stranger promptly slung his gun in line with Murphy's stomach. "*Three!* Where's the other man — or are there more of you somewheres around? Now speak true, else we'll surely blow you fellows apart!"

Maddox spoke up in a hurry. "Take it easy, Mister! 'Fore God, there's only Sam Mason behind yonder ridge; he's guardin' our nags."

"All right, you kin come on in. But don't make no sudden motions."

Maddox and the rifleman then shuffled forward, light snow spraying rhythmically from under their bear-paw shoes. Solemnly, they stripped off their mittens to offer filthy, claw-like hands.

Eyes bright and restless, the strangers rose from behind the buffalo and advanced slowly, watchfully. Both were stockily built, brown-bearded and appeared to be in early middle age. One, wearing a shaggy wolfskin coat secured by a wide, brass-buckled belt, had a frayed and broken turkey feather stuck into the back of his cap; the other was protected from the weather by a long-skirted and dingy white Dutch blanket circled by a blue band. For a moment the four men lingered on this vast white plain with sharp snow particles eddying about their legs.

Finally, Tim inquired, "You fellers trappin'?"

Said he in the Dutch coat, "Naw. We're huntin' meat out of Kasper Mansker's place."

"Mansker?"

"Yep. The Dutchman's building a station hard by Sulphur Springs."

"That far off?"

" 'Tain't close. Barrin' another storm it lays at the end of two, mebbe three days' hard travel."

"You mounted?" Dan demanded in carefully subdued anxiety. Men a-foot might go to any lengths to get horses.

"Yep. Got a pair of tackeys tethered hard by. Oh, I forgot to say," the bushy-bearded fellow wearing the wolfskin tapped himself, "me, I'm Haydon Wells and this here no-good son of a woods colt goes by the name of Humphrey Hogan."

"Pleased to meet you."

"Say, that friend of yours up there in the scrub, what's he called?"

"Goes by the name of Mason — Sam Mason." Maddox almost added that he was a doctor but checked himself barely in time; to try to reasonably explain why a physician should have left the main body to go off meat hunting would not be easy.

Red-rimmed and yellow-encircled eyes narrowing, Hogan said sharply, "You really tried to find Robertson?"

"Sure did," Tim assured. "We've been wandering about this blasted country for over a week. Don't any of us know 'come here' from 'sic-'em' about the landscape so we'd be downright pleased if you'd let us trail along with you back to Mansker's. Likely we can help bring down some game. Got a pack horse, too; for all he's damn' skinny I reckon he c'n walk a while longer."

The strangers drew aside and conferred briefly but earnestly while a pair of chickadees sauced a bluejay feeding on pips in a tangle of wild roses.

Hogan grinned and in his turn offered to shake hands. "Me and Haydon would admire to have you along. The both of you look like you know how to handle a rifle."

Tim chuckled, "Brother! If you only knew how well! Believe me, Wells, you and Hogan ain't going to regret this."

Dan slung Ilsa across his back, then jerked out his skinning knife and pointed to the buffalo which lay with tongue lolled out and steaming and glazed black eyes staring fixedly on squadrons of ragged, silver-gray storm clouds which had begun to charge out of the northwest. "Let's get this critter's skin off whilst he's still warm."

When the gory job was completed Hogan slowly wiped his blade on fringed elkskin leggings. "Wal now, reckon we've plenty to stay our bellies with till this new tempest blows over."

"Let's hope so," Wells said, then turned to Tim, who was cutting out the tongue. "Your hatchet sharp? We'd best start cuttin' up."

Dan said, "Mine is, so I'll help butcher. Meantime, Tim, you trot back and fetch in *Mister* Mason —" he stressed the "mister" — "and the mounts. Hurry; looks like we'll get hit by another mean storm before long."

He was right. The new blizzard proved even more vicious and prolonged than that which lashed the expedition after crossing Mad Bear Creek. During four whole days, the men were forced to huddle, half-frozen, in a shelter contrived of the buffalo's hide and blankets stretched over a rough frame contrived of willows growing around a frozen pond. The horses, however, fared better, being able to crop their fill on sere brown buffalo grass and to drink all they wanted at a spring which remained open on the pond's far side.

When the sky finally cleared, the men were filled with food and had regained much of their strength, not to mention confidence in the immediate future.

They were loading their scant possessions and what remained of the meat when Mason said thoughtfully, as if thinking aloud, "I'd be surprised if either party has survived this long."

Curtly, Wells shook his head. "If they were caught 'way out on the Barrens I reckon there won't be anything seen of 'em except bones when the spring thaws uncover 'em. They were plain crazy to try traveling in mid-winter."

Dan Maddox finished cinching his ribby horse before drawling, "Think you're at least half wrong; bet you even money most of Jim Robertson's party will win through."

"What about Rains and Phillips and their people?" Hogan queried as he caught up his reins and prepared to lead out.

The gunsmith shrugged. "Sorry as I am to say it, I won't grant 'em the chance of a snowball in hell!"

Mason nodded. "I fear you're right and that's bad; I must recover my records. I can't afford to wait for 'em to be forwarded hit-or-miss and at no particular time. They've got to reach General Knox in the spring if they're to serve any useful purpose."

"Just how you fixing to recover 'em?" Tim demanded while slinging his famous rifle.

"Don't know, but I've *got* to. Right now I'm chiefly interested in remaining alive."

When the daylight came and the wolves had retreated to a reassuring distance — much to the relief of the huddled and frost-whitened horses, Maddox yawned cavernously, then trained a speculative eye on the doctor. "Didn't sleep so good last night, did you?"

Before making reply, Mason struggled out of snow-crusted blankets and began slowly to flail his arms. "What prompts you to say that?"

"Watched you rise up four-five times during the night, then walk around awhile after you'd fed the fire." The expression in the rifleman's badly bloodshot blue eyes was both curious and sympathetic. "What was eatin' you?"

Dr. Mason's shoulders rose briefly under his rusty-black coat, which by now had lost half its buttons, then stared unseeingly at the scouts from Mansker's Station at present engaged in spearing lumps of half-frozen buffalo hump onto roasting sticks. Everyone in the party was sick to death of buffalo meat — of all game, for that matter — but they'd have to eat more of it or go hungry.

The physician passed a bony and dirt-glazed hand over his thick, inch-long, dark-red beard which served, aside from shielding his face from bitter winds, to conceal many of the harsh lines that had become engraved upon it. His dark-brown eyes had retreated even deeper into their sockets while his cheekbones now stuck out like hatchet blades, but his voice remained clear and strong. "I was wrestling with that uncomfortable thing called a conscience," he explained simply.

In a gesture unusual for so undemonstrative a man, Dan Maddox placed a hand on his friend's shoulder. "Come on. What in hell's troubling it, Sam?"

"— Whether or not I should make an attempt to find Rains and Phillips. You see, if they keep on in the southeasterly direction they were keeping when we — er — when we parted, they'll be attempting to cross the Barrens at their widest point, or so Hogan tells me."

"Wells says the same," Maddox said, then turned aside and unconcernedly relieved himself onto the snow. "He allows they'll never live to reach the far side. When them old-time Indians burned off this country for a buffalo pasture they sure did one fine job. Been at it for ages, so they tell me."

"Do you think anything ought to be done about locating our former companions?"

"I ain't sure," drawled the rifleman. "Hate to think of all those poor fools dyin' so slow and painful after all they've been through."

Once the men had eaten and began to flap snow from ragged blankets preparatory to rolling them, Sam Mason raised his voice, "Hold it a moment, fellows, I've got something important to say and I hope you'll hear me out."

"Spit it out," Hogan rasped. "Time we was movin'. What's on yer mind?"

"— That I've decided an effort must be made to locate Phillips's party."

Tim's bearded jaw sagged. "My God, Sam! You gone clear out o' yer wits? Why, those people will surely shoot you like a dog the minute they recognize you!"

Haydon Wells's shaggy head snapped about so fast that the horses raised their heads. "What's that?" he demanded sharply. "Why fer would anyone want to kill Sam Mason?"

There was nothing for it now but to tell, as simply as possible, the whole sorry and complex story. Maddox did a good job, omitted no pertinent fact, then steadily regarded Haydon Wells, whose permanent half-smile had vanished. "Well, there you have the whole story, boys, as short and plain as I can make it. You'd best make up your minds who's right in a hurry."

Wells fingered his salt-and-pepper-colored mustache. "Don't know what Hump thinks, but, as for myself, I think the Doc's been done dirty by."

Hogan's gap-toothed grin lifted grease-shiny round spots on his cheeks. "Reckon ye're right, Haydon. Me, I figger that two good men who've knowed the Doc for so long wouldn't have elected to take their chances along with him if he'd been a wrong one."

For the first time in many days Samuel Mason's smile was genuine. "I thank you both for this confidence far more than I can say!" His voice swelled, his manner grew brisker. "I take it you will listen to me while I propose a plan which you'll probably decide is utterly mad."

"We'll decide that when we hear your mind," grunted Hogan.

The men returned to the dying cook fire and kicked a few wood ends together. The rack-ribbed horses, standing knee-deep in snow, without interest watched them sink onto their heels and extend hands towards the rekindled flames.

Mason considered the two scouts. "You fellows know the Barrens well?"

"Not well, but better'n most," Wells admitted. "This is a damn' hard country to find yer way about in. Why d'you ask?"

"Think you know which direction an old Long Hunter like Tom Spencer'd be apt to take if he wanted to reach the Frenchman's Bluff?"

"No tellin', because Tom can't hardly know this land a-tall," Hogan drawled after momentary deliberation. "He traps and ranges considerable further north."

"Even so, do either of you think you could find Spencer?"

Under his round lynx-fur hat Humphrey Hogan jerked a nod. "Maybe, if we needed to, real bad — which we don't. Our job is to kill meat for Mansker's Station."

"And you've killed a lot?"

"Plenty. Got meat cached in five or six places along the way back to Sulphur Creek. Say, Doc, what're you drivin' at?"

Mason batted swollen and granulated eyelids a couple of times. "Suppose I ask you to lead me to Rains and Phillips. Could you?"

"Perhaps." Wells spat into the fire, watched his spittle boil, then growled, "But why should we?"

Maddox spoke up, "Because they've got with 'em people — women and youngsters among 'em — who are sick and about ready to die of starvation."

Hogan then heaved himself erect. "Hell, that ain't nothin' onusual out here, and after the way they treated you boys and the Doc, here, I'd tell Phillips and Rains to go hump a 'possum."

Mason also stood up and precisely rewound his muffler. "I suppose they do deserve their fate, but, somehow, I just can't stand aside and let them die." He looked Wells in the eye. "Suppose I promise that you'll both be very well paid for your time and trouble?"

"In hard money?"

"Yes. In hard money. Rains has got a fairly rich man for a partner."

Tim laughed. "Meanin' that old blow-hard Squire Valentine?"

"Who else?"

"What'd he pay us to get him out of this mess?" Hogan asked.

The physician shrugged. "My guess would be around fifty pounds. Would that be enough?" he inquired, although he was pretty sure that such a sum would be more cash than either man had seen during his lifetime — or was likely to.

"That'd be fine," Wells said quickly, then he frowned. "How d'you know he'll pay so well?"

"— His money'd be of no use to him," Maddox hurriedly pointed out, "if him and his family were to freeze or die of hunger."

Wells turned aside, conferred briefly with his fellow scout, then came back.

"All right, it's a deal. Me and Hump will help you search for three days, but no longer; after that we'll have to turn back or Kasper will have our hair."

"That's fair," Tim admitted. "That train can't have gone very far, no matter where they went."

Hogan scratched under his fur hat. "I still can't rightly figger out, Doc, why you're so all-fired keen to help folks who turned you out to freeze. You don't owe 'em a thing."

"I know I don't," agreed the physician, "but, well, I'm a doctor and I look at it like this: by this time there are bound to be a lot of very sick people among those immigrants. I fear some already may be dead." He spread mittened hands as if in apology. "So, well, I feel it's my duty to go back and see what can be done to save innocent victims from their leaders' stupidity."

"Don't suppose you've any interest in recovering yer papers, either?" came Maddox's dry comment.

"You always were smart, Dan. Very well, I will admit that their recovery is also a mighty serious obligation which must be discharged — no matter what the risk."

Tim spat disgustedly, then heaved his blanket onto his saddle and commenced to fumble at its cantle straps. "I sure hate watching you stick that educated, handsome head of yours in a noose like this — but I'll string along and let's see what happens."

Mason grinned faintly through his frost-flecked bristly beard. "Is it my imagination, Tim, or aren't you just a little eager to see a certain Choice Valentine again?"

"Reckon so. I — well, I been missin' her somethin' fierce."

After deliberation, it was decided that in case Spencer, for some reason, had elected to depart from his original route, Haydon Wells would guide Mason and Murphy to the southwest while Hogan and Maddox would search due south. It was reaffirmed that, if three days' scouting produced no sign of the column, all hands would turn back and rendezvous at the nearest meat cache the scouts had established on the way to Kasper Mansker's station. Nobody even mentioned the grave possibility that none of these men so stiffly loading their horses might ever be seen again.

⌒

27. Camp Misery

MANY times during the past fortnight, Choice Valentine had imagined that she'd touched the ultimate depths of despair, but right now she realized that she'd been quite mistaken. Nothing which had occurred in the past could even compare with the appalling conditions at present prevailing in "Camp Misery," as this desolate, disorderly encampment aptly enough had been nicknamed.

Three days back so many immigrants had taken scurvy or had otherwise fallen sick — with several lingering close to death — and losses among the remaining skeleton-thin livestock had become so serious that, when the head of the column entered a wide natural bowl created among a group of low ridges on which a good supply of brown buffalo grass was visible, the harried and increasingly desperate leaders decreed a long halt.

Perhaps it was the death of Agnes Valentine that prompted this decision, but, more likely, it was the fact that Tom Spencer, their principal guide, at last had succumbed to snow blindness which was afflicting everybody, more or less. In addition, he'd fallen victim to a mysterious complaint in his bowels that, for hours on end, kept the giant groaning and doubled up in agony.

Choice glanced across the tent, in which many rents and holes were admitting daylight along with penetrating draughts of icy air. Lips compressed, the girl considered a tumbled heap of bedding under which Rosemary lay, semi-conscious from hunger and exhaustion induced by untiring efforts to nurse the many sick. Demands for her well-intentioned but often useless or incorrect ministrations had doubled once Josh Freedly, the banished doctor's assistant, had become incapacitated by a whole bootful of frozen toes. Her twin's long, dark-lashed eyes, ringed in purple-brown, stared fixedly at a triangular tear glimmering in the worn, brown canvas above her feet.

In a way, Choice was relieved that poor, dear Mamma had died so suddenly — of what nobody seemed to know — but now, at least, she wouldn't have to go on starving and freezing.

She wondered how much longer Papa would remain absent. Over an hour ago he'd been called to another of those interminable councils which never seemed to arrive at a decision — right or wrong — and usually ended in wrangling as futile as it was bitter. Despite her wretchedness, Choice was becoming aware that Papa — who now was weighing forty pounds less than he had three months ago — had become influential among the leaders.

If only he'd been able to prevent that stupid driving away of Sam Mason and Tim and Dan Maddox! Until recently she'd not appreciated how much the last two had done for her family. Choice snuffled, then wiped a red, badly chapped nose on her sleeve. Admittedly she missed Tim, with his easy laughter, eager lips and ready virility whenever a moment's privacy became available, but to her growing surprise it was of the gunsmith she had thought the most often of late. Maybe it was because Rosemary definitely was "sweet" on him? All her life she'd set out to win whatever her twin wanted. Dan Maddox, she decided, she'd have for her own.

How very inconsiderate it had been of Black Sally to go die just a few days before her mistress! With Rosemary so miserably sick it was now up to her to tramp through dung-splashed snow over to the supply tent and there draw the family's pitiful daily ration which undoubtedly again would consist of a meager double-handful of precious seed-grains — peas, squash, corn, wheat and rye — which would never sprout and flourish in Middle Tennessee.

Employing the jerky motions of a woman thrice her age, the girl wearily pulled Mamma's best cashmere shawl over her own dirty gray one, then braced herself and stepped out into blazing sunlight to be momentarily blinded. Lord! How her eyes ached and burned from continual exposure to acrid wood smoke and the fearful glare of sunlight glancing off these interminable snow-blanketed Barrens.

The first person she encountered was young Jonathan Robertson, who, supporting himself on a staff — he'd suffered a touch of frostbite in both feet — was stolidly limping along driving the ram and three surviving ewes out to graze. Poor little fellow! He tried to smile even though he knew he'd be out in the wind all day ready to use that funny old pistol of his on any predator that dared to come too close. Wolves — and there were several sizable packs of them prowling about — daily were growing bolder, perhaps because they no longer could feed on that long line of carcasses dotting the division's tortured route.

When Old Scratch started to stray among the sagging, smoke-stained tents, Jonathan used his staff to fetch the ram a resounding *whack!* which, a few weeks earlier, certainly would have earned him at least an attempted butt, but today the ram merely coughed before lunging heavily across a snowbank in the right direction; dispiritedly, the ewes followed.

In making for a certain brown patch of grass showing on one of those low, rolling ridges which so forcibly suggested swells on a frozen ocean, the boy, through burning eyes, decided on a route along which, experience told him, the snow would likely prove shallow.

Once blood started pumping through him Jonathan felt somewhat better. By grabs! He was still here, alive and kicking and as determined as ever that, come what might, someday he'd herd these contrary, blatting fools of sheep right up to the top of the Frenchman's Bluff!

By now he'd become so expert in the management of his undersized, bear-paw snowshoes that often he had to slow down to allow his floundering charges to catch up. On reaching the exposed patch, he felt considerably encouraged to find the buffalo grass both rich-looking and plentiful. Immediately the sheep had begun to graze he tried to forget constant gripping hunger pains by climbing a low ridge from the summit of which he could spot any wolves that might attempt to come sneaking in from downwind.

Criminently! The glittering, diamond-bright glare seemed worse today than usual and his cruelly stung eyes already were swollen half-shut. The boy lifted a mitten and separated the thumb from the rest of his fingers in order to create a crack through which he might peek without suffering too much. There wasn't much to see, only an occasional charred stump protruding above the crust like a sinister forefinger and a few patches of weeds revolving halfheartedly in the wind. Away off in the distance the outlines of a few stunted and lonely-looking trees now and then relieved the horizon's monotonous whiteness.

Briefly, Jonathan wondered what the outcome to today's council would be. Would the head men decide to stay where they were awhile longer or try to move on? If only Joe Drake, Cash Brooks or some of the other old-timers hadn't gone with Pa! For some time Jonathan had suspected, privately of course, that neither Tom Spencer nor Ed Jennings had been too sure about where they were going. If only there had been a few unmistakable landmarks around to set them right; but there hadn't been a one. Jennings, at least, had admitted that he was lost.

Jonathan painfully started to traverse his gaze but suddenly checked the slow turning of his head. Were his eyes tricking him or had three dark specks appeared to move slowly along the summit of a ridge running roughly parallel to the one on which he stood? Shading his eyes with both hands the boy stared until burning tears started to draw cold lines down his cheeks.

Shucks, what if those were only a few stray buffaloes! He caught his breath and stared harder at those distant silhouettes. No, by grabs, those *were* horsemen yonder and, better still, they couldn't possibly have come from Camp Misery! Criminently! Maybe big Tom Spencer had been right all along and a settlement lay somewhere nearby?

Air bit at his lungs with icy teeth when he filled them to yell, but he sensed that his high-pitched shouting wouldn't travel anywhere near far enough. Besides, dang the luck, those strangers were riding upwind and away from him!

Jonathan started to snowshoe wildly down the slope, but halted halfway down, aware that this effort would prove futile. Those horsemen must be riding at least half a mile off. Worse still, it now looked as if they were headed away from Camp Misery and about to disappear below the crest. Oh, God! How could he attract their attention?

Then he remembered his pistol and, praying that its priming was good, leveled in the strangers' direction and squeezed the trigger.

Eternal seconds seemed to elapse before the smoke cleared away. Had they heard? Yes. They'd reined in and were swinging their mounts to face him.

He waved and jumped up and down like an oversized jumping jack, all the time yipping shrilly, Indian-fashion.

Indians? A sobering thought: what if those tiny dark figures turned out to be redskins scouting for a large party? If such proved to be the case, would he be allowed time to snowshoe back and raise an alarm?

But, almost immediately, he became sure those were white men whose horses now were rearing and plunging often breast-deep through deep drifts covering the floor of that little valley which separated the two ridges.

Pretty soon Jonathan began to knuckle his eyes and to believe that his empty belly must be tricking him. Danged if that tall fellow riding in the lead didn't look a lot like Doc Mason — and — by grabs! that *was* Tim Murphy all bundled up in a tight-belted bearskin coat. The other man he couldn't recognize.

Snowshoes kicking up successive sprays of dazzling white, Jonathan plunged down the slope. "Doc! Doc! Is that really you?"

"In body if not in spirit," called the foremost rider. "By God, Jon, I'm delighted not to find you frozen stiff!"

The boy grabbed Mason's leg out of the stirrup and hugged it.

Tim's grin widened as he inquired, "How's everybody in camp?"

"Gee, Mr. Murphy, we're powerful bad off. Hungry and lost, I reckon. Doc's going to be awful busy." Then he remembered something. "One of Squire Valentine's girls been took terrible sick."

"Which one?" Tim and the doctor demanded simultaneously.

"Why, 'tis Miss Rosemary; she's been poorly ever since her Ma died. She's been bedridden three-four days now." The boy's windbitten features peered up through a cloud of breath vapors. "You'll come quick and fix her up?"

"I expect so — if I'm allowed."

Once the four of them had come up with the grazing sheep the rifleman queried, "Now look, Jon, what, well, what kind of a greetin' kin we expect?"

Wells asked sharply, "Are they hungry enough down there to listen to reason?"

"Yep. Reckon they'd do most anythin' fer a good feed."

Murphy gathered braided rawhide reins while his gaze flickered across the glaring plain and came to rest on the encampment's irregular dark outlines. "If that's so, I reckon, Doc, you'd best play it safe and keep these here sheep company whilst me, Wells and the boy go find out whether it's safe for you to come in. Maybe we can talk sense into Rains, Phillips and the rest of them numskulls."

The emissaries were absent only a short while and returned to give Samuel Mason, M.D., a brief account of what had happened since he'd been expelled.

"The Squire says they want you back," Murphy stated.

"On my terms?"

"Guess so," drawled the rifleman. "That's why they're sendin' out a dep — dep —"

"— Deputation."

While Old Scratch and his diminished harem continued to paw snow from the browse, those on the ridge watched a party of horsemen quit Camp Misery and head for the grazing ground.

Suddenly, Jonathan fixed bleared eyes on his companions. "Any you fellers spare me a charge of powder and shot? Used my last to signal you."

His crooked smile widening, Haydon Wells bent in his saddle and offered a powder horn along with a pair of dull-gray musket balls which seemed small enough to fit into the bore of the boy's antique weapon.

"Thanks, Mister. Thanks a lot!"

The scout chuckled. "Ye're welcome, but tell me, Bub, what're ye reloadin' fer?"

Jonathan squared thin shoulders under a sheepskin cloak fashioned from the fleece of that ewe which had died of eating ivy. "I figure to kill the first man who tries to hurt or drive the Doc away again!"

As matters turned out there was no call for Jonathan to use his pistol. Squire Valentine, suggesting a gaunt, bearded and not unattractive caricature of his former self, appeared astride an equine scarecrow a few yards ahead of hollow-eyed and fuzzy-bearded Major Phillips and a pair of bundled-up heads of family Mason recognized only by sight.

While pulling in his frost-rimed mount, Valentine managed a vague salute and then dismounted to offer his hand. "Ah — Doctor. I, well, I trust that you will be sufficiently generous enough to — er — overlook suspicions which now appear to have been quite baseless."

"That's very handsome of you, sir." Mason's tone was sardonic. "Do I take it correctly that you speak for your colleagues as well?"

Major Phillips forced a bleak smile onto long and somber features. "We do, sir. Pray forgive our hasty decision and action. It's, well, it's just that during this war we've suffered so damned much from treason that —"

"I quite appreciate that, sir," came the physician's cold assurance.

Valentine then broke in, "May I say, sir, we are more than eager to have you resume your very skillful ministrations! Incidentally, Tom Spencer and my daughter should receive your first attention."

"Is — is Rosemary badly off?"

"She is gravely ill, I fear."

"I regret to hear this." Then the physician recalled the other obligation, demanded crisply, "You will return my portfolio with its contents intact?"

"It will be returned the moment we reach the encampment. You have my word on that, sir."

"Good. Now, before we proceed further there is one more matter — a very important one — which must be settled here and now."

The Squire's bushy, brown brows elevated themselves to the lower rim of a ratty-looking fox-fur cap. "And what is that?"

Mason pointed to Haydon Wells, then described how Maddox and Hogan at present were searching in another direction.

"Now, listen well. Either of these scouts can lead us to Kasper Mansker's Station — provided they're well paid. They must be reimbursed for failing to bring in all the meat Mansker hired them to kill."

Major Phillips began to look anxious. "I'd gladly pay 'em, but, so help me, I've no hard money of worth." He shrugged. "Only Continental scrip and my veteran's land warrant."

With something of his former orotund manner, Virginius Valentine boomed, "Ahem. Please, Dr. Mason, allow me to assure this worthy fellow that he and his mate will be amply rewarded the moment our party arrives at a settlement."

Wells's red-lidded, steel-gray eyes as well as his mouth remained unsmiling. "Talk plainer, brother. Just how much do we get?"

Valentine drew a deep breath, narrowly studied the wild-looking, leather- and fur-clad figure before him. "Shall we say, well, thirty pounds apiece?"

The scout blinked, then looked suspicious. "Hard money?"

"No. You will be paid half in coin and the rest in Continental notes. How does that sound?"

That the scrip being offered was nearly worthless Haydon Wells was well aware, but, after all, fifteen silver and gold pounds apiece sounded mighty inviting. "That's a fair offer, but, all the same, I'll want half of our hard money paid in advance, else it's no deal."

"Very well, you'll be paid what you want in advance. And now that we're agreed, Mr. Wells, how soon can you furnish us with some food? Most of us haven't eaten even a half-meal in over a week."

Deliberately, Wells passed the back of a mitten across his long and nearly toothless jaw. "Well, Mister, you're goddam lucky we come across you so quick after we started lookin' fer ye 'cause me and Hogan hev a tall stack of elk and buffler meat and marrow bones cached less'n two days' easy travel from whar ye're standin' right now."

BOOK II

No Band of
Brothers

1. *Ricelands*

THE day was so exceptionally warm and pleasant for early February that Captain Barry Colcord told his wife to fetch little Patrick out onto the half-finished porch where the baby could enjoy the sunshine. Having just pulled off boots muddied during a ride around his property, the dark, well-built young Carolinian relished the comfort of going about like this in stocking feet; it was even better to drop into a wicker armchair, relax and just sit for a while; he'd been out since sunup inspecting dikes being raised to enclose a series of new rice fields situated along his plantation's northern border.

Again Barry experienced exasperated frustration that this seemingly endless war should so seriously have slowed and otherwise have hampered the development of Ricelands, the well-situated and otherwise promising plantation he'd bought on the Sampee River just before his marriage to Laura MacDonald. The property lay due north of the little town of Georgetown, South Carolina.

They'd only been married a few months when news of the Battle of Breed's Hill had arrived from the North along with a ringing call to arms. In quick response, he and his brothers, Augustus and Robert, had mounted their hunters and had ridden away, lightheartedly enough, during the summer of '76 to enroll in Francis Marion's newly formed Partisan Legion. At that time "the Swamp Fox," as he now was becoming known, had been a mere lieutenant-colonel with most of his brilliant career still before him.

When Laura led Patrick, staggering happily, out onto the still unrailed porch he pulled his chair over to sit in contented, family-man silence beside his wife until the child took it into his two-year-old head to toddle over towards the porch's unguarded edge. Before Barry could even pull his feet under him, Laura had pounced upon the tousle-headed adventurer but due to her noticeably distended abdomen her movements were by no means as graceful as they would have been a few months earlier.

"Reckon we'd better snap a halter shank onto that foal," drawled Colcord, a twinkle in his wide-set and dark-blue eyes. "Hold him while I fetch one."

Striding indoors he brushed by a brass helmet topped by a crest of faded black horsehair which, with other headgear, dangled from a set of ten-point deer antlers that had been nailed to the wall. It also supported a double-caped riding cloak and a thick but threadbare cavalry tunic of dark-brown flannel turned up in dingy white facings on cuffs and collar. After coiling a picket rope used in the field to tether his charger, the tall young officer sought the kitchen in search of tumblers and a pitcher of cool milk which he carried to the porch.

His wife raised that ruddy and angular but far from unattractive face which so clearly revealed her Highland ancestry and reached up to pat his cheek, murmuring, "Ah, Barry, Barry, my dearest, 'tis fair to have you by me. How much longer can this idyll continue?"

Pouring milk, Colcord replied gravely, "Another full week — if my luck holds. Rob and I were granted the same leave; 'Gustus, too." When he grinned some of the weary lines disappeared from his powerfully modeled features. "When the Colonel wants to get shut of the Colcord clan he don't believe in doing it piecemeal!"

A small smile curved Laura Colcord's wide and pleasantly-shaped mouth. "Of course it hasn't occurred to you that Colonel Marion might feel that three men going on leave together might travel safer?"

"Good of him — but unnecessary. Since we chased Prevost from before Charles Town last fall that esteemed general and Colonel Campbell appear quite content to remain in Georgia waiting to find out what Lincoln and Moultrie may have in mind. Actually, I expect that both sides must be waiting for reinforcements before undertaking serious operations."

Frowning, Laura tilted milk into the baby's shiny rosebud of a mouth; next, she smoothed gleaming, raven hair, tightly braided about her head. "That's good, so long as British or Tory patrols don't start raiding this far north. What really worries me is that —"

"— Is that some of our dear Loyalist neighbors will begin to make trouble before long? Well, I'll admit they're a force to be reckoned with since we failed to recapture Savannah and took that licking at Briar Creek — which I'll not forget in a hurry. Yes, the King's friends *are* growing steadily bolder and more outspoken. It's unfortunate, also, that the Governor's finding it hard to raise new militia companies."

"Why?"

"Because they're afraid to enter Charles Town since that outbreak of smallpox killed so many people last fall. On the bright side, a good many volunteers are coming into Charles Town and Lincoln's camp at Purysburg. Beyond this," he continued seriously, "we've heard news that General Washington already has ordered south the Virginia and North Carolina Continentals who have been serving with him."

Laura's fine, bright black eyes sought the porch's unpainted flooring. "I may sound timorous and cowering, my dear, but, without you around, I've been feeling strangely fearful of late."

"There's no call for that. Father's here, hardly a mile away, and he still has plenty of dependable men on Tranquility." He chuckled. "Lately, he's been drilling them in tactics he learned during the old French War."

Barry's gaze sought that large iron bell which, rigged a-top a stout pole, daily roused or told field hands that their long day's work was at an end. "You have only to ring that and Pa's people will gallop over here hell-for-leather. Besides that, you've my overseer and his son right here on the place; further, I feel that our slaves are to be trusted."

"Why so? Aren't the poor creatures held here against their will?"

Colcord reached down and began to pluck sand burrs from his stockings. "I'll tell you why. It's because they've learned through that mysterious grapevine of theirs — beats me how news spreads so fast — that the British are shipping Negroes captured in America to the West Indies." He straightened and smiled faintly. "I'll admit that a slave's life here ain't exactly a bed of roses, but 'tis sheer bliss compared to the treatment they can expect in Barbados or Jamaica. Yes, my dearest, ox-stupid though they are, they still know where they're best off."

Barry sighed; what luxury it was simply to sit like this on his own front porch, watching great, dark, ever-shifting strings of ducks, reed birds and other waterfowl continually climb, dip and swirl like smoke above the broad and tawny Sampee flowing so leisurely to join the Pee Dee above Georgetown and then to drown itself in the Atlantic.

Aye. He knew now that he felt more than a little surfeited with going half-starved a lot of the time, with bivouacking night after night in the cold mud and camping among poisonous snakes and insects and, worst of all, going for days on end without dry, let alone clean, clothes.

Downstream a dim cluster of white rectangles indicated the where-abouts of Tranquility, Squire Frederick Colcord's extensive plantation house and its complex of outbuildings. Probably, on a fine winter's day like this — provided that 'Gustus had sufficiently recovered — his broth-ers would be out gunning waterfowl or possibly riding to hounds after deer.

Ducks were especially easy to kill; the poorest shot in the country could, with a single blast from his fowling piece, bring down at least a dozen canvasbacks, redheads, scaups or any other kind of raft duck. In fact at this season waterfowl were so overplentiful that slaves grumbled as loudly as they dared whenever a cartload of fat, big-breasted canvas-backs was dumped among their cabins; nor did they fancy any better being fed too often on diamondback terrapins or blue-fin crabs. On the other hand, the Negroes yearned for even a scrap of any wild pig that could be trapped, shot or pulled down by dogs.

Increasingly well pleased with the moment, Barry Colcord debated whether or not he'd go inside and sample a glass of his all but exhausted stock of fine Madeira. Yes. At the very first opportunity he'd better ride down to Charles Town and see if he couldn't maybe flatter or wheedle a pipe or two out of Uncle William's stock if, indeed, the old connoisseur had any wine left in his once magnificent cellar.

Laura, abruptly aware that, despite his tumbler of milk, young Patrick was beginning to make hungry noises, untied the front of her dress, pulled down her undershift and, without comment, set about nursing her sturdy, tow-headed offspring.

After a while she murmured over the baby's avid suckling noises, "Tell me, dearest, since we have suffered so many defeats of late how do most of our people — of the ordinary sort, I mean — feel about who is going to win this eternal war?"

Colcord's look of contentment faded and, for a brief instant, he eyed his wife almost cautiously. "Why ask about that? Have you heard news I haven't?"

Her nod was curt. "Yesterday afternoon, while you were riding the fields, a stranger stopped by here."

Colcord's voice grew edged as he watched a flush suddenly creep out over his wife's prominent cheekbones. "What did he want? Why haven't you mentioned this before?"

"Because I didn't want you needlessly upset; not while you're on leave."

"Well, then, why did this fellow come here?"

"He was bearing a message from my brother."

Straightening abruptly in his chair, Barry demanded, "The Whig one, I hope?"

"Aye. 'Twas from Jamie. He sent word that, with the British now holding Savannah in greater strength than ever and having won control over all Georgia, enemy commanders are very busy recruiting among the Loyalists. Also, their agents are traveling in our hill country and rousing the mountain Scots of North Carolina — my people."

Colcord's lean, red-brown and weather-roughened features contracted; he looked her in the eye. "That's no recent news. Wasn't there anything else this messenger had to say?"

"Yes, that's not all." Nervously, Laura began to stroke her son's head. "Jamie has heard reliable reports that last fall Sir Henry Clinton gathered a strong fleet and a great army up in New York and he thinks that, at this very moment, it is sailing south to Savannah."

"What!" Barry jerked a nod. "It stands to reason, doesn't it, that Sir Henry would want to join forces with the British in Georgia?"

"Jamie feels sure that the enemy will attack Charles Town as soon as they can." Laura summoned an uncertain smile. "Of course, as we both know, Jamie *may* have been listening to wild rumors, but he says that my — my other brothers are all excited. Charles is reported to be raising a Loyalist company while Colin has mysteriously disappeared. He is supposed to be riding southward."

A barking laugh escaped Barry and his squarish mouth thinned itself. "Ha! So it's to be 'King George and the Broadswords' all over again? The poor, deluded idiots! Thought the mountain Scots had learned their lesson for good after we mowed them down at Moore's Creek Bridge and again at Kettle Creek!"

"I fear they haven't. Oh-h. I'm so sorry for poor Jamie — outcast from his own family. He's gone to enlist in the North Carolina Continentals."

Some of Barry's anger dissipated. "Poor Jamie"? Say rather, "Poor Laura"! Was it any fault of his wife's that she'd been born a MacDonald? A member of that clan which, after the disastrous defeat of Culloden, had learned the hard way what tragedies could befall British subjects who dared to defy Royal authority. Aye. She was MacDonald born, but never yet had he found the least cause to question her loyalty to him or to the Cause for which he'd been fighting. And yet — and yet — blood-ties so often *did* count for more than politics.

He started to speak out, but contented himself by reminding her that Benjamin Lincoln, the portly, lethargic but often brilliant New England general whom Congress had sent down to command its Southern army, had captured Beaufort and had won a smart minor victory at Kettle Creek — that same battle in which the Colcord brothers had led their light-cavalrymen in a successful charge.

Barry sighed and wiggled his toes under coarse gray woolen stockings knitted by Laura during his most recent absence in the field and allowed his gaze to wander over to where Juno, his favorite foxhound bitch, contentedly was suckling half a dozen nearly round and still blind puppies. As if to participate in a period of general refreshment, a sleek Maltese cat appeared from indoors and preceded its gracefully waving tail in the direction of the still unpainted cowshed in which gnarled old Uncle Aneas must have begun the afternoon milking.

As if catching the trend, Laura shifted the baby to her other breast, then, for a long moment, stared unseeing out over the Sampee.

Straightening, Barry made an effort to break the tension. " 'Twould appear that our young soldier has drawn sufficient rations for the moment." He reached out and, with awkward gentleness, wiped milk from Patrick's chin before briefly stroking the baby's curly blond hair.

Replete, Patrick refused to rouse even when his mother draped him over a shoulder and began to pat his back. All at once, Barry, deeply moved, bent to kiss his wife, but was checked by a suddenly intent look in her large, black eyes.

Following her gaze, he spied a faint, cone-shaped cloud of yellow dust arising above a narrow road which followed the tops of dikes separating his rice fields from his father's.

He felt a small chill creep down and spread over his back. That rider was coming in a hurry. Um. People didn't ordinarily spur like that over trifles.

Among the slave quarters cur dogs roused and, baying and barking, galloped down the driveway to meet the horseman. Wandering game chickens took fright at their racket and flew like quail into a patch of leafless raspberries. Juno heaved herself up, left the roly-poly puppies to whimper and squirm on the winter-killed lawn and, with milk-swollen dugs a-sway, lumbered heavily after the pack.

Frowning, Barry Colcord jerked on his boots before descending from his veranda and strode down the rutted driveway which ran between a double rank of young magnolias he'd planted while his home was being built. Almost at once he recognized the rider by his immensely wide and powerful shoulders and the characteristic way he sat, rather than posted in the saddle, as his younger brother, Robert.

"Mercy! I'm a sight! Tell Rob to wait. I'll be out as soon as I can."

Still buttoning her blouse Laura carried Patrick indoors. She trod heavily because of the unborn child's not inconsiderable weight and, at the same time, struggled to keep from bursting into hysterical sobs; so grim were her premonitions. She succeeded in remaining dry-eyed only because Feyther, austere old Ian MacDonald, had forbidden his only daughter the luxury of tears ever since she could remember.

Hurriedly, Laura tried to reassure herself. Of course, Rob's mission might well be another case of much ado about nothing. Ever since she'd known him, Rob always had been in a hurry about whatever he was doing. Aye. His galloping over like this might mean nothing more serious than an invitation to visit Tranquility for a day of horse racing, cock fighting or just a session of genteel drinking. The Fates simply must not tear Barry away before his leave was up.

---

2.   Sails off Tybee Island

SINCE childhood Robert Colcord never had been given to minimizing his account of any event — no matter how trivial; in fact, his friends long since had claimed that Rob could stumble over a stick and make his report of that incident sound more important than the Second Coming of Christ. His broad, good-natured features a-gleam with sweat, Rob flung himself off a lathered gray hunter and, after looping his reins over an arm, hurried to his brother.

"From that unusually serious set on your silly phiz," Barry observed acidly, "I judge you're bringing some news of real importance."

Panting slightly, Lieutenent Colcord burst out, " 'Fore God, Barry, it couldn't be more serious!"

"Well, are your tidings good or bad?"

Rob kicked aside an over-curious hound, then dashed sweat from his eyes. "They're both!"

"For God's sake, don't riddle me at a moment like this! What's this all about?"

"Seem's a courier passed through Georgetown this morning carrying news that a great fleet of enemy transports and men-of-war — over a hundred of 'em — has been sighted off Tybee Island heading for Edisto Inlet!"

"Oh, my God! All that many! Are you sure about this?"

"Oh, yes! Yes. General Lincoln is sending word for all militia and state troops to report to Charles Town as soon as may be, so we're off again."

"What's the good part of the news?"

Grinning hugely, Rob clapped his brother on the shoulder. "Cheer up! This means that we're going to get another crack at the Lobsterbacks and square accounts for Briar Creek and Savannah! Ain't that wonderful?"

Grimly, Barry shook his head. "What's so wonderful about that? I'm heartily sick of campaigning."

The younger brother's elation vanished. "Sorry — since I ain't married I'll admit I don't see things the way you do, but I do understand you hate to leave Laura in her — er — present condition."

"— And that's not the half of it!" Barry drew a slow, deep breath. "Well, Rob, I suppose this means we're bound for Charles Town in a big hurry."

"Aye. Tomorrow we're to arm and mount as many true men as we can recruit. Heyo, girl!" He stooped to pat Juno's head when she sidled up to sniff at his handsome new English riding boots. "How's our canine Diana of Ephesus?"

Flattered, the foxhound lolled out her pink tongue to its full length and seemed to smile.

Resentment welled into Barry's being like a bitter tide. How in God's name could Rob remain so damned offhand, so almost childish about soldiering after he'd killed at least three men and had taken two serious wounds?

"Who are we supposed to report to?"

"Colonel Moylan's Horse — if we can find them. If not, to a Major Vernier who commands what's left of Pulaski's dragoons."

"Why dragoons? We're light-horse."

"I've no idea, but those were the orders I got. The message wasn't written out, so maybe the fellow was mistook. As for myself, I'd say we'd better attach ourselves to the first organized cavalry force we come across."

"That makes sense till we learn more."

Barry sighed. "Well, that being that, suppose you come in and help finish the last of my '58 Madeira. You'll find time for that, I expect."

Rob laughed. For a long time he'd prided himself on being the Colcord family's most wholehearted, if not selective, drinker. "Since when have I ever passed up your Madeira?"

They tramped into the house to find Laura changing the baby's diapers in the unfinished dining room into which Patrick's cradle had been placed because of the large fireplace and its accessibility to a temporary kitchen in which the house slaves sheltered. There were now but three domestic servants remaining at Ricelands; two of the younger retainers mysteriously had disappeared before Barry had returned, exhausted and emaciated, after the retreat from Briar Creek. So, nowadays, the staff was composed of a half-blind, blue-gum Negro who once had been a footman at Tranquility and the cook, Becky, his toothless wife. An angular and heavily freckled mulatto girl combined the duties of being Patrick's nurse, a waitress and a chambermaid.

A soft sigh escaped Barry's wife when she straightened up and slowly shook her head. "Glad to see you, brother Rob, but I'm terribly discouraged over your news." She looked away quickly with wide but narrow lips compressed. "Oh! Rob! Rob! This isn't right! This isn't fair! Our time together has been too short, too happy. Why must you go again? Haven't you two done more than your fair share of fighting?" she almost wailed. "Why, oh why, couldn't you have enjoyed your entire leave?"

Rob went over diffidently to pat his sister-in-law's back. "Don't take on so, honey. Near as I know, a war ain't never been designed to fit any particular man's convenience. Take heart, dear girl. This time we're surely going to smash the Redcoats and Tories so hard they'll just have to holler quits! Then we'll be home for keeps."

"Pray God you're right!" Laura almost ran to arrange a coverlet higher over Patrick. "You can't ever know how much I despise to see you go off again. When a woman is in love and new-married, three years is all eternity — especially when there seems to be no end to this killing in sight.

"Well, Barry, expect I'd better go now and start patching your shirts and small clothes."

Once her heavy figure had departed laboriously climbing the stairs,

Barry, from that handsome old Scotch hunting board which had formed part of Laura's dowry produced a cut-glass carafe of red-brown Madeira. Only after they'd ceremoniously touched glasses did Barry detect a touch of unfamiliar gravity in his brother's manner.

"Why so serious, Rob? Whenever we've gone campaigning before you've acted gay as a catbird on a pump handle."

The muscular and taller younger brother frowned before lowering his voice, "Reckon this time it ain't quite like before."

"Why not?"

"Heard anything lately about those poor whites who live down in Shell Town?"

Over his glass Barry nodded. "Now and then. What about them?"

"Well, those rascals have managed to arm themselves — God knows how."

Barry's dark-blue eyes met his brother's of clear gray. For all Rob inevitably had aged during the past three years, his curly, roughly clubbed, collar-length brown hair and his smooth, almost unlined features continued to lend him an almost boyish aspect.

"Towards which side do those swamp rabbits incline?"

Frowning, Rob gnawed his lip. "Can't answer that; no one can. But Pa and I expect they're waitin' to see which way the cat's going to jump before they choose sides."

"Who leads 'em?"

Rob slowly revolved his wine glass between short but powerful fingers. "A mean-looking, yellow-beard fellow name of Jasper Skelton; it was he who, at the head of a gang of scalawags, rode up to Tranquility, bold as brass, yesterday morning and, grinning like a horse collar, told Pa he wasn't to fret if us boys got called back into the field; he and his neighbors stood ready to protect all Colcord property."

Rob's voice deepened, "Next, could Papa see his way towards finding some good mounts for a few deserving Shell Town Patriots who couldn't afford decent horses? And maybe Papa would let him borrow a few bars of lead and some powder?"

Standing in a bleak stubble field back of Ricelands, a mule commenced to bray like a bugle blown by a beginner, sent its strident plaint echoing far out over a landscape fallow with winter.

"What did Papa do?"

"You know how easy-spoken the Old Man is. Well, he stayed insult-

ingly polite and told that mangy swamp rabbit that he'd no mounts or
supplies to spare and that he'd be entirely satisfied if the good Patriots of
Shell Town merely undertook to protect themselves against the King's
men — should any show up."

Robert's eyes began to shine. "As for himself, the Old Man snapped,
'I'm ready, willing and damn' well able to protect any and all Colcord
property.' Skelton — he's scrawny, sallow-faced and a little cockeyed —
sneered, 'Well, it's just as you say, Squire — but these days ain't nobody
can be *sure* about nothin'! We just might have to call on ye to supply us
someday, willy-nilly.'

"Damn the sassy fellow!" Rob rasped. "I only hope he grants us an
excuse to burn that human hogsty flat! Should have been done a long
while ago."

They were savoring the last drops of the Madeira when Barry queried
casually, "Will 'Gustus be well enough to ride with us?"

"Don't know. But I doubt it. He ain't really over that swamp fever he
took after Briar Creek. You going to take along any gamecocks this
time?"

"A couple, maybe. Nero and Mars, they're in shape. How about you?"

"I've half a dozen stags that ought to whip some of those barnyard
roosters they call fighting cocks down in Charles Town. What about a
body servant?"

"Think I'll take along Saul Black Buck."

Robert's brows went up. "Saul? You mean that mustee hunter you
bought last year?"

"He's the one. While Saul's a little long in the tooth, he's still damned
knowledgeable in swamps and wooded country."

"He's part Indian, ain't he?"

"Yes. Half Creek, half nigra — or maybe less. He don't know himself."

"He own a firearm?"

Barry put away the decanter. "No, but I'm lending him that German
rifle-gun I picked up at Kettle Creek. He's learned to shoot it pretty well,
but he's still handier with a bow."

"Well, Barry boy, I'm off now to see who can be coaxed or threatened
into enlisting."

Long after the hollow sound of hoofbeats had faded along the dike
road Barry remained silent, slumped in his chair and feeling all of ten

years older. Why in God's name had Rob had to add to his anxieties by
mentioning Jasper Skelton's visit and his implied threats? Everybody
in this part of Georgetown County for a long time had considered Shell
Town, that unimportant hamlet downriver, as no more than a squalid
disgrace to the community. Most Shell Towners certainly were smug-
glers and probably pirates as well. Granted the opportunity, they were
reported ready to row out under cover of darkness to plunder defenseless
little coasters.

Of late, some of the Shell Town "swamp rabbits," as they were con-
temptuously referred to, had been seen riding blooded horses that could
not honestly have been come by. Earnestly, Barry attempted to reassure
himself by recalling that plenty of his recruits who'd appeared no more
respectable than Shell Towners nevertheless had become hardy and usually dependable irregular cavalrymen.

John, the half-blood butler, worked till the candles guttered at bur-
nishing "de Cappen's" brass helmet, sword hilt and horse metal into
presentable brightness.

Laura, although looking uncommonly pale and drawn, manufactured
cheerful conversation while darning the same pair of light but warm
woolen blankets he'd so appreciated during that last luckless campaign.
Next, she patched and mended his light-horse officer's short-skirted
tunic, which was dyed a sensible butternut brown, set off by pewter buttons and cuffs and revers of sadly dulled white nankeen.

Barry himself took apart and expertly cleaned the locks to his heavy,
brass-mounted saddle pistols. After that he stitched tight a fraying seam
in his saddle of fine English pigskin. He ended by poking up the fire and
running bullets to fit his carbine and side arms. By midnight the young
captain's saddlebags bulged with fresh underwear, stockings and even a
ruffled dress shirt against the possibility that it might be required for a
formal occasion.

Barry felt increasingly sure that his decision to take along Saul Black
Buck was sound. Aside from acting as a body servant, the half-breed was
certain to prove invaluable in scouting or on patrol duty. He cast a look
across the room at Black Buck, as he preferred to be called, busily braid-
ing a fresh pair of bridle reins. How strange that, in a cross between an
Indian and a Negro, characteristics of the former race should almost invariably predominate. Saul's slightly hooked nose was thin and high-
bridged, and his grizzled hair wasn't really kinky — only wavy — while
his skin was the hue of copper-black velvet.

By the pearly first light of a clear and frosty dawn Laura Colcord pulled an old MacDonald tartan shawl higher about her shoulders before carefully descending Ricelands's front steps. Even by this uncertain half-light Barry could make out the great mass of raven hair cascading down his wife's back, also the haunted expression on her strong-boned features.

"I feel hesitant, my dear, about taking Saul away from you; however, since Rob and I've been given orders to bring along every reliable man we can find, I feel justified.

"Besides, the mustee can care for our horses. That will help me no end. You've no idea what it means to a commanding officer to have to water, groom and feed his mount at the end of a long day when he should be resting to make decisions which may decide the effective use of his command."

Nothing was said when the old mustee silently appeared around the house leading Barry's favorite hunter, Eclipse — so named, rather un-originally, because the long-legged mare hadn't a single white hair on her. For himself, Saul Black Buck had found a bigger-than-average brown tackey which, judging by its long legs, might have counted a blooded animal somewhere among its ancestors.

Only when Barry began to pull on his gauntlets did Laura, for the first time in her life, begin to quiver and then burst into uncontrollable tears. "Forgive me," she choked, "I — I fear I'm acting like a silly child and no part of a good soldier's wife, but I — I can't help it." Almost angrily she slapped her bulging abdomen. "Perhaps this is to blame for my weakness."

He put gentle arms about Laura, hugged her to him and kissed her wet features again and again while gamecocks in their walks behind the house announced the breaking of the new day. "Ah — darling, dearest, please don't take on so. Look. Right now I swear to return in plenty of time to greet our new heir."

She forced a pathetic attempt to smile. "Oh, Barry, Barry! I'll live in the hope that you really will. For no reason I — feel so foolishly fearful of — of, oh, I don't know what."

He kissed her again, then, setting his riding cloak a-flutter, he swung up onto Eclipse, wheeled and, with the day's first light drawing dull gleams from his helmet, reined the mare about and clattered off towards Tranquility. At a more sedate pace Black Buck and the pack horse moved out after him.

Behind Ricelands the foxhound Juno began to emit doleful sounds.

3. *Rebel! Rebel!*

WHEN the Colcord brothers, with crested brass helmets glinting, left behind the small but fast-growing port of Georgetown, they were leading what was termed a "half-troop," consisting of twenty-four passably well-mounted recruits. They set off along a sandy, little-used back road which led less comfortably but more directly to Monck's Corner than did the comparatively wide and roughly graded King's Highway.

Only a few of the troopers were clad in parts of uniforms from several units. Although this was winter, most of the men, who, for the most part, were hard-eyed farmers or small tradesmen, wore fraying broad-brimmed straw hats, sleeveless jackets of strouding, frieze or osnaburg. The rest of their costume consisted of knee breeches or pantaloons of coarse linen and stockings of heavy thread. Without exception, these new cavalrymen's footgear was well worn and home-cobbled.

To wear a sergeant's green worsted shoulder knot, Barry Colcord designated taciturn Gavin Wilcox, a silent, grimly efficient, sheep-faced veteran of the Siege of Charles Town in '76. For corporals he selected Paul Skene and Oliver Peete, both time-expired militiamen who swore that they'd served last year under Colonel Laurens during General Lincoln's costly and unsuccessful attempt to recapture Savannah. For his lance-corporals he selected a quartet of hard-looking characters said to have fought in Georgia with Patriot Partisans under Captain John Dooley against Tory forces led by the redoubtable and able Colonel Boyd.

Lending the half-troop a slightly professional air were several swords and sabers of varying design and a few battered helmets of brown or black leather.

The balance of Barry's recruits admittedly were riding to war for the first time and, as usual, were full of brag and impatience to close with the enemy. To the Colcord brothers' deep but unexpressed satisfaction their half-troop, on the average, proved better mounted than most of the levies they'd led in the past. A majority of their followers bestrode deep-chested and long-legged horses which in most cases certainly must represent their owners' principal asset; consequently, these animals always were well fed and cared for.

In following this little-traveled road on which deer and pig tracks were plentiful, the Ricelands Rangers, as the half-troop had nicknamed itself for want of a better designation, rode in a column of twos and made no pretense of maintaining a military bearing; weapons and personal gear were slung or worn any which way — just so they didn't inconvenience the rider. At the brief column's rear, Trooper Black Buck, his jet eyes never still, rode herd on the new unit's three sleepy-looking and lop-eared baggage mules.

This inland section of the South Carolina coast was flat as any platter, sandy and overgrown with useless slash pines, pin oaks and palmettoes. An occasional grove of huge, moss-draped and silver-gray live oaks helped to relieve the landscape's depressing monotony. The half-troop continually was forced to ford or even swim across a seemingly interminable succession of brooks and creeks flowing eastward to feed those vast marshes which lined the coast all the way up to North Carolina.

Hereabouts, what farms there were looked poverty-poor. Few and far between, they usually consisted of no more than a ramshackle slab shanty or an old-time log cabin standing lonely amid sandy-gray fields on low, brick supports, with only a privy, a cowshed or a rickety corncrib to keep them company.

Rob, jogging along beside his brother, all at once raised a hand to shade his eyes against the pale winter sun. "Notice all those buzzards wheeling up ahead? Wonder what interests 'em?"

"Probably someone's butchered a hog — or maybe they're just waiting for some sick horse or cow to die."

For quite a while now the track, aside from plentiful spoor of wild creatures, had shown only faint ruts caused by cart wheels obviously made a good while ago. Now the road led in apparent aimlessness across a wide and desolate barren of slash pine and scrub oak which must have looked very much the same when the first white settlers cautiously had begun to grope their way inland.

All at once Black Buck rode up alongside with so intent an expression that Barry straightened in his saddle, asked quickly, "What's wrong?"

"Me know this place, sar. Is little public house around next bend. Vultures swinging low close by."

Reacting with an alacrity learned during many campaigns, Captain Colcord sounded a low note on the little silver whistle he invariably wore at the end of a lanyard. Next, he arm-signaled his men to form as skirmishers in line abreast and passed word for them to look sharp and to report if they noticed anything out of the way. They fanned out in a silence so complete that a pileated woodpecker's hammering on a hollow tree sounded loud as drumbeats.

A moment later the sandy track straightened sufficiently to reveal a great swarm of black-and-brown turkey buzzards flapping, wheeling and planing above the charred skeleton of a small structure standing under the scorched limbs of a gigantic water oak.

"Look alive!" called the sergeant. "Prepare to charge!"

Weapons were yanked out of boots and holsters and were held at the ready as the Ricelands Rangers closed in and trotted forward, all the while studying the surrounding piney woods until it became apparent that the scene was deserted save for a few chickens and a couple of ribby curs slinking about in the underbrush. All else was still.

Sergeant Wilcox suddenly rasped, "Jesus Christ! Look over yonder!"

A furious yell went up when the horsemen followed Wilcox's out-thrust arm.

Lieutenant Rob Colcord's broad face went scarlet. "Oh, no! Oh, God!"

From the lower limbs of a nearby tree three attenuated, half-naked bodies dangled six feet clear of the ground. They remained quite motionless except when brushed into gentle motion by the wings of buzzards swooping and striking at the dead bodies with gruesome patience. Because they'd no way of obtaining purchase, thus far they hadn't had much success.

While kicking forward Eclipse, Barry, as well as his followers, realized that a ragged piece of paper had been affixed to the shirt of each corpse. Most of the veterans present guessed what had been scrawled on those placards. It would be something like "A Rebel Dog," or "So, to all the King's enemies."

What particularly chilled the troopers was that the smallest corpse, suspended with dirty, bare toes rigidly pointing to the ground as if in search of some nonexistent support, was that of a yellow-haired youth who could scarcely have passed his fourteenth birthday. The second cadaver was that of a plump, gray-haired man whose sparse chin whiskers showed forlornly below horribly bulging eyes and a black, protruding tongue. The third victim in life had been lean as a rail. He must have put up a fight against Fate, for a long, brown-red wound encrusted with busy bluebottle flies ran across one long-unshaven cheek.

Cautiously, the half-troop searched the immediate vicinity.

"What do you make of this?" demanded Captain Colcord while un-cocking his pistol.

"Reckon the destructives couldn't ha' been here later than yesterday," volunteered Corporal Skene. "Nothin' burning. Ashes are cold."

Disregarding his orders to report to Monck's Corner with all speed, Captain Colcord ordered his men to dismount, then in a gruff voice instructed Sergeant Wilcox to cut down the murdered men and start digging bury holes.

While the men were looking about for shovels and pickaxes, they made two shocking discoveries. One was the frail body of an old woman who must have been shot while trying to escape. Her pitiful remains weren't pretty, because wild hogs had found the body some time ago. Later, among the pungent-smelling ashes of the tavern, the charred corpse of what could have been either a young girl or boy was discovered.

While others were digging, Sergeant Wilcox and Black Buck rode along the destructives' trail until they lost it along the edge of a great, gloomy swamp, but not before it seemed clear that the murderers were heading almost due west. By this time they must be so far away as to be beyond pursuit.

The half-troop's veterans, having already viewed similar atrocities, worked in grim silence while a row of shallow graves were being scooped out of the sandy soil, but the recruits raged, cursed and vowed terrible revenge.

Through a quick inspection of half-burned bills and invoices scattered about the clearing, the Colcords concluded that the murdered tavern-keeper's name had been Bernard Piggott, and since there was no hint of the identity of the victims, they lettered the date in charcoal on head-boards hastily improvised from pine slabs and marked them Piggott No. 1, Piggott No. 2 and so on.

After a delay which had lasted about an hour Colcord pulled on his helmet and told Sergeant Wilcox to remount the command.

"Stand to horse! Prepare to mount! Mount!" bawled the sergeant, then in the customary column of twos the Ricelands Rangers trotted off along a road which, if a weathered finger board was to be trusted, even-tually should bring them to Cobb's Mill; the road sign, however, gave no indication of how far off the place lay. Possibly they might, at Cobb's Mill, encounter other troops on their way to join General Lincoln — or a band of Tory destructives? Devoutly, they hoped to come upon the latter.

Sure enough, later in the day they came upon a tatterdemalion militia company slogging along over the sandy ground. They looked tired, bent as they were under shapeless packs and lugging long-barreled muskets, most of which weighed around fifteen pounds apiece. These levies didn't in the least resemble those gaudily uniformed, fire-eating volunteers who'd turned out in '76.

From the expressions on their brown and generally bearded gaunt faces it was inescapable that they were anxious over what soon might occur to unprotected families in and around Charles Town.

<hr/>

4. Tory! Tory!

COBB's Mill, South Carolina, consisted, in the winter of 1780, of about sixty largely wooden dwellings, three churches, a dozen-odd shops and stores; well and handsomely constructed of red brick were the Eagle Tavern, the County Court House and the adjacent jail. The prosperous little town's population nowadays numbered three hundred souls of all ages and various colors; but for this war, its inhabitants undoubtedly would have numbered many more.

Sheltered by a magnificent grove of water oaks, Cobb's Mill had been built on the convex bank of a wide and leisurely bend in the Upper Cooper River. Nowadays the services of a clumsy, flat-bottomed ferry-scow was much in demand. One Hubert Rugely owned a rough wharf with a shed standing at its land end which accommodated pirogues, canoes and small flatboats bringing deerskins, furs and other products in from settlements springing up in the back country farther west. Dingy little sloops, snows and pinkies which managed to sail up from Charles Town also tied up at Rugely's Wharf.

Cobb's Mill as the Colcords quickly perceived was busy and evidently prospering thanks to the intermittent passage of troops on their way to the coast. For the most part these irregulars, often weirdly garbed and even more oddly equipped, were glad to break their march to bivouac for a night or so on empty cotton fields fringing the outskirts of town, then march on and use Rugely's ferry to cross the tawny-gray Cooper and disappear on the far shore.

Wise through experience, Captain Colcord selected a campsite for the

Ricelands Rangers removed as far as possible from the little town's dubious entertainments to thus limit opportunity for his followers to become involved in sometimes serious drunken brawls with neighboring troops.

Early on the morning after their sundown arrival on the Cooper's east bank Barry, after exercising his gamecocks and staking them out to feed and stretch their legs, called aside Corporal Skene and Black Buck to give them instructions about collecting fodder and inspecting all mounts for saddle sores and loose shoes.

He then placed his brother in command of the half-troop and, beckoning Sergeant Wilcox, rode off towards Cobb's Mill. With his helmet's black horsehair crest whipping gently under a breeze out of the west, he jogged past an infantry company and a platoon of shaggy, wild-looking riflemen fresh out of the backwoods; these waved in friendly fashion.

By the time Barry and Wilcox *clip-clopped* into the town's dusty and unpaved main square almost all soldiers had moved out so it appeared that, for a while at least, the inhabitants of Cobb's Mill would have their pretty little tree-shaded town to themselves.

Hopeful of purchasing sufficient cloth of any shade of brown to make uniform jackets for his followers, Barry pulled up before a shop marked A. BENBOW, DRAPER, swung lightly off Eclipse and, passing his reins to Wilcox, said, "Sergeant, reckon I'll go see if he's got anything useful in there."

He had started to climb the draper's gritty stoop when he halted, puzzled by a clamor of many angry voices rising somewhere out of sight but certainly in the near vicinity.

The outcry swelled until people slammed open windows and craned their necks about the square. Suddenly a church bell commenced to toll slowly, ponderously, as for a funeral. Doors banged open and citizens, men and women alike, appeared pulling on coats and shawls and started hurrying, even running, over to the brick building which, because of its barred windows, Barry took to be the jail.

The Captain continued up the draper's steps, only to collide with the proprietor, a fat, round-faced little man wearing square-lensed, steel spectacles.

"— One moment, sir," Barry began, "d'you have brown-dyed yard goods of any description?"

"Lord love you, no, suh. Not anythin', any color. Been cleaned out of all yard goods since near a year ago." The draper was selecting a brass key when he noticed the frayed silver epaulet on Colcord's right shoulder, said, "Sorry, Cap'n, but bein' as how I don't aim to miss what's about to happen, reckon I'll lock up for a space."

Under the visor of his helmet Barry's dark, wide-set eyes narrowed. "What's all this fuss about?"

"Why, sir, there's about to be a trial."

"What are you talking about?"

"Well, sir, last night our Committee of Safety finally got around to arrestin' George Walker."

"Who's Walker?"

"Why, sir, 'tis him who owns and runs The Golden Lion."

"What's that?"

"Why, sir, 'tis a fine big tavern on the ferry road."

"For what did they arrest this man?"

"Why, sir, plenty of people livin' around here take George Walker for a Loyalist sympathizer," the shopkeeper blinked short-sightedly while putting away his key, "but near as many others stand ready to swear he ain't a Tory." The draper chuckled and began to button up a well-cut gray overcoat. "Be that as it may, sir, in a little while we aim to make sure about his politics."

A Tory! Yesterday's scene returned in full and horrifying detail. Under his chin strap Barry's jaw set itself.

Now more people began to hurry by; boys whooped and yelled so excitedly that despite Sergeant Wilcox's soothing voice and hands Eclipse showed the whites of her eyes and began to snort and shuffle nervously.

Not without difficulty Colcord remounted, saying shortly, "Come along, Sergeant. Might be wise to find out which side the people here really favor."

What had prompted this decision was an abrupt realization that by no means all of Cobb's Mill's inhabitants were hurrying towards a pair of lofty, moss-draped oaks towering above the Court House and the jail alongside. A good number of angry-looking persons had gathered into little groups and were talking in savage undertones.

Through the advantage of being on horseback, Barry could see from the edge of the crowd a growing throng jostling and shoving about a plain pine table which, along with three stiff wooden chairs, had been set under one of the oaks' low-sweeping branches.

"Sir," grunted Wilcox, "looks like some of these folks already have made up their minds what the verdict's going to be."

"What's your meaning?"

"Just look over yonder, sir." The sergeant pointed down a rutted side street in which an iron cauldron of tar was being lowered over a fire so big that men working there had to keep shielding their faces against the soaring, crackling flames.

An excited, ugly sound went up when a slovenly, hang-bellied fellow in an old blue Continental uniform coat came out of the jail and set a glass and a battered pewter pitcher on the table. Briefly, Barry wondered what the latter might contain.

"Give him the Test Oath!" someone's big voice yelled. "Force that goddam innkeeper to take it!"

Another great, discordant shout went up when the jail's ponderous, nail-studded door cracked open again and a quartet of semi-uniformed militiamen in broad hats and cross belts tramped out and at once lowered their muskets to the horizontal in order to force the screaming, fist-shaking mob to back away from the table and chairs.

"Hurray fer Judge Thompson!" someone shouted. "Hurray! Hurray fer justice!" "Come on, yer worship," howled another decent-looking citizen. "Make George Walker swear or just hand that dirty King-lover over to us!" "That tar hot yet? Somebody fetch a feather pillow! Get a rope ready in case he won't swear!"

The next figure to appear provoked such an explosive outcry that horses shied and women stopped their ears. From where he sat vainly attempting to calm his mare, Barry could tell that the prisoner was a tall, well-built fellow who still appeared distinguished though his chin showed a purple bruise and his light-brown hair hung like a gapped fringe before blazing black eyes. The prisoner wasn't able to brush aside the dangling locks for the simple reason that his hands were tied behind him.

Pandemonium swelled. "Tory! Tory! Test the goddam bloody Tory!"

All at once the church bell stopped clanging, which, oddly enough, had the immediate effect of subduing the outcry.

The next to appear was the sheriff, a bittern-thin fellow whose long beak of a nose emphasized the similarity. He was followed by a short, plump individual who, judging by the quill pen he carried thrust over one ear and the folio of papers tucked under his arm, must be clerk of the court. Judge Thompson parted the skirts of his long black coat and gravely seated himself behind the table under the tree.

Barry and his companion slowly worked their mounts forward with the crowd readily giving way before Eclipse's nervously dancing hoofs until they were close enough to read sullen defiance written all over the prisoner's rather handsome features, which by now had turned a sickly, cheese-yellow hue.

The suspect held up his head and glared down his nose at his persecutors. Barry estimated that George Walker must be nearing early middle age.

The sheriff honked ludicrously in blowing his beak of a nose on a red bandanna. When he'd finished, he signaled to a big fellow wearing a corporal's red worsted shoulder knot. "All right, Toby, bring the accused forward."

Only the excited yipping and snarling of dogs and an undertone of angry voices on the square's far side broke a comparative stillness when the judge donned gold-rimmed spectacles and queried briskly, "Your name?"

"Why ask that, Edward Thompson? Ain't we served on the same vestry for going on ten years? If your memory's that poor, you ought to give up law."

The judge's already taut mouth contracted into a thin and colorless line. "Never mind the advice, George. Answer me!"

"Very well, your worship. My name is Walker; George Huger Walker — and be damned to you! How can you, presumably a man of law and integrity, dare to countenance the arrest of a peaceful, law-abiding citizen without a warrant?"

The clerk hammered on the table with a heavy leaden inkwell. "Speak respectful, you! And keep quiet lest ye're answerin' a question."

Walker snorted, then yelled at the onlookers, "I appeal to any honest man among you to halt this illegal nonsense! I tell you I have been denied the basic rights of a British subject and a taxpay — O-o-h!" He gasped and swayed when, with vicious energy, a guard smashed his metal-shod musket's butt between the prisoner's shoulders.

The sheriff half-arose, growling, "That'll do, Billy! Now, untie the accused's hands."

The corporal hesitated. "Aw, Roger, what for you want me to do that? This feller's a desperate man."

"Do as you're told!" Judge Thompson thundered, then continued in grave, almost sad tones, "George Walker, you stand before this tribunal accused of entertaining Loyalist sympathies inimical to the cause of American independence. How plead you?"

"This ain't a proper court of law!" wheezed the prisoner still deathly pale and fighting for breath. "So, Ed Thompson, I'm damned if I'll plead one way or another!"

"You better change your mind or 'twill be made up for you," advised the sheriff, again mopping his juicy nose. "Smell that?"

A pungent reek of heated tar had begun to drift across the square.

The tavernkeeper merely glared straight ahead.

"See that?" rasped the big corporal. "See what's comin' fer ye?"

Out of a side street rumbled a two-wheeled farm cart drawn by an aged and heavy-footed white horse. Its ungreased axles screeched like fiends undergoing torment.

"Quiet, everybody!" roared the sheriff. "His worship will now administer the Test Oath!"

While waiting for the shouting to die down, the clerk picked up the pitcher and filled a glass with an amber-hued fluid which apparently was a rum toddy.

Solemnly, Judge Thompson got to his feet and, merging heavy brows, picked up the glass. In a clear, rich voice he said, "George Walker, will you swear before the ever-living God and the world that our war against Great Britain is just and necessary? That you have not and will not aid or abet the forces of Great Britain? Will you pledge faith and true allegiance to the Sovereign State of South Carolina?" He held out the toddy glass. "Will you seal this solemn oath by drinking to the health of George Washington, of the Continental Congress and to the damnation of King George III and all the rascals about him?"

A taut stillness descended in which people elbowed, shuffled and craned necks to obtain a clearer view of that small, cleared space before the jail.

The tavernkeeper, breathing noisily, continued to stare straight ahead, made no sound.

Angrily, the sheriff prompted, "Get on with it, Walker! Before we're done we intend to find out where your true sympathy lies!"

Two guards had started to hustle the prisoner forward when, all at once, the publican shook off their hands and, of his own accord, advanced to the table and cried in a strangled voice, "All right, I *will* drink!" His hand shot out and seized the glass which he held poised be-

fully, they'd turned aside would-be recruits who were too old or too young or were mounted on those short-legged but durable tackeys found in profusion all over Georgia and the Carolinas. While such beasts were wonderfully tough and could live on almost nothing, they couldn't run very fast or far carrying any considerable weight — as many a dragoon commander had discovered to his sorrow.

The only inducements Barry could offer to prospective recruits was the promise of some good meals in the immediate future and liberal pay in Governor Rutledge's nearly worthless South Carolina "Proclamation scrip." Apparently, what counted most with these prospective troopers was a solemn promise that when, as, and if Loyalist properties were seized, everyone would receive a fair share in the resultant plunder.

So, on this dreary morning Barry Colcord could congratulate himself on leading, exclusive of his brother and himself, a force of forty-one tolerably well-mounted and physically able men.

After some rearming and re-equipping in various directions, the Ricelands Rangers, granted an opportunity to learn some drill and rudimentary maneuvers, might develop into a useful unit.

During the two-day ride from Cobb's Mill the slowly growing Troop had overtaken disorganized bands of volunteers. For the most part these foot soldiers were clad in rough civilian clothes and otherwise were miserably equipped; on a few occasions, however, Barry's little column had seen soldierly-looking, blue-uniformed units which, to his no great surprise, had proved to be detachments of Virginia or South Carolina Continental regiments plodding doggedly through the mud on their way to Charles Town.

Towards midday the Troop, riding in the usual column of twos, neared a crossroads beside which a pair of discouraged-looking vedettes in rain-soaked capes were slouching in their saddles. Off to the left, as Barry knew through long experience, lay Governor Edward Rutledge's mansion, a handsome, white-porticoed structure of red brick effectively revealed against a background of moss-hung live oaks.

Gentle pressure by Colcord's knees sufficed to set Eclipse trotting to the Troop's head in time to halt his command on the main road, at present flanked on both sides by deep ditches overflowing into adjacent tobacco fields.

One of the vedettes was wearing a hussar's busby covered in ratty-looking fur and a frogged, once-brilliant blue uniform. When he splashed by the other vedette, a wiry, short-legged fellow whose pointed, yellow-brown features suggested a fox's mask, he was offered a vague salute.

Barry glared. "You can do better than that!"

The fellow stared, then stiffened and offered a regular's crisp salute, which Colcord returned with equal precision.

"I'm in search of Colonel Moylan's cavalry regiment. Where is it?"

The hussar's sloping shoulders rose under his long and mud-splashed cape as he replied in an unintelligible language which Barry, through his service before Savannah, reckoned must be Polish — there had been a lot of Poles among the French and other foreigners in Count Pulaski's Legion. The hussar crooked a finger to his companion, who under his cape was wearing the dark-brown-and-red shell jacket of Colonel Daniel Horry's South Carolina Light Dragoons.

"Sorry, suh, he's jest another dumb ferriner. Kin I he'p you?"

"I'm looking for Moylan's Regiment. He commands the Virginia Continental Light Horse, I believe."

"Yessuh, but he's went into Charles Town; rode off early this mornin'." The dragoon brushed a beading of crystalling raindrops from the visor of a weather-beaten leather helmet before tilting his head towards the driveway leading to the Governor's mansion. "Howsumever, the most of his men is camped over yander."

"Who's in command around here?"

"Why, right now, suh, 'tis Cunnel Washin'ton, but they do say Gen'ral Huger —" he pronounced the name "Hew-gee" — "will soon come to take over."

"You are referring to Colonel William Washington?"

"Yessuh."

"Where is he?"

"On a mean day like this reckon you'll find him holed up in the big house."

When Colcord led his volunteers off the highway his followers straightened in their saddles and in dull curiosity began to look about them.

To veterans like Sergeant Gavin Wilcox and Corporals Skene and Peete, the fairly extensive encampment scattered about fields on either side of the driveway appeared entirely familiar. There were the usual rows of weather-beaten tents among which fires built with wet wood smoked and steamed, and low, canvas-covered piles of fodder. Near cooking fires protected from rain by tarpaulins a squad of bloodied men were busy butchering the carcass of a black-and-white cow. Beyond the tents, long lines of dejected-looking, blanketless horses stood drowsing at the end of halter shanks attached to picket lines which had been stretched tautly between the trunks of tall, arrow-straight, long-leaf pines.

Rob splashed up alongside. "Say, Bro, looks like that old tobacco shed over yonder and slave quarters behind it ain't occupied. Suppose I lead the boys over and take possession while we've the opportunity — they're pretty cold and weary and would be the better for a bait of hot food." He grinned. "Know *I* would."

"All right. I'll go try and find out what we're to do."

Accompanied by grizzled and hollow-cheeked Corporal Skene, Barry continued to follow the driveway. His gamecocks, in little wicker cages protected by specially designed canvas covers, clucked indignantly when he dismounted and handed his reins to Skene, then made his way up to the portico under which a pair of dragoons, wearing black leather helmets and long gray watch cloaks, saluted smartly with heavy, curved sabers and allowed that, "Sho 'nuff, Cunnel Washin'ton is inside."

From a side room appeared an attractively ugly young officer who inquired the visitor's business and, on being informed, led off with spurs jingling along a tessellated floor of black-and-white marble, the once-gleaming surface of which had become sadly scarred and filmed by dirt and debris.

Of the four officers who, with tunics unbuttoned and sashes loosened, were seated around a card table before the fireplace of Governor Rutledge's library, Barry at once recognized two: one was that hard-bitten veteran, Lieutenant-Colonel George Baylor, shrewd and generally successful commander of Baylor's Virginia Light Horse; the other was a short, almost boyishly slender officer clad in the dashing sky-blue, silver-frogged and fur-trimmed hussar uniform of the late Count Casimir Pulaski's Legion. This he knew was the redoubtable — and easily excited — Major Vernier who more than once had distinguished himself in action before Savannah by making reckless, headlong charges. Although a Frenchman, Vernier affected the typically Polish powdered braids which swayed to either side of a scarred, red-brown face. Barry remembered that Paul Vernier spoke tolerably good English and generally affected an air of tolerant *ennui*.

Barry clicked muddied brass spurs, then pulled off his helmet, tucked it in the crook of his left arm, bowed and addressed a big-bodied, broad-shouldered individual who had a long straight nose and the same bold, aggressive jaw as his Cousin George. "Colonel Washington, sir?"

Deliberately, Washington finished his play, then faced his cards before looking up. "Well, sir, and what might your business be?"

Once Colcord stiffly had reported his troop's arrival, the Colonel smiled while reaching for a delicately etched brandy glass that appeared to be engulfed by his powerful, brown hand. "Delighted to welcome you among us, Captain. 'Tain't every day we receive a well-mounted troop led by experienced officers — and more's the pity. Sorry Moylan ain't around right now, but, in any case, I wouldn't assign you to him. Too many other regiments are seriously under strength."

Washington's big, dark-brown head swung to his left. "Captain Colcord, meet Colonel Horry — Daniel Horry." He elevated a quizzical brow. "You won't object to serving under a fellow South Carolinian, eh?"

Colonel Horry, who'd undone his neck cloth and looked to be feeling better for a few brandies, arose to offer a hairy fist. Some time ago he must have taken a saber slash across the face; there was a deep nick in the bridge of his nose and his left cheek was almost caved in. He grinned like a friendly dog. "How do, Captain Colcord. You're more than welcome to my command; what with one thing or another, my regiment right now has less than a hundred men ready and able to ride against the enemy."

Colonel William Washington gestured towards the fireplace. "Shed that damn' wet cloak and go stand over there. We've enough puddles in here already." Next, he shouted for an orderly to bring in another glass, after which he held out a squat brandy bottle which, if the thickness of the dust coating it meant anything, must be of respectable age.

Once a secretary had prepared orders enrolling the Ricelands Troop — Colcord quietly requested that it be so designated — into the service of the State of South Carolina, Washington over one shoulder bellowed for his aide. "Walker! Write requisitions for such rations, blankets and fodder as Captain Colcord may need for the moment. We'll see about arms and other equipment when and if that damn' supply train ever arrives from Charles Town."

He glanced at Barry, warming his hands before the flames. "Anything else you stand in immediate need of, Captain?"

Hesitantly, lest he appeared to be crowding his luck, Barry mentioned the need of sufficient cloth to uniform his men — at least from the waist up.

Queried Major Vernier, twirling his brandy glass, "Why this urgency to uniform your men?"

"Well, sir, I feel it's important if I'm to maintain the kind of discipline I want." He smiled faintly. "As you know, Major, uniforms help build and maintain discipline."

"*Mais oui*. Of a certainty, uniforms help."

Colonel Baylor grinned at the hussar officer. "What with your presently reduced numbers, Paul, I presume you might spare our friend sufficient tunics?"

The Frenchman parted long, expressive hands. "*Oui*. That is possible, *mon ami*, but *hélas*, they are certain to prove much too small for your tall American bumpkins. They always have."

"In that case," Colonel Washington said, "Captain Colcord, you'd better go in town tomorrow and see what cloth — if any — you can come across." His wide, thin-lipped mouth spread in a brief smile. "Oh, by the way, tell Mr. Walker that I expect you and your brother to mess with me until further notice."

In an obvious gesture of dismissal the commandant of General Lincoln's cavalry picked up his cards; his companions also returned their attention to the game.

6. *Threatened City*

FOR all that the morning dawned silver-dimmed by fog and posing the threat of continued rain, Lieutenant Robert Colcord was feeling, as his brother was fond of putting it, "as happy as a flea in a fox's ear." Noticing everything of significance, Rob rode past those inadequate raw earthworks which had been thrown up so hastily last summer when General Augustine Prevost's small army of British regulars reinforced by hundreds of Tories had threatened to capture Charles Town.

The muddy, deeply rutted highroad was crowded by a vast variety of traffic moving slowly in both directions: driven cattle, pedestrians, horsemen and troops. In addition there were forage wagons, civilian vehicles of all sorts and even pieces of limbered artillery drawn by six horses which kept looming eerily out of the sour, ever-shifting mist that reeked of mud flats and swamps. A pity this fog continued so impenetrable; heretofore, Rob invariably enjoyed viewing the wonderfully slim and graceful white steeples of St. Philip's and St. Michael's; today, he could barely discern the outlines of houses less than a block away.

Once he reined Hector into Broad Street Rob commenced a systematic canvass of draper's and clothier's shops, but invariably, proprietors shook their heads, mumbling, "Sorry, sir. Got sold of all yard goods long ago." This remained the usual reply until one said, "Might have some, sir, once they've auctioned the cargoes of those transports our cruisers prized last week, but there ain't no telling what kind of cloth it might be or of what color."

How considerate of dear old Barry to send him in town in his stead, saying that there were many requisitions to be filled and important information to be gleaned at Cavalry headquarters. Brother Barry, of course, had sensed that he just might be eager to catch another glimpse of Amelia Trefont, that lovely young girl who'd been completely orphaned because her mother had perished of smallpox only a few weeks before her father had been killed during Sir Henry Clinton's first siege of the city during '76.

Uncle William, a distant relative of Amelia's father, generously had taken the girl under his roof, ostensibly as a companion for seventeen-year-old Betsey, that child of his later years whose bearing had cost him his wife's life.

While on duty in Charles Town the previous summer, Rob at first had taken only a passing interest in the gay young orphan with the gently oval features, curly red-gold tresses and wide, pale-blue eyes, but, gradually, he'd come to pay her more heed; not that he'd advanced beyond the formal kissing of her hand. But just once, on the eve of his departure to join the Allied armies besieging Savannah, he'd lightly kissed her cheek. Even so, the aspect of pert little Amelia Trefont had the trick of appearing, unbidden, in his mind's eye; especially when he was about to waken or to go to sleep.

Dark-haired and self-centered Cousin Betsey, however, remained in his estimation just another saucy, empty-headed chit who, as he laughingly maintained, should have been drowned at birth.

Twice, he had to steady his tall, dappled-gray hunter when groups of drunken sailors off the feeble little squadron of privateers and Continental men-of-war presently anchored off Battery Point came reeling and yelling out of grog shops and taverns. Fog-veiled Broad Street continued to be obstructed by creaking wains, carts and covered wagons laden with every imaginable sort of freight.

After turning into Church Street, the broad-shouldered young officer continued riding towards Battery Point, on which stood Uncle William's familiar and quietly elegant white-trimmed brick dwelling. Arriving before the Colcord residence he reined left down a short, cobbled drive towards a pretty little garden which, in a few weeks time, again would burst into a symphony of carefully planned color. How smart of the Charlestonians to ensure privacy by building their homes with the public rooms facing towards the side or the rear, safely removed from the street's dirt and noise.

Seizing an elaborate silver knocker which, in happier times, had had the name Colcord engraved upon it in flowing script by a famous London silversmith, he knocked loudly, because Uncle William's venerable butler, Euripides, recently had grown very hard of hearing. The gleaming white door, therefore, was drawn back with commendable promptness. "Why, Mistuh Rob! Do please come in, suh. Sho' is one measly day, ain't it? Dey's a blaze in de library, suh. Better you go in dere."

Bowing continually, Euripides backed indoors, reporting that his owner had gone out to attend a meeting of the Fellowship Society.

"Yassuh. Jes' wait a little; Massa gen'rally come home to eat, lessen —" the butler grinned, blinked rheumy, yellowish eyes — "lessen Massa doan stop at Misto' Strickland's tavern."

A tinkle of feminine voices upstairs caused the caller to raise his brows in unspoken query.

"De young Mist'is an' Miz Amelia is busy fixin' up fo' a socialable."

Rob handed the Negro his mud-spattered cloak and then a long-peaked forester's hat of green felt. "Pray inform the ladies that I am below and would be pleased for an opportunity to offer my respects."

Euripides bowed once more, obviously proud of a brand-new livery of canary yellow long-skirted coat, red-striped waistcoat and pewter-buckled nankeen knee breeches, then murmured, "Would Massa Rob enjoy a drink of somethin' warmin'?"

Rob laughed. "I've always believed, Euripides, you enjoy second sight. What d'you recommend by way of a libation?"

"Well, suh, dey's some right tasty arrack what was fotched in by a privateer last week. It do mek a lively toddy, suh."

" 'Do it'? Good. That will be fine; but, mind you don't spare cinnamon and cloves — always providing there still are any."

Heaving a grateful sigh, Rob collapsed onto rather than seated himself in a worn but wonderfully comfortable wing chair upholstered in Turkey-red leather. Sighing, he then unbuttoned the lower buttons of his tunic while gazing about this musty-smelling but subtly companionable little room which he'd always enjoyed.

Following a time-honored rite, he nodded solemnly three times to a dusty marble bust of Virgil occupying a pediment above the library's entrance. The big young man yawned, then stretched lazily. God's love! How absurd for supposedly civilized people to get so mad at one another that they'd voluntarily leave such comforts behind and go off to the miseries of war!

On a small table beside him he noticed a copy of the *Gazette of the State of South Carolina* now reduced to a single sheet of coarse, grayish-white paper. Idly, he noted it was dated February 9, 1780. While the room's warmth gradually commenced to penetrate his damp and sour-smelling garments, Rob picked up the *Gazette* and scanned its contents.

A notice attracted his attention:

> Peter Muzon of Bay Street has for Sale a Number of Pipes of exceeding good Madeira and a few Dozens of best Batavia Arrack.

Um. Barry must hear about this Madeira at once. God send it hadn't already been sold!

Next he read that:

> Mr. Pierre Lafitau-Gimon intends to leave the State beginning March next. He desires all Indebted to him to Pay, those to who he Owes to Call upon him and Receive their Respective Dues.

Another item caught his eye:

> Married, Edw'd Davies, Esq., to Miss Rebecca Lloyd, d. of Thos. Lloyd — a most amiable Young Lady.

Disinterestedly, his gaze drifted on until he encountered an announcement that:

The Continental Ships of War, *Providence* and *Ranger*, and tender, *Eagle*, have return'd from a Cruize of Tybee where they encounter'd 5 Brit. ships at Anchor & 3 other Ships under sail. They prized two Sloops, *Revenge* and *Henry*, which were on their Way to Ga. from N.Y. Captured: 14 Officers, 32 other Ranks belonging to Lord Cathcart's Light Dragoons, Passengers & much Horse Furniture.

Hum. Undoubtedly this would be the source of that cloth and the liquors he'd heard about. In rising curiosity Rob wondered in what strength the enemy had landed on low-lying Johns Island across Charles Town's spacious harbor. Rumors heard in Colonel Washington's headquarters had it that Sir Henry Clinton's army numbered anywhere from five to ten thousand and just recently had captured the all-important Stono Ferry which linked Johns and James Islands. The latter island, being higher, larger, and lying much closer to the threatened city, would, once siege batteries were raised, present a deadly menace, for from there Charles Town lay within easy range of heavy guns and even of some field pieces.

Frowning, he went over to peer out of the window and judged that the fog must be lifting because now a pallid yellow radiance was gilding the withered lawn and leafless rose trees looking so forlorn in Uncle William's garden.

From somewhere in the distance came a sudden, dry-sounding rattle of musketry which, after a moment's reflection, failed to alarm Rob. Many units, in hopes of making tolerably good marksmen out of new men, were given to target practice at odd hours.

The screech and whine of ungreased axles and the *clip-clop* of hoofs on Church Street became less noticeable once Euripides fetched in a pineapple-shaped carafe of pale yellow arrack together with a plate of spices, lemon peel and a copper pot of steaming hot water.

"De young ladies send wu'd, suh, dey soon be down." The slave's liver-colored lips twitched. "Reckon you knows, Massa Robert, dat 'soon' don't mean 'di-rekly'."

"Ah yes. Tardiness is a feminine failing — and privilege, I presume. At least they think so."

Before leaving, the old Negro went over to place more logs on the fire, but, being damp, they hissed and steamed a good while before reluctantly taking fire.

To savor its fragrance Rob held the steaming toddy under his nose before taking a swallow and allowing its heat to warm his belly. He was conjecturing whether Amelia Trefont might have matured a bit since he'd last seen her, when the front door knocker banged insistently. At a quick shuffle the butler hurried to draw a pair of brass bolts; in these uncertain times no Charlestonian in his right mind ever left any ground-level door unlocked — even during the daylight — as he would have during those blissful, almost forgotten years of peace.

Rob guessed who was causing all that racket even before a deep voice boomed, "Beelzebub's balls! A fine to-do when a man has to wait in the wet outside his own home! Damn you, Rip, why're you so slow answering? Rheumatics worse?"

"Nossuh, Massa Tom, Ah come de quickest Ah could."

"Bah! Trees grow faster than you move these days."

"Tom!" Rob surged to his feet and ran out into the hall to fling arms about his favorite first cousin, who was nearly of the same age and was about as big-framed as himself; he also had the same weathered look and his red-faced, blue uniform reeked just as pungently of horses and wet leather.

Delightedly, Tom beat upon Rob's shoulder blades. "By God, this *is* a wonderful surprise!"

"When did you get back from the frozen North?"

Tom finally ceased pounding his cousin's back. "Less than a week ago. When spies told Light-Horse Harry that Clinton was collectin' troops and ships fo' a Southern campaign he let me go on detached duty — indefinitely."

"Good thing. How is Colonel Lee these days?"

"Busy as a fox in a forest fire and still the best cavalry leader we've got on our side — barrin' Francis Marion, of course."

Once Rob had mixed Tom an arrack toddy and a second for himself, the long-legged cousins fetched chairs up to the fire. After a considerable exchange of news concerning births and deaths among relatives and friends and an account of the formation of the Ricelands Troop, Tom abruptly abandoned his light manner and looked his brown-clad cousin steadily in the eye. "You've heard how many men the Redcoat generals already have brought against us?"

"Only hearsay. As I said, we only reported in to Billy Washington's headquarters yesterday. What can you tell me?"

"Plenty. I've just left a staff meeting at General Lincoln's headquarters. Oh, by the way, I've only today been assigned to duty with Colonel Theodorick Bland's regiment. They say he's a real piss-cutter."

"Well, to return to the subject, it's been reliably reported that Clinton and Cornwallis right now have with 'em at least six thousand of the King's regular Establishment and near twenty-five hundred Northern Tories they've brought down from New York, New Jersey and Pennsylvania — real mean fellows by all accounts — and lots more are reported to be on their way South."

The dark-faced young man hunched forward, elbows on knees and locked fingers around his glass. "When you add these numbers to General Patterson's regulars, who are due from Savannah any day now, you'll appreciate our side's up against one hell of a lot of excellently trained and equipped troops. Worse still, strong reinforcements under Lord Rawdon are on their way from New York. And so far I've not even mentioned their naval forces."

"When's Rawdon supposed to arrive?"

"It's anybody's guess."

Rob, by rubbing his chin, caused a soft rasping sound. "How many men-of-war do the Lobsterbacks have on hand?"

Beneath chestnut-colored bristles Tom Colcord's chapped and concave cheeks flattened. "At headquarters just now they circulated a tally." He fumbled in a side pocket and pulled out a crumpled sheet of paper. "Here's my copy. Read it, my lad, and weep."

Frowning, Rob scanned the names of an awesome number of ships-of-the-line headed by Vice-Admiral Mariot Arbuthnot's gigantic flagship, *Romulus*; ten frigates also were identified, along with a depressingly long list of brigs, sloops, bomb ketches and transports. The fleet presently anchored off Johns Island numbered well over a hundred vessels mounting at least a thousand cannon of varying weights and ranges.

" 'Twould appear," Tom remarked while employing a jack to remove sodden knee boots, "that Messrs. Clinton and Arbuthnot — don't you admire that name? — are in sufficient strength not only to blockade this port tighter than a bull's ass in fly time but also to blow our pitiful little squadron to kingdom come. Then they'll be free to come in to bombard the hell out of this port."

Rob frowned over his half-consumed toddy. "And what do we have to oppose this armada?"

His cousin pulled out a second piece of paper. "Very few real men-of-war of any consequence. Our best are vessels bought from the French when they pulled out from Savannah last year." He wrinkled his brow, read on. "Well, there's the *Bricole*, a forty-four-carriage-gun frigate, the *Queen of France*, a twenty-eight-gun sloop, *La Truite* carries twenty-six pieces, the brig *Notre Dame* with sixteen, and then there are one or two small craft which mount about a dozen cannon between 'em."

"And what do we have for American-built ships?"

"Says here, the *Providence*, and the *Boston*, both sloops carryin' thirty-two guns; the *Adventure*, a brig mounts twenty-six; the *General Lincoln* and the *Ranger* are schooners which together mount around twenty old cannon."

A spark snapped out of the fireplace; Tom yelped when he tried to extinguish it with a stockinged foot.

"Who commands our squadron?"

"Commodore Whipple, a lanky, blue-nosed Yankee."

On a brass fender enclosing the fireplace Rob absently scraped a curd of black muck from his boot. "What about Whipple?"

"They say he's both able and brave and so far has had a fine record. Be that as it may, all you've got to do is contrast the weight of broadsides on each side and you'll appreciate how hopeless Whipple's position is. What makes it especially bad for him is that his rag-tag crews are made up of ex-smugglers and privateersmen — rascals who won't put their hearts into a fight 'less there's enough prize money in the offin'."

Once the cousins had refilled glasses and packed yellow Maryland tobacco in yard-of-clay pipes lifted from a mahogany rack above the hearth, they reseated themselves.

After a while Rob asked through a cloud of smoke, "What sort of horses do they breed up north — in Pennsylvania, I mean?"

"Hardly any thoroughbreds exceptin' around Philadelphia; aside from that, they only rear heavy-boned farm stock or saddle horses we wouldn't even look at twice." Tom pursed weather-cracked lips to expel a perfect circle of gray-blue smoke. "Yes. Harry Lee's been very hard put to mount his men even reasonably well." He sighed. "What few good animals there were got swept up by British and Tory raiders early in seventy-seven."

Tom further eased his short-skirted, blue-and-buff cavalry jacket revealing a light blue waistcoat lacking several buttons. "By the bye, speakin' of raiders, have you heard that that devil, Banastre Tarleton, is reported to be among the officers Clinton's brought from New York?"

The harsh quality which entered his cousin's voice caused Rob to elevate an eyebrow. "And who, pray, is Banastre Tarleton?"

A grating laugh escaped Tom. "Seems he's a young, hell-for-leather, damn-all London rake who at present is supposed to be servin' with Lord Cathcart's Light Dragoons. He's brimful of ambition, a first-rate tactician and a magnificent swordsman — but he's got no more sense of honor in a bedroom than on a battlefield."

"Meaning —?"

"Captured officers report that, whenever opportunity offers, this Tarleton fellow will bed a brother officer's wife or mistress quick as a buck rabbit and never mind the consequences.

"Nevertheless, the 'Green Dragoon,' as they call him up North, is a darin' and a successful leader. Seems he's got boundless energy and is so ruthless he's been known to saber a surrendered man rather than bother to take him prisoner. He took a major part in that horrible massacre of Mad Anthony Wayne's men at Paoli."

"Paoli?"

"It's a hamlet near Brandywine in Pennsylvania.

"Nevertheless, Light-Horse Harry swears Tarleton's the best cavalry leader on either side."

Tom took a long swallow of his toddy. "Wish to God we'd Tarleton fighting against the Crown. He's a remarkable man, no matter what you think of him.

"Can you imagine it? He's barely twenty-six, yet, without benefit of influence at Court, he's been promoted from cornet to lieutenant-colonel in less than two years! There's no doubtin' that his havin' played a big part in the capture of our eccentric General Charles Lee in New Jersey had much to do with so amazin' an advancement."

Rob was about to inquire the whereabouts of Bland's Horse when light footsteps and a sibilant swishing of skirts and petticoats sounded on the hall staircase a moment before plump little Betsey Colcord ran in with a jauntily flowered bonnet bobbing from its ribbon ties over her shoulders. Dark eyes lighting, she flung arms wide and, skirts flying, rushed towards her cousin. "Oh, Cudd'n Rob! What a *wonderful*, wonderful surprise!"

Because Betsey was only a young sixteen Rob felt it still proper to catch her in a bear hug, sweep her clear of the floor, then kiss her resoundingly on both cheeks.

Set down, she burst into a torrent of questions. "How is Cudd'n

Barry? And Uncle Frederick and Juno? Has she had more puppies? If she has, may I have one?"

Tom groaned in derisive disapproval. "Try to forgive her, Rob! I fear the brat won't ever learn manners. Too bad she's too big to spank — used to be lots of fun."

All at once Tom checked his ribaldry and offered a slight "leg" when into the library floated a slight, straight-backed figure clad in mint green taffety which contrasted effectively with short, reddish-gold curls bunched to either side of pale, gently oval features.

"And how are we today, Amelia — Mistress Trefont, I mean."

Rob released his cousin and hurriedly attempted to recover a measure of dignity before offering the Trefont girl a bow infinitely more courteous than Tom's. She made a graceful little curtsy and lowered her gaze as became a well-bred young lady, then she looked him full in the face and summoned a bright smile. " 'Tis fine indeed to see you looking so well, Mister Colcord," she murmured, happily unconscious of the banality of her words.

He was right. By God! Amelia Trefont's eyes *were* a baffling shade of greenish-blue and the passage of half a year had done quite a bit towards filling out her bodice. But what a tiny thing Amelia remained. Even on tiptoe she couldn't stand above five feet. Suddenly he knew now how to describe her complexion — it was the delicate pinkish-white of newly burst apple blossoms.

"Good day to you, sir." She merely tilted her nose in Tom's direction. She didn't much like Betsey's brother; he was such a clumsy tease and never would take anything she said or did in the least seriously. Besides, the big oaf invariably reeked of sweat, horses and liquor of some kind.

"Mercy!" giggled Betsey, setting straight her bonnet. "I declare, Cudd'n Rob, you look even handsomer and more distinguished than ever."

" 'Out of the mouths of babes and sucklin's,' " Rob laughed without removing his eyes from Amelia. "Tell me, where are you young ladies going in such a flutter?"

Betsey whirled a light camlet cloak about her shoulders. "Oh, dear! We must leave for Mistress Mazyck's this very minute! She and her friends there are going to teach us how to tear bandages, pick lint and fashion pledgets."

"Lawd! Lawd! Such serious work for dainty hands," grunted Tom, then stalked over to the fireplace and used tongs designed for the purpose to relight his yard-of-clay with a coal from the grate.

Full skirts a-sway, Amelia swirled up to Rob, who suddenly wished his tunic weren't quite so badly wrinkled and stained. "And, sir, how have you fared since we last met?"

"Barry and I had a hard time following that awful whipping Pat Ferguson and Colonel Prevost handed us at Briar Creek. We were very lucky to escape with enough men to keep on campaigning till the New Year, when we were ordered to disband."

"— And how is Cudd'n 'Gustus?" Characteristically, Betsey refused to keep quiet even for a moment. "He's much the nicest of all of you at Tranquility. 'Gustus is quiet and polite, even to a silly little chit like me."

Relaxing, but with his attention still on Amelia, Rob went on to describe how, just before Christmas, his older brother had been stricken and become bedridden by a severe attack of fever taken while riding in the swamps after Briar Creek. No, 'Gustus hadn't recovered sufficiently to go along when he and Barry had left home, but, undoubtedly, with the return of warm weather he'd be able to take the field again.

Amelia's long lashes fluttered several times before she peered almost boldly up at Rob's broad, red-brown features, then said a little breathlessly, "Will you excuse me a moment? I'll be right back."

She departed running upstairs with unladylike speed and returned almost immediately carrying his brass helmet in one hand and a short, emerald-green ostrich plume in the other.

"Amelia!" burst out Tom's sister. "How dare you to be so — so bold!"

"You see, I noticed that that pretty, bright helmet of yours is lacking a plume." Smooth cheeks flushed, she said hurriedly, "So I wonder whether you would care to wear this until you find a more suitable one?"

Good Lord, thought Rob, in Horry's Horse an officer's plume is supposed to be either yellow or dark blue. Nevertheless, he bowed, smiled and spoke softly, "I shall be most honored to wear your gift, Miss Trefont. Since I deem this a lovely lady's favor, I trust you will put your plume in place?"

Cousin Tom snickered in the background. Rob cast him a warning look. Good God, couldn't he appreciate that this girl was entirely in earnest and quite unaware of the implications of her act?

Once the bright green feather's quill had been well seated in a short, brazen tube, Amelia, holding out the garnished helmet, offered it with a bright but tremulous smile that Rob wouldn't forget in a hurry.

"Miss Trefont, please accept my earnest thanks. I — I hope that I shall always wear this with honor."

Beelzebub's balls! thought Tom, that kitten's got her claws sunk into poor old Rob quick and deep.

On the driveway sounded a soft rasping of iron tires, whereupon Euripides shuffled in to announce that the ladies' chariot was ready and waiting.

"Do you expect to be stationed around Charles Town awhile, Mister Colcord?" demanded Amelia, gracefully raising the hood on her cloak. "There is so much I — I want to hear about — and this is such a pokey little visit."

"There's no telling, ma'am, but be sure that I'll return as soon as possible. I must pay my respects to Uncle William, you know," he added hurriedly, then flushed. "I will try to send word in advance."

Again the Trefont girl considered him steadily while little dimples appeared to either side of a naturally sensuous mouth to create a right triangle with a third in the center of her chin. "Indeed, sir, I shall anticipate such an occasion." She returned to her ridiculously formal manner. "And I'm sure Betsey will, too."

"Oh, for heaven's sake, 'Melia, do come along! We're already terribly late and I really *must* find time for a chat with Sally Colleton and her mother." She flashed a gleaming smile at Rob. "They're *ever* so genteel."

"Maybe so," grunted Tom, leaning resignedly with one elbow on the mantlepiece, "but everyone around here knows Sir John Colleton's just another damn' King-lover."

Betsey flared right up. "That may be true, my dear brother, but nevertheless, Sir John remains a true son of South Carolina. Nobody can truthfully say he's taken part in any Tory activity."

Tom inquired acidly — he didn't like to hear of any relation of his defending a Loyalist — "Why are you so all-fired eager to gab with Lady Colleton?"

Hurriedly, Amelia broke in, "Why, Tom, 'tis this way. Lady C. has kindly invited us to visit at Fair Lawn and keep Sally company if — well, just in case Charles Town grows too — too crowded to be safe, or if —"

"— Or if the Redcoats start to bombard us," snapped the lieutenant of Horry's Horse, "which they're surely goin' to do just as soon as they complete their batteries across the Ashley. 'Twon't be over-healthy here once they start."

Tom interjected, "Well, let's hope we can dislodge 'em before that happens, but if we fail, you should hurry out to the Colletons. You'd be a lot safer there."

Amid a soft flurry of skirts Betsey pecked Rob on the cheek, then stuck out her tongue at her brother before disappearing into the hall. Amelia, however, lingered long enough to offer the men a hurried curtsy before she, too, disappeared.

Once the dull *clunk!* of the chaise door closing was heard Tom grinned and stripped off his tunic, which he tossed onto a couch before referring again to the arrack bottle. "Ain't female relations, 'specially fillies like those, a real plague out of Egypt? Expect the Good Lord inflicted 'em on families just to remind 'em life ain't to be a continual round of pleasure."

Rob relit his pipe, puffed comfortably, then drawled, "Speaking of families, Tom, maybe you don't know it, but, come a couple of months or so, Laura aims to make me an uncle again."

Tom clapped his cousin's shoulder. "Now, ain't that *somethin'*? Pray convey my congratulations to Barry; he always was a capable lad on the cornhusks. I'll stop by Harper's tomorrow and pick up a silver christening cup or maybe a porringer — always provided the old rascal's still got any. How's Laura takin' to this second time around? Came through well enough the first time, near as I can remember."

With toddy glass halfway to his lips Tom said, "Speakin' of your sister-in-law, funny thing happened this morning; thought I spied one of her brothers on my way home, but it was so foggy I couldn't be sure."

"Which one did you think you saw?" Rob demanded, experiencing sudden, sharp anxiety.

"Damn' if I can recall his name, but seems to me I saw him at Barry's weddin'."

"What's he look like?"

"Got a red face, jug ears and badly bowed legs."

Rob was at pains to keep his voice casual despite the cold current which began to descend his spine. "'You got a *good* look at him?"

"No. 'Twas too foggy and we got lost in the crowd before I'd time to take a second look." Tom frowned and tugged an ear lobe. "All the same, I almost vow that the man I saw was one of Barry's groomsmen. Still remember he wore a kilt and side whiskers that sprouted almost down to his chin — you know, like those wild Scots fresh from the Old Country we used to see around here once in a while. What *is* his name?"

"If he's really the man you saw he'd be Colin MacDonald, Laura's next-to-youngest brother. How was he dressed?"

"Like a backcountry horse jobber, wearin' a long, linen smock coat, durant britches, cowhide boots and a big, wide-brimmed hat. Last I saw of him he was makin' fo' Jacob Volk's tavern, where as you know, slave dealers, vendue masters, horse buyers and other rascals of that kidney like to hang out."

Rob kept on questioning until he became regretfully convinced, although he didn't say so, that unless some amazing resemblance was accountable, his fire-eating Loyalist brother-in-law must be in town. If it really had been Colin, what would bring him to Charles Town at just this time? Rob masked his uneasiness by changing the subject to the Madeira he'd seen advertised in the state *Gazette*.

"You mean that lot at Peter Muzon's? Well, you'll be glad to hear that Pa's bought some and finds it so good he's put aside some pipes for Barry and Uncle Frederick."

When at the end of an hour Uncle William still had failed to put in an appearance, Rob regretfully drained the last of his arrack, called for his horse and made ready to depart. "You'll ride out to see us, eh, Tom? Barry would be that pleased!"

"Sure 'nough. Where are you?"

"Bivouacked on the Governor's property — but how long we'll stay there I've no idea. Come over real soon and fetch along some of those measly gamecocks you're always bragging on. Might fix up a main and do a little serious drinkin'."

The sun had begun to peer timidly through high gray overcast but plenty of puddles remained on the unpaved streets when Rob Colcord dismounted at a hitching post in a crowded and evil-smelling little square before Jake Volk's hostlery; judging by the number of wheeled vehicles and saddled or barebacked horses in sight that fat old German must be doing a rushing trade.

There could be no doubt that Colin MacDonald in his role of horse dealer — if indeed it was he — had been shrewd enough to select the most logical place in which to stay.

In Volk's big taproom scarcely a uniform was to be seen, only rough, smelly and bearded or long-unshaven fellows wearing clumsy boots, manure-splashed ankle-long coats or calfskin jerkins that had hair still on them.

Not wishing to attract attention through queries, the tall young dragoon gradually circulated in the crowd, his eyes stung by billows of rank tobacco smoke and acrid fumes escaping from a huge fireplace to one side of which a spotted spit-dog was trotting on a small, loudly clacking treadmill that caused a leg of lamb to revolve, dripping, on a spit.

He was about ready to question one of the hard-working barkeepers as to whether anyone fitting Colin's description had lodgings here when, momentarily, the jam of patrons parted and afforded him an opportunity to decide that, beyond a doubt, Colin MacDonald, red face, side whiskers and all, was sitting alone in a far corner. He was nursing a battered pewter beer mug between his hands and listening to all that was being said about him.

Rob lingered a moment, realized that, for all his raw-beef complexion, angular features and huge ears, Colin wasn't really at all bad-looking; his mouth was generously wide and well formed while his blue eyes were clear, wide-spaced and steady.

Taking care to blend with the shoving, hawking and spitting crowd, Rob backed away feeling as sick as if he'd had much too much to drink. Poor Barry.

7. *Brother-in-Law*

ON learning that Laura's Tory brother had been seen in Volk's Tavern, Barry Colcord seemed to age by ten years. Almost desperately he repeated, "Are you *sure?* How good a look did you get?

"Volk's place *was* pretty smoky and crowded, but I got close enough to swear in court that the man I saw danced at your wedding."

"But did you see him on his feet? Colin is bowlegged as all get out. Without seeing that, there's still room for doubt, isn't there?"

"He was sitting," Rob admitted, while staring out of their tent into the lantern-dotted dusk. "Didn't want him to notice me so I didn't linger; I just took one long, hard look then eased back into the crowd."

Barry gnawed his lip. "How much d'you recall about Colin at my wedding? All kinds of strangers were there, remember? God knows how many of Laura's kinfolk were among 'em. Besides, as I recall," he smiled faintly, "nobody at Tranquility was even halfway sober — you and me included." With a note of desperation in his tone he pleaded, "Ain't it possible you might have been mistaken?"

Rob shook his well-formed head. "Anything's possible, of course, but I'd recognize those bright blue eyes and jutting cheek bones of his anywhere." The younger brother's voice hardened, "And that being that, what's to be done about him? You and I and a lot of others *know* Colin's a red-hot Tory, along with his father and most of his kin."

Fixedly, Barry stared at the tent's trampled groundcloth and sighed. "True enough. If Colin's in Charles Town and wearing civilian clothes, there's only one explanation. We both know what it is, but before I make a move I'll have to find sure proof of what he's up to."

Rob felt desperately sorry for his brother; why couldn't he think of something clever to say or do to help him? Too bad that he'd never been anywhere near as quick-witted as either 'Gustus or Barry.

At length, Barry got up, said heavily, "If Colin's guilty, he's got to be arrested and turned over to the provost's men."

"— Who won't waste any time in stretching his thick Scotch neck."

Barry caught up a cape and hat and strode out at the same time yelling for Black Buck to saddle Eclipse and for Sergeant Wilcox to ready himself to ride into town in short order.

On nearing Volk's Tavern they stabled their horses in a public stable situated across the small square.

While easing cinches amid ammonia-tinctured gloom Barry spoke quietly, "Wilcox, I've brought you along because I'm about to tackle a most delicate matter and I take you for a man who can hold his tongue."

The sheep-faced sergeant backed out of the stall, grunting, "Aye, sir, I've never been called a blabbermouth."

"Good. Now remember this. You're to say nothing about whatever may happen in Volk's. Got a pistol?"

"No sir. Ain't yet come across one."

"Then take this saddle gun."

"How about you, sir?"

Barry touched a side pocket, tested the outlines of an elegant little pocket pistol he'd won at cards from a French officer during the Siege of Savannah. "I'm armed, Sergeant. Now let's get going."

As expected, they found the inn's ground floor jam-packed with noisy, scruffy-looking patrons. When a cautious reconnoitering of the taproom revealed no sign of the man Barry was dreading to find, he consulted the innkeeper's blowsy wife who, seated behind a sort of low pulpit, was attempting to make change out of a wild variety of currencies. Until Barry placed a silver shilling before her she remained disinterested in his inquiries, but then she became cooperative.

Aye. To be sure, a Scottish-talking gentleman with bushy side whiskers and bowed legs had taken up lodgings about two days ago, but, she stroked a perceptible mustache, the guest's name had been Charles Mac-Donnel — not Colin MacDonald. Aye. She remembered the tenant clearly because, for a horse dealer, he'd talked uncommon polite and was ready to spend a tidy sum to secure all to himself a tiny room with a cot, rather than share a comfortable wide bed with two other patrons. Mr. MacDonnel's room, she informed, was Number 12 and situated under the eaves on the top floor.

Just before they started to climb a set of narrow and very steep stairs Barry was struck by a sudden inspiration, so sought the bar where, for an outrageous price, he succeeded in purchasing a half-bottle of dark and violent-smelling Demerera rum. Halfway upstairs Barry paused, said softly, "Now Wilcox, since I'm about to enter a possibly dangerous situation, I don't wish the gentleman I'm seeking to take alarm, so from now on, try to put your feet down exactly when I do. He mustn't suspect that more than one man is mounting these stairs. Once we reach the top landing you'll wait very quietly outside the door and make no move unless I call out."

By the half-light he watched Wilcox's cavernous pale eyes narrow in concentration as he whispered, "That I'll do, sir."

"After I've gone inside you're not to allow anyone to enter Number 12, not even a chambermaid or a pot boy."

Once the sergeant's gaunt and shadowy figure had taken post, Barry rapped on the greasy panels before him and, by listening hard, heard faint rustling sounds before a deep voice called, "Who's yon?"

"Barry Colcord."

"Barry!" More noises as of a piece of furniture being quickly moved. "What in the wor-rld brings ye here?"

Barry experienced a ghastly sinking feeling; beyond the shadow of a doubt Laura's brother was inside.

"My brother, Rob, thought he glimpsed you downstairs this afternoon and told me about it. Since I was coming in town anyhow I thought I'd find out if it really was you he saw." He felt his heart hammering as it had not since that forlorn charge at Briar Creek. "It's been such a damn' long time since we last saw each other, I thought I'd bring a bottle and stop in for a chat."

"Losh, mon, come in and be welcome." Colin's voice sounded hearty and untroubled.

The door swung back, disclosing a dingy little room feebly illumined by a pair of smoky and bad-smelling mutton-fat dips which stood jammed into tarnished brass candlesticks.

Colin offered a hard hand. "Come in! Come in, laddie." He stepped back, linen smock coat swaying gently. " 'Tis a waesome time since I've seen or hear-rd aught of you or Laura." The bandy-legged Scot's big rich voice sounded completely natural.

Once the two had gripped hands as if it were the most natural thing in the world, Colin grinned and with his toe shoved forward a three-legged stool. "Wull, wull, Barry, 'tis fine to see ye again. What's that ye've got in yon bottle?"

"Demerera I bought downstairs, so I don't know whether 'tis tolerably good or not fit to wash a pig with." Barry passed over his gift, which Colin deftly uncorked with his teeth before tilting the thick, mahogany-red liquor into a pair of earthenware teacups lacking handles. Wisely, he added generous measures of water from a cracked pitcher. While his brother-in-law was thus occupied, Barry stole a quick glance at a thin pile of papers on the squalid chamber's only table. He decided that they consisted only of receipts, invoices, and dog-eared bills of sale.

Warily, Colin's brilliant blue eyes bored through the feeble candle-light. "And how was my sister-r the last you saw of her?"

"Well enough, for all she's getting ready to present me with another heir before long." He relaxed a trifle. "Sorry you've not yet been to see our little Patrick and the new home I'm finishing." He raised his cup and was surprised to find his hand so steady. "Well, here's to old times. May we soon live in peace again."

"Aye. Yon's a bonny toast to which I'll drink wi' pleasure."

Next Colin inquired casually into the health of Barry's father and that of Rob and Augustus. The Scot's manner continued disingenuous even if, as Barry suspected, he must be wondering how and why his brother-in-law had penetrated his crude alias and had looked him up.

While the fiery raw rum burned its way down to his stomach Barry drawled, "Oh, by the way, about a fortnight ago a traveler from your part of North Carolina stopped by my place. I wasn't there, but Laura told me he brought news of your family."

Almost imperceptibly alertness entered Colin's manner. "Aye? And what had he to say?"

"Among other matters he reported that your youngest brother, Bruce," Barry said slowly and distinctly, "has gone to enroll in the First North Carolina Continentals."

Colin's bold features turned a darker shade of red and his eyes grew white-ringed as, violently, he shook his head. "Nay! Brucie would ne'er do such a thing whilst the rest of us —"

Barry straightened suddenly. "— While the rest of you damn' Tories support the King!"

Colin glared and started to snarl something but, by exerting a mighty effort, managed to control himself and finally said, quietly enough, "Aye, Barry, ye're right! Most of us MacDonalds *are* loyal tae the King, but as for-r meself, I've not yet made up my mind on that question." At best a transparent liar, Colin didn't sound in the least convincing. "In the meantime I've come here tae buy mounts big enough tae carry dragoons and such are verra difficult to come by as, nae doot, ye ken well enough."

Briefly, Barry wondered what Wilcox was making of all this; of course he couldn't help but overhear all that was being said. He fought down an impulse to inquire bluntly into the intended destination of Colin's purchases but ended by asking calmly, "Mind if I glance at the list of animals you've already bought? Might find some suitable for my troop; God alone knows how badly we need such remounts." He tossed off the last of his rum, set down his cup and picked up the papers.

"How many animals have you bought so far?"

"Aboot a dozen."

"If you'll sell me some, I'll give you better than fair prices."

Some of the bandy-legged Scot's alarm subsided. "How d'ye pay?"

"I've still some silver and a few gold pieces Pa's lent me."

Although a film of fine perspiration was breaking out on Colin's bony forehead, he nodded almost too readily. "Verra well. Meet me here tomorrow morn and you shall have yer pick. After all, are ye no' family?"

"This is most handsome of you," Barry smiled, then refilled their cups. "So, Colin, suppose we drink to American liberty?"

Colin nodded and raised his cup to his lips, but only wetted them and didn't swallow a drop.

Thinking furiously, Barry settled back onto his stool. "Too bad you couldn't find more comfortable accommodations. The vermin must be fierce in a rat hole like this."

"That they are, laddie, but the town's full to overflowing, so if a body wants privacy he canna afford to be choosy."

For a little while they continued to talk generalities, while an indefinable tension mounted. Barry said at last, "I just heard on the street that General Patterson has come up from Savannah to join Clinton at Stono."

"What's his strength?" Colin asked eagerly.

"They say he's got with him two thousand regulars of the line and about five hundred of the British Legion's infantry."

"The British Legion?" Colin queried. "Ain't that Colonel Tarleton's command?"

"So we've heard."

On the grimy wall behind him Colin's shadow mimicked his nod. "Oh, so ye've heard of him? D'ye ken that Tarleton's reputed tae be as fiery and deceitful as auld Clootie himself?" In his enthusiasm the Scot lost all sense of discretion and his Highland burr thickened. " 'Tis reported he lost all his heavy horses on the voyage doon from New York, so, Barry me lad, yer cavalry will have to look alive else they'll find the Green Dragoon helping himself to yer picket lines."

Re-experiencing a curious buzzing sensation in his fingertips which usually manifested itself during tense situations, Barry returned his attention to a paper's end he'd noticed protruding from the pocket of a riding cloak hung to a peg let into the dormer window's side. Sipping all the while, he crossed as if to peer out the window into the court below, then plucked what appeared to be a printed map from the cloak.

Instantly, Colin roared, "Damn you! Leave that be! Ha'e ye no respect for a mon's private papers?" He plunged forward, but not before Barry had seen that what he held was a map of Charles Town Neck liberally marked by inked-in symbols and blocks of handwriting.

"Sorry you object to my glancing at this," rasped Barry, at the same time dropping a hand into his side pocket. "I've never before seen so accurate — and interesting — a map of this town. I feel it shouldn't be kept from the provost."

"Damnation! Gi'e me that!" snarled Laura's brother. He snatched up a heavy brass candlestick and sent its candle flying across the room while he started forward. But even as Colin's hand closed around the candle holder, Barry jerked out his pocket pistol and held it level with his brother-in-law's belly. "Hold where you are! If this map's meaningless, you've no cause to get excited."

Glaring furiously, Colin checked his advance to assume a half-crouch which lowered his hands almost to a level with his knees, where a flash of brass winked in a woolen stocking's top just above his clumsy drover's boots.

Barry snapped in a low but carrying voice, "Wilcox! Come in here!"

Instantly the door swung inwards and Wilcox ran in, the saddle pistol cocked and ready. "Yes, sir?"

"Sergeant, cover the gentleman whilst I take a better look at this map. If he makes the least move, shoot him!"

"Och! This is a kerlish, Sassenach way to treat yer own wife's kin. Laura'll be verra proud o' ye!" Colin protested in a furious undertone and appeared to be gathering for a spring but straightened when he felt the muzzle of Wilcox's weapon driven into the small of his back.

With quivering hands Barry held Colin's map to the remaining candle and was sickened to note how accurately the positions of various new batteries and earthworks defending the peninsula had been sketched. Behind each gun emplacement was listed the number and weight of the cannons it contained. As further and completely damning evidence, the names and strengths of newly arrived American regiments, as well as their present encampments, had been listed on blank spaces in the map.

Dear God! What *can* I do? How will Laura take it when she hears, as surely she will, that I personally caught Colin spying and turned him over to the provost marshal's men for hanging?

As if appreciating his brother-in-law's dilemma, Colin relaxed somewhat, said with an uncertain grin, "Losh, Barry, ye're not going to let the Rebels hang a mon who's doing naught but what his conscience dictates?"

Barry, standing taller than ever amid the dim candlelight, hesitated a long instant while this musty-smelling room seemed to shrink until its walls appeared ready to crush him. He ended by catching his breath with a little *click*. "Wilcox! Back the prisoner against the far wall, lay your pistol on the table, then wait outside till I call."

"But — but, sir, is that wise? This here feller's desperate. Just look at him!"

"Do as I say!"

Once the door had closed, not quite completely, Barry sighted along his pistol's barrel at young MacDonald's blazing blue eyes.

"What in God's name are ye up to?" Colin muttered. "Ye're not going to shoot me down in cold blood?"

"No. Even though I swing for it I'm about to grant you a chance to escape hanging; after all, you *are* my wife's brother. Now listen carefully. When I give the order, you'll advance *slowly* toward the table until you stand six feet short of it. Then halt. See that you do exactly what I say. Now 'tis for you to decide whether I turn you over to the provost's men or we settle this business in a more genteel fashion."

The silence became electric. For some reason the blurred undertone of voices rising from the taproom reminded Wilcox, waiting miserably on the landing, of the rumble of swells beating against a distant seashore.

"What are ye up to?" Colin repeated, while almost imperceptibly commencing to resume that stooping position which allowed his unusually long arms to dangle even with his knees.

Barry directed in a cold, hard voice, "When I tell you, you will advance to within six feet of the table. Then I will place my pistol on the table with the other and retreat a similar distance. This done, I will begin a count of three. After the word 'three' we will both try to seize a pistol and find out who's quickest and the best shot."

Beginning to quiver like a leashed bird dog which scents game, Colin demanded hoarsely, "And if I win, what aboot yer kerl ootside?"

"You still will have a loaded pistol while Wilcox has none. An you're not able to escape with such an advantage you don't deserve to." He stood straighter than ever, demanded tautly, "Well, Colin, what's your decision?"

"Aye. I'll fight yer daft duel."

Unhurriedly, Barry placed his weapon beside the saddle gun, then backed away until he and the Scot stood equidistant from the little candlelit table.

Urgently, Wilcox called. "Please don't sir! 'Tis not right that you should —"

"Be still! And stay out!" Laura's husband balanced himself on the balls of his feet, dark eyes riveted on his antagonist.

"Ready?"

"Aye." The young Scot had begun to breathe hard, as if he'd just finished a long foot race.

"One! Two!" Barry was about to complete the count when, with incredible speed, Colin MacDonald stooped, snatched a slender Highland dirk from his stocking's top and sent it flashing past the candle.

When he lunged for his pistol and fired point-blank, the grimy little chamber became vividly revealed for an eternal instant and Barry felt a tap on his shoulder. His own weapon's report, intensified by confinement, deafened and dizzied him. While he swayed, coughing hard amid blinding billows of acrid fumes, he heard, but did not see, his brother-in-law crash onto the floor.

Wilcox dashed in, pale eyes wide. "My God, sir! Are you hit?"

"No. See how he is." Ears ringing painfully, Barry in a detached sort of way watched his sergeant drop onto one knee and bend low over the Scot's motionless form.

Wilcox peered up through the drifting smoke. "He's stone dead, sir!"

8. *First of the Green Dragoon*

DURING the month which followed the arrival of the Ricelands Troop — as the unit now had become designated officially — the Colcord brothers did not endlessly drill their men or scheme for supplies in vain. Few cavalry units under General Benjamin Lincoln's command could boast a comparable improvement. Further, the troop had been recruited, selectively, to a strength of seventy enlisted men, which made it one of the largest on duty in the vicinity of Charles Town.

Through cultivating the friendship of Major Paul Vernier, commanding the remaining cavalry of Count Pulaski's Legion, Barry obtained arms and equipment impossible to come by elsewhere, for, at the Siege of Savannah, he'd noticed that the Polish nobleman's forces had been excellently well equipped.

In quite another fashion, Rob's skill in the frequent cockfights and games of whist and faro at Headquarters paid off in the form of saddles, bridles, blankets and other horse furniture.

From his Uncle William, Barry secured sufficient funds to purchase a number of good horses, some of which, ironically enough, had been collected by Colin MacDonald — whose death never was mentioned in the family. Through an understanding with the provost marshal, it was given out that one Charles MacDonnel had been killed in a brawl among horse traders who, as everyone knew, were a parcel of tricky and unpredictable rascals — especially when drinking.

To top things off, Barry finally had come across an ample supply of fine duck sailcloth brought in by the last privateer able to pierce Admiral Arbuthnot's now impenetrable blockade. Next, the Troop commander searched until he found a dyer who could and would stain the tough white material a weatherfast butternut brown.

Once the Troop's new jackets had been faced with white duck out of the same lot and ornamented with some of the late Count Pulaski's buttons, the Ricelanders strutted about, mighty proud of uniforms which wouldn't have won any praise from a competent military tailor.

The Colcord brothers were hard put to keep straight faces when for the first time the Ricelands Troop paraded in the new finery; their boots and breeches remained so hopelessly civilian. Some men were wearing dented French dragoon helmets of brass, others had donned fur-covered hussar busbies which, being too small as a rule, rode high on unruly shocks of oily shoulder-long hair. At least half of the troopers still clung to the shapeless, broad-brimmed felt hats they'd worn when leaving home. Some of the younger men, however, had attempted to smarten up such headgear by pinning the brim up on one side by means of a cockade which might be of any color.

By now the Troop had become comparatively well armed: cumbersome long-barreled muskets and fowling pieces had gradually been replaced by short-barreled carbines or naval blunderbusses. At short range the latter weapons had a murderous effect — and were infinitely easier to handle on horseback. In addition, all troopers by now had been issued either a sword or a saber of some description, but few of these were supported by proper frogs or slings; they dangled loosely secured by rawhide whangs and straps to any convenient part of a rider's saddle.

The Colcords even became cautiously optimistic about the Ricelanders' future efficiency — especially since they'd secured the services of a veteran drill sergeant borrowed from Colonel Moylan. This tobacco-squirting martinet used bursts of inspired profanity to instruct these gangling and ruggedly independent fellows in the rudiments of close-order cavalry drill, plus a few simple evolutions likely to prove useful in combat.

In a clean new tent presented by Colonel Horry, the brothers were enjoying French brandy laced with icy spring water and poured over sugar and crushed mint leaves — now that winter was over no ice was to be had for love or money. This delectable drink Major Vernier called a "jelappe," which potion, he declared, had been well and favorably known in Normandy since the Middle Ages.

An orderly came galloping up to the Troop's bivouac near Lieutenant-Governor Thomas Bee's modestly attractive residence on the Ashley's west bank. Without dismounting, the red-faced rider shouted that Colonel Horry wanted the Ricelands Troop prepared to ride inside of an hour.

Since Black Buck had not yet unsaddled the captain's mare after the afternoon's drill period, Barry soon came cantering up to the Lieutenant-Governor's ivy-covered mansion. Just inside, he encountered Colonel Horry, whose eyes were bright with excitement.

"Glad ye've reported so promptly," Horry observed in his curiously high-pitched voice. "Most of our people are off on patrol."

An aide hurried up. "Gentlemen, General Huger and Colonel Washington present their compliments, and will you please come with me?"

They hurried into Thomas Bee's pine-paneled study to find the general and several of his staff questioning a mud-splashed cornet of Bland's Regiment who looked as if he'd just been hauled backwards through a bramble-filled swamp.

Absently, General Huger was stroking a strong, deeply cleft jaw while Colonel Washington, with brow furrowed, riffled through a sheaf of morning reports.

The general wasted no time. "G' day, gentlemen. Mr. Boyle, here, has just fetched in intelligence of considerable significance which is to the effect that Sir Henry Clinton's main force is advancing in this direction behind a screen of British and Tory cavalry commanded by that same Colonel Tarleton who surprised and cut up Boyle's outpost on the Edisto two days ago. Boyle was taken prisoner but managed to escape last night. Mr. Boyle, pray convey your information to these gentlemen."

Wearily, the ex-prisoner passed the back of a dirty, thorn-raked hand over a forehead smeared with black swamp muck and addressed Horry. "Sir, I was held under guard close by Colonel Tarleton's tent, so close in fact that, just before I got away, I overhead plans being made for a raid on Sir Toby Gascoyne's stud farm with the object of seizing as many tall horses as possible."

Colonel Horry looked startled. "Why should they do that? I've always deemed Sir Toby as an avowed neutral."

Colonel Washington's big, white-wigged head inclined. "So he is.

Nevertheless, Sir Toby is about to suffer the usual fate of a neutral — which is to get hurt by both sides."

Daniel Horry cast a quick glance at the pale and hollow-eyed cornet. "Did you form any impression of when the enemy expects to call on Sir Toby?"

The slim youth, who looked as if he had neither slept nor eaten in many hours, swayed a little but continued to stand at attention. "Sir, I can't be sure, but my guess is that the raid will take place sometime this afternoon. Colonel Tarleton was most insistent that no time be lost in securing remounts."

General Huger arched heavy, iron-gray brows and demanded crisply, "Mr. Boyle, approximately how far from here does this stud farm lie?"

"Sorry, sir. Not being from these parts, I wouldn't know."

Colonel Horry spoke up. "Sir Toby's property lies on the Edisto Ferry Road about ten miles away."

"That's good," snapped the general. "Horry, see that every effort is made to cut off Tarleton's retreat. Every tall horse that falls into enemy hands will cost us dear. I'm told Tarleton is determined to capture animals strong enough to carry those big dragoons he's brought down from New York."

Well within the stipulated time, the Ricelands Troop, reinforced by two half-troops from Colonel Moylan's Light Cavalry Regiment, set out at a trot along a rough track which ran in a southeasterly direction through piney woods over flat and uninteresting country.

That anxiety was evident among his newer men Barry observed without comment. Apparently they were coming to realize that at last they were riding towards a fight in which men were going to get killed. Loud-mouthed bragging dwindled, then ceased.

The Colcord brothers now rode tight-lipped, wondering what their untried followers would do once bullets began flying in two directions. Possibly some of them were beginning to wish that they hadn't been so reluctant about learning to use those long sabers now clinking and rattling by their sides.

It seemed difficult to realize that Death was lurking somewhere among these sunlit, early spring woods in which wild cherry, dogwood and Judas tree buds were beginning to burst. Migrating songbirds — towhees, tanagers, bluebirds, cardinals and an infinite variety of warblers whistled and sang while flitting from tree to tree but Sergeant Gavin Wilcox noticed them not at all. He was again experiencing a gradual tightening of muscles crisscrossing his lean belly. The veteran was devoting disapproving attention to the noisy and haphazard fashion in which Lieutenant Ballard and the men from Moylan's regiment were advancing in a wavering line of skirmishers through myrtle and honeysuckle tangles and around stands of holly and red-trunked slash pine. Here and there a cottontail rabbit or an occasional deer would bound away with white stern flashing.

The afternoon continued so uncommonly warm and lovely that Barry felt prompted to jump Eclipse over a series of fallen logs. Grinning, Rob spurred Hector and followed his brother's example.

According to a moon-faced tenant farmer who'd been forced, most unwillingly, to act as guide, raiders retreating from Sir Toby's stud farm would be likely to follow a little-used woods road which led northeast towards Goose Creek, where, according to Colonel Horry, the enemy's advance guard had halted in order to allow General Clinton's main body time to come up.

Barry, having recovered from his burst of exuberance, fixed the guide with a hard look. "How far to this road?"

"Why, sir, 'tain't but a half-mile further on," the guide informed, all the while glancing nervously about. Least of all, he was liking a certain gleam in Private Black Buck's narrow jet eyes. "Ye'll come on it before long. It curves around a low, woody ridge which you ought to reach, easy, afore the raiders come up. If ye're nippy about it, ye can hit him sidewise. Now kin I leave? Got to get home by milkin' time; got two heifers come fresh this week."

"You can go when we find the road, my friend, and then with my most sincere thanks. Black Buck, ride on ahead and see what you can see before all this racket we're making alarms the enemy."

Presently, Barry arm-signaled a halt, then, with newly burnished helmet a-gleam in dappled sunlight, rode over to confer with chunky little Lieutenant Ballard, who appeared anxious and not at all sure either of himself or of his troopers.

After issuing detailed instructions, Barry showed his silver whistle. "Now remember, Mr. Ballard, at all costs keep your men quiet till I sound this. After they've fired a volley, they're to mount and charge with the saber down onto the road. Make 'em whoop and yell like the Devil was after 'em."

When, finally, the mustee rode back to report that the road lay not far ahead, the cavalry deployed along the crest of a low, thickly wooded ridge, then dismounted, unevenly spaced for the sake of cover. Just behind and below the ridge crest stood knots of horse holders, each man holding four animals in addition to his own.

Barry was encouraged to see how effectively Rob, his green plume jauntily a-sway, along with Wilcox, Skene, Peete and other veterans, steadied troopers, reminded them that after they'd fired the first and only volley they'd have time for they must mount quickly, draw sabers and charge, making all the noise they could.

While Private Black Buck, his wrinkled features devoid of expression, expertly soothed Eclipse a few yards behind him, Barry eased himself into the depths of a clump of holly already bright with shiny new leaves and was cautiously thrusting the branches aside to see better when the mustee hissed and pointed to the right. An instant later the captain thought he heard faint sounds coming from that direction. Softly, he cursed, because a squirrel had started to chatter furiously somewhere down the road.

Soon the faint jangle of curb chains, the clink of iron stirrups colliding and a low and continuous thudding made by many hoofs became clearly audible. Veterans among the ambushers wriggled as flat as they could amid the underbrush, then checked flints before snugging carbine stocks tight against their shoulders. Sweating in streams, green men followed their example.

In Rob's imagination eons seemed to elapse before a knot of men wearing forest-green jackets and black-crested helmets banded with brown fur trotted briskly into sight around a bend in the road. That the enemy's point was alert Rob appreciated at once and felt his mouth beginning to go dry, as it usually did in anticipation of a fight. The point kept peering carefully at both sides of this narrow sunlit track.

The raiders' advance guard now appeared riding four-abreast carrying their carbines with brass-shod butts supported upon their hips.

Moments later the main body rode into sight; they were big men who mostly were wearing green, but there were a few scarlet jackets among them, also a number of men in drab-hued civilian clothes. These last, Rob decided, must be local Loyalists who'd just joined up and hadn't yet found time to get into uniform. Behind them appeared a single figure. Short but powerfully built, he was wearing a Lincoln-green dragoon tunic, buckskin breeches, glossy knee boots and a brass helmet resplendently crested in white-and-crimson horsehair.

The stallion this solitary rider bestrode was the most magnificent piece of horseflesh Rob had sighted in a very long time. By God, that thoroughbred down there must stand well over seventeen hands!

There was something about yonder officer's erect, almost arrogant posture in the saddle as he trotted nearer which instantly attracted and held Barry Colcord's attention. Now the smoothly posting figure drew near enough for the ambusher to make out light-brown side whiskers sweeping down almost to the point of a short and almost femininely rounded jaw. Barry couldn't tell anything about the other's eyes, they being hidden below the helmet's visor. Just the same, he felt certain that Lieutenant-Colonel Banastre Tarleton, the Green Dragoon, was riding into pistol range.

A few yards in Tarleton's rear rode half a dozen officers, all high-ranking individuals were one to judge by the amount of gold and silver lace adorning their tunics of scarlet and green. Fleetingly, Rob was reminded of a clump of sugar maples he'd seen last fall while campaigning up North.

Fervently praying that his still uncertainly disciplined troopers would keep quiet and otherwise obey orders, Barry grinned widely when, through a haze of dust, he sighted a small herd of riderless and unsaddled horses being driven between outriders covering either flank. The Ricelands Troop's captain made a hurried count of the captured horses and estimated that around ten or fifteen fine animals were drawing near.

The knot of officers riding a few horses' lengths behind Tarleton trotted nearer to an accompaniment of softly creaking saddles and stirrup leathers.

Barry waited for the enemy's point to pass Ballard's end of the ambush and at the same time marveled why some woodswise Tory among the raiders hadn't taken alarm at the racket raised by that fool squirrel; a homegrown Britisher, of course, couldn't be expected to notice such a sign. Once the raiders' rear guard began to round the bend Colcord clapped the whistle between his teeth, drew a deep breath and aimed a long-barreled saddle pistol at the nearest officer before sounding three shrill, ear-piercing blasts. He fired, but even before the ponderous weapon roared and its recoil jolted his arm clear up to the shoulder, he sensed that he'd missed. Meanwhile the ridge, for a distance of two hundred yards, bloomed with puffs of woolly gray-white smoke. The reports of small arms firing a ragged volley sounded like a gigantic pile of dry brushwood set afire. Beyond a curtain of burnt powder smoke sounded the wild trampling of hoofs followed by yells, shouts and the screams of wounded men and horses.

Without delaying to learn what might be happening on the woods road Barry dashed back, grabbed his reins from the mustee and swung into the saddle bellowing, "Draw sa-a-bers! Charge! At 'em, Ricelands — keep on yelling!"

As he kicked forward his horse, Black Buck threw back his head and raised a heart-stopping scalp yell: *"Whoop! Whoop! Hi ya-a-h. Yah!"*

While his mare buck-jumped down the slope Barry jerked out his sword, caused a rasping *zweep!* as he spurred Eclipse at Colonel Tarleton's small figure.

Although his stallion had begun to lash out with its forefeet, the Green Dragoon was standing in his stirrups, kept shouting like a maniac for his men to stand firm, all the while making a glittering windmill of his sword blade.

Indescribable confusion prevailed upon the road. Everywhere, horses were neighing, rearing, plunging and bumping into each other. To the ringing clash of meeting blades and a barking of horse pistols, more saddles became emptied.

Ignoring pistol balls that hissed past, Barry lay out on the mare's neck, bunched his weight behind his sword point and aimed at that muscular little officer with the brown side whiskers.

Barry wasn't two horses' lengths short of his target when, out of dust clouds raised by the mêlée, dashed a wounded trooper who charged into him and sent Eclipse staggering off balance for a few strides. Despite everything Barry kept his attention on Tarleton's long-nosed face, now become visible beneath his visor.

Correcting his aim, Barry yelled, "At you, sir!"

Tarleton heard. Baring his teeth, the Green Dragoon swung his charger about, whirled his blade high above his head, then spurred to meet his attacker. All the while Tarleton kept screaming for his men to rally.

Only a split second before Barry counted on driving home his point, a wild-eyed riderless horse blundered into his opponent and knocked him aside at the critical moment. Before the Carolinian could manage to wheel, a tangle of cursing, slashing, stabbing men became interposed.

When next he sighted the Green Dragoon it was to see him galloping towards the head of his column all the while striking at his men with the flat of his sword and shrieking for them to stand fast.

But the retreat wasn't to be checked. British and Tories alike bent over their horses' necks and, raking their flanks with bloody spurs, thundered away in the direction of Goose Creek, leaving the road littered with equipment, dead men and groaning wounded.

Rob had the good sense not to chase very far and returned to set his and Ballard's men to rounding up loose horses after they'd secured a handful of dazed and scowling prisoners. Among these was a gorgeously uniformed officer who turned out to be a Lieutenant-Colonel Hamilton. Disgustedly, this haughty fellow admitted belonging to Sir Henry Clinton's military "family" — a member of that general's personal staff.

A quick tally revealed the cheering fact that not one American had been killed or seriously hurt! What especially delighted Barry was the fact that neither his Ricelanders nor the men of Ballard's troop had panicked. In fact, the outcome of this brisk little skirmish proved so amazingly satisfactory that Barry Colcord felt prompted, later on, to dance a jig and get gloriously drunk with his brother.

9. Letter to Laura

AFTER hunting up a piece of planking for a desk Captain Barry Colcord seated himself, rested his back against a tree and braced for the ordeal of penning a letter; his writing always had been deplorable, while his spelling had been the despair of every schoolmaster under whom he'd smarted. Brow furrowed, he unscrewed the small leaden ink bottle he used in preparing reports and other official documents. Laboriously, he then used his penknife to shape a new point on his quill but paused to cast a look at the fast-darkening afternoon sky; briefly, he debated whether he might not justifiably postpone the letter, but the call of duty prevailed, so after smoothing a sheet of foolscap on his improvised desk, he scribbled painfully:

> Munk's Corner,
> S. Carolina
> 13th Aprill, 1780

Respect'd Madam:

I trust by this time you rec'd my last Letter in witch I enformed you of the Tragickall death of yr. bro. Colin in a Tavern fight in Charles Town. I hope, my Deerist, you have not been undully Greeved but How sad it is to think of such a Fine yung Man cut down in the very Flour of yuth.

Nearly 3 Weeks have passed since I last wrotte you and what a Tragickall 3 Weeks theese have been.

Our ennemies are said to Nummer above 10,000 Men now and only 2 days ago succeeded in crossing the Ashley and are now on Charles Town Neck ware they are throwing up Earthwurks at a furius rayte.

Worse News piles up on the Bad. 2 days ago a scoutt-Sloop out of Georgetowne sightted a strong Fleet of Ennemy Men of Warr with many Transportts saling towards Charles Towne. This is thought to be Lord Rawdon bringing neer 3,000 more Reglars to join Gen'al Clinton in the Seege. Theese, added to the 10,000 men already under Sir Henry's Command, plus 5,000 Seemen makes a very formidibel Force for our little Garrison to stand off — Gen'l Lincoln has only 2700 Contintal Soldiers and about the same number of Millitia who may, or may Not be Dipendable! We, the Cavalry that is, have been drove back untill now Wee are camped near Munk's Corner wich lyes about 30 myles above the Towne.

We have nearbye 2 small Reg'ts of Infantrie garding Biggen Bridge. Everyone is in low Spirrits because iff Gen'l Lincoln is to save our last reel Army in the South he must *Retreat at Once!* whilst wee still can keep open a lyne of Retreat for him to the Cooper River Crossings. This is a verry difficult feet, thanks to the Acktivittys of that devill-on-Horseback, Colonel Tarelton who seams to have now found sootable Mounts for all his Men.

I am pleezed to say our Troop maintains its Discipline and Courage. My Bro, as usuall, is a Very Tower of Strengthth.

We howrly expect to engage Tarleton who is reliable Reportted to be sumwhere in the Vicinity and in grate strengtht. Would to God wee knew just where he is!

Momentarily, Barry raised eyes to watch a tall and neatly dressed mulatto go galloping by on the road to Charles Town. He had no difficulty in recognizing the rider as Cudjo Jim, General Huger's trusted mulatto body slave. He thought, yonder perhaps goes the last man who stands a chance of winning through to the city.

He shifted his gaze to watch Black Buck grooming Eclipse, which, with Rob's gray, stood tethered apart from the rest of the Troop's mounts, at present drowsing along a picket line tautly stretched between stout trees.

After unnecessarily flexing already smudged fingers, Barry resumed:

My thots are so offen with you, Deer Hart, especiall because I know yr Tyme is growing close. Oh, this currsed, currsed warre! which keeps me from yr side att this Tyme.

How is Papa? Is 'Gustus any Bettar now? I hope they will be verry wachful for thanks to Gen'l Clinton's Advance, all Torries and otherwise disaffeckted Persons are taking Hart.

How are Juno's puppys turning out? Rob has promised One to our Cousin Betsey. How is Planting going forward in the new field? I trustte Papa's Overseare is making sure that itt is.

When a shadow crossed his letter he glanced up to find Sergeant Wilcox standing at a respectful distance with his long sheep's face set in a mighty anxious expression. After saluting, he broke out, "Sir, I just returned with the watering detail and I feel you better hear about something that happened down by the stream."

Glad to be relieved of penning, Barry nodded. "What was it? You've never been one to bark at a knothole."

Gilded by the sunset the ungainly, semi-bald figure looked uneasy. "Sir, you remember that time up to Cobb's Mill when that Tory got tarred and feathered?"

Barry stuck the quill over one ear. "Yes. 'Twas a fellow called George Walker if I remember right. What about it?"

Wilcox forgot himself long enough to scratch vigorously under his new dark-brown tunic. "Well, sir, just as we was finishing watering I chanced to look across the stream and saw, not thirty yards off, a trooper in a green jacket sitting his horse on a little knoll, bold as brass. How long he might have been there I got no idea; might ha' been quite a while 'cause he was pretty well disguised among the trees and bushes."

"What makes you think that that fellow you saw may have been Walker?"

"Because like I said, sir, he weren't far off and I got a good, long look at him. At first sight I thought he looked kind of familiar." Wilcox paused to ease his saber's sling. "And then he was wearing a dark patch over his left eye. Remember what that peddler said, sir? That was the eye that Tory got gouged out during his tar and feathering."

"Yes. I recall his telling about it," Barry said getting to his feet and stoppering his ink bottle. "Did you give chase?"

An unhappy expression appeared on Wilcox's weather-beaten features. "We tried to, sir, but by the time me and a couple of the boys got across the stream the feller had faded back into a thick woods. We looked everywheres but couldn't find no sign of him. Think likely, sir, he was a enemy scout?"

"Seems entirely likely," Barry admitted and gratefully dropped his piece of plank. "Come along. Headquarters ought to hear about this."

While hurrying to his tent he folded his letter, then buckled on his sword and snatched up his helmet. At the same time he yelled for the mustee to saddle Eclipse.

Twenty minutes later, hot and breathless, the master of Ricelands was demanding an interview with the cavalry commander. He found General Huger in heated conference with his staff. Perpetually haggard and sallow from recurrent malaria, he cut them short, then curtly demanded Colcord's errand. Although still red-faced and short-tempered, the commanding officer kept quiet long enough to hear an account of Wilcox's experience.

A tall, one-eyed major glared at Colcord. "Impossible! The enemy *can't* possibly be scouting this far north! More likely 'twas just some deserter or straggler of ours your man saw. Remember, sir," he turned to Isaac Huger, "plenty of our units are wearing green these days — Baylor's Fourth Troop, for instance."

The general turned on George Baylor, snapping, "That correct?"

"Aye, sir. My Fourth troop have green jackets turned up in red."

"Was this fellow wearing red facings?" sharply demanded Colonel Washington.

"I don't know, sir. Wilcox didn't say. But —"

"— So your man may have been mistaken," growled Colonel Horry. "Still I think —"

"Oh hell!" persisted the one-eyed major. "Not even Tarleton can possibly have advanced so close! Why, only this noon he was reported bivouacked near the siege lines, which, as we all know, lie thirty-odd miles away!"

"Nevertheless," Colonel Horry pointed out acidly, "the fellow disappeared when the sergeant and his men crossed the stream."

"If he was a straggler or a deserter he wouldn't be apt to linger, would he?"

"Be that as it may," Horry insisted, "seems to me the better part of wisdom is to order our pickets and patrols to be advanced a good distance in the direction of Charles Town."

Colonel Washington rapped an angry curse and changed the subject. "Oh, to hell with such trifles! What I want to know is why Ben

Lincoln doesn't get off his fat arse and get to hell out of Charles Town
sometime tonight. Tomorrow will be his last opportunity to save his
neck. After that 'twill be too late. If only he weren't keeping back the
North Carolina and Virginia Continental Line — the only real soldiers
we've got left. God! To think of those veterans penned up like sheep
behind those feeble earthworks."

With hands slapping each other behind his back, General Huger took
a short turn over the Red Hart taproom's bricked floor — that rough and
ready little tavern recently pre-empted by his adjutant. Grimly, Huger
halted and faced his staff.

"Gentlemen, please believe that I've done everything possible to persuade our commander-in-chief that he *must* abandon the town at once!
This same afternoon I have written to emphasize his dire peril, and to
encourage him, I described the location of our supporting patrols as well
as the disposition and strength of my forces." Angrily, Huger flung up
his hands. "Yes. Not an hour ago I sent my servant, Cudjo Jim, to him."

"My God, sir," cut in Baylor, "you didn't entrust such a message to a
nigger?"

"Yes, I did, because I figured that being black he'd stand a better
chance of getting by any British patrols he might encounter.

"To add weight to my plea I requested Major Vernier, here, to add
the warning of a veteran campaigner."

Paul Vernier vigorously inclined his narrow, dark head. "*Mais oui.* I
wrote to *le général,* begging him in the name of common sense to retreat
at once, while he can. Also I advised him that only for a short time
longer will we be able to keep open his route to the river crossings. *Nom
de Dieu!*"

Everyone in the crowded, smoke-filled taproom, thought Barry, looked
as gloomy and depressed as if he'd lost his last friend. They would, however, have appeared infinitely more anxious had they known that, at this
very moment, Cudjo Jim, General Huger's dispatches and all, was being
hustled into the presence of Lieutenant-Colonel Banastre Tarleton.

10. Monck's Corner

BARRY Colcord's dream was a jumbled but frighteningly realistic reconstruction of the Battle of Moore's Creek Bridge. In awful clarity he heard once more the sharp, vicious crackle of musketry, the thunderous roar of cannon and, more particularly, the eldritch wails of bagpipes and nerve-crisping shrieks from the wounded.

He heard again Campbell's kilted Highlanders screaming "King George and the Broadswords!" as they launched their valiant, foredoomed charge across the bridge's naked stringers. Again, all the world seemed to be staring eyes and red, wide-open mouths lurching through the battle smoke.

God above! *This was no dream!* Convulsively, the Ricelands Troop's commander flung aside his blankets and sat up. By the brilliant blue-white starlight he glimpsed a black, shifting pattern of half-seen figures eddying confusedly among the tents. Then arose a gale of frightened howls, curses and shouted commands, followed immediately by the *boom! bang!* of heavy horse pistols going off interspersed by the sharper sounding *crack! crack!* of carbines.

Out of the shadowy woods appeared a wave of screeching, saber-swinging cavalry who charged headlong into the encampment and began slashing and pistoling down their half-awakened and hopelessly confused enemies.

Coatless and stocking-footed, Barry had barely time to snatch up his sheathed sword in one hand and his French pocket pistol in the other. He had started out of his tent when a yelling, brass-helmeted horseman blundered into it and buried him under wildly flapping canvas.

His wind effectively knocked out, Barry Colcord lay writhing, vainly struggling to fill his lungs and only half aware of hoofs trampling all about him. Now shrill, frightened yells arose: "Quarter!" "I surrender." "Quarter! Grant me Quarter!" "No! Don't!" "Can't you see I've surrendered?" "Quarter! Spare me! Quarter!" Followed by screams of "For God's sake have mercy!" "No! No! Don't!"

Vaguely, he heard his brother shouting, "Ricelands! This way, Ricelands! Rally to me! Quick! Quick!"

He thought also to recognize the voices of Skene and of Peete; all else remained a dim confusion and an agonizing pain paralyzing his diaphragm.

All at once the sour-smelling canvas was yanked aside and hands were thrust under his armpits. Saul Black Buck was hissing like an angry bobcat, "Quick! Quick! Hostiles all about."

An arm about the old mustee's bony shoulders, Barry managed to stagger along and became able to draw a little wind into his lungs. The general tumult seemed to be increasing; more ragged volleys split the night; everywhere, it seemed, shone brief, brilliant streaks of yellow-red fire.

A hoarse, exultant voice kept roaring, "That's it, lads! Feed 'em the saber! Ride 'em down! Cut 'em down!" More and more loose horses raced about, utterly terror-stricken. Gradually, Barry became aware that this was more than a horse-stealing raid carried out by a small force. In fact, General Huger's entire command had been taken by surprise and now was under an attack as effective as it was merciless.

From the direction of the tavern and those few scattered houses which formed the hamlet called Monck's Corner came more sporadic bursts of musketry, more sounds of a hot conflict. In every direction showed indistinct black tangles of fighting men weaving about to the ringing clash of steel. Here and there small but orderly detachments of the enemy galloped through the stricken camp on their way to carry out orders.

A big dragoon riding a very tall horse loomed out of the gloomy confusion so suddenly that Barry, as he staggered along towards the woods, barely found time to level and fire his little pistol. The enemy trooper screamed once before falling from his saddle, but his mount kept on and shouldered Barry so hard that the pistol flew out of his hand and was lost in the dark.

By the time he'd regained his balance there was no sign of Black Buck, while the enemy — who probably were Tories because they kept *whoop-whoop-whooping* like Indians — were charging at will through the encampment.

In all directions limp or slowly writhing bodies now littered the trampled ground. Quite a few erect figures were darting furtively from one clump of bushes or tangle of wreckage to another.

Avoiding the nearest groups of struggling men Barry began to call. "Ricelands! Ricelands! To the swamp! Rally in the swamp!"

He unsheathed his sword and, using its scabbard for a cane, started to limp as fast as he could towards a shadowy row of trees marking the swamp's rim.

Small groups of the enemy pounded by, but for the moment they ignored this lone, bare-headed and half-dressed fugitive.

More screams, stark with terror, filled the night. "Don't hit me!" "Can't you see I've quit?" "God blast you for bloody butchers!" "Quarter! For Christ's sake, grant me quarter!"

But Banastre Tarleton's men were yelling: "No quarter to Rebel dogs!" "Ride 'em down!" "Hack 'em!" They were repeating the butchery at Paoli. "Goddam it, kill that man — he's only shamming surrender!"

Finally, a quartet of Tories wearing battered tricorns and dark-gray tunics closed in on the stocking-footed Carolinian.

"Surrender, you Rebel bastard!"

Barry dropped his sword, then, shaking like an aspen, raised both hands shoulder high. "Quarter!" he called out as steadily as he could. "Grant me quarter! I'll cause no trouble, you've an officer's word on it."

One of the shadowy figures panted, "What say, boys, shall we cut the bugger down?"

"Naw," snapped another Tory. "Us Virginians don't aim to take on Tarleton's ways." The last speaker, evidently a noncommissioned officer, then leaped from his horse and with practiced ease bound the prisoner's hands tightly behind him. "Now, Rebel, just you get a move on. Don't stumble or try to hold back else ye'll get yer skull split."

At a brisk trot that taxed Barry's endurance to its uttermost the quartet set out for the Red Hart, around which a savage mêlée was taking place. Judging by the noise and a throbbing glow of flames against the sky near the Cooper, American infantry guarding Biggen Bridge must also have been pounced upon.

After a while Barry was turned into a peach orchard, flowering and fragrant with spring, to join other dazed and disheveled prisoners who were being guarded by a detail of foul-mouthed and jubilant mounted infantry belonging to Tarleton's British Legion.

None of the prisoners yet seemed capable of grasping the true magnitude of this disaster.

Dawn took so long to break that the dozen-odd officer-prisoners — minus watches stolen by their captors — calculated that Tarleton's squadrons must have struck around three in the morning. While attempting to make an estimate of their situation, the miserable group stood about the flowering trees and blinked owlishly at Tory guards clad in a fantastic miscellany of uniforms.

Prisoners carrying limp, feebly groaning wounded in blankets, on wheelbarrows or on shutters wrenched from nearby dwellings, deposited their dripping burdens with rough carelessness in a big carriage shed facing the Red Hart's stableyard. Although the stricken men kept moaning and calling out for water and medical help, not one of the enemy paid them heed.

Meanwhile, strings of captured horses with all manner of gear and equipment slung any which way across their backs were driven in; once stripped, these animals were turned in to join a growing herd held in the tavern's well-fenced barnyard.

Unshaven and otherwise slovenly guards lounging about the captured American headquarters stood to attention when out of the Red Hart's front door strutted Lieutenant-Colonel Banastre Tarleton, whose short and stout but wiry figure Barry recognized immediately.

Flushed and swaggering, the Green Dragoon was bareheaded so his curly, red-brown hair fell in untidy coils to brush his shoulders. The victor stepped out into the sunshine and at the same time peered for a long minute at the scarecrows standing, still bound, among the peach trees. After taking a deep pull from a pewter pot of liquor, he bellowed, "Guards! Any of their so-called officers out there?"

A big, raw-boned Tory sergeant saluted. "Yes, suh! An they h'ain't been lyin' in their teeth, there oughter be a major and a couple of capt'ns 'mongst them."

"Very well. Fetch the mangy rascals inside. I want to talk to 'em."

When he was shoved inside, Barry saw that several severely wounded American officers had been placed on the taproom's long oaken serving tables. They were moaning or just breathing stertorously while their blood, flowing unchecked, caused a soft pattering noise upon the bricked floor.

The most hideously mangled of all the prisoners was the Frenchman, Major Paul Vernier. The hussar was suffering from at least half a dozen deep saber cuts, one of which had shorn off his right ear and had sliced away most of the flesh from his jaw; another had caved in his whole left shoulder, creating a hideous area of gory flesh and splintered bone.

From where he stood Barry Colcord heard, all too distinctly, the dying Frenchman curse the Americans first for having allowed themselves to be surprised and then for having panicked and for running away in so cowardly a fashion. Even more bitterly, Vernier then damned their leaders, Lincoln, Huger and others, for being no better than puffed-up amateurs and stupid Sunday soldiers. When, suddenly, the ghastly figure managed to struggle up onto an elbow, his once-beautiful silver-frogged, light-blue jacket became so bathed with gushing blood that he appeared to be wearing the King's scarlet.

As in a bad dream, Barry noticed, oddly enough, that the saber cut which had mangled Vernier's face also had shorn off one of those little powdered pigtails he always wore to either side of it.

Although the late Count Pulaski's aide was close to death, as so often happens he found sufficient last-minute strength to rally and cry out in a terrible voice, "I call on all of you to believe I had thrown away my sword and had called for quarter, but these English barbarians kept on sabering me even after I had fallen and lay helpless on the ground!"

The gory figure actually reared himself higher. "*Je prie le bon Dieu* to lay an everlasting curse on all such dishonorable savages." He recognized Tarleton. "An' you, you heartless butcher, may you forever roast and burn in hell!"

Casually, Banastre Tarleton turned his head and stared, then laughed. "Well said, Froggie. Couldn't have laid on a better curse m'self." He turned to an aide. "Dashed poetical fellows, these Frog Eaters, eh Creighton? Can't match 'em in that direction."

"*Espèce de canaille!*" choked Vernier, then sank back gasping, "*Ah-h, Seigneur Dieu!*" He died with crimson froth oozing from between contorted, lavender-hued lips.

Aching in every muscle along his hurt side, Barry Colcord remained much too exhausted and miserable to get any sleep in a corner of that dusty, half-filled corncrib into which he and three other officers had been shoved to join a multitude of rats.

In the near distance wounded men under the trees still were making noises like thirsty cattle; from around the Red Hart sounded bursts of drunken laughter and singing.

Finally, the night grew unexpectedly quiet save for the croaking of frogs and the shrilling of peepers — so still in fact that Barry could hear the footsteps of a dragoon on guard wearily circling the corncrib.

Bitterly, the Carolinian berated his own stupidity in not having taken Gavin Wilcox's warning more seriously. How could he have been so incredibly lax — so incautious? What sheer hell it was that a conscientious and able officer could remain wary and alert ninety-nine times out of a hundred and then on the hundredth occasion he might lower his guard for only a moment and suffer disaster. It was hard work to face the fact that, because of his error, the majority of his followers must be dead, wounded or taken prisoner.

What could have befallen Brother Rob, Wilcox and the other dependables who'd created reasonably disciplined and steady soldiers out of a mob of unruly recruits? How well he now understood the Roman emperor Augustus Caesar's anguished cry of *"Varus! Varus!* Give me back my Legions."

Worst of all came the awful realization that the Southern States would be lost from the moment General Lincoln, inevitably now, signed an instrument of surrender. Soon stiff-necked Royal governors would be returning to their palaces protected by British arms and men-of-war. Worse yet, a mass of hitherto neutral Tories would spring to arms; next, mused the battered prisoner, dispossessed Loyalists would ravage the countryside, aided, no doubt, by gangs of deserters and common robbers.

He was too deeply plunged in an orgy of self-reproach to notice a faint *thud!* as if someone had dumped a sack of grain behind the corncrib. But he did notice what seemed to be a large rat's persistent squeaking.

Barry raised his head, listened with care. What the hell? Weren't these squeaks too rhythmic and too often repeated to be natural?

Squirming towards the corncrib's rear over the sprawled bodies of his companions, he pursed lips and squeaked back — one long, two short, one long note; next he cupped a hand to his ear and caught sounds as faint as the whispering of a wild duck's wings high in a night sky. Black Buck was murmuring, "Cappen? Mistuh Barry. You there?"

Pressing his mouth against a ventilation slat let into the building's whitewashed side, Barry muttered, "Yes. What's up?"

"Guard dead. Me unlock door now. You come out quick."

"Right. But first I must rouse the rest."

"Sure. But don't let fellas make noise nor follow too quick."

It proved difficult to awaken the others snoring in exhausted slumber, but somehow he managed to impress on the suddenly hopeful but sleep-befuddled men that they must quit this crib at not less than two-minute intervals.

When the plank door's crude lock clicked and its hinges creaked, Barry slipped out into the starlight, and on hands and knees, crawled as fast as he could around to the rear, where he glimpsed the dead guard lying on his side as if suddenly overcome by sleepiness rather than eight inches of razor-sharp steel between his ribs.

Gapped teeth faintly a-gleam, the mustee passed over the dead guard's carbine, but kept his saber for himself. Black Buck beckoned towards a dense holly thicket. Silent because he was in his stocking feet, Barry plunged into the woods, where it proved hard work to keep his slave in sight. The mustee must be able to see uncommonly well in a dim light, so unerringly did he follow a faint footpath which evidently led to a big swamp lying behind the village called Monck's Corner.

Following careful reconnaissance, Black Buck, wading most of the way, presently led to a small wooded and bush-covered island which at the moment was occupied by an indeterminate number of bedraggled officers and men. Present were tragic-faced and tight-jawed General Huger, Colonel Washington and a handful of regimental commanders. Few carried arms of any description and all were dressed just as they'd been when Tarleton had swooped. Many were bootless and some were wearing only underdrawers.

A few horses, mostly minus saddles, were standing listlessly among the shadows off to one side; Barry's heart gave a joyful surge when he recognized Eclipse's familiar outline.

Brigadier General Isaac Huger began to speak slowly, tonelessly, like a man who is just coming to realize his responsibility for an overwhelming and, worse still, inexcusable defeat. "Gentlemen, I feel that our most sensible course is to scatter before daybreak and individually make our way across the Cooper as best we can."

He peered about at faint white blurs created by the faces surrounding him. "You will collect as many survivors as you can and then, as swiftly as you may, rendezvous with me at Lenud's Mill."

"Where's that, sir?" someone queried.

"On the Santee River behind Georgetown. Good luck, everyone."

As they were splashing back to solid ground Barry beckoned the mustee alongside. "I think it's better that you scout around here. Round up all of our men you can find and tell them to get to Lenud's Ferry as fast as they can. Those are General Huger's orders."

11.　Fair Lawn, I

THE clanging of the big iron bell set on a post in front of the slave quarters awakened Amelia Trefont from a comfortable sleep. She was lying, warm and cozy, beside Betsey Colcord in a big, brocade-canopied four-poster. Blinking like a sleepy kitten, Amelia turned onto her side and peered groggily about. "What's that?"

Betsey moved, reluctant to rouse, but when she did, the chubby little creature sat bolt upright, clutching the bedclothes before her. "What — wha' amiss? Why, 'tis still dark. Oh, that awful bell! Make them stop!"

"Must be a fire," Amelia hazarded, then raised her fallen night rail to cover pink-pointed breasts and slender, sloping white shoulders.

Round-eyed, both girls, holding hands over ears, endured the bell's wild clangor until it ceased with almost shocking suddenness. Only then were they able to identify a clatter of distant musketry which seemed to originate in the direction of Monck's Corner. Although the crossroads village lay better than a mile distant, a stiff breeze was blowing which, with startling clarity, carried sounds of battle to Fair Lawn.

On both floors of Sir John Colleton's house could be heard the padding of feet and excited Negro voices. Quickly, the girls realized that, one by one, candles had begun to glow outside the guest-room door.

Amelia, her long, red-gold hair streaming loose down her back, forced quivering fingers to tie on the first petticoat that came to hand right over her night rail; next she tugged on a riding jacket she'd worn the afternoon before. Betsey, dark eyes huge and white-ringed with fright, hurried to pull on a few garments.

Someone knocked hastily, then Lady Colleton appeared shading a candle with one hand. The old lady was wearing a rose-tinted nightgown over which she had pulled a loose, lace-trimmed housecoat. Although she must have known that her gray hair was sprouting in ludicrous elf locks from under an enormous nightcap, she remained calm and patrician.

"Good girls! It's fine that you've kept your wits enough to get dressed. I've no idea what is taking place at the village, but rest assured, my dears, everyone will be safe inside this house!"

"But, but what *is* happening?" Betsey wanted to know, hastily clubbing her black hair with a ribbon.

"I only wish I knew!" snapped Lady Jane. "It would appear there's some sort of an engagement taking place over at Monck's Corner."

"— Do you believe, ma'am," Amelia cried, "that the battle will come this way?"

"How should I know, child? Shouldn't think so, this property lies pretty well away from the river. But then, I'm no general — not even a good corporal!" She laughed nervously, and, returning to the landing, beckoned to a half-dressed and very frightened-looking house boy. "Peter! Run out to the overseer's quarters and tell Mr. Parkinson I must see him right away."

Pale-haired Sally Colleton now appeared, suggesting an animated ghost in a dressing gown of flowered yellow lawn. "Oh, Mamma, Mamma! What are we to do?"

"Stop whining and keep your wits about you!" cried her mother. "Above all, keep quiet. Oh, dear! If only your Papa hadn't insisted on riding over to Cobb's Mill yesterday. Drat the man! Why does he have to be away at a moment like this?" Lady Jane Colleton appeared to be talking more to herself than to the three wide-eyed young girls she was leading down a broad, gracefully winding staircase towards the ground floor.

Curtly, the old lady ordered her trembling and white-eyed butler to locate the footmen, a pair of young, strong Negroes, and to close and bar all doors and windows opening to the outside on the ground level. Unfortunately, not every window shutter in the place could be secured; a lot of them simply wouldn't close due to the careless application of paint.

Once these precautions had been taken, the straight-backed old lady marched the girls, pale and subdued, into Sir John's handsome, walnut-paneled study.

Lady Jane thrust her disheveled head out of the study door and called down to the servants' hall, in which the house slaves were huddled weeping and moaning. "Where *is* that idiot Peter? Why hasn't Mr. Parkinson appeared?"

Peter emerged from the hall and ran up, gray-faced with fright. "Ah done hunted ev'rywhere fo' Misto' Pa'kinson, but, Missus, he ain't nowheres 'round. Reckon he tek de blood horses and lit out fo' de swamp wit' de field han's."

"Now there *is* a fine bit of loyalty," snorted Lady Jane, who as certain astute but unkind relatives had observed, rather resembled a horse, albeit a blooded one. "Tell Sukie to heat some water at once and fetch us some coffee the minute it's ready."

For the ladies in déshabille to pretend that nothing out of the ordinary was taking place proved difficult, but somehow they managed to talk of trivialities until a frantic knocking began on the front door. The butler hurried in, yellowish eyes round as marbles.

"Take the poker and go find who's there," Lady Jane directed in a strained but steady voice. "Unless you recognize 'em, don't let 'em in."

The butler summoned a brawny footman who, gripping a billet of firewood, followed him to the front door.

A moment later young and darkly handsome Mrs. Greenslit, who lived on an adjoining property, hurried in, followed by a bony and much older sister — a confirmed spinster named Dayton. Their eyes were red and streaming and their hair flying witch-wild.

"Oh dear, oh dear!" wailed the tall young woman. "It's so dreadful!"

"What?"

"Soon after the fighting began," Mrs. Greenslit began to sob, "our carriage house was set on fire. Paul went to put it out and, and he — he hasn't come back — nor have any of our servants." She ran to fling arms about Lady Jane. "Oh dear! Oh dear! I hope you don't mind, but we were all alone and so — so frightened by all that smoke and flames. When the fire began spreading to the barn and dairy house we ran out of the back door and came here. I — I hope you don't mind. You're so strong, and always know what to do."

"There, there, my dear! Of course you're welcome, both of you. Here, take some hot coffee."

Within the next half-hour two other groups of women and a pair of young children reached Fair Lawn, so, by sunup, over a dozen bedraggled people sat about the study talking ninety to the minute and attempting, without much success, to reassure one another that soon everything would turn out all right.

There seemed room for hope when, around seven, the last shots to be heard at Fair Lawn were fired away over towards the river. The refugees breathed easier when the sun appeared, warm and reassuring, above flowering fruit trees and newly leafed water oaks growing in that great swamp which stretched to the east and south.

Amelia was pleased and also surprised to find herself so calm by comparison with Betsey and Sally, both of whom were acting "jumpy as a pair of fleas on a hot stone," as Mrs. Greenslit's unattractive sister acidly put it.

Once her guests had munched buttered beaten biscuits washed down with steaming hot acorn coffee, Lady Jane Colleton quietly excused herself and disappeared upstairs; presently she returned carrying a silver-mounted dueling pistol. From the way she held it Amelia could tell that her hostess didn't understand the first thing about the use of such a weapon. But the visitor did, thanks to her father's having served many years as a sapper officer in the King's regular establishment. The veteran had shown his only child, even when only a wispy, big-eyed little thing, how to clean, to load and even fire his pocket pistol — a small, light-weight affair. How many times had the late Major Trefont concluded his instruction by saying, "I know it ain't a bit ladylike, 'Melia, for you to handle such things, but you never can tell when this kind of knowledge may come in handy." How right dear Papa had been!

"I am about to make a tour of the property," announced Lady Jane, "and I invite anybody who understands the use of this — this thing to accompany me."

Delicately pointed features flushing, Amelia spoke up. "I do, ma'am."

"You?" Betsey, Sally and the rest began to laugh. "You, of all people!"

"Yes! My Papa taught me. He was a soldier," she added with pride, "and a fine one."

"Capital!" smiled Lady Jane. "Then take this, my dear, and come with me. We shan't venture far, but I feel I must make an 'estimate of our situation,' as Sir John would say."

A brief inspection of the property revealed that apparently all the slaves, including house servants, had vanished into the swamp. They weren't likely to emerge from it, remarked Lady Jane, until all was peaceful.

Amelia's misgivings returned when she and her bony-faced hostess sighted single riders or small groups of armed and uniformed horsemen in the distance. As a rule these men were trotting across fields which stretched away from Fair Lawn on three sides but were staying comfortably well away from the mansion.

Apparently, observed Lady Jane, the King's troops at present must be occupied in running down survivors of the defeated forces. Since it seemed unlikely that more fighting would take place in the vicinity of

Fair Lawn Lady Jane led her guests out to the semi-detached, deserted cooking house and there supervised the preparation of a breakfast which quickly was carried into the big house.

Betsey ate like a hungry fledgling and Amelia also made a good meal now that the danger appeared to be by, but Sally Colleton, always a pallid and colorless little creature, refused to touch her food. Instead of eating, she kept crossing to an unshuttered window to peer out.

All of a sudden she emitted a gasping cry. "Oh, Mamma! Mamma! Some riders are coming this way!"

Amelia ran to another window and, by peering through a crack in its shutter, glimpsed some twenty green-coated horsemen in crossbelts and dirty white breeches. Several were wearing red fox-tails in their broad hats. They were closing in on the mansion in an irregular line abreast. Short cloaks a-flutter, they circled the mansion to its rear and made straight for the stables. Almost at once their disappointed curses could be heard on finding nothing more useful than a pair of worn-out, gray-muzzled mules.

Led by a gray-haired officer with alert bronzed features, the detachment clattered back to the front of the house. The officer then dismounted and went up to hammer on the wide white door with the pommel of a brass-guarded sword.

"Open up!" he roared. "Open up and be damn' quick, else we'll burn down this Rebel rat's nest with everybody inside of it."

"Hold hard, sir!" called Lady Jane, then unbolted the door, swung it open and stood glaring defiance.

The green-coated officer, who was no longer young, stared in amazement at this apparition standing framed in the entrance. "And who might you be, you scrawny old hen?"

"I, you unmannerly lout, am Lady Jane Colleton. I blush that any servant of our King — by your jacket you must be a Tory — should prove so uncivil." She glowered down her long, broad nose. "This is my home and since you are uninvited guests, you and your verminous rascals had better get off this property at once or you'll wish you had when Sir Henry Clinton hears about this inexcusable discourtesy." She then added, "Sir John Colleton always has been loyal to His Majesty."

Something in the straight-backed old woman's uncompromising attitude must have carried conviction, for the officer passed the back of a hairy hand over his brow. "I have heard about your husband, ma'am, and personally have no quarrel with his convictions. However, ma'am,

you must give me your solemn word of honor that no Rebel fugitives are
sheltering in your home."

"There are not!" snapped Lady Jane while the sunburnt Tory horsemen shifted in their saddles and edged closer to the front door. Gorry!
What a place to plunder!

Unwisely, Jane Colleton continued to talk. "For that matter, not a
single white man is on this place at the moment — not even my poltroon of an overseer."

Among the dragoons lounging on tired and dull-coated mounts was a
well-set-up and not unhandsome middle-aged man who was wearing a
corporal's shoulder knot of red worsted — also a brown leather patch to
conceal a missing left eye.

Amelia noticed that this somehow educated-looking fellow wore a
hard smile on his stubble-covered mouth; also that he seemed to be listening carefully to all that was being said.

While running a finger inside his helmet's sweat band, the officer
jerked a nod. "Very well, ma'am, I'll accept your word on that. Servant,
ma'am. I'm sure you'll be safe here till the Crown's authority is re-
imposed."

"Better not believe her, sir," called Corporal George Walker. "The
people around here need only the least excuse to turn their coats when
the wind blows to suit 'em."

The brown-faced officer turned and spoke in acid tones. "That will do!
If this lady passes her word that there ain't no Rebel soldiers in her
house, that's all there is to it — no matter what people of your kidney
may imagine."

The Tory offered a sloppy salute and just had remounted when, in the
distance, an outpost raised a fox-hunter's view-halloo and, standing in his
stirrups, pointed to a brief and badly scattered stream of horsemen galloping heavily across a field green with new vegetation.

"There go some Yankee bastards! Come on!" The Tory officer pulled
out his sword and spurred down the driveway followed by his detachment.

After pushing his men and desperately wearied horses to the limit of
their endurance the Tory leader decided to abandon the chase and ordered his patrol to fan out and reconnoiter a dense patch of woods in
which enemy stragglers might conceivably have taken refuge.

When the patrol was well into the grove and deployed into a thin line abreast, Corporal George Walker deemed it a good time to veer out of contact and set about his own business, along with three other Carolinians who had suffered much and lost everything.

On a signal from the one-eyed man, they pulled up, listened to diminishing noises made by their companions in crashing through the underbrush. Once certain that no one would notice them, the deserters wheeled their mounts and at a brisk trot set off in the direction of Fair Lawn.

Since the occupants of Sir John Colleton's home had failed to resecure the mansion's front door following the Tory patrol's departure, it was simple for the corporal and his hard-faced companions, Troopers Barker, Middleton and Rolfe, to march indoors. They stood in the hall, muddied boots marking the gleaming parquet floor while they stared at gilt-framed portraits, crystal candle sconces, a handsome bull's-eye mirror and well-polished mahogany furniture such as George Walker once had owned.

Stung by memories, he shouted down the deserted hall, "Everybody listen to what I want done! I want every nigger out of here inside of two minutes; everybody else will come to the drawing room *at once!* God help anybody who tries to delay or escape."

In their bedroom on the second floor to which they had retired in order to dress more properly, Amelia and Betsey heard harsh male voices below and exchanged frightened glances.

"Who's that?" the Colcord girl quavered. "Oh dear, oh dear! Those Tories must have come back! What *are* we to do?" Betsey's plump and rosy features crumpled as she hid her face between her hands. "Oh-h, I'm so fearful!"

"Heaven knows. But perhaps they're some of our people —" she encouraged — "maybe your brother or your Cousin Rob."

A string of resounding curses beat up the stairwell. "Get down to the drawing room, you addle-brained bitches, and bring your whelps along, else we'll take the lash to you!"

Amelia remembered her soldier-father. "You do as you please," she announced in a small, taut voice, "but I'm going to stay up here. See? I've got Lady Jane's pistol."

In the frozen silence of utter terror the girls heard women begin to wail shrilly below.

In Lady Jane's small but elegantly furnished powder-blue, white-trimmed withdrawing room stood a clump of tearful children and females. Among them now was Mrs. Douglas, the corpulent and already hysterical wife of a prominent physician with a practice in Charles Town. Quietly, Lady Colleton assembled her companions under a handsome crystal chandelier which was effectively reflected by the highly polished parquet floor.

His remaining eye red and narrowed, George Walker rubbed his stubble-covered chin while, with the careful deliberation of a housewife about to select from a coop a fowl suitable for her table, he surveyed the weeping and terrified captives.

Finally, he rasped, "Is everybody here?"

"Everybody!" snapped Lady Colleton in icy tones. "Now, what do you want of us?"

Rolfe, a brutally handsome blond young fellow who had new and old pimples standing out all over his face, drawled, "Say, George, reckon there still must be somebody upstairs; heard a noise from there just now."

Sally Colleton lost her head, whimpered fearfully, "Oh-h, please don't be angry. Everybody's here except Betsey and Amelia."

Walker emitted a snarling laugh. "So that's how it is? Well, since we're in a hurry, Barker, just you get right up there, find those shy little ladies and bring 'em down instanter — drag the bitches if they won't come peaceably!"

Because Amelia had been careless and had only half-cocked her pistol she couldn't fire it when, after several attempts, the bedroom door burst open and in lurched a dark-complexioned, shock-haired fellow who had tufts of chest hair spurting through an unbuttoned green-and-white tunic. Like a hawk stooping on a wood pigeon he pounced on Amelia Trefont and wrenched away her pistol before slapping her so hard across the face that she reeled across the room.

"Try to shoot me, eh?" Wearing a slack grin, he closed in on her. "Now ain't you the bobcat's kitten? C'mere!"

For both Betsey and Amelia it proved most unfortunate that they should just have removed those few garments they'd donned so hurriedly when, early that morning, the slave bell had begun to clang and not yet had found time to dress properly, so now they were fluttering about wearing only short and semi-transparent lawn undershifts.

Gesturing like a farm boy shooing chickens to the door, the deserter demanded, 'C'mon along, my pretty little pullets. Really, ye should have obeyed orders."

"Oh! No, no!" screamed Betsey, and tried to dodge aside, but Barker's hand promptly closed over her wrist. Ineffectually, Tom's sister tried to brace bare feet on the rug, but got hauled along all the same.

The invader turned to Amelia, "You comin' quiet-like or — ?"

"Don't touch me!" Amelia cried in a small, flat voice. "I — I'll come without your help."

When the girls arrived in the drawing room in loose white garments they suggested nymphs animated from a Greek frieze. The doctor's fat wife uttered a scream of mortal fear and started a frantic dash for a side door. Without compunction one of the green-jacketed men blocked her path and gave her a swinging slash with his saber that dropped her quivering and moaning onto the gleaming floor. Blood gushing from her shoulder soon created a wide and shiny pool of scarlet.

One of the Tories started towards the fallen woman but Walker's grating voice checked him. "Let her lie! Nobody helped me when *I* got hurt!"

The one-eyed corporal then tramped over and dropped onto a fragile gilded parlor chair that creaked under his weight while he balanced a naked saber across patched knees. "All right. The old hens among you take your brats, get off this place *and keep running!* The boys and me have business to transact with a mind towards squaring accounts for what your gentle, high-minded Patriots have done to us and our folks."

Like sleep-walkers, Lady Jane, the old-maid sister, the other women and their children prepared to depart. Mrs. Douglas, clutching a shawl to her wounded shoulder, was among them. Her course across the drawing room was marked by a series of small, round red splashes that looked like miniature setting suns.

Once they'd downed the contents of a brandy decanter, the invaders, laughing uproariously all the while, employed the flat of their blades to drive the unwanted captives out-of-doors. Left behind were Betsey, Amelia, Sally and that handsome young matron named Greenslit. All four remained in the drawing room's center pressed together, their eyes huge and unseeing.

For all of a minute Walker and his fellows studied their captives, then the one-eyed corporal kicked over his chair, strode forward and grabbed

Amelia's wrist, announcing in a thick voice, "I want this one! You boys take your pick of the rest!"

He hauled the Trefont girl, wildly struggling, out of the parlor and up the staircase. "Come along, Sissy. Since we're going to have fun together we may as well enjoy ourselves in comfort."

Amelia tried to scream, but she seemed to have lost control of her throat muscles and could only gasp and gurgle. Not so the other females; once the hot-eyed invaders seized them they shrieked like pigs being hoisted for butchering. Only Mrs. Greenslit made an attempt to struggle, but it was no use; squalling and kicking futilely in her captor's arms, she was carried out towards a couch in Sir John's study.

The raiders had started to scatter to various rooms when Barker sang out from the landing, "Hey, fellers! C'mon upstairs. There's a plenty of fancy beds up here."

At that Betsey fainted, but Barker carried her plump, pink figure, already half-revealed by the disorder of her lawn undershift, up Sir John Colleton's gracefully designed hanging staircase.

Amelia tried to go limp and heavy but at once felt herself clutched so tight to Walker's chest that his uniform's buttons dug painfully into her newly budded breasts. Moreover, his body was giving off a reek of stale sweat and horses so nauseating that, amid a semi-daze, she gagged and struggled only ineffectually.

On gaining Sir John's bedroom the Tory set her down; deliberately seating himself on an armchair still covered with feminine garments, he ripped off a filthy neckcloth. Next, without once removing his gaze from the girl, Walker slowly undid his sword belt and stripped off his torn and faded green tunic and a flannel shirt dark with sweat stains.

After that he said softly, "Now, honey, you can start walking back and forth before me." He sat studying Amelia while she hesitated, barefooted, in the middle of the room all unaware of how effectively sunlight beating through French windows was revealing her body under a nimbus of white lawn.

"D'you know," announced George Walker, "I've always admired watching a likely filly parade before the judge's stand?"

Lost in a frantic turmoil of emotions, Amelia could only shake her head and mumble, "Oh-h, I — I don't understand wh-what you want."

When she hesitated, the one-eyed man leaped towards her and, causing a brief, snarling sound, ripped off her shift, left her swaying in the center of the room stark naked save for long strands of gold-red hair with which she vainly attempted to conceal her private parts.

"Start moving! I told you to dance," he rasped. "Dance, damn you!"

When she only turned horrified greenish eyes in his direction and made a pathetic little gesture did George Walker use his sword belt to smack her twice, thrice across the thighs. "Dance, you Rebel slut!" he choked, ravaged features working and going scarlet. "You'd better dance real good — till maybe I feel better about Cobb's Mill!"

Amelia gasped and attempted to comply with a few steps from a Christmas masque she'd once performed but her slender white legs could execute only stiff and halting movements.

"Jesus Christ!" snarled Walker, "I've seen gracefuller trulls prance about my tavern many's the time! Well, Sissy, since you can't dance, let's see if you make love any better!"

He caught the slim young figure about its waist and flung her, hair flying, to lie whimpering and spraddle-legged across that same canopied bed from which Lady Jane had roused so hastily long hours ago.

12.   Fair Lawn, II

Simply because he'd been up inspecting the Troop's picket line Rob Colcord had not been quite as surprised as the rest of the Ricelanders when outposts — who had not, despite Major Vernier's earnest advice, been sent out nearly far enough — came tearing wildly through the lightless woods yelling that a great force of enemy cavalry was hard on their heels.

Rob barely had time to grab up his sword and shout at the top of his lungs, "Turn out! Turn out!" then, "Wake up, Barry! Enemy's here!" just before Tarleton's men appeared in a howling, saber-swinging mass of indistinct figures.

Only Rob, Sergeant Wilcox and possibly a dozen alert fellows had time to snatch up the nearest weapon and make for the picket lines, where they cast loose the nearest horses. Since there wasn't time to bridle, let alone saddle, their mounts, the beasts had to be guided through the starlit camp by the pressure of halter shanks alone. Nevertheless, Rob and his men raced across the tented fields spreading the alarm to other regiments, which at once began turning out in wild disorder.

Out of nowhere Black Buck appeared through the darkness. He was riding bareback and reported that he'd seen the captain taken prisoner and carried off God knew where. Then the mustee disappeared into the gloom.

When a handful of wild-eyed men increased Rob's scratch force he led them in a charge at a thin, dark line of horsemen who suddenly approached whooping out of the woods and across the fields.

It was just as well that Lieutenant Colcord's half-armed force encountered only the extreme tip of the enemy's right flank. Nevertheless, the enemy, amid a clatter of shots and hard-swung sabers, brushed aside the defenders and scattered them in all directions — like quail "bounced" by a poorly trained bird dog.

With Wilcox and a few others strung out behind him Rob headed towards that great swamp which lay behind Monck's Corner.

Dawn revealed his hatless and sadly bedraggled little party which, ominously enough, now numbered thirteen, occupying a small, thickly grown islet situated near the swamp's rim. There, Saul Black Buck rejoined them, reported the captain's escape and his order to rendezvous at Lenud's Ferry.

When broad daylight broke, Rob was forced to agree that this improvised command seemed about the wildest-looking gang of sullen and dispirited wretches he ever expected to see. Not a single man wore a hat of any sort; most had on neither boots nor jackets; a few, lacking even breeches, went about uncomfortably bare-arsed. But what concerned Rob most was his discovery that over half of his following carried no arms whatever. Such being the case, he decided he had no alternative but to remain in hiding until darkness fell. Cursing softly, the stragglers watched Tarleton's troopers ride by herding many disconsolate-looking prisoners towards the Red Hart.

Only late in the morning did the enemy finally make casual efforts to collect the last of many wounded Americans. Dead men were left lying where they had fallen; already, they were attracting the attention of huge numbers of leisurely wheeling turkey buzzards.

Around midday Black Buck returned from a cautious scout about the vicinity to report that most of the victorious troops appeared to be crossing the Cooper at Biggen Bridge, undoubtedly to further harry and disperse the remnants of Isaac Huger's cavalry division.

By late afternoon Rob Colcord decided it might be safe to move out in search of food, weapons and clothing. Nothing living remained in sight except for a few stray pigs, skulking dogs and some wounded horses limping and grazing about the fields.

Rob took Wilcox aside, said, "I reckon our best bet is to slant back away from the Cooper awhile, then we'll head upstream and try to cross somewhere near Cobb's Mill. I doubt if the enemy can have got *that* far upstream already."

Accordingly, the semi-naked and insect-tortured survivors set off close to the swamp's edge in a northwesterly direction. Now and then they sighted Negro faces — which ducked instantly out of sight — and an occasional white man peering from among bushes and tangled vines. The stragglers, however, were too tired to pay much attention to these furtive creatures.

Before long, Rob sighted a thin column of bluish-white smoke climbing from behind an oak-grown peninsula jutting boldly out of the swamp.

Rob turned to the mustee. "Wood fire?"

"No, Mastuh. That house fo' sure."

"Wonder why that place should be afire?" Sergeant Wilcox grunted when the pace was increased to a trot. "It's a long way from the Corners."

"I've no idea," Rob admitted, then shifted his weight. By damn! Riding bareback on such a bony brute was no fun. What had happened to Hector? Most likely one of Tarleton's officers had claimed him and was astride the big gray hunter right now. His sense of depression deepened.

The survivors had come within half a mile of the conflagration when they sighted a gray-haired woman stumping along, stiff-legged with fatigue. She was using a broken sapling for a walking stick and was following a cart path that skirted the great swamp.

Rob trotted forward, then slipped off his nag and bowed to this pathetic old lady with the wildly disordered hair. Incredibly, she was wearing a tattered housecoat over what appeared to be a nightgown.

He was shocked and surprised to learn that this harridan was Sir John Colleton's lady.

"Lady Colleton!" A fearful possibility struck home. "Please, ma'am, is Amelia Trefont visiting you?"

Tiredly, Lady Jane's reddened eyes raised themselves. "Yes, unfortunately she is."

"Please, ma'am, where is Mistress Trefont now?"

"Still at Fair Lawn — I fear."

" 'Fear'? What do you mean by that, ma'am? What has happened?" he demanded while his scarecrow companions rode up.

The barefoot, bedraggled old lady leaned more heavily on her staff as if to prevent herself from falling. "Sir, I wish to God I knew! And then again, I'm glad *I don't!*"

"For God's sake, ma'am, can't you tell me *something*? I'm Betsey Colcord's cousin, Robert."

"*You* are Robert Colcord?"

"I am."

"Oh, my God! Not long ago four ruffians in Tory uniform invaded my home; my daughter, Amelia and two other young ladies were detained when those villains drove us older women and the children out of my house."

The moment he heard the sum of Lady Jane's garbled and semi-hysterical account he ordered one of his followers to surrender his horse for her use. The trooper, who for some time had been saying that he lived in the vicinity, was only too eager to oblige; now he'd be quit of the goddam military for good and all! He disappeared into the swamp as effectively as a hunted deer.

Being English and born of a sturdy, fox-hunting family, Lady Jane hiked up her bedraggled housecoat and climbed aboard the nag, where she seemed more at ease than most of the survivors.

At first glance Fair Lawn was seen to be intact, but several outbuildings on an adjoining property, Will Greenslit's place, had been reduced to smoldering ruins.

Four horses were drowsing and switching flies before a hitching rail before the mansion. Listlessly, these raised heads when the newcomers clattered up.

Rob had begun to feel a trifle reassured when inside the handsome ivy-grown brick mansion sounded a thin, choking wail redolent of fear and pain; this was followed by a burst of raucous laughter.

Rob didn't delay to secure his mount, but slipped to the ground and, carrying only a naked sword, rushed up the front steps. Just then a burly, yellow-haired young man appeared in the front doorway. Although boot-less and stripped to the waist, he was holding ready a brass-barreled carbine.

From behind, Wilcox shouted a warning, but Rob raised his blade and kept on. Just as he mounted the last step the half-dressed fellow fired and Rob's life ended amid a blinding sheet of flame; his body went bumping and rolling back down the front steps.

Snarling incoherent curses, Gavin Wilcox started to rush the murderer but someone screeched, "Turn back, Sergeant!"

Wilcox checked his stride and cast a backward look when Black Buck yelled, "More hostiles!" The mustee already had started to gallop towards the haven of the swamp.

Less than a quarter of a mile away, a line of horsemen, this time wearing red coats, were deploying across the fields at a fast trot.

13. *Flotsam of Defeat*

CAUTIOUSLY Captain Colcord reined his mare at the edge of a steep, heavily wooded ridge in order to view a wide stretch of the coastal plain of South Carolina. In vain he attempted to ignore the insistent throbbing of a long though shallow gash in his scalp — the result of a saber cut only partially parried. At length he dismounted, and when Black Buck came forward to take Eclipse's reins she at once extended her long neck, no longer sleek or well filled, to nibble at nearby tufts of grass.

One by one the wounded officer's haggard, ill-clad companions followed his example, stretched legs and then checked the condition of their mounts' shoes and hoofs.

Barry noticed that Gavin Wilcox's pale-brown and sheep-like features had grown increasingly emaciated since he'd learned from a chance-met straggler that, some weeks ago, a party of raiders belonging to Major Patrick Ferguson's American Volunteer Regiment of Tories not only had burned his home to the ground but also destroyed the small tannery he'd owned. Worse still, they'd carried off his entire family to an unknown destination; they might even be dead for all poor Wilcox had been able to find out.

Three of Barry's ragged and wild-appearing followers were of the original Ricelands Troops who'd enlisted at the start; all of them lived in the immediate vicinity of Georgetown. The sixth and last member of this weary little party was a smallpox-scarred major of infantry named Spurling. His property, he claimed, lay on the seacoast some twenty miles northeast of Tranquility and Ricelands.

Like Barry and his handful of veterans, Spurling barely had escaped with his life following Colonel Buford's sanguinary defeat at the Waxhaws. With Buford's undoing, the last force of organized American troops remaining in South Carolina had been shattered and scattered.

So horrible had been the cold-blooded massacre of surrendered men after the Waxhaws defeat that, for the balance of the war, Banastre Tarleton invariably became referred to as "Bloody Tarleton." "Remember the Waxhaws!" became a rallying cry and "Tarleton's Quarter!" a warning to the enemy that no prisoners would be taken under any conditions.

Unhooking a wooden canteen from his pommel, Barry took a swig of flat-tasting, lukewarm water while employing his free hand to fan away swarms of bluebottle flies which persisted in buzzing about the lumpy, bloodstained bandage secured about his head. Meanwhile, dusty horses cropped halfheartedly at tough, yellow-brown grass — this summer had proved to be the hottest ever known — while their riders sought shade to sit staring dully on a light blue haze which danced and wavered above a seemingly boundless sea of treetops.

Bone-weary and never so discouraged, Barry fell to worrying over what he would find when and if he ever reached Ricelands again.

For a fact, he hadn't felt so utterly sick at heart since that day when Sergeant Wilcox and Saul Black Buck had ridden into Lenud's Ferry to report Rob's murder and describe the outrages committed on Sir John Colleton's property.

Later on, the Carolinian heard that Major Ferguson, on learning about the rapes and the sabering of the doctor's wife, had wanted to hang Walker and his fellow criminals out of hand. Colonel Tarleton, however, had persuaded the British High Command to delay quick justice, with the result that the guilty troopers were taken into Charles Town. There, a court-martial had allowed them to escape with nothing worse than a severe flogging.

Chewing slowly on a stalk of sweet grass, Barry lay sprawled in the shade and found himself still unable to admit that Rob really could be dead. Surely, some day he'd come riding into sight with a big grin spread all over his face?

What a nightmare this summer campaign had been! In the past he'd experienced and survived some pretty hard going — but nothing comparable to what he'd just been through. Nowadays the country was crawling with little groups of dispirited soldiers struggling furtively

homewards as best they could. Such stragglers had to remain eternally
alert to avoid British and Tory patrols combing the backcountry.

Soon after Lincoln's surrender, Lord Cornwallis, for him, had made
unusually swift and skillful use of the forces left under his command by
Sir Henry Clinton after that general had sailed for New York, confident
that the Rebellion, in the South at least, had been crushed for good.

Listlessly, Barry tested the security of his head bandage improvised out
of a dirty old shirt sleeve. He knew he should feel pleased, because yesterday, he and his fellow fugitives successfully had escaped yet another
defeat. A brisk little action had been fought near a meager hamlet called
Rocky Mount, which generally was supposed to lie in North Carolina
across the state line. There, Colonel Davies's scratch force of cavalry had
fought successfully until, hopelessly outnumbered, they'd been forced to
run or die where they stood.

Round-shouldered Major Spurling approached and stood looking silently out over the heat-blasted piney woods below. Finally, he said in a
nasal voice, "Tell me suthin', Capt'n Colcord. How much of a chance
d'you figure we got of reachin' the coast 'thout being noticed?"

"Fairly good, Major, provided we travel at night. Stands to reason the
enemy can't have near enough troops on hand to really patrol a country
as big as this."

The infantry officer batted sunken, red-rimmed eyes. "How much farther d'you figure it is to Geo'getown?"

"Black Buck allows it must be twenty miles, and he ought to know."

Stiffly, Barry arose and beckoned Wilcox. "Reckon the best thing we
can do before it grows dark is to water the horses, rest and eat whatever
we've got along."

Followed by the old mustee, he then shambled towards a brook leaping cheerfully over a succession of mossy green rocks. "Once it's dark,
Saul, we'll ride down onto the plain. You got any idea where we are?"

Black Buck nodded impassively. "Yes, Mastuh. Us see home come
daylight."

By way of provisions there wasn't much found in the men's frayed and
shapeless haversacks — only a few charred pones, chunks of greasy boiled
beef and a slab or two of greenish-white salt pork.

Once they'd devoured the last of their rations, the stubble-bearded
fellows stretched out under trees and promptly fell asleep.

Barry remained awake long enough to dip a rag in the brook and attempt to remove flecks of dried blood marking his jacket's lapels; no point in frightening Laura any more than he had to. Too bad he couldn't conquer this mounting anxiety over what he might find at Ricelands; his only encouragement was to remember that, in so vast an area, the enemy might have occupied themselves with more tempting targets than a half-finished plantation house. Thank God, he'd not much longer to wait to find reassurance.

From where he lay he could see several smoke columns rising lazily into the blistering August sky, but he wasn't disturbed. By their blue-white hue he recognized their origin as ground fires which always seemed to be burning somewhere in the piney woods. High above the coastal plain a few lonely-looking buzzards were soaring endlessly on motionless pinions; still higher, a pair of huge bald eagles circled the brazen sky.

Laura must have borne their second child by now. How had she weathered the ordeal? Who had attended her? Papa, of course, would have made sure that she'd receive the very best of care. How shameful to realize that he'd not the least notion whether his wife had presented him with a son or a daughter.

How would the news of Colin's death have affected her? — if, indeed, she'd ever received his first letter. Could she possibly have learned about the manner of Rob's death? He prayed that Laura hadn't. Better that he soften the blow. She'd been so very fond of him.

When big black ants began to nip at his wrists he got up and shifted to another tree, but nobody roused and the horses dozed on. What bothered Barry most was that, for the life of him, he couldn't see how this war might be won now. Just before that fight near Rocky Mount he'd heard a rumor that the Congress had entrusted a veteran major general by the name of Horatio Gates, who, it was said, had won a great victory up North, with the task of creating a useful army out of hastily raised militia levies and the badly scattered fragments of General Lincoln's forces.

Everyone on the Patriot side grimly agreed that something *must* be done — and in a big hurry — to check Lord Cornwallis's projected conquest of Virginia and North Carolina. To conduct this campaign, the new British commander-in-chief could rely upon plenty of capable subordinates, among them Lord Rawdon, Banastre Tarleton and that great if vindictive Tory leader, Patrick Ferguson.

While fanning insatiable flies from his head, Barry closed his jaws convulsively. Oh Lord, if only those more than two thousand fine Continental troops hadn't been surrendered so stupidly, so needlessly at Charles Town!

Thanks to the light of a full moon the fugitives were able to travel rapidly through the piney woods and made even better time after Saul Black Buck became able to identify private landmarks along the headwaters of the Sampee. In the distance brush fires glowed redly and, keeping well clear of them, 'coons, wild hogs, deer and smaller animals scurried off into the safety of darkness. There was no sign of human activity.

The false dawn found Colcord's raggle-taggle gang following an old Indian trail skirting ghostly-looking swamps which gave off the roars of bull alligators and the croaking of frogs and herons.

The riders took it as a good sign that the few small farms they sighted, while lightless, seemed undamaged and lonely-looking cows awaited daybreak in small stump lots.

Ruinous hat riding on the back of his head, Black Buck appeared out of the gloom. "Home direckly after sunup, Mastuh."

"How d'you know?"

"Done fished off little island plenty times — *that* one."

Barry recognized the trail the moment it swung away from the river in order to short-cut a big bend made by the Sampee a few miles above Ricelands.

"All right. Let's pick it up," he called. "I know where we are." At a smart trot he led off along a track that led across a wide stretch of marshy and treeless flatland which, long ago, he'd planned someday to convert into rice fields.

Marsh birds commenced to raise liquid morning songs, summer ducks squeaked in reed-choked sloughs and, in the distance, roosters began to greet the day as the stars winked out and a pearly sky commenced to redden.

The local men perked up and began to crane their necks about, trying to see through a light mist which was beginning to form over the river and sloughs. Everyone knew it would burn off directly the sun came up. Even the horses raised shaggy heads and cocked ears as if sensing that this long, hungry march was coming to an end. Not very far away a farm dog commenced to bark conversationally, which most likely meant that some farmer had turned out to start another day's milking.

While retying his queue Spurling called softly, "Well, Capt'n, reckon you're pleased to be comin' home. Wish to God 'twas me."

At that moment the distant report of a firearm penetrated the stillness so delicately that the sound might have been let in by a needle's point on the horizon. Immediately, the survivors reined in on recognizing a brittle spatter of shots. They sounded like giant hailstones striking a tin roof.

14. Nadir

BECAUSE Eclipse had been, and probably still was, the fastest horse foaled in Georgetown County in many a year, Barry Colcord raced along the Sampee's shore leading Sergeant Wilcox by a good hundred yards. The rest of his following became strung out over a quarter of a mile.

A strangled, breathless sensation seized the Carolinian when, on rounding a bend in the road, he sighted Ricelands for the first time — in an eternity, it seemed.

The house itself, standing among great oaks, appeared to be intact although flames were beginning to curl up from the horse barn and the slave quarters behind it. However, as he was turning into his driveway a tentative wisp of smoke rose from Ricelands's western exposure and he sighted a swarm of dark figures hurrying in and out of his home like ants about a disturbed hill.

In a frozen, deadly rage, the Carolinian roweled his mare until she began to run as she had not since the start of the war. His remaining saddle pistol he knew to be useless, it recently having suffered a broken lock — so he wrenched out a heavy dragoon saber he'd picked up after the Battle of Waxhaws and, in deadly silence, charged straight at a milling crowd of looters clad in parts of uniforms or rough civilian clothes. They were too busy piling furniture into a pair of farm wagons pulled up before the front entrance to notice him until he got quite close.

A mad gleam in his eyes, Colcord slashed at raiders lugging Laura's chest of drawers down the front steps. Screaming, they dropped their loot and tried to protect themselves, but two of them immediately went down under the thick, curved blade. Next, the berserk master of Ricelands made for a bearded, narrow-shouldered fellow who hurriedly dropped a chair he was preparing to heave onto the nearest wagon and tried to get away.

Barry felt his arm jarred all the way to his shoulders as he brought his saber crashing down squarely onto the looter's head and split his skull to a level with his brows. Wrenching free his weapon, Barry raced about the wagons. Then, for the first time, he wished he'd delayed long enough to allow his companions to come up, for now a group of mounted men appeared around a corner of the house and rode straight at him. Their furious yelling penetrated the crackling roar caused by flames consuming wood dried by the long and rainless summer.

"Laura! *Where are you, Laura?*" screamed Colcord, then wheeled to meet a wide-shouldered and pale-bearded fellow in a tattered red tunic. He came rushing up a few yards in advance of his companions, jeering, "She ain't goin' to see you, Cap'n — nor anyone else anymore!" Barry got a brief but indelible impression of burning blue eyes, a long jaw and a ruddy, stub nose rushing toward him behind a leveled pistol.

He swung his saber in a short arc — no time for a full swing — and struck with all his strength, but Eclipse was moving too fast to permit his hitting the target fairly. He was carried past the red-coated rider before he knew it. All the same, he knew he hadn't missed altogether; his point had encountered brief resistance and he glimpsed his enemy reeling in his saddle while clutching at a crooked cut that had started blood spurting through his sparse yellow beard.

Barry tried to turn back, but couldn't; Eclipse was too outraged by his merciless spurring to heed him. In desperation the frantic Carolinian again and again threw his weight against the bit in a series of violent jerks which opened his wounded scalp and sent a warm rivulet coursing down his neck.

By the time Colcord succeeded in wheeling, his companions, although heavily outnumbered, had commenced a mêlée in front of the house. Above the ever-increasing roar of flames, he heard scattered shots, then blades began to flicker in the sunrise. Horses backed and lunged in all directions. By the time Barry could close in again, several figures lay still on the dusty ground and wounded men were trying to pull out of the fight.

Barry thought he recognized the sandy-haired man he'd slashed; he was dismounted and running towards a row of horses snorting and rearing at a hitching rail.

When, through shifting clouds of dust, Barry realized that Wilcox,

Black Buck and two others were falling back, he charged for a third time, but this time a swarthy fellow in a black-and-white calfskin jerkin saw him coming and sang out, " 'Ware! Heah comes the young mastuh ag'in!" and whipped a carbine to his shoulder.

Barry dropped flat along the mare's neck and drove his point into the fellow's hairy chest barely in time to spoil his aim, but then another musket roared and it seemed that his whole left side was caving in. By instinct alone, he clung to his saddle until a red-streaked wave of blackness engulfed him.

Gray-haired but still athletic Lieutenant-Colonel Frederick Colcord leaned forward in his saddle keeping his gaze on those woolly, bronze-blue columns of smoke beginning to mount lazily from his second son's home. Fervently, he cursed that slave lookout who probably would pay with his life for having been found asleep on the watch.

Well-fleshed but nevertheless quite vigorous at sixty, the veteran felt pleased to recognize the stirring of certain exhilarating if un-Christian and bloodthirsty impulses he'd not experienced since the close of the old French War. In his rear galloped a heterogeneous column of retainers he'd trained and equipped for just such an emergency. Alas, most of them were suffering from disabilities which had kept them from service in the field.

While his good gray hunter covered the ground with easy, space-eating strides, Lieutenant-Colonel Colcord, late of His Majesty's 42nd Foot, mourned that at least one of his three sons couldn't be riding beside him. But that wasn't possible; Rob had perished so futilely, unnecessarily at Fair Lawn and 'Gustus had gone back to the fighting only to die at the Waxhaws and Barry hadn't been heard of in weeks. The veteran's fine, aquiline features contracted as to physical pain.

With the sound of many hoofs drumming behind him along the sun-dried dike, Frederick Colcord fought to contain himself enough to think clearly. Oh God! *Why* hadn't he been warned earlier about this attack on Ricelands?

What could be happening to Laura and, damn it, to *his* grandchildren? An icy wave of anxiety chilled the veteran. What could he find to say when Barry came back to find his home a ruin? Then he realized that the raiders, whoever they might be, had sighted his party, for they quit loading plunder and ran to scramble aboard their horses.

Experienced, the colonel let his followers catch up, then unsheathed that same lion-guarded sword he'd carried up to Louisburg. Flourishing it above his head he bellowed, "Cha-a-rge! Grant quarter to nobody!"

To the veteran's astonishment, a trio of horsemen he'd seen hovering undecidedly at some distance from the house came galloping to meet him, although the rest were hurrying off to the westward.

Major Spurling, bareheaded and scarlet of face, swerved his lathered horse off the road, panting, "For God's sake, sir, don't shoot! We're none of them!"

Barely in time, Frederick Colcord noticed this wild-eyed rider's blue-and-red tunic as that of the Virginia Line, yelled, "Fall in behind!"

The men from Tranquility closed in on the burning mansion so fast that the old colonel was able to recognize Jasper Skelton's bloodied, lanky figure among the fugitives. The rescuers chased long and hard and, thanks to lucky shots, succeeded in emptying a pair of saddles, but there was no overtaking the main body — their stolen thoroughbreds were just too fast; soon the outlaws vanished into a scrub pine forest with the ease of ants disappearing into a rotten log.

Obeying willingly enough Colonel Colcord's command that no prisoners be taken, his overseer lost no time in executing three captured Shell Towners, but only after the hairy fellows had been forced, savagely enough, to admit that Jasper Skelton had been their leader.

Long since, Frederick Colcord had abandoned the pursuit and, followed by a few retainers, had raced back to Ricelands, the whole second story of which now was ablaze.

"Mastuh! Mastuh!" On bowed legs Saul Black Buck appeared running out of Ricelands's dairy house into which he'd dragged his unconscious commander. "Come quick, suh! Cap'n Barry he lose much blood!"

" 'Tend to him best you can!" the veteran shouted over the conflagration's rolling roar. "Must try — find — wife — children. Seen anything of 'em?"

"No, Mastuh. Not been in house."

As Frederick Colcord clattered across a veranda littered with a wide miscellany of household property, scorching flames began to buffet his face.

"Laura! Laura!" As if preparing to dash out into a heavy rainstorm the veteran bent his head and, shielding his face in the crook of his arm, dashed into the hall against a whirling blast of gas and smoke. "Laura! Where are you?" Through smarting, streaming eyes he peered in all directions but saw nothing beyond Barry's wildly scattered possessions.

Beginning to choke, the elder Colcord dropped onto his hands and knees and crawled into that room which Barry had intended to become the library. "Laura! Laura! Where — you?"

Then, through acrid smoke clouds, he glimpsed Laura, lying loosely sprawled on the floor. At first glance he knew she was dead — she lay too flat to have any life left in her. A wide crimson pool was creeping away from beneath her shoulders.

After thrusting his daughter-in-law's body into a half-seen figure's arms, the old man disregarded searing lungs to conduct a quick search for his infant granddaughter. Nothing was found of her until, next day, a small black lump of flesh was discovered among the charred remains of a cradle.

At length the veteran, with throat and eyes afire, had to give up and feel his way back to the entrance hall. So deafening had the roar of flames become that it was a miracle that the singed and staggering old man heard a faint whimpering come from a long, low clothes chest standing just inside the front door.

Despite tearing coughs, Frederick Colcord managed to raise the lid and make out the small, tear-streaked face of Patrick, his grandson.

He barely had time to pull the child from his hiding place before the staircase leading upstairs burned through and collapsed, creating a fiery maelstrom. The master of Tranquility just was able to stagger across the porch with most of his hair singed from his face and his clothing smoldering in several places. He passed the child to one of his bookkeepers and then reeled rather than walked towards the dairy house.

15. The Fugitives

SERGEANT Wilcox and Saul Black Buck unloaded the unconscious and deathly pale captain from a spring wagon and placed him on a mattress which four husky Negroes maneuvered up a winding staircase to the room Barry had occupied during his youth.

Old Dr. Jessup, fetched from Georgetown in a racing chaise, made a careful examination, then stated that a heavy bullet had passed cleanly through the patient's side, but, in doing so, had cracked two, possibly three ribs. He was forced also to stitch the reopened gash in Barry's head.

Thoughtfully fingering a long, silver-gray beard, the physician drawled, "Well, Frederick, I wouldn't worry overmuch if the boy weren't in such a damnably poor condition. Even so, he may be riding in two months' time. D'you know what really concerns me?"

"No, Edward, I don't. What is it?"

"How will your son react when he learns about the doings at Rice-lands?"

Two days dragged by during which the old colonel spent much time pacing about his big and now strangely empty-sounding house with griz-zled head bent and hands clasped behind him. Try as he would, Freder-ick Colcord couldn't bring himself to admit that the voices of two sons would never again be heard in Tranquility. Tranquility? Bah! What a tragic misnomer the name had become!

Only through great efforts did the veteran of the old French War force himself to organize his neighbors and retainers as a home guard of sorts. He met with little success. First off, Major Spurling, not un-naturally, had ridden on his way to learn what might have happened to his family and property. Returning or discharged soldiers proved apa-thetic, if not downright disinterested in further military adventures. The war had been lost for good and all, said they, nor could anyone foresee what might happen in the immediate future.

Most people confessed that they intended to accept a general amnesty just as soon as it was offered by Lord Cornwallis and return to the Old Order quickly and peacefully as they might.

As for Barry, he lingered in a curious half-world. Much of the time he felt light-headed and feverish because the weather continued windless, hot and dreadfully sultry. Endlessly, he muttered, turned and twisted on sweat-sodden sheets.

Whenever she could, old Aunt Minnie from Ricelands — she had es-caped Skelton's raid because she'd been out looking for a strayed calf — came up to fan him and place cool cloths on his brow and wrists. In vain she tried to get him to taste all manner of his favorite dishes pre-pared in the mansion's semi-detached kitchen.

Following a brief period of noisy lamentation, Minnie, with typically Negro resignation, had given over worrying about her "man" and their half-grown son, who'd been carried off by the Shell Towners. Aunt Minnie knew very well she wasn't going to lay eyes on either of them again.

On occasion the old slave would find the patient lying with eyes wide open, unblinking and apparently seeing nothing. Despite her best efforts, he soon would lapse into a semi-stupor which he seemed unable or unwilling to shake off.

Dr. Jessup was sent for every day to change dressings and to bleed the man he had tended to since birth. Dutifully, the snuffy old fellow would delve into a bag of medicines and produce foul-tasting tonics, cordials and elixirs which Barry would refuse to swallow.

After Dr. Jessup's second visit Frederick Colcord followed him out to the mounting block and asked quietly, "Now, Edward, not as a doctor but as an old and dear friend, is Barry making any progress — will he recover?"

Dr. Jessup merged slender, silvery brows and heaved a deep sigh. "I could answer that better were I certain that Barry *already* knows the worst — that his wife and the baby girl are dead, that his home and outbuildings have burned to the ground."

The colonel fingered his strong, box-like jaw. "While I can't be positive, Edward, I *feel* that he knows."

"Why?"

"Understanding my son as well as I do," the old officer said heavily, "I think that since he hasn't tried to rally enough even to ask questions, it seems obvious that he's aware of what's happened and that he's unwilling to make the effort to recover."

Briefly, the doctor rested a blue-veined hand on his friend's shoulder. "You never were a fool, Frederick, so you may be right about that, but it's not Barry I feel the sorriest for — 'tis you. It ain't right that you, a widower these many years, should have raised three fine sons and now, through no fault of your own, stand to lose the last of 'em."

The colonel straightened, said with a touch of asperity, "Well, since I don't intend to lose Barry, suppose you tell me what I must do?"

"Somehow you're to rekindle Barry's interest in life. Possibly constant reminders that Patrick is alive and well and needs him may do the trick. Failing that, Frederick, you must find some other incentive."

Barry awoke around twilight, then lay staring blankly at the antlers of the twelve-point white-tailed buck he'd shot on his fourteenth birthday with the new rifle-gun Pa had given him. For the first time he noticed that a lot of dust had collected on the rack of which he'd been so proud.

But what did it matter? Nothing mattered, nothing; not anymore. In that case why not retreat into that half-sleep, half-stupor in which he was finding the peace and respite his mind needed so urgently. Well, in a moment he would drift off again, just before Aunt Minnie came waddling with her tray and wearing a spuriously cheerful smile.

He experienced a faint stirring of anger: so this was to be his reward for all the hunger, pain and misery he'd endured during the past four years? Where was that divine justice they lauded and prated about in church? Had God rewarded the merciful, the valiant and the faithful and those quietly enduring in this war? Not by a damn' sight!

Why had the Lord in His infinite wisdom seen fit to inflict on the Patriot armies so many hard-drinking, self-seeking or hopelessly incompetent senior officers? Why should He have awarded victory to such red-handed butchers as Banastre Tarleton and his like?

Aye. Something was very wrong with a world in which men like Rob and 'Gustus bravely gave up their lives while all too many cowards, brutes and traitors went unpunished. Why should Cousin Betsey, the Trefont girl and the others be forced to pay so terribly for barbarities inflicted on George Walker — a man they had never known to exist?

Suppose he decided to go on living? What was left for him? Barry Colcord continued to stare at the dim and shadowy ceiling ten feet above. Should he attempt, if the British permitted, to raise a new home on the ashes of Ricelands, on the graves of Laura and their second child? Or should he take Patrick and strike westward to homestead on those rich lands waiting beyond the green ramparts of the Alleghenies? Come to think on it, after Monck's Corner he'd heard a lot of talk about taking such a course.

His musings ended when on the driveway below his window sounded a trampling of hoofs as if three or maybe four horses were being pulled up. Losing interest, Barry decided that this probably was only the return of a scouting party Pa had sent out to continue the hunt for Jasper Skelton's marauders. Shell Town itself, when searched, had produced nobody who knew anything at all about the raid on Ricelands. Of course not.

Only vaguely he recalled snatches of a conversation between his father and a neighbor who'd brought in a report that British patrols also were in pursuit of Skelton. The Shell Towner, it would appear, entertained no compunctions about whether they should kill and loot neutrals, Patriots and Tories indiscriminately. The neighbor had concluded his visit with an observation that Skelton, along with other bands of desperadoes who had taken to harrying the Tidewater, was beginning to find the vicinity too hot for him. Most of these outlaws were heading towards the sparsely settled interior or up into North Carolina where nobody would be likely to identify them.

The hoofs sounded closer, then golden rays cast by a lantern wavered across the bedroom's ceiling. Next, Barry heard his father's strong voice calling, "You, out there! Stand fast and raise your hands, else we'll blast you! Are you Britishers or Loyalists?"

Someone down on the driveway laughed harshly. "Not guilty on either count, your honor."

Another rather pleasant voice then pleaded, "Let us in, *pour l'amour de Dieu!* We and our 'orses are ready to perish through 'unger and fatigue. We assure you, *Monsieur*, that life 'as been most uncomfortable since our defeat."

"What defeat?"

Barry was surprised to find himself straining to catch the reply. "Why, near Camden, sir," the first stranger said. " 'Twas for us a disaster of the first magnitude."

Camden? So the American defeats were continuing!

Suspicion still in his tone, Colonel Colcord called out, "When was that?"

"Three days ago — or was it four?"

"You're sure you're neither British nor Tory sympathizers?" Barry's father insisted.

"Anything but; besides, there are only the three of us — all too dog-tired to put up any kind of a fight."

"In that case I'll accept your word, sir." Door bolts *click-clacked*, then Negro grooms led the strangers' horses off to the stables.

Camden? Where in hell was Camden? Through the effort of trying to remember, Barry's head wound commenced to throb again. Oh, yes; Camden was that pretty little town up in North Carolina where he'd stopped one night while on his way to court Laura — old Ian MacDonald's considerable holdings lay only a scant day's ride beyond it to the northwest. Barry stifled a moan. That was when he'd first met Colin MacDonald. To his amazement he could recall in clear detail just how Colin had looked while going for his dirk.

Suddenly nauseated, the wounded man was content to re-enter a vague maelstrom of semi-consciousness in which he whirled until he lapsed into a profound sleep.

The sun was up and already making its heat felt when Barry opened gummy eyes and realized that today was so windless that even minor noises could be heard beyond the mosquito bar of white muslin protecting his bed. Reaching out, he rang a silver hand bell and almost at once recognized Aunt Minnie's elephantine tread on the back staircase.

"Lawd be praised!" She beamed like a dusky moon when she saw him for the first time sitting somewhat propped up among his pillows.

He managed a wan smile framed in a dense growth of dark stubble. "Want to eat something, Auntie; real food, mind you — no invalid's hogwash."

"Nossuh! Oh, praise de Lawd! Ah fix you de bestest omelette eveah Ah make! Anythin' else, suh?"

"Present my respects to my father and ask him to come and see me at his convenience."

Frederick Colcord's rugged, deeply lined and ivory-tinted features lit when he beheld his second son regarding him with a clear light showing in his sunken, brown-ringed eyes. "Oh, Barry, Barry! Thank God you're getting better! Should have known you would, but I — I've been so — so goddam bloody fearful you mightn't — well — want to live." Colonel Colcord offered an apologetic shrug as he crossed to take the invalid's hands very gently between his. "You never were any part of a coward, my son." The veteran thumbed a trace of moisture from his cheek and his manner underwent an abrupt change, became brisk. "I must leave you now to speak to some uninvited guests. You may have heard them arrive last night?"

"Yes, Pa, but only in a vague sort of way."

The hollow-cheeked captain of the late Ricelands Troop barely had downed Aunt Minnie's omelette plus some delicious biscuits and a mug of powerful real coffee when Colonel Colcord returned to seat himself on an embroidered taboret dragged to the bedside.

Following a stilted conversation on generalities the older man said carefully, "I hesitate to bring up a painful subject, but —"

"Yes, sir?"

Frederick Colcord drew a deep breath. "How much do you recall about what happened at Ricelands — the fate of Laura and her new baby?"

The bandage-swathed head inclined almost imperceptibly. "Yes, Pa, I've overheard enough to guess most of what's happened."

"Good. That spares me a dreadful task." He smiled. "By the bye, you'll not have to listen hard to hear Patrick playing a game of tag with pickaninnies back of the house."

Barry blinked. "Thank God at least he was spared. How did that happen?"

Barry listened to a militarily succinct account, nodded, then said, "What about those people you spoke of, sir? I mean the ones who came here last night?"

"They're fugitives from another terrible defeat we've suffered. At the moment the poor devils are still sleeping like dead men. The senior officer is a Colonel Armand. With him are a lieutenant from Maryland named Tarrant and a Frenchman who calls himself the Chevalier de Buysson; seems he was an aide to a foreigner called Baron de Kalb. He says the baron was killed at Camden."

"Why have they come this way?"

The old man glanced out of the window over a succession of rice fields waving yellow-green under a torrid sky. "It's a long story, but if you're prepared to hear more bad news, why, I'll bring our visitors up and let them tell you in their own words about what happened at Camden. Shall I?"

"Pray do, but only after they've finished their rest. I can guess how exhausted they must be; it's a long ride here from Camden."

16. *Colonel Armand*

LATE in the afternoon Colonel Colcord ushered in two of his visitors. One was Colonel Charles Armand, who not only was an aristocrat from Virginia but, like his host, had served for many years as a regular in the British Army during which he'd done extensive campaigning in the Low Countries, aside from having taken part in General Wolfe's famous siege and capture of Quebec.

Otherwise, Charles Armand was a hatchet-faced, wiry individual who stood almost as tall as General George Washington, on whose staff he had served for over two years as a personal aide. The Virginian, because his tunic was being mended, at present was outfitted in one of his host's velvet housecoats. His were level but penetrating gray-blue eyes, deep set in a narrow head which appeared to be close-shaven under a short and yellowed campaign wig. Because remarkably few wrinkles creased the visitor's fine, patrician features, his age might lie anywhere between fifty and seventy.

Colonel Armand's companion, Major le Chevalier du Buysson, was Norman and as French as French could be — although not typically so, he being big of body, blue-eyed and quite deliberate of speech and manner. Moreover, his plentiful hair was coarse and straw-colored, as was his large and ragged mustache.

Later it came out that the Chevalier du Buysson had reached America quite early in the war in the retinue of the Marquis de Lafayette and, because he spoke fluent English — for all he hated the "Goddams" with a passion — he had been attached almost immediately to the commander-in-chief's headquarters, where he'd served until that unlucky day when he and Colonel Armand had been detached and ordered South in a desperate attempt to reach General Horatio Gates in time to help him devise a plan of campaign which would be to drive the enemy out of Georgia and the Carolinas and, in so doing, destroy Lord Cornwallis's army.

Once the guests had been introduced and had found seats near Barry's bed, Colonel Colcord courteously invited Colonel Armand to speak.

"I feel," the veteran commenced, "that perhaps what the chevalier and I have to tell you, Captain, is best related in two parts. The first concerns a major engagement fought near the village of Camden in North Carolina." He inclined his head towards the big Norman who sat on a ladder-back chair with arms folded across his chest and thick, hairy legs sticking out from an old, brown-and-blue banyan of Augustus's. "Since Major du Buysson was longer in the thick of battle than I was, I shall ask him to give you an account of what happened."

Beyond opened windows familiar noises such as the chopping of firewood and the beating of a rug continued as the chevalier, in almost unaccented English, began a terse account of the battle.

According to most of the staff, explained the Norman, General Horatio Gates, after receiving his orders from the Congress, had come down from Virginia full of self-importance and still preening himself over his undoubtedly great victory at Saratoga. Eager to add laurels to his brow, that high-living and stubbornly opinionated old man had refused even to consider the true strength of forces hurriedly scraped together for him to command. Complacently, the new commander-in-chief had closed his eyes to reports of desperate shortages in all sorts of essential supplies and munitions. Worse still, du Buysson said bitterly, Gates, ever "full of sound and fury," had allowed himself to be tricked into hurrying after Lieutenant-Colonel Lord Francis Rawdon when that astute tactician had feigned a retreat with the dual purpose of allowing his reserves to catch up while enticing the American into committing his forces before they were even partially organized or supplied.

The big Frenchman leaned forward elbows on knees and stared at the floor while Barry, despite himself, listened to his every word in slowly mounting rage.

Of all things, snorted the chevalier, this ineffable general made up his mind to conduct a night march — a risky and difficult maneuver even when executed by well-trained troops — to Sanders Creek lying some seven miles to the north of Camden. In vain had the commanding general's aides and adjutant pointed out that, although certain unreliable strength returns *did* indicate that he had some seven thousand troops on hand, rather less than half of such a number actually were present and fit for duty.

Rasped the tall, blond Norman, "I am very pleased, *Monsieur le Capitaine*, that you were not there to 'ear what that pompous bag of wind said when informed of our actual strength — or weakness: 'Gentlemen, these are sufficient for our purpose!' *Figurez-vous! Monsieur le Général* then boasted: 'Tomorrow I will breakfast in Camden with Lord Cornwallis at my table.' "

Du Buysson's large features gradually turned red while he went on to relate how, resisting all arguments and protests, Horatio Gates had ordered this general advance on a stiflingly sultry night — a march which became almost immediately disorganized because, for supper that evening, General Gates had decreed that his hot, tired and bewildered men be issued generous rations of molasses in place of the usual heart-warming gill of rum. Of course the hungry troops eagerly devoured rations of half-cooked salt beef along with plenty of coarse-ground corn-meal mush mixed with molasses; the poor devils might as well have swallowed stiff doses of jalap or any other strong cathartic!

As a result, when the march began, the sweating and chigger-bitten troops soon were forced to fall out by the hundreds in order to relieve themselves. Once they did so they stood little chance of rejoining their units. To make matters worse, no moon was shining and the weather and the insects could not have been more insufferable.

Du Buysson paused and brightened when a servant entered carrying a tray of dewy silver goblets containing mint and brandy and a pitcher of cold spring water.

Frederick Colcord told his son, "Have a little. It's the best cognac I have left. Can't harm you."

When Colonel Armand raised his goblet, the rest did the same. Said he, "To your swift recovery, sir."

Once the men sitting about in the darkened bedroom had swallowed a few sips, the Frenchman continued, "We 'ad marched for about four hours along a narrow, sandy and wood-cloaked road that ran between mosquito-filled swamps when, suddenly, the night became streaked by musket flashes." Angrily, the Norman broke off, tilted back his big yellow head and took a long gulp. "Our advance guard 'ad blundered into the enemy, who also were undertaking a night march in the 'ope of surprising us at dawn. *Voilà!* They were as astonished as we, but much better trained."

Du Buysson bowed towards his companion. "Since Colonel Armand was in command of the American Legion, 'e can tell you better than I what 'appened to our van when the infantry of Tarleton's Legion came up and opened fire."

"No, Emile, I would prefer not to dwell on that painful moment, so pray continue your account," growled the old Virginian and bent to pat one of Juno's handsome puppies which had wandered upstairs in search of a cool spot. The young dog sighed, flopped down at Armand's side and promptly went to sleep.

Obediently, the Chevalier du Buysson went on to describe how, during a fight between the advance guards, they had blazed furiously at one another for a few minutes then had broken off because in the dark neither side really knew what they were doing or what they were up against. Both sides were ready to postpone further action until daybreak.

"— A moment, sir," Barry's weak voice broke in. "I don't quite grasp the situation — the terrain, I mean."

The Frenchman nodded, described how the armies had chanced to clash in a dense woods growing up a narrow neck of land running

between two large swamps; how at the first hint of dawn the American
Legion, plus Gist's and de Kalb's troops, hurriedly had deployed to form
a line across the neck, but then Redcoat regulars were seen advancing
through the morning mists with bayonets fixed.

Although neither side had many cannon along, the few they had
opened fire and added their smoke to the poor visibility and the mounting
confusion. Nevertheless, the British and Tories, raising deep-throated
cheers, had surged forward through the uncertain gloom. Some raw Virginia militia units were ordered to meet them, but these, du Buysson said,
had moved out only slowly and reluctantly but had advanced to within
forty yards of the British line when Lord Rawdon's regulars fired a series
of well-spaced volleys which halted most of the bewildered Americans
in their tracks.

Still weak from diarrhea, the disorganized Americans took one look at
those lines of scarlet-and-white-clad figures advancing steadily behind a
hedge of twinkling steel points and around two thousand of them
dropped their muskets and, without so much as pulling a trigger, fled in
a headlong panic which at once communicated itself to a Maryland bri-
gade held in reserve.

"*Alors, Monsieur le Capitaine,*" the Norman spread hands in a gesture
infinitely expressive of disgust — "being a veteran yourself, you readily
can perceive the sudden 'opelessness of our situation with our left and
center in complete confusion and terrified men running in every direction save towards the enemy. In vain did my chief, the Baron de Kalb,
send for the remnants of our reserves. These Maryland men came up
bravely, but, *hélas*, by then it was far too late. Milor' Cornwallis 'ad
launched his best regulars in a furious attack upon our left flank which
crushed it —" Slowly, the Norman shook his head. "I ask you, what
choice 'ad we but to fall back?"

Du Buysson sat up on his chair with blue eyes flashing and more color
welling into blunt, weather-beaten brown features. "*Hélas,* the Baron de
Kalb's 'orse soon was shot from under him so 'e fought on foot. *Mon
Dieu!* 'Ow 'e fought — like a Roland or a Bayard! What an 'eroic figure
that giant made as 'e laid about with 'is sword while I fought on 'is
left side. 'Aving received no orders of retreat, we 'eld our ground so
successfully that *le baron* wished to attempt a charge *à la baïonnette,*
but just then 'e was 'it by a musket ball, and others struck 'im till 'e collapsed bleeding from eleven wounds!" The Frenchman's voice strength-
ened until it filled the shadowed sick room. "*Mon Dieu!* I stood over 'im

and beat aside bayonet thrusts until Milor' Cornwallis chanced to ride by and at once caused the Baron de Kalb to be attended by 'is personal surgeon.

"I, too, would 'ave been taken 'ad not some Marylanders at that moment staged a brave but unsuccessful counterattack. During it I caught a loose 'orse and continued fighting."

Under Augustus's faded banyan, the guest's muscular shoulders drooped a little. "Later, I 'eard that, after 'aving for three days endured the greatest of pain, the baron died. *Que le bon Dieu reçoive son âme bien tendrement!*"

"A very gallant gentleman died with him," Armand agreed softly — "and a damned capable officer, too."

"What followed?" Barry murmured after a brief silence.

"Disaster, complete disaster! *Figurez-vous, mon Capitaine*, of our poor little army more than a thousand men were killed, wounded or captured, along with all of our baggage train, supplies and artillery."

Colonel Armand's wigged head swayed slowly from side to side. "In other words, gentlemen, we must face the fact that we have no organized troops left south of Virginia — nor is there much possibility of forming a new army before Cornwallis crushes our remnants, once and for all. Nevertheless," he looked up and spoke briskly, "we and a few other diehards are here to see what can be done about that — and another matter of equal importance."

A stillness prevailed in the high-ceilinged bedroom in which were clearly audible a droning of flies, the far-off braying of a jackass and the crowing of gamecocks strutting in their walks back of the mansion.

Finally, Barry asked, "And what, may I ask, was General Gates doing during the battle?"

Father and son were taken aback by the violent curses which erupted from both visitors. Their vehemence so startled Colonel Colcord that he arose and hurriedly ordered a fresh round of drinks.

"Well may you ask, Captain, how our valiant commander-in-chief occupied himself!" Charles Armand, with bony jaw jutted, commenced to stride agitatedly back and forth on slippered feet. "Believe it or not, sir, the moment the battle was joined that vast, lily-livered poltroon became so numbed by fear that he could not issue a single order! During the entire engagement he sent never a word to his subordinates! Instead," snorted the Virginian, "the general — I, myself, saw him do it — mingled with the first flood of runaways which, as the chevalier has told you, were green, half-sick volunteers from North Carolina.

"That miserable coward completely lost his head, and being mounted on Fearnaught, the fastest horse in the Army —" he glanced at Frederick Colcord — "which is a son of Colonel Baylor's famous racer of the same name, you'll no doubt remember, sir — our general soon outdistanced his fellow fugitives and never drew rein till he reached Charlotte, which lies a long sixty miles to the north of Camden."

An all-too-familiar sense of disgust and outrage forced Barry to sink back among his pillows. God above! What hope remained for the American Cause when the Victor of Saratoga in person set so miserable an example?

"— And there, sir, you have the whole ugly and disgraceful story of Camden!" concluded Armand, angrily draining his second julep. "Never was a victory more complete nor a defeat more total! What remains of our troops now have become all but hopelessly dispersed, hiding in swamps and forests. Most of 'em, we fear, have abandoned their weapons and are too disgusted to even dream of taking them up again — and after what's happened this last year who can blame the poor fellows?

"Aside from this, our Continental paper currency is altogether worthless, while in the South there remains no reserve of arms, ammunition or other materials of war.

"What with the French," he bowed to du Buysson who made a rueful grimace, "having retreated to their West Indies and displaying little inclination to continue the war, the future couldn't appear more hopeless, especially since one hears persistent rumors of disaffection and even mutiny breaking out among troops serving in the Northern states."

Colonel Colcord's iron-gray head drooped a moment, then he looked up. "Tell us, sir, *is* it true that the New Englanders are willing to quit the war provided they, themselves, are granted independence?"

The puppy woke up, wandered over to sniff at the commode and, catching the idea, started to cock a leg but Colonel Colcord discouraged him in time. Courteously, he turned to Armand, "Sorry. You were saying, sir?"

"That the Yankees are dangerously self-centered is all too true," Armand admitted, "but there are several notable exceptions — Nathanael Greene, Henry Knox, Ethan Allen and many other New Englanders remain unswerving Patriots."

The Virginian fetched a long, long sigh. "To render our situation more desperate, hardly an American man-of-war now remains at sea, so our ports are subject, at will, to enemy raids. Meanwhile, the enemy's vigorous blockade of our coasts is strangling our commerce and cutting off aid from abroad while the Congress continues to prove itself ineffectual — incapable of acting with either wisdom or vigor."

Noticing the disappearance of what slight color had tinged his second son's features, Frederick Colcord went over to a bell pull, and when it jangled somewhere in the depths of Tranquility he said, "Gentlemen, my son needs repose. May I suggest we seek refreshment below?

"If you feel up to it, Barry, we will return after dining, but only because our guests have — er — a matter of critical importance to take up with you."

17. Last Resort

Barry had had a long nap when Aunt Minnie rapped and peered inside, beaming because she was wearing a new orange-and-blue 'kerchief knotted neatly over kinky gray hair. "De gennamuns say dey be up direckly, suh — if yo' cares to see dem."

"Send them up by all means. I'm feeling much better."

On this occasion Barry's previous visitors were accompanied by a small, jockey-sized young lieutenant named Tarrant who, as the chevalier explained humorously, had been sleeping like six dead men ever since his arrival at the plantation.

After offering courteous greetings Colonel Armand lost no time in coming to the point. Barry prepared to listen with bandaged head resting against a mountain of pillows.

"As you must have gathered from what we told you earlier, Captain Colcord, our Cause at this moment totters on the edge of ruin." The Virginian's hard, steel-gray eyes fixed themselves on Barry's dark-blue ones. "Many of our best and most intelligent leaders, both civilian and military, are now convinced that, barring a miracle, the forces of the Crown cannot fail to destroy what is left of the United States, and that within a few months' time. However, as I have already indicated, there are others in high places, George Washington among them, who do not concur with this dismal view and have sworn never to surrender or to accept a Royal government."

The Chevalier du Buysson waved the blackened briar pipe he had brought upstairs. "*Mon Capitaine*, what my distinguished friend says is true. Many of us who 'ave serve' on le Général Washington's staff 'ave formed a grand plan to be put into effect in case the war is truly lost."

Young Lieutenant Tarrant, having nothing to say on the subject, occupied himself by moving quietly about to study the antlers, the fox mask and brush which flanked them, along with a silver-mounted riding crop and a well-burnished copper hunting horn resting on pegs let into the bedroom walls.

"Shortly after news was received of that inexcusably stupid capture of General Lincoln's troops," Colonel Armand continued after casting a curious glance at his host, who sat staring moodily out into the night, "a secret council of war was convened in His Excellency's headquarters, one which only the ablest and most trustworthy of his officers were invited to attend. It was then that weighty decisions were arrived at and agreed upon."

The Virginian paused long enough to permit Colonel Colcord a question. "And what were these decisions?"

Barry struggled up on his bed, Lieutenant Tarrant turned to face the speaker and Colonel Colcord stopped looking out of the window as Armand said, speaking slowly and impressively, "Among other things we decided that, if all were lost in the field, we would under no conditions tamely lay down our arms and submit to the King's pleasure!"

From behind Tranquility came the despairing squawks of fowls about to be killed for the next day's table.

Young Tarrant laughed nervously. "Damme if those poor birds don't sound just like our generals after a defeat."

Colonel Armand couldn't help smiling. "That's an apt simile, young fellow, curs'd if it ain't." He inserted a finger under his wig and scratched absently. "Well, gentlemen, this council was held very shortly before the chevalier and I were ordered to serve on the staff of the gallant General Gates, but before we left we were, in the deepest secrecy, entrusted with plans the first steps of which are now to be put in motion."

Fascinated in spite of himself, Barry drew a deep breath and wished he hadn't. His cracked ribs caused such stiletto-like stabs of pain that he gasped, "Oh, damnation!"

Misunderstanding, the Virginian cast him a sharp look. "Shall I desist, sir? Or does what I'm saying meet with your approval?"

The haggard young officer caught his breath and nodded. "It does, sir. Kindly continue."

"Very well. Certain of us who escaped from the defeat at Camden now feel justified in carrying out the Council's first instructions."

"— And they are?" queried the master of Tranquility from among the shadows.

"We, sir, are to scatter and range through the South to find groups of stragglers and time-expired veterans and fragments of broken regiments to tell them two things: first, those who are willing to fight on must remain in small, mobile groups which will be capable of avoiding British and Tory patrols. These are gradually to work their way into North Carolina where they are to assemble in the vicinity of Hillsboro, or at some other rally point to be determined later on."

"What about those who've had a bellyful of the war?" queried Barry. "I fear they will form the great majority of the fugitives you seek."

"Such men who refuse to fight but don't intend to live under British rule will be instructed to prepare themselves and their families to cross the mountains when spring comes, settle beyond them and thus enable us to continue our form of government in this new land."

Colonel Colcord stroked his chin a moment, then asked, "So is it the intention of the Council you've mentioned that patriotically-minded people should emigrate to settle in Kentucky and Tennessee?"

"That is our intention."

"— And what preparations, if any, have been made to accomplish this migration successfully?" This was a veteran field officer speaking.

"Surveys of possible routes across the mountains have been and still are being made. For example, Mr. Tarrant, here, was sent West earlier in the summer on just such a mission."

"Then why is he here?" Barry asked unexpectedly.

Tarrant flushed and looked acutely unhappy. "Why, sir, I was making my way towards the Watauga settlements when my party — which numbered only six in all — was surprised by a band of outlaws who murdered all of us saving myself. I was lucky enough to have been off exploring a nearby ford at the time they struck."

Barry reached for water to quench a suddenly burning thirst. Meanwhile, his father said, "So you failed in your mission?"

"Only partially, sir; I was able to bring back valuable information about the state of the Charlotte Pike as far as the Smoky Mountains which lie about two-thirds of the way to Watauga."

"Wherein, then, did you fail?" Barry asked.

Tarrant sighed and slapped a mosquito. "In that I had orders to locate certain agents who had been sent last winter to find out about what preparations had been made to receive immigrants and troops retreating from the South and East."

The diminutive officer hesitated and glanced about the darkening room. "It isn't generally known, sir, that, last autumn, the Council dispatched certain agents to the westernmost Watauga stations and urged settlers already established there to take along any newcomers and push farther west — all the way out to the mouth of the Cumberland River. On arrival, they were to build forts or stations — as I believe they call 'em — clear land and start plantations sufficient to feed immigrants arriving from the East."

Young Tarrant looked increasingly embarrassed. "My failure lay in that I did not reach Sycamore Shoals, which is the chief settlement of the Watauga country."

"— And because of this," broke in the chevalier, "we of the Council remain in ignorance of what 'as 'appened beyond the mountains. For all we know, expeditions led by Colonels Robertson and Donelson may 'ave been wiped out, or may 'ave been so decimated before reaching their destinations that the survivors 'ave been reduced to 'elplessness."

"On the other hand they might conceivably have got through," commented the Virginian. "If they have, we must swiftly find out how they are faring. We have heard absolutely nothing definite nor have received any maps of their routes or a description of the country they traveled through, although such were promised us."

A servant knocked, then brought in a pot of fragrant real coffee, glasses and a gleaming decanter of cognac. Conversation briefly was suspended in favor of banal comments on the weather and an exchange of topical jokes everyone seemed to have heard.

Finally, Colonel Armand set down his cup and addressed Barry. "Suppose, sir, that I come directly to the point? In the light of what you have heard from us you can understand why the Council must dispatch a few dependable and experienced officers across the Alleghenies. Our agents must evaluate the situation in the West and then, as quickly as possible, send us the maps and information we need — and *make sure* that they get to us."

Leaning forward, he lowered his voice, "Captain Colcord, we very much hope that you will consent to be one of these men."

Barry uttered a short, mirthless laugh. "Why me, sir? I know nothing about the frontier."

"Nevertheless, you have campaigned for years in wildernesses no less difficult than those to which I hope you will go."

"But," insisted the wounded man, "I speak no Indian language at all and know nothing of the savages' ways."

"— But your mustee manservant does," promptly stated the chevalier. "I 'ave 'ad some interesting conversations with 'im. This Saul Black Buck 'e speaks Creek, Cherokee and Shawnee and several dialects. And, of course, 'e is part Indian. Is that not so, *Monsieur le Colonel?*"

Barry's father inclined his handsome head. "That is so, and besides, Black Buck hunted with the Creeks and Cherokees until he was captured and enslaved."

Curious, young Tarrant inquired, "How in the world did he ever come here, sir?"

"I bought him years ago from an Indian trader who happened to be passing through Charles Town. At the time I stood in need of a good hunter for this place. I gave him to my son when Barry got married."

"— And so," Armand resumed, "if Black Buck accompanies you, you will, in effect, have at your disposal the special knowledge required for a successful mission.

"Aside from that, Major du Buysson and I are agreed that you are excellently well qualified in matters of integrity, courage and intelligence — let alone military experience." He stood up. "Will you undertake this mission?"

Barry hesitated, then half-shook his head. "I really can't give you an answer, sir. Not now."

The big Norman said quietly, "After all you 'ave suffered and lost, one can understand why you may refuse. Perhaps you feel that you should remain on your land — undoubtedly you 'ave ties 'ere you may not wish to sever."

Barry Colcord's gaze wandered beyond the windows; while he couldn't actually see those twin chimneys rising, black and stark, from the ruins of Ricelands he knew just how they'd look — he'd seen too many like them. Finally, he spoke, in a flat, weary voice, "Sir, most of the ties you mention already have been cut."

Frederick Colcord broke in, agitatedly, "Come now, Barry, don't say such things! Remember, you are now my only son; also, there is Patrick to be considered."

"I'm remembering that, sir, but somehow I feel it's impossible to start over and live here again — especially under British rule."

"Don't be hasty about this matter, Barry. Among other objections, you'll be in no shape to undertake such a mission for a good while."

Barry sat completely upright for the first time and studied the solemn faces surrounding his four-poster. "Gentlemen, I am no more ready to call quits than you are. So, to the best of my ability I will endeavor to oblige you."

"Oh, God," sighed the master of Tranquility. "Must you go? You've already done so much!"

"No more than many others, sir. Pa, I — I'm pretty tired, so please advise me. What would *you* do in my place?"

The old man sighed. "Just what you're going to do, I expect."

"Thank you, Pa. And now, gentlemen, do you care to inform me further about this assignment?"

The Virginian said, "As soon as you are able, you will follow the Charlotte Pike to Sycamore Shoals in the Watauga country. You will take Saul Black Buck with you and not more than two other companions — a larger party might attract unwelcome attention. Feel free to adopt any expedient which will get you surely to the Watauga country as fast as possible.

"Upon arrival you will endeavor to find either Colonel Sevier or Colonel Shelby — both of whom enjoy the Council's complete confidence. Once you have obtained the required intelligence, maps and reports, you will forward them at once to General Washington's headquarters."

The Chevalier du Buysson added gravely, "*Mon Capitaine,* there is still another matter which requires your investigation. Last fall we ordered to Fort Patrick Henry a Dr. Samuel Mason with secret orders to attach himself to Colonel Robertson's expedition before it set out for the Frenchman's Bluff."

"Where is that?"

"It lies somewhere near the middle of the Tennessee country. A similar agent accompanied Colonel Donelson's waterborne expedition which was intended to descend the Tennessee and other rivers to the Ohio and then proceed up the Cumberland to join Robertson's people at the Bluff. Although both parties are rumored to 'ave reached their destination, we 'ave 'eard nothing at all — no maps, no news, either from Dr. Mason or our other agent. You can comprehend our desperate need for definite information, *hein?*"

Colonel Armand jerked a nod. "Yes. One of your principal duties will be to discover what has become of these men and their information.

"There is no need to point out that yours will be a most perilous journey, for, as Mr. Tarrant here has discovered, the hill country, and the whole frontier for that matter, are swarming with banditti, masterless men and gangs of outlaws wanted by the British Crown and our own government."

After a long pause the big Frenchman queried, "Now, 'aving 'eard all this, *mon Capitaine,* are you still prepared to cross the mountains?"

"I am. As quickly as I'm able to travel I'll set out with Saul Black Buck." His gaze then sought his father's erect figure. "Speaking of outlaws, sir, has there been any news of Skelton?"

Colonel Colcord snapped his fingers. "Damn my forgetfulness! Only this morning my overseer told me that a straggler had ridden in to beg a meal and said that just a few days ago he'd passed a party fitting the Shell Towners' description. He said they were hurrying towards the mountains as if eager to get beyond them."

BOOK III

Phoenix Republic

1. Over the Crest

F OR all this was only mid-September it was inescapable that fall was setting in. On and near the summits of Stone Mountain Range hardwoods, showing as bright patches on a dark blanket of evergreens, were turning yellow, orange or red — especially the maples, beeches and birches.

On the Charlotte Pike, a rough trace which wound in a generally northwesterly direction over the Stone Mountains from Morgantown in North Carolina, Captain Barry Colcord of the dispersed and defeated Ricelands Troops reined in Eclipse, his long-limbed mare, on the range's highest crest.

To pull up he had to use his right arm because, after a few hours in the saddle, his left side still pained like an infected tooth. Probably he'd left Tranquility a good deal too soon. True, the gunshot wound had closed, but those ribs the bullet had cracked were yet almighty tender under continued exertion.

Briefly, he wondered what instructions Colonel Armand, the Chevalier du Buysson and young Tarrant now were issuing to wandering bands of American soldiers.

Turning in his saddle, Barry Colcord peered back along the Charlotte Pike — so-called even though it remained impassable for wheeled vehicles over most of its length — and perceived that Tom Calloway, a hungry-looking young Georgian who usually wore a cheerful expression on his flat and sallow face, had dismounted to tighten his saddle's girth.

It had struck Barry as significant that Calloway when he'd asked if he might go along out West hadn't volunteered any details concerning his immediate past.

Saul Black Buck also had halted. Odd, mused Barry, how many subtle changes had taken place in the mustee since they'd set out from Tranquility. Of late Black Buck had taken to wearing his slightly kinky, gray-white hair in twin braids and had mounted a pair of eagle feathers in his battered straw hat. His hooked beak of a nose and thin lips more than ever resembled those of a full-blooded Indian. Ever since they'd entered the foothills of the Stone Mountains the mustee's jet eyes had begun to flicker, ceaselessly probing his surroundings.

With his ragged cloth hunting shirt billowing in an updraught from the valley below, Calloway led his horse to stand staring out over these many ridges, which, all blue with haze, lay ahead.

"Say, Cap'n," drawled the Georgian, "how soon you figger we'll come to the first o' the Watauga settlements?"

"No telling. Maybe tomorrow, or the day after, or the day after that. Why?"

"Just been wonderin' why right-minded people ever would want to settle in such a God-awful, lonely wilderness!"

"They tell me that about fifteen years ago a Colonel Sevier and a surveyor called Alexander Brown explored this country and took such a fancy to it that they moved in their families and settled down."

Calloway reached under a floppy black felt hat and scratched hard at a thatch of sand-colored hair. "Now I never! Say, suh, to what colony — I mean state — does this here land belong?"

"Well, Tom, some folks say Watauga belongs to Virginia but a lot of others are ready to swear it belongs to North Carolina. Nothing's been settled yet, as far as I know."

Briefly, Colcord considered a magnificent succession of towering, deeply forested hills and age-blunted mountains. Stiff puffs of wind beating up from the valley ahead now began to stir not only the horses' manes but also Colcord's hair, grown shoulder-long during his convalescence.

He beckoned Black Buck. "Ever hunt this country?"

"No, Mastuh. Me lived more west 'mong Creeks and Cherokees on edge of Great Hunting Ground."

Colcord turned to Calloway. "What about you?"

"Naw, suh, ain't never been this way afore, but I done heard plenty 'bout the Watauga ground from my Uncle Sam. Him and old Jacob Brown wintered and trapped out this way back in '71. When he come back to Georgia to fetch his family out there he told us young 'uns all about the Watauga country; said they's plenty of game and rich land out that way."

Captain Colcord's newly lined features relaxed a trifle. "It's magnificent, all right. How far ahead of us would you say the next party is traveling?"

The mustee grunted, " 'Bout two, mebbe three mile."

A few thin columns of gray-blue smoke rising in the middle distance suggested that other groups of emigrants already had pulled off the Pike to make camp for the night.

Since setting out from Ramsay's Mills in North Carolina over a week ago, Colcord had encountered many groups of military stragglers; discouraged and hungry-looking, these men slogged along carrying next to nothing by way of supplies or equipment. They displayed no interest whatsoever in Colcord's party beyond inquiring if this track did indeed lead to the Watauga settlements.

Among these ex-soldiers there were not a few honorably discharged veterans on their way to take up land warrants issued in lieu of pay. Also traveling the Pike were family groups of small merchants who'd been ruined by the war; then there were all too many shifty-eyed fellows who kept their mouths tight shut and rode tackeys while their gaunt and slatternly women trudged along on foot often towing a tired child by the hand and at the same time leading a scrawny cow, or maybe herding a few thin pigs, which were reported to bring good prices on the far side of the Alleghenies.

Time and again Captain Colcord's party passed wrecks of carts and wagons which had broken down once the Pike had become nearly impassable for wheeled vehicles. Beyond Morgantown Gap more and more pathetic items of furniture were to be found amid the Stone Mountains' rugged foothills.

It was encouraging, however, to recognize a good many leather-faced and obviously experienced frontiersmen among the emigrants. These generally traveled in small, fast-moving groups.

The mustee remarked softly, "Fum now on, Mastuh, us bettah look out sharper'n we bin. Plenty Cherokee live beyond this gap."

"What of that? They made peace five seasons ago with Colonel Robertson."

"True, but dey plenty Creek 'round here, too, and 'breeds an' white outlaws. None of 'em goin' pass up takin' a easy scalp." The mustee's narrow and nearly lashless jet eyes slitted themselves. "Mastuh, now us must journey like we scoutin' Tory country."

"All right." Colcord mounted Eclipse, swearing softly at barbed pains shooting through his tender side.

Accurately, Tom Calloway squirted tobacco juice at a stump and began to wonder what in hell had happened to start this grim-faced young captain riding towards the frontier. Was a feller to judge by Cap'n Colcord's well-cut civilian garments, elegant weapons and blooded mare, he must be *real* quality and not just a gentleman by Act of Congress — like many officers he'd served, and suffered, under.

That a sizable party of some description must be traveling not too far ahead became evident from piles of horse droppings which still gave off pale feathers of steam. To increase pace to come up with these strangers had been a considerable temptation, but Barry Colcord resisted the idea. For all he knew, these travelers could be deserters or outlaws like Jasper Skelton's Shell Towners.

On sighting a fairly level little clearing hemmed in by lofty evergreens and carpeted with frost-killed ferns, which should offer easily-come-by bedding, Barry pulled up and announced that this night would be spent here.

Once the horses had been unsaddled and their single pack animal off-loaded, Black Buck was preparing to use a flint and steel on a small pile of shredded cedar bark when two shots sounded not very far away. Almost before the reports ceased to echo and re-echo through the fragrant-smelling fir forest, Colcord and his companions were behind trees with weapons cocked and ready.

"How far off?" breathed Tom Calloway, small, pale-brown eyes intent.

" 'Bout a whoop off," muttered the mustee.

Colcord listened a long moment, then spoke softly. "Tom, you mind the animals whilst Saul and I take a look. Most likely 'twas nothing more than some fellow shooting his supper."

Noiselessly as panthers stalking a grazing deer, they started along the Pike a few yards out on its either side. They had progressed only a short distance when a series of shrill and unearthly screams that lifted the hairs on a man's neck beat through the purplish twilight. At the same time Barry heard a loud crashing as if several horses were traveling downhill at a gallop.

Drifting, shadow-quiet, from tree to tree, Barry closed in on that point from whence had come the shrieks.

He glimpsed Black Buck's dark outline keeping abreast, then saw a fire burning in a small open space barely visible through the trees. When, cautiously, Barry parted a clump of laurels just enough daylight remained to reveal a man's long-legged body lying loosely sprawled on the ground; a slender youth was kneeling and keening shrilly beside it.

Once Barry had made sure that no one else remained in the vicinity, he ventured into the clearing, at the same time calling in a soft undertone, "Don't be afraid, lad. We're friendly."

Briefly the mustee exposed black-and-yellow tooth stumps in a flat, tight grin. "Saul's eyes may be growin' dim, Mastuh, but he kin tell dat ain't no boy, for all dem britches an' short hair."

2. *Woods Colt*

ONLY vaguely did Parthenia Bryant recognize the sound of advancing footsteps, then raised her eyes from the body lying so incredibly flat, and through blinding tears watched the approach of a tall, wide-shouldered figure.

When the stranger drew near, Parthenia leapt to her feet with catlike speed, at the same time unsheathing a long, slim-bladed knife. Emitting a squalling snarl, she sprang at the apparition with such violence that, had she been any heavier, the impact must have sent Barry Colcord staggering off balance.

As the blade flickered towards his throat Barry brought his carbine's barrel down on the girl's forearm, forcing her to drop her knife. By the shrill way his sharp-featured and freckled assailant screamed Barry knew Black Buck was right; this meagerly built individual with slanting, hate-filled pale eyes and short, dark hair was no youth but a girl of about eighteen.

When his assailant staggered aside, Colcord flung an arm about her waist, but she must have known something about wrestling, for she escaped his grasp and started to run. She might have escaped had not the mustee tripped her so effectively that she fell hard enough to knock out her wind and lay on the fallen leaves writhing spasmodically, like some small animal run over by a wagon.

Barry picked up the girl's knife, then stood peering down at her through the fast-deepening dusk. "My God, Saul, I've met up with gentler bobcats."

Leathery, deeply seamed features impassive, the mustee called from beside the body, "Mastuh, this feller bin shot thu de heart — from behind. 'Nother ball took him high in de leg."

Since spasms of breathless agony still were convulsing the girl's thin body, Barry put down his carbine to straddle her; after placing palms against her rib cage he began to pump air back into her lungs and at the same time noticed that this body was firm yet surprisingly soft in places. Even by the uncertain light he realized that his prisoner had wide, ruler-straight brows, a short and narrow nose and a well-formed mouth distinguished by an intriguingly brief upper lip.

The minute Parthenia recovered enough breath she began to struggle and kick; when Barry attempted to pin her down by her wrists she spat full into his face. Provoked, he slapped her sharply.

The mustee grunted, "Mastuh, better me tie her up?"

"No! No! Please — don't tie!" The girl stopped struggling and began to sob wildly. "You — you've broke m-my wrist, y-you bloody murderer!" She sat up glaring about. "You aimin' to slay me, too?"

Colcord snapped harshly, "Suppose you stop talking nonsense and tell me what's happened here."

"I — I won't! Y-you're one of the k-killers!"

"What's your name?"

"Parthy Bryant, and be damned to you!"

He pointed to the roughly dressed corpse. "Who was he?"

"Billy — my brother."

Colcord kicked together the remains of the Bryant's cooking fire. When it blazed up he could tell at a glance that this brother and sister — if indeed they really were related — must be poverty-poor; only two threadbare blankets lay half unrolled on the bare ground while their cooking implements included only a skillet and a small kettle, both of cast iron.

Barry began to wonder, why should a couple, so seemingly destitute, have had at least five horses in their possession? He had counted as many severed halter shanks dangling from nearby trees.

"Saul, go fetch in our animals."

When Tom Calloway and the old mustee loomed out of the darkness it was to find the girl crouching, apparently alone, beside the fire. Neither Colcord nor the dead body were anywhere in sight. While securing the horses Calloway peered uneasily about and started violently when, on a nearby hilltop, some woods buffaloes began to bellow.

Presently Colcord re-entered the zone of gold-red firelight, explained, "I've dragged the corpse under the bushes. In the morning we'll fix the poor devil a grave."

Without being told, the mustee left the fire to hunker down and guard the animals hitched to those same trees the Bryants had used.

While Colcord undid blanket rolls and got out a folding tin candle lantern Tom concocted a stew from lumps of greasy and slightly tainted venison boiled with Indian cornmeal and a rasher of salt pork.

Once the stew had begun to simmer, Colcord carried a gourd dipper of it over to the sullen-faced girl. He sank onto his heels. "We had nothing to do with your brother's death, so eat this, you pathetic little fool, and maybe you'll feel better."

From under dark lashes the girl's faintly slanted and pale gray eyes peered upwards; a fleeting half-smile appeared on her clearly delineated lips. "Thanks, Mister. Guess I — I must ha' been too shook up to think straight. I won't cause no more fuss, really I won't."

As Parthenia Bryant's slim and grimy hands closed over the gourd she seemed to shrink in size and to appear even slighter and thinner than ever. Although the stew remained smoking hot this wild, barelegged creature in the tattered and shapeless homespun shirt and breeches used black-nailed fingers eagerly to cram lumps of meat into her mouth.

No one spoke. Tom Calloway circulated a blackened tin can of bitter but warming acorn coffee.

The girl licked clean her fingers, then, employing quick, dainty dabs reminiscent of a raccoon washing itself, she removed most of the sauce from her mouth. Colcord fished out a short-stemmed clay pipe, said quietly, "Now, Missy, suppose you give me a truthful account of what's happened and why you're traveling the Charlotte Pike."

"Like I told you, I'm Parthenia Bryant."

"Parthenia?" smiled Barry. "I've never heard the name before."

"Reckon not. Ma got it outen a book, but folks mostly call me Parthy." Briefly, the girl's well-modeled features relaxed. "My Ma came from somewhere in the East. She could read and write pretty fair." She balled a handful of dead leaves and commenced halfheartedly to scrub at dark smears of blood on her almost skin-tight durant breeches.

In his deep and slightly hoarse voice, Calloway said, "Say, Sissy, you say yer last name's Bryant?"

"Aye. My Pa was Long George Bryant — one of the firstest Long

Hunters." Then she added with a hint of pride, "Him an' Dan'l Boone was cousins — sort of."

The mountain wind began to blow cooler, so Calloway got up and fetched more sticks for the fire. Black Buck didn't like to see that much light in this sort of country and grunted complaint from his thicket.

"Yep. Oncet Ma told me how Pa'd traveled farther west than anybody'd ever been before, along with Dan'l Boone, Joe Drake and a feller named Bledsoe. They must ha' trapped and hunted clear 'cross Tennessee and a land to the north they called Kentucky.

"Later on," continued the girl, "Pa and a German feller named Kasper Mansker made a real long hunt 'twixt the Tennessee and the Cumberland."

Pushing scuffed and dirt-glazed squaw boots closer to the fire, Parthenia then described how her Pa and Mansker had discovered lands so rich in game that a man had to jump from back to back of bison herds in order to get across a living river of animals bound for the great salt licks.

"That no lie," Black Buck called from the background. "Seen 'em so."

Feeling uncommonly good-natured, Calloway invited, "Go on, Sissy. You talk a heap like my Uncle Sam."

"Don't go on callin' me Sissy," snapped Parthenia. "I ain't got a brother now."

Barry relit his pipe and expelled billows to join the campfire's smoke. "All right. From now on we'll call you Parthy. What else about your father?"

"Pa give up trappin' after a while and went back to New River where he came from — that's in Virginny — and married Ma, but some folks claim he didn't really, 'cause he'd already got a Christian Injun wife out in the Creek Nation." Parthy shrugged and sighed, "Reckon that's why mean folk sometimes call me a 'woods colt.'

"Well, Pa, he tried farmin' a while but he weren't much good at it, so when game got scarce, he moved us acrost the Blue Ridge into North Caroliny and settled hard by Salisbury.

"When the trouble with the Redcoats begun, Pa took down his long rifle, filled up his war bag with possibles and told Ma, 'Ye c'n expect me back, Millie, when you sight me.' "

The horses must have scented a prowling bear for they commenced to snort and skitter about at the end of their halter shanks but nobody heeded them; unless starving, no sane bear would venture close to a fire.

Wearily, Parthenia pushed strands of greasy brown hair from before eyes circled by lavender shadows. "Well, in near two years' time Pa come home but he weren't nice to look at or hear, 'cause he was half-crazy and had a great shot hole in his neck that never did heal up; said he'd took that hurt in a great battle fought 'way up in Pennsylvany — wherever that is."

Colcord extended hands towards the flames and nodded. "I take it he never recovered?"

"Naw. 'Though Billy, the neighbors and me nursed him bestest we knew how, Pa kept on failin' till he perished."

"— Where was yer Ma?" Calloway drawled while picking broad, yellowish teeth with his knife's point.

"She'd died a piece before Pa got back."

"How long ago did yer Pa perish?"

The girl shrugged thin, gracefully sloping shoulders. "Don't rightly recall when, but 'twas towards this summer's end. He gave Billy —" Her oblique, light-gray eyes filled as they sought that patch of leaves yet darkened by her brother's blood. "Anyhow, all Pa left of worth was his gun and his soldier's land warrant. Me and Billy decided to move on, so we sold Pa's cabin and got hardly enough to buy a little travelin' gear and a couple of no-count tackeys.

"Well," her voice grew strained again and she glowered at the flames, "we was ready to set out for Watauga when Billy chanced to fall in with some trifling fellers who claimed they was quittin' the war 'cause they reckoned us folks sure 'nuff was going to get licked. Anyhow, they got Billy to join 'em in a raid on some Tory's farm in the valley next to ours. Well, they pulled it off all right an' come back with some valuables and a herd of real good horses."

Propping himself on an elbow, the gaunt young Georgian peered across the fire. "Didn't know there was any Tories livin' near Salisbury."

Parthenia's pointed chin tilted aggressively. "Well, Mister, all *I* know is that Billy and his new friends *said* they took only Loyalist horses."

"And after that?" Colcord prompted.

"After resting and drinkin' for a couple of hours the other fellers took their share of the horses and rode off without no by-yer-leave."

Barry roused a little. "Did they say where they were going?"

"Naw. They just lit out, like I said. I was glad. They were a mean lot and even tried to pester me some, but Billy wouldn't let 'em — nor would I.

"We lit out the very next day for the mountains fixin' to settle somewheres out there."

"Are you sure those men weren't just common horse thieves?" Colcord suggested casually.

Abruptly, Parthenia broke into another freshet of tears. "Oh-h, I — I don't rightly know! Even if them horses mightn't truly have belonged to a Tory, my brother weren't no thief!"

Calloway yawned cavernously. "Say, Parthy, ain't it possible that them horses' rightful owner might ha'e caught up with ye?"

"Who knows? All I know is they slew poor Billy 'thout no warnin'!"

Colcord stretched and sighed. It had been a hard day but he'd no intention of going to sleep just yet. "Did you see anything of the attackers — enough to recognize them, I mean?"

"No. I — I was mindin' my business 'in the bushes' when those cowards killed Billy; reckon that's the only reason I ain't dead, too. I was just tying up my britches when, next thing I know, I heard shots, then a big feller came ridin' fast right past me towin' some of our horses towards the Pike. The others was further off."

"Others? How many were there?"

"Mebbe three of them."

"Tell me, how well did you see this man?"

The girl, whose loose shirt seemed to be only moderately filled, jerked a nod. "For all the poor light I think he was tall, like you, only he'd a yellow beard which weren't so thick I couldn't spy a big red scar."

"Shaped how?"

"Like a pot hook, kind of."

Barry Colcord's voice sounded harsh as a blade being dragged across a steel sharpener. "Like a pot hook?"

Parthenia blinked. "Sure. Like I said, I spied a scar shaped like that through the feller's beard."

"How tall would you say he was?"

"No tellin'. He was a-horseback while — well, I was still kind of scrooched down low among the bushes."

"Was he narrow-shouldered and long in the body?"

"Yep. Kind of." Parthenia's interest rose. "Why? Think maybe you'd know him?"

"Not from what you've said so far. I suppose you'd no chance to notice the color of his eyes?"

Lips pursed and level brows knit, Parthenia considered a moment.

"Come to think on it, I *did* notice. They looked small and was blazin' blue."

"What was he wearing?"

"Some kind of a old green soljer's jacket."

"Can you remember anything else? Try. It's important," Barry urged, aware that a muscle in his cheek had begun to tick.

"Why, he was wearin' a black leather cap with a red foxtail tied to it and Injun leggin's pulled over high, store-bought boots." She peered at him like a suspicious puppy. "Why?"

In the top of a giant beech nearby a great horned owl commenced its eerie ululations.

"I'm looking for a fellow who looks something like that," Colcord admitted, then added with a harsh little laugh, "Back where I come from he was called Skelton, Jasper Skelton. I'm mighty keen to come up with him."

Calloway asked drowsily, "Was he a — a Tory?"

"I'm not sure about that. All I know about Skelton is that he's a cold-blooded murderer."

3. The Movers

ALL morning long a fine, cold rain fell and didn't stop while Colcord's party, now proceeding with increased caution, followed the Pike downwards from the crest of Morgantown Gap.

Nobody talked much, least of all Parthenia Bryant, for during the night a marked change had taken place in her manner. When spoken to she now returned a blank, slack-jawed stare as she sat slumped on the pack horse with shaggy head bowed.

On the day after Billy Bryant's murder the party entered less mountainous country which gradually became characterized by a seemingly endless succession of steep, heavily wooded hills.

From both sides of the Charlotte Pike sounded the music of hurrying brooks and the pretentious rumble of insignificant waterfalls swelled to importance by prolonged autumn rains. More often than not, the horses slipped and splashed along, fetlock deep, in watery, well-trampled black mud. Hoof prints caused by cattle, pigs and horses only a short time before became increasingly noticeable; also, there were tracks which must have been made considerably earlier. According to the old mustee these had been left by horsemen riding in a hurry and leading a number of spare mounts.

Parthenia, astride the pack horse, rode behind its canvas-covered load with small feet dangling slack from her knees. Barry noted, however, that the girl's reflexes remained unimpaired; whenever her mount slipped or stumbled her long, sinewy legs instantly clamped themselves around the beast's barrel.

All in all, Parthenia Bryant presented an unlovely if pathetic figure, for if the girl possessed a comb she hadn't used it to untangle her boyish dark-brown locks which appeared to have been hacked off rather than trimmed above small, flat ears.

The gray and cheerless afternoon was well advanced when Black Buck, who had been riding a few rods ahead of the rest, halted and pointed to a ravine over which a lacy stratum of gray-blue smoke was drifting just above the treetops.

The mustee blinked. "Careful, Mastuh. That plenty people."

Could Skelton be in the camp below? Barry turned to young Calloway. "You and Parthy stay here. Saul, come with me."

Maintaining a brisk lookout, Colcord kicked forward Eclipse. It seemed advisable to warn these strangers of his approach, so he started to sing in a strong but sadly off-key baritone.

He barely had commenced a second stanza when a gruff voice warned from the depths of a thicket, " 'Bide right there! Don't you move!"

When the former cavalry officer halted, Saul Black Buck slipped off his horse, quick as a pouncing lynx, to take shelter behind a thick oak; already he had an old carbine ready for use.

Colcord made no effort to shift his own weapon from its crosswise position on his pommel. "Take it easy, friend. We mean no one harm." Desperately, he tried to visualize the challenger; too bad he'd never heard Skelton speak.

"How many do ye number?" the unknown demanded from among a stand of blue spruces.

"There are two of us here and a couple more — one's a girl — waiting on the Pike. We're peaceable folk on our way to Watauga."

"You better be tellin' strict truth."

Colcord could see the speaker now; he was black-haired and didn't in any way resemble Skelton as he crouched among the spruces leveling a long-barreled Tower musket. His garb was a hunting shirt of coarse brown linen and a jockey cap of black leather that had its peak pinned up in front with a sprig of evergreen tucked into it — ranger fashion.

Barry raised a hand in casual greeting. "Come on out, stranger, and let's get acquainted."

"Well, seein' as you put it that way, I just might. But don't make a quick motion; the same goes fer yer tame savage behind the tree."

Out of the thicket stepped one of the biggest men the Carolinian had ever beheld. He must have stood at least six foot three and was broadly built. This clean-shaven stranger's complexion was a healthy red-bronze hue and he wore his black hair braided into a single, orderly queue bound by a greasy, black ribbon.

To complete the unusual this big fellow's knife, war hatchet and cartridge box, along with a bayonet — of all things — were supported by once-white canvas crossbelts of the type worn by British grenadiers. With a start of surprise, Barry recognized an oval pewter ornament stitched to the fellow's cap.

Bending in his saddle, Barry shook hands, saying, "Seem to recognize that badge of yours — North Carolina Rangers, ain't it?"

"Well, I'll be dogged! That's right. How *d'you* know that?"

"Seen some fighting down South."

"Who air you?" After a perceptible pause, he added, "sir."

"Barry Colcord, late Captain of the Ricelands Troop — Colonel Horry's Light Horse." He called over his shoulder, "Saul! You can come out."

Walking lightly on the balls of his feet the mustee sidled into the open, elevating his carbine's barrel as he advanced. His battered brown hat and the two feathers on it were still drooping and soft from rain.

The big man's full lips curved. "Me, I'm Arthur Jennings, recently sergeant in Major Dixon's company of North Carolina Rangers."

Somehow a warm, indefinable current passed between the veterans when they struck hands.

"Suppose, sir, you and your tame Injun and the rest of you —" he paused, raised a bushy brow — "sure there's only two more?"

"Sure, and one of them, as I've said, is a wild sort of girl we found beside the Pike. If you're interested, friend Jennings, I'll tell you more about it later on."

"All right. Since night's nigh, suppose you camp with us? My wife and the rest of us are halted in yonder hollow."

Barry couldn't suppress a grin. "Somehow I'd guessed that you've women with you. How many?"

" 'Bout a dozen — all ages. Got some sprats along, too."

Wasn't this sheer, bull luck? Now, perhaps he could get rid of Parthenia and go on with his mission.

"Thank you, Sergeant. We'll be happy to join you. Saul, ride back and bring along the others."

Several families were busy about a clearing in which a couple of tents stood pitched on a level, grassy section on the bank of a swift-flowing little river. Two men were dressing out the pink-red carcass of a deer which had been hoisted to a big sycamore. Others were splitting firewood and drawing water.

Several large hunting dogs of indeterminate ancestry raced up hurling threats of death and destruction, but promptly subsided at Jennings's command. The former ranger then beckoned forward a scrawny, bow-legged individual introduced as George Harrison. Grinning diffidently, Harrison offered a calloused hand as big and tight as a fox trap.

"George was a Ranger, too. Hails from Virginny, but don't go holdin' that agin him — he's mighty handy with an ax and can shoot the eye out of a gnat at fifty yards."

The next man to come forward interested Barry because his clothing immediately set him apart. His jacket was of dark gray serge and had a city cut to it, while his legs were protected by muddied broadcloth gaiters buttoned from knee to ankle. Also, he was wearing a linen shirt with a rumpled stock and a dingy, Turkey-red waistcoat lacking several flat, brass buttons.

"Cap'n, I want you should meet Mr. Tom Drayton."

The other, a square-built and slightly pop-eyed individual, offered a curt head bow. "Your servant, sir."

"Mr. Drayton," Arthur Jennings explained, "is a surveyor. He's going to Sycamore Shoals, where he's supposed to meet some fellow surveyors from Virginny. Together, they're supposed to run a boundary line 'way out west. Way things stand nowadays, ain't nobody in Watauga knows whether his land lies in Virginny or in God's country —" he laughed — "which is North Carolina. Mr. Drayton's been sent by our legislature to make sure us Carolinians don't get to hold the dirty end of the stick. It's important 'cause there'll be a pile of people headin' this way from now on."

A faint smile flitted over Mr. Drayton's squarish, insect-mottled features. "If running a true line is *all* I'll have to worry about I'll be well satisfied."

Something in the surveyor's voice prompted Barry to inquire politely, "What are you driving at, sir?"

"— Why, just before leaving Edenton I read a report that Georgia and South Carolina have been conquered and that a pair of British Indian agents by the name of Stuart and Cameron are busy trying to raise the Cherokees, Chickamaugas and Chickasaws against us. Seems these gentlemen are spreading reports that fugitives from the East intend to establish a number of settlements in the Indians' Great Hunting Country. Naturally, the savages don't fancy the idea."

Three women herding children of varying sizes, all round-eyed with curiosity, drew near.

Jennings patted a broad-faced, alert-looking young woman on the shoulder, and his expression softened. "This is my wife, Lucy, and I'll vum no man ever had a finer one. Lucy, girl, this here is Cap'n Colcord from South Caroliny. We figger it's all right fer him to travel with us."

That Lucy Jennings must be descended from a good English family was Colcord's immediate, if unexpressed impression; although her body was big-framed, her hands and feet were small and her lightly tanned features were delicately shaped.

"I'm very pleased to meet you, sir," she smiled and actually dropped a little curtsy rendered awkward by the heavy footing and a thick woolen skirt.

When suddenly all the dogs in camp started to bark, the men jumped for their weapons while, with practiced swiftness, the women dragged their offspring into the underbrush.

"Rest easy," Barry called out. "Those are only my other companions coming in."

When Calloway and Parthenia rode into sight, Lucy Jennings at first was fooled into believing that the latter was a lanky boy, but then recognized her mistake and caught a quick breath. "Good Land of Goshen! Why, that lad's *female!*" Then she turned to Colcord, demanded sharply, "What's wrong with her? Why don't she pay attention? Is she sick?"

As briefly as he could, Barry described the murder of Parthenia's brother and the theft of the Bryants' horses. In conclusion he shot a sharp glance at the former sergeant. "Now, perhaps, you'll understand why I must know if anyone has overtaken your party in the last day or so."

"Well," Jennings said, "ever since we crossed the mountains we've been passed by a lot of soldiers — mostly stragglers and maybe some deserters, I'd say. Howsumever, they all minded their own business and went on by, peaceable and friendly — like they weren't looking for loot or trouble and only wanted to get shut of the war."

George Harrison glanced at Jennings, said, "That's so, but only this mornin', just before sunup, we heard a passel o' horsemen — sounded like there might ha' been five or six of 'em — ride by our camp along the Pike. We wondered why they didn't halt for news and a bait of food. Folks goin' over the mountains gen'rally do."

Colcord studied the sunburnt faces around him. "Did any of you actually see those men?"

"No, we didn't," Harrison admitted. "We were busy watering the stock and the womenfolk were getting breakfast, so, as I said, we only heard 'em pass by. Why are you so curious, sir?"

Barry's mouth tightened. "Because it's possible those people you heard are the ones who murdered Parthy Bryant's brother." He made no mention of Ricelands.

A big woman whose vast bosoms rode easily under a calico shirtwaist approached Parthenia, said, smiling, "I'm Betty Harrison. Come on, Sissy, we're friendly folks — as you can see — so there's no call to look so down at the mouth."

She patted Parthenia's shoulder. "First thing is to get some real food into you, then we'll find you female garments of some sort. No decent girl should go about in boots and britches. Come along." But when she attempted to slip an arm around Parthenia's waist the girl roused violently from her apathy.

Snarled Parthenia, slanted eyes glittering, "Don't you dast touch me!"

"Why, you pert little baggage! I only —"

Jennings's wife intervened, soothingly, "Don't take on so, my dear. Nobody's going to force you to do anything. Land of Goshen! You *must* have had a hard time lately, you look *that* starved and weary. Come along to my tent."

A sigh of relief escaped Barry when Parthenia nodded and obediently trudged off after the former sergeant's wife.

Millions of blue-white stars began to glitter while in the depths of the forest wolves raised their mournful wails. Barry Colcord listened to them, his stomach comfortably full of Virginia ham cooked with bear grease, potatoes and some sort of greens washed down with scalding-hot sassafras tea. He lit his pipe, then attempted to augment his store of information about what was taking place along this road to the Watauga settlements.

"Guess you people are tired of the war?"

"Sure are, sir," Harrison admitted. "We've done our turn in the Army — two years of it — and for thanks we've lost all we ever owned save what we've brought along."

"You think our side is licked?"

"Seems like it. But none of us here aim to holler 'Uncle' just yet."

"Why not?"

Harrison swilled the last of his tea, then lit a charred corncob. "Whyn't you start off with an easy question, Cap'n? You might just as lief ask why the Lord created this here world in seven days!" The Virginian hunched forward and his rugged features became tinted golden-red by the flames. "All I know is that we're heading for 'fields of green and pastures new,' as the Good Book says, which are sections of fine farming land somewhere along the Cumberland River in Tennessee."

4. The Road to Watauga

BY now September was so far advanced that brooks had started to form skim ice along their edges at night and long V's of migrating geese could be seen flapping southward; their musically eerie honking was to be heard at almost any hour.

Now that Barry Colcord and his companions were acting as scouts in front of the column, Jennings and Harrison devoted most of their time caring for a small but precious herd of brown-and-white milch cows and a rambunctious little red Durham bull which, on account of his truly magnificent genitals, was known as "Gentleman Johnny Burgoyne."

Parthenia, still uncommunicative and moody, tried to help Lucy Jennings about the cook fire but wasn't of much use. Her gaze was so blank that three Negro slaves belonging to the party wondered whether this mysterious young female weren't "tetched in de haid."

Betty Harrison remarked acidly, "That Parthy's a real queer one; she don't seem to even half-understand women's work."

"Yep, that's true," one of the other wives agreed. "But she sure can skin game and handle horses to a fare-thee-well."

Barry found amusement in watching Lucy Jennings's expression when one evening she saw Parthenia, who had been splitting kindling, suddenly straighten and hurl a hand ax at a sapling growing nearly fifty feet away and sink its blade inches deep into her target. Unconcernedly, the "Woods Colt," as with innate cruelty the children called her, went over, jerked her hatchet free and then spat on its blade before continuing her task.

It occurred to Barry Colcord that the Jennings camp was the quietest he'd ever been in. Here, no one ever talked loudly or exchanged friendly insults.

Perhaps the women were acting subdued because for the most part they had come from well-settled regions and found this country desperately empty and lonesome. Out here, a body never sighted a cabin's smoke, let alone a fence or a clearing.

Shortly after the parties merged, Jennings and his men became insistent that Captain Colcord assume overall command. Former rangers Jennings and Harrison and their sober, grimly determined fellows guarded the main body while Black Buck and Tom Calloway scouted well out on the column's flanks.

Parthenia begged for scout duty, but Colcord curtly ordered her to the rear to herd the livestock. The rangy young thing looked daggers at him but ended by obeying sullenly.

On this third day after the union the sun must have risen but couldn't be seen through an endless mass of dark, gray-white clouds which dimmed bright autumnal colors among the foothills.

The farther the emigrants toiled towards Watauga the more the column got strung out, despite Colcord's continual urgings. He wasn't by any means happy. Why in hell had he allowed himself, with his responsibilities, to become guardian to these nearly helpless people — unless it was to take advantage of support in this unknown country; after all, wasn't it his first duty to arrive safely at Sycamore Shoals?

Colcord had turned the point over to Black Buck in order to ride back to see how the main body was faring when he glimpsed Parthenia Bryant riding well out to one side and cantered over to her.

"Why aren't you where you're supposed to be?"

Her pale eyes shone coldly from under a ratty fur cap someone had given her. "I ain't no soljer. I — I guess I c'n ride where I please."

Colcord grabbed her bridle, snapped, "Whilst I'm responsible everyone does what they're told, you included! Now, get back where you belong and keep on herding the stock or I'll paddle your backside."

Parthenia scowled before turning her mount and heading for the rear. She'd lived in a black mood ever since Mrs. Harrison had warned that once they reached the Shoals she'd have to wear a skirt and otherwise act like a decent female. While she'd said nothing, rebellion had begun to seethe in her soul.

Around noon Black Buck came back to report that he'd sighted a dead horse lying beside the Pike; apparently it had died so recently that wild beasts had had no time to tear it.

Nobody in the column heeded the carcass lying, stiff and forlorn, in a little gully beside the track until Parthenia drew abreast. When she saw it, she uttered a thin scream, leaped off her mount and ran over to clutch the fallen animal's head to her chest. She began to curse and weep.

Exasperated at such nonsense, Colcord rode over. "What the hell ails you, girl?"

"He was my horse. They've killed him, damn them!"

"How d'you know he was your horse?"

Parthenia raised streaming eyes. "S-see that c-cross-shaped b-blaze on his forehead? I — I'd know it anywhere 'cause I p-picked him for my own from among the herd Billy and those fellers b-brought back."

After dashing tears from golden-brown cheeks, the girl, her jaw set, peered through foliage as bright as gold coins dropped on a green-and-red counterpane, then got up to stand over the stiff-legged carcass.

Colcord noticed that this animal hadn't perished from sickness or hunger. There was a red-black hole in the center of that cross-shaped blaze. Next, he realized that one of the animal's forelegs had been broken.

Parthenia checked her sobbing. "If I'd been ridin' him he'd not have broke that there leg." Convulsively, she fingered her long-bladed sheath knife. "For that I'm goin' to slay some of them villains."

Tom Calloway drawled from behind her, "That'll take time, Sissy, so 'bide yer chance and get back to drivin' stock."

Parthenia cast the Georgian a look of pure hatred before swinging back onto her tackey. "I'll kill 'em! By God, I will — and sooner'n any-body thinks!"

To Barry this discovery of the stolen horse's carcass was significant; didn't it stand to reason that Skelton — if indeed it really were he — and his companions hadn't left the Pike? Probably, they still were mak-ing for the Shoals. How long the Shell Towners would linger there was a matter for conjecture.

Later in the day a furious equinoctial storm broke. Rain sluiced down in blinding freshets, branches thrashed, trees whipped and bent. Before long the storm so blinded the point that they had to pull up; they couldn't see where they were going any longer.

The Carolinian ordered his followers to take shelter in a grove of oaks which offered protection of a sort. The children by now were too cold even to whimper and clung blindly to pack straps or tugged at someone's hand.

Soon the wind became awe-inspiring; it drove small, hard raindrops before it with a stinging velocity. Horses and cattle turned rumps to the blast and huddled together in loose rings with heads held low.

During a lull, Barry, just as he always had after a long march, ordered a count of heads — animal and human. Only then was it discovered that Parthenia had disappeared together with a horse, a carbine, and some ammunition. No one had seen her depart.

When the storm finally diminished to a driving rainstorm, Colcord, followed by the mustee, sought Eclipse and mounted.

Harrison saw him, cupped hands and bellowed, "Where you going?"

"After that fool girl. Be back soon. She can't have got far."

"You're crazy to go out now," shouted Drayton. "You're needed here. Wait a while."

Black Buck was growling under his breath. He didn't fancy setting out like this to hunt for a strange young squaw who didn't belong anywhere or to anyone.

Before covering a mile Barry felt pretty sure that they weren't going to catch up with Parthenia — at least not right away; her tackey's hoof prints were being erased or concealed by wet leaves and fallen branches.

Soon, he couldn't even be sure whether gaps which appeared in the dripping woods were natural blind alleys, game trails or the Pike itself.

Without warning, the mustee pulled up and sat listening with head half-turned.

"Horses."

Soon a dim shape materialized in one of the openings. So Parthenia had found sense enough to turn back? Barry felt curiously relieved.

Almost at once he realized that this wasn't the fugitive, but a stranger who carried a handsome long rifle slung in a fringed leather scabbard under his left leg. He was riding with head lowered against the rain and apparently was relying on his mount's ability to follow the Pike. In his wake splashed a pair of muddied pack horses.

When the big-bearded fellow saw waiting figures he reached for the rifle but checked his motion when Barry yelled, "Easy there! Who are you?"

"Sam Calloway," replied the gray-bearded apparition. "Been trappin' the lower Holston."

"Where're you headed?"

"Morgantown."

"Where from?"

"Sycamore Shoals and Fort Pat Henry."

Colcord moved Eclipse alongside, although she didn't like the looks of this stranger's mean-looking gelding. "Met anyone on the Pike today?"

"No. Who'd be fool enough to travel in such a tempest — aside from me — and you?"

"Sure you haven't noticed anyone? A girl riding alone?"

"Hell, no," the other grunted. "My eyes been so all-fired stung I ain't looked about, bein' out o' Injun country — I hope." Long leather thrums running across either breast of his hunting shirt squirmed under the wind like little snakes.

"You're Sam Calloway?"

"Ain't no one else. Never have been."

"Have you a nephew named Tom?"

The trapper thought a moment, then spat tobacco juice. "Yep. He was a real wild colt last I seen of him. Why for?"

"You'll meet him when we reach camp."

"Well, I'll be dogged. Ain't heard of Tom in the longest time."

During their leader's absence the emigrants had managed to rig a few pack covers among the trees and were huddled in their lee to warm themselves before smoky fires.

Tom Calloway didn't recognize his uncle at first, but then the young

Georgian broke into a gap-toothed grin and sidled up to offer his hand. "Heyo, Unk! How's trappin' these days?"

The bush-bearded figure spat sidewise into the nearest fire. "Only tolerable. I wuz doin' real fine till some goddam Shawnees raided my camp whilst I wuz off tendin' traps. Red bastards stole most of my gear and half the winter's crop o' cured pelts."

At the word "Shawnees" the surveyor looked up. "Any war parties out?"

"Naw. None I know about. This season they ought to be workin' back to their villages but you cain't never be sure. Lend me that tobacco bladder, Nevoo; ain't had a chaw of flue-cured tobaccy since time out o' mind."

Sam bit a generous chew off the twist. "Say, ye air Luke's boy, ain't you? Or air you one of brother George's mistakes?"

"Luke was my Pa," Tom admitted, at the same time wondering how Pa, who'd been so straight-standing and handsome, could have had a wrinkled, bent and hairy old timber beast like this for a full brother. Pa always had looked a man in the eye when he talked, which was more than one could say about Uncle Sam.

"Where's Luke nowadays?" Sam Calloway cocked a brow as furry and gray as a squirrel.

Tom glanced aside. "Pa, well, he perished last year of a wound he took up in Noo Jersey."

"So Luke went for a soljer, did he? Never did think he was real bright. Where's the profit in soljerin'?" Briskly the trapper shook his head, whereat drops of water flew from his bearskin cap as from the hide of a wet dog. "'Pears like ye must take after him if ye're really intending westwards."

Harrison asked, "How far is it to the Shoals?"

"You'll be there come a couple of days if you travel steady." The Long Hunter then peered curiously through the slowly dripping rain at the ring of disheveled people gathered about to hear him. "Any of ye who's got the wit God give a bug-tit will turn right around and make tracks back East. Bad as it may be back there, ye'll find it a damn' sight worse the farther west ye go."

Former Sergeant Jennings pushed forward, his big, always close-shaven jaw outthrust. "Stow that, Mister! We don't favor such talk."

Sam Calloway snorted and picked at a hairy nostril. "Have it yore way, Mister, but I been in and 'round the country ye're expectin' to settle on — land warrants and all — and, well, while it *may* seem safe right now, ye'd better not be there come next spring."

"Why?" Colcord demanded over the diminishing patter of rain.

"Only 'cause 'bout ten thousand Injuns won't let you settle there."

"Why not?"

Sam Calloway's flat black eyes crinkled at their corners. "Christ, Mister, ain't you ignorant! That's their Great Hunting Country; for huntin' and trappin' ye'll not see the likes of it anywheres else."

George Harrison asked, "If the hunting out there's all that good, why are you going back? Too unhealthy out there for you?"

Calloway bristled like an angry lynx and jumped up clapping his hand to the use-shined handle of a tomahawk slung to his belt. "If ye're tryin' to name me a coward, ye lousy Eastern jughead, ye'd better crawfish else I'll cut ye up and swaller ye whole 'thout butterin' yer ears!"

Aware that a valuable source of information was being affronted, the surveyor grinned and shook his head. "No, I didn't intend that the way you took it. No coward could have lived as long out there as you have."

Sam Calloway subsided and fell to warming moccasined feet. Finally, he resumed. "I been rangin' that there country off and on for ten years so you-all better listen when I warn you not to settle west of the Holston or the Clinch Rivers; keep on, and you and yer families will wind up hairless and dog food 'round some Injun torture stake."

Harrison, looking mighty worried, spoke up. "Why's that? We were told there's a treaty of peace in force with the Creeks and Cherokees."

"Treaties have been broke before," grunted Tom's uncle. "What with winter comin' on the peace likely will last a while longer. No. 'Taint likely there'll be big war parties out till next spring; all the same, they's always some restless young bucks driftin' about on the lookout for easy hair. Just wait till the winter snows run off, then you'll see a mort of scalpin' and murderin'."

The trapper's shaggy head traversed in a slow semi-circle as if inviting contradiction. "Now, maybe, ye'll understand why I'm headin' East?"

Jennings's strong and wind-reddened chin went up and out. "All you say may be true, Calloway. I don't question your word, but we — well, we're going out to fix a refuge where liberty-loving folks can settle out of the King's reach."

"Have it yer way," grunted Sam Calloway, "but I mean to keep my hair in place. Are any you fellers minded to come along with me?"

Ex-Ranger Harrison, standing straight as a ramrod, snapped, "Thanks for yer counsel, Calloway, but me and a lot of others who was in the Army didn't quit even when the goin' got awful rough. We don't aim to start now."

5. *Frail Nemesis*

WHEN she sneaked back to the Jennings camp Parthenia Bryant, along with a carbine and powder and bullets, had also stolen a square of old tarpaulin cloth which had been slit near its middle to make what later would be termed a poncho. Only this kept her slender, shivering body from being completely soaked as, using a broken branch for a whip, she drove her tackey splashing along the Pike at its best pace. The animal was a clever little brute, which was fortunate, because it seemed able to follow the track when she herself couldn't see through the blinding storm more than a yard or two ahead.

Long before the beast slowed to a walk, then halted, Parthenia had been listening and, with ears sharpened by the frontier, thought to detect faint sounds other than those made by the wind and rain.

Barely in time she was able to rein off the Pike and into a clump of balsams; heart hammering, she watched a big man ride by. He had his head bent into the storm and wasn't looking where he was going; like her, he was leaving things up to a big, bony gray which plodded ahead of two heavily laden pack horses following in single file with heads held low.

Once the little column had vanished amid a wild welter of lashing rain and flying leaves, Parthenia delayed a good while before returning to the Pike — no point in getting jumped by anyone who might be following that lone rider.

Shielding her eyes and peering between fingers stiff with cold, the girl kept on. She guessed she might have felt as miserable before but she couldn't remember when. By now she was soaked to the skin, shivering violently and, worst of all, because she was riding bareback — she hadn't dared delay long enough to swipe a saddle — her wet buttocks were beginning to chafe and ache like fury. Her main concern, however, was to keep an oily rag she'd wound around the stolen carbine's lock in place and, at the same time, to not lose the bullet bag clutched under her poncho.

She was growing so terribly hungry that her stomach grumbled and griped while she cursed herself with quaint Elizabethan oaths that she hadn't delayed long enough to take along a few morsels of food. Water from her drenched rabbit-fur cap kept purling in frigid trickles between her scant breasts and down her back as well. All the same, Parthenia was only partially aware of her misery, so gripped was she by her deep and overpowering rage.

It was good to know that, by God, the men who had slain her brother and who had killed her horse still were on the Pike; in weather of this sort it wasn't likely Billy's murderers would travel fast or far. Savagely, she goaded herself to maintain as lively a lookout as possible.

Obscured by endless silvery sheets of rain, the Pike wandered on, up hill and down dale through threshing woods and over infrequent little meadows. How long Parthenia rode like this she couldn't have told, but eventually she aroused to an encouraging fact; the wind and downpour were beginning to slacken. Before long rain ceased to fall and the clouds broke. Soon shafts of sunlight began to lance through, revealing details of the storm's damage.

She must, Parthenia reckoned, have covered about another two miles before the sky cleared completely and the lowering sun's rays drove a measure of chill from her bones, but she kept on shivering; huge trees kept on dripping and trickling onto her as heavily as a spring shower.

The tackey splashed doggedly along rivulets which, all too often, followed the track's trampled, manure-browned course. Still there was no sight or sound of the men she was seeking and she was feeling almighty low when, on rounding a bend, she noticed, about a hundred yards ahead, a curl of bluish smoke hanging above a shallow ravine that cut across the Pike.

She pulled up and listened, but hearing nothing, urged forward her ribby animal a few paces. The instant she heard quarrelsome voices she turned off the track into a dense thicket of sumach and yellow birches. Stiffly, she slid off the tackey and forced numbed fingers to tie it to a stout tree. This done, Parthenia flailed arms and did knee bends until she panted and felt blood hurrying through her. Next, she struggled out of the tarpaulin and used strong long hands to wring it out, then repeated the operation on her sodden rabbit-skin cap. After that, she'd have felt better but for that gnawing emptiness in her flat little belly.

To wait proved difficult, but she thought about Billy and her horse and forced herself to stay quiet until dusk began to gather; while it still was light enough to see clearly she set out through the underbrush making no more noise than a hunting vixen. True darkness was about to set in as Parthenia gained the lip of a little ravine from which smoke still was rising. Ah! She caught a faint glimmer of flames beyond the black pattern of sodden leaves.

To manage her carbine without making noise — it now felt heavier than lead — was hard work but, heart pounding, she succeeded and presently squirmed silently into the heart of a laurel bush overlooking her objective.

Tethered between her and the campfire were three of the horses Billy and his companions had brought back. She recognized them beyond any shadow of uncertainty so lay flat and kept as still as a hiding rabbit while making a careful survey of the group huddled about the fire. A fresh sense of outrage surged through her and momentarily dropped a transparent scarlet veil before her eyes. In this hollow were lounging those same villains who'd murdered Billy without granting him the least chance of defending himself.

Easily she recognized the tall, thin, yellow-bearded fellow, but not before she had mistaken Skelton for another bearded individual who also was wearing a ragged green uniform jacket and closely resembled him in build.

There were two other whiskery fellows down there wearing the roughest kind of frontier garb. All four were seated on logs around the campfire, smoking and drinking one after another from a stone jug they'd acquired God knew where. What immediately attracted Parthenia's attention was a hand ax someone had driven into a tree trunk once he'd done cutting firewood. Ah! Parthenia's slanted eyes narrowed and her teeth met with a little click; that looked like a fine hatchet with a gracefully fashioned handle.

From where she lay, there was no telling what the men down there were arguing about, but they sure were mad about something and kept yelling and making short, angry gestures. After a while the fellow who resembled Jasper Skelton got up and went over to dip a calabash bowl into a pot steaming beside the fire. Then he threw sticks on the flames and went back to squat on his log.

Parthenia carefully selected a route past a pile of stones and a bush or two down to the hollow's bottom. If she remembered right, the moon ought to come up pretty soon after darkness fell.

While she lay with teeth clenched to keep them from chattering the girl thought about a story told long ago by a very old man. She recalled that many years back a woman named Hannah Dustin had been captured by Indians somewhere up in New England and had been forced, along with her children, to undertake a long, hard march towards Canada. Parthenia recalled the old gaffer's saying that Mrs. Dustin had waited one night till her captors all had fallen asleep. Then that old-time frontierswoman had seized the nearest tomahawk and successively had slain each and every one of her captors! How strange that she should remember the ancient adding, "What's more, Hannah scalped them redskins and brung home their hair!"

She lay there, trying to keep herself warm by recalling how poor Billy had lain on the leaves, all bloodstained and spread out flatter than a buffalo-skin rug.

Pretty soon the usual night noises of the forest commenced, then some of the horses lay down, the rest just stood with heads held low and occasionally shifted their weight from one side to the other.

Parthenia hoped that since these men had been drinking hard, they should fall asleep early. Soon they obliged her, and, after throwing wood on the fire, rolled up into shapeless outlines around the firelight's perimeter.

The girl was preparing to make her move when, without warning, a panther higher on the hill screamed so loudly that the men awoke and grabbed their guns while the horses began to whinny and dance and plunge about in fright.

Some time was required to quiet the animals and for the men to settle down again — which was just as well; Parthenia was granted additional time to plan her movements.

At length everyone seemed to have fallen asleep and, fortunately, the fire still burned brightly enough to show where the sleepers lay. Cautiously, she got to her feet but was so wet and stiff she could barely move during the several minutes required to unwind the carbine's wrappings.

Fierce joy surged through her while with infinite care and delicacy she drew back the icy-feeling hammer through half, all the way back to full-cock. For the first and only time that day she blessed the rain which had so drenched this hollow that no twig snapped nor did any leaf rustle.

Lugging the carbine in her left hand Parthenia soundlessly parted branches, dodged bushes and otherwise made her way towards that hand ax stuck in the tree.

It proved vastly encouraging to discover that she'd still the strength and skill to quietly ease the weapon free. Then she circled the drowsing horses without rousing them and, treading very carefully, made for the nearest huddled figure. After the panther's squall the men had moved about, so she no longer retained a clear idea of who was lying where, nor was there any way of identifying the man she particularly wanted to kill.

Bent well forward, Parthenia neared the fire until she found herself standing directly above a fellow who lay face down, with his hat fallen off. The same half-strangled sensation she'd suffered when her brother had been murdered returned, only stronger this time. Expertly, her cold hand hefted the hatchet as she straightened and while raising her arm remembered what a Long Hunter once had said — that the only sure way of killing a man outright, without raising an outcry, was to strike him squarely on the center of his poll.

Parthenia put all her weight and muscle behind the blow and did just that. The hatchet caused a soft *ta-chunk!* as if it had only split a ripe melon. The sleeper never even stirred.

To free the blade proved more of a task than the girl had bargained for, but by planting a foot on the fellow's shoulders, she succeeded and was preparing to strike again when, much nearer this time, the panther screeched again. Immediately, the three remaining outlaws roused from their blankets, cursing and fumbling for their guns as they peered stupidly about the hollow.

"Ye bastards!" Parthenia threw at a figure who was halfway erect. Her hatchet caught him flush on the side of his head and sank in deep; emitting a hoarse, choking cry the fellow swayed an instant and fell heavily.

At the same moment Parthenia whipped the carbine loosely to her shoulder and, recognizing Jasper Skelton, fired a snap-shot. The weapon kicked like an angry mule and flew out of her grasp amid billowing smoke. She saw Skelton convulsively fling wide his arms and go staggering backwards until he collapsed across the dull red campfire.

Parthenia didn't delay but wheeled and tore off through the sodden woods back to the Pike and began running and tripping towards her tackey.

6. *Sycamore Shoals, I*

IN very few ways did Choice Valentine resemble that delicate young lady whose family had set out from Bethlehem, Pennsylvania, well over a year ago. Her body, rid of adolescent fat, had lengthened and narrowed while her pretty pink-and-white complexion had turned a not unpleasing shade of light brown. Her now stringy honey-colored hair had turned a shade darker. The only things that remained unchanged about Choice were the fullness of her generously rounded breasts, the hue of her black-fringed somber eyes and the dark-red contours of her small, full mouth.

In skirt and breeches of bleached buckskin bright with beads and quill work she suggested a proud young Amazon who thought nothing of carrying a knife and a brace of little pistols clipped to her belt.

Slouched comfortably in her saddle she heard Dan Maddox ask a fellow who was returning to Sycamore Shoals from Fort Patrick Henry how much farther on lay their destination.

"Ten, mebbe fifteen miles, I reckon," drawled the wizened old man. "Ought to git thar in time to watch the sun set." His effort to bite off a chew exposed ruinous black-and-yellow teeth. "Ye'll find it quite a place. Yep, this last year the Shoals hev growed into a considerable burg. Above five hundert folks live there, or real close by, and there'll be more refugees showin' up all the time till winter sets in fer keeps."

Dr. Samuel Mason, astride a ribby bay gelding, only half heard the ancient's observation; he was much too preoccupied in wondering how his wife might be coming along. Wouldn't it be just his infernal, continual bad luck to be away when Rosemary would be delivered of their child? Of course, he had given Josh detailed instructions about what to do if anything really went wrong; but nothing should. There were plenty of "wise women" among those feeble stations which, during the spring of '80, had sprung up around the fairly sound fort James Robertson had built on the Frenchman's Bluff. Now the place was known as Bluff Station and provided a refuge for nearby weaker stations.

Poor Rosemary! How able, good and calm she'd proved through everything. Perhaps it was those qualities which had decided him to marry her — along with an inarticulate but nevertheless sincere feeling of devotion. Of course, he told himself once again, Rosemary would be as safe as anyone out there, installed in reasonable comfort at the Bluffs.

Lulled from his anxiety by the warm sunlight and the autumnal beauty of these rolling hills, Sam Mason again considered his wife's father. *Certes!* Considerable changes had reshaped Virginius Valentine; no longer was he half so loud, pompous or purse-proud. Certainly his nose was no longer as florid and pulpy; otherwise, the Squire appeared years younger than when Mason first had sighted him and his twin daughters outside of Carpenter's ill-placed and probably doomed settlement.

Trust the Squire, mused Mason, to appreciate, early-on, that, for a long time to come, there would be little political power wielded from Middle Tennessee; there just weren't enough votes out there to carry any weight — not yet at least.

He reined to allow ex-Sergeant Dan Maddox, big, calm and steady as ever, to ride up beside him.

Tim, of course, was keeping Choice company, but everyone around Nashborough — as some people were beginning to call Bluff Station in honor of General Francis Nash, a patriot who'd got himself killed in action early in the war — was aware that whatever might have passed between them during the winter march was now over and done with.

The gunsmith was feeling more contented than he had been for some time, in fact, ever since a trapper had appeared at the Bluff bringing the exciting rumor that Dan'l Morgan was about to reassemble his riflemen in a desperate, final effort to save the Republic. Unexpectedly, several immigrants had volunteered to return to the wars but hadn't been able to get themselves equipped in time to accompany Dr. Mason and Major Valentine to Fort Pat Henry.

This country sure looked a deal more companionable than where he'd settled. Why, around here one could at the same moment spy several habitations. These stood in the center of cleared spaces in which crops had been planted. In time, he guessed, such little fields would eat farther and farther into the woods, but right now what grain there was had been grown among fire-blackened stumps.

Yes, sir, if what that trapper had said about Dan'l Morgan's returning to the war was true — well, he and Tim Murphy were figuring to be among the first to rejoin "The Old Wagoner." But, of course, no one could credit even a little of the rumors which sometimes seeped across the mountains.

By cracky! Wasn't it fine to sleep soundly again, to see and hear humans about him instead of silence or the cry of wild beasts?

Some Eastern-born officer at Fort Pat had taken his friend Mason aside and had talked with him until late in the night. After that, the doctor had appeared more silent and thoughtful than ever. All Dan had been able to get out of him was that the British had licked the tar out of the American Southern Army and had forced it into a disgraceful surrender at a place called Charles Town.

After that, the Lobsterbacks had beaten the Patriots again and again and now were advancing through North Carolina, wreaking death and destruction as they came.

Absently he stroked Ilsa's glowing tiger-striped maple stock, but frowned over the presence of too many bruises and scores marring that beautiful satiny surface. Yep. First thing he'd do when he reached the Shoals would be to find a gunsmith and borrow the use of his tools for awhile. For some time Ilsa had needed a new pan cover and a set-screw to hold a flint firmly in the cock's jaws. Nor had he been able, with all his skill and the tools at his disposal, to fashion a first-class frizzen out of nothing. Tim's double-barreled Goucher also stood in need of considerable attention; the right barrel's lock by now simply couldn't be trusted any longer to handle more than a moderate powder charge.

He pulled aside and dismounted, sensing that a pebble must have found its way under one of his bay's shoes.

"Getting saddle-sore?" Choice called lightly, all excited over the prospect of beholding something like civilization again.

Grinning, Dan shrugged and, using a pick, dislodged the stone. Then he remounted.

Tim came up growling, "That gal's so all-fired set-up with the idee of meetin' some fancy new men she won't even pass the time of day with an old friend."

Why in God's name, he wondered, hadn't Choice said the word? If she had, by God, he'd never have even glanced at another woman — for a while, anyway. Why, when they'd known each other so damn' sweetly on so many occasions, hadn't the memory of them made a difference? Maybe it was because she'd never got pregnant, for all he'd tried his best to bring that about. A terrible possibility struck him for the first time. Was she afraid he was sterile and couldn't father a brat?

Choice, riding up to join the leaders of the little party, pulled in beside the doctor. It had proved quite a blow to the girl's vanity that, despite proven wiles, she hadn't been able to lure Sam Mason from Rosemary. Of course, some small-minded folk could claim that Sam and Rosemary weren't *legally* married yet. Colonel Robertson had felt himself qualified as a civil official to preside in the absence of an ordained minister, so, solemnly enough, he had read the marriage service one blustery March morning when the log palisade protecting Bluff Station was only half raised.

Yes, during the summer a few other stations had gone up. For example, most of Colonel John Donelson's people, after completing their long and torturous river journey, had settled on a rich flat called Clover Bottom lying some twelve miles from the Bluffs. Both Freeland's and Mansker's Stations were more distant. Ike Bledsoe had put up a weak little fortified farmhouse which, in time, he hoped to enclose with a palisade, provided he could persuade enough people to settle nearby.

It was a mighty good thing, mused Choice, that Donelson had arrived just when he did, for with his coming the white population of Middle Tennessee had been trebled. Not that these little communities represented more than a microcosm in a vast and empty wilderness; still, with more and more immigrants arriving, she wouldn't be surprised if there weren't now around seven or eight hundred souls settled in Tennessee.

Choice frowned. Too bad that towards midsummer redskin bands had taken to killing, burning and stealing horses and precious cattle. Tom Spencer, who had returned to his solitary life, Cash Brooks and Joe Drake and most of the other old-timers warned that what had happened already was but a faint forerunner of what would take place come next year; then, for sure, the savage hordes would attack in earnest and settlers' blood would flow in torrents under torture or by sudden death.

Well, she was mighty glad to be away and had no intention of returning to the Station. Surely, among all the people in Sycamore Shoals there must be some well-bred officers? How wonderful it would be to hear decent English spoken once more.

Major Valentine rumbled to the old guide, "Do we sight the Shoals from the top of the next rise or don't we?"

"Likely you will, Squire, or I don't know my way around these parts."

Sam Mason shifted in his saddle, glanced at a waterproof bag protecting the original black portfolio he'd compiled despite so many difficulties and dangers. What could have happened to the copy he'd forwarded to Fort Patrick Henry in Captain Blackmore's care? Even now, he'd learned nothing except that Blackmore had disappeared and that the papers never had reached their destination. God send they'd fallen into the hands of truly wild Indians unable to comprehend their importance. Yes. Probably Blackmore's scalp and that of a Long Hunter sent along to protect him right now were decorating some Shawnee's smoke-filled wigwam.

Bitterly, Samuel Mason, M.D., lamented those weeks which had elapsed before the arrival of a messenger sent by Colonel Sevier to inquire why his information had never reached the Fort. Well, this time Sam Mason intended to place his data in John Sevier's own hands or in those of his immediate deputy.

The physician switched this somber train of thought to a pleasanter subject — for instance, today was near perfect; the air was crisp without being cold while the deep blue sky was marked only by little flecks of scattered white clouds which looked like nothing so much as a basket of cotton bolls spilled onto a vast, bright-blue counterpane.

On several occasions during the past few days Mason's party had encountered riders heading west. They'd all said Colonel Sevier would very likely be found in, or near, Sycamore Shoals unless he were off inspecting one of several properties he owned in the Watauga Concession.

From the brow of a steep little hill the saddle-weary travelers from Middle Tennessee obtained a fine view of the town called Sycamore Shoals. Established on land purchased from certain Cherokee chiefs of questionable authority, the place soon had become populated largely by sturdy Scotch-Irish immigrants from the hills of North Carolina, but there were also a good many rough-and-ready backcountry Virginians and more than a scattering of sober, industrious and curiously superstitious Pennsylvania Dutch.

Nowadays this burgeoning little town included over a hundred log cabins and pine-slab habitations of varying sizes built on rich bottomlands created within a wide sweeping bend in the Indian River. The sprawling town lay under the guns of a well-built fort which had risen right after the still-disputed Treaty of Sycamore Shoals had been signed back in 1772.

To Dan Maddox's considerable surprise a good many huts and houses lay dangerously far from the fort. Here and there ox carts or wagons could be seen crawling along dusty roads; but what did him a world of good was to see how many recently harvested grain fields and other cleared lands were driving back the woods.

"What an admirable situation for a town," Virginius Valentine commented. "I'd venture yonder's a natural focus for trade routes crossing the mountains."

"Aye," nodded the old guide. "We got mebbe five or six pikes, traces and roads all leadin' straight to the Shoals."

Dr. Mason made no immediate comment because he was experiencing a lifting sensation on sighting a crude version of the Stars and Stripes fluttering above the Fort's lookout tower. All at once he realized he hadn't beheld an American flag in nearly two years. In fact, he'd continually been astonished that so few of the people going out to Tennessee had ever even seen the flag of their country.

The physician gathered his reins and called over his shoulder, "Since it's downhill and not much farther to go, suppose we take up a trot?"

7. Sycamore Shoals, II

NEWS of Parthenia Bryant's amazing exploit had preceded the Jennings party into Sycamore Shoals, with the result that when a lone, hard-looking individual herding several good-looking horses appeared, the surviving Shell Towner promptly was arrested for confinement in the Fort's guardhouse. Meanwhile, the animals were impounded pending his trial.

In a way, Barry Colcord was feeling well pleased because Parthenia's arrival was diverting curiosity from himself and his mission, and also, he'd no longer feel responsible for this pathetic, half-wild young female.

Strangely enough, once Parthenia had achieved her revenge she'd quit being quite so bristly and unfeminine; she'd even taken to hiding her worn and patched breeches beneath a short, fringed skirt of buckskin pressed upon her by Mrs. Jennings.

That this raw frontier town was pervaded by an undercurrent of uneasy excitement Barry perceived before he'd spent an hour in the place. Its rutted streets swarmed with frontier types busy about their affairs. Every so often small groups of shaggy and generally leather-clad horsemen would ride into town whooping, making their horses rear and otherwise showing off as on a holiday. Significantly, none of these parties were accompanied by women or children, and the gear they carried slung to their saddles was of a sort useful only for campaigning.

Once the Jenningses and their companions had pitched camp on the edge of that rich plain on which Sycamore Shoals had risen, Barry signaled Saul Black Buck and Calloway and, followed by them, made for the Fort, which when one got close to it, didn't look like much — at least not from a regular soldier's point of view; nevertheless, the palisade was high and stout, while its curtain walls and corner blockhouses mounted a respectable number of cannon and swivels.

If any sort of interior guard was being maintained it wasn't noticeable, Barry decided; only a pair of long-haired fellows wearing dirty crossbelts and faded blue jackets seemed to be on duty before the main gate. Both had stood their muskets against the palisade and, watched by a circle of boys and stray dogs, were flipping knives in a game of mumblety-peg.

After passing the gate without earning even a questioning glance from the guards, Colcord left his companions to watch the horses and made for a door marked Orderly Room. He found it occupied only by a tired-looking clerk who drawled that Colonel Shelby had gone over to Jonesborough to race some of his horses.

"Is Colonel Sevier in the Fort?" Barry asked stiffly. God above! Discipline around here seemed to be even worse than in Carolina.

"Yep. Ye'll find Johnny up in the commandant's office."

Barry crossed the grassless, sunburnt parade ground which, no doubt, was designed to double as a refuge for settlers and their stock during an Indian raid.

He found Lieutenant-Colonel Sevier bent over a table desk and immediately was impressed that the commandant's blue-and-white uniform really fitted him and that his gold epaulets and buttons were clean and shining. Perhaps because of his crisp white wig, John Sevier's long, clearly chiseled features appeared coppery-hued as any Indian's.

Smiling, the tall North Carolinian heaved himself to his feet and offered a hand. "And whom have I the pleasure of addressing, sir?"

Standing to rigid attention, Barry stated his name, rank and former command, though it hurt to mention the Ricelands Troop.

Sevier waved to a seat of rawhide laced over a hickory frame. "Please to sit, sir, and tell me more of the situation in Carolina."

After dispatching an orderly to fetch leathern jacks of scuppernong wine, Colonel Sevier permitted penetrating gray eyes to consider his caller.

"— And now, Captain, suppose you tell me what's brought you here?"

Once Colcord had given a cautious description of the mission on which Colonel Armand had sent him, the commandant nodded thoughtfully.

"So that's it. Well, Colcord, I presume you know that both Shelby and I share the Council's confidence, so I'll say it's timely you've shown up this soon after Dr. Mason's arrival."

"*Dr. Mason's here?*"

"Yes. He only reached this place yesterday evening, along with some people from those new settlements along the Lower Cumberland River.

"After identifying himself, the doctor made only a preliminary statement, but he left some — er — documents in my custody." He studied the younger man with care. "After I have studied them and when Colonel Shelby returns, we'd better talk again.

"I presume," resumed Sevier, quite deliberately rearranging some papers before him, "after what you have told me, it'll be a pleasure to witness the hanging of the only rascal to survive that remarkable Bryant girl's attack. She was one of your party, wasn't she?"

"She was. Yes, sir, I'll attend the execution; you see, I've a private reason to take pleasure in watching him die."

"Why, may I ask?"

As briefly as possible Colcord described the Shell Towners' brutal descent and the destruction of Ricelands.

Sevier sighed, shook his dark, leanly handsome head. "It's a vast pity, sir, that you're far from being the only one to suffer such an outrage. Tarleton and Ferguson's Tories are raging through the backcountry as pitilessly as any Indian war party."

"Have you seen the Bryant girl yet?"

"No. But I'd surely admire to shake her by the hand — for all she took the law unto herself." Sevier eased back into his armchair, which creaked under his weight. "Ah me, God knows how long 'twill be before we can live under the rule of law and order again."

"Sir, to which state does your county belong?"

"Some tell me it's Virginia, some say North Carolina. At the moment," Sevier said carefully, " 'tis believed we belong to the latter state, but no one can be sure till surveyors, already at work, have run a line out west."

"And what, sir, is Colonel Shelby's responsibility? I gather you are in joint command here?"

"He's Colonel of Sullivan County, just as I suffer the same responsibility here in Washington County."

"— And just what is the kind of colonel you speak of?"

Sevier laughed briefly. "Why, in effect, we're sort of half-arsed, civilian-military sub-governors with only temporary authority from the State of North Carolina. Damned if either of us has any clear idea about our powers."

Outside a dull hubbub began. The lounging guards caught up their arms and ran to block the gate but were too slow. A short, thick-bodied man on a fast-looking badly lathered horse already had pounded through it. He dismounted immediately and, after yelling something at the sergeant of the guard, ran up to the commanding officer's door.

His face and beard were speckled with dust. Wide dark sweat marks showed on his back and under the arms of a faded brown canvas uniform coat.

"Well, Mister, what's yer business?" snapped Sevier. "Why ain't you been properly escorted up here?"

"Them lunkheads downstairs don't understand the hurry I'm in," panted the stranger.

"Why the big rush?"

"Sir, Cunnel Cleveland's done sent you a proclamation just wrote by Major Patrick Ferguson — damn his Tory soul to hell!" growled the messenger. He spat savagely, then fumbled in a shot bag and pulled out a crumpled sheet.

"Where did you come by this?"

"Near the Cowpens. An officer of the cunnel's done give it me two days back and he says, says he, 'Ride like hell to Watauga and give this to the commander there.' "

Sevier's heavy black brows merged. "Where is Colonel Cleveland now?"

"Cain't say. Only he was headed for Morgantown Gap and herdin' a gre't passel o' homeless folk from Carolina; they're bein' chased by the Tories so hard there ain't no tellin' just where they're to be found right now."

"About how many folks is Cleveland guarding?"

"Mebbe a thousand souls, mebbe half ag'in that many more." Without invitation the messenger plunked himself down on a three-legged stool. "Ain't ye goin' to read what I've rid so hard to bring ye?"

"Haven't you read it?" demanded Sevier.

"Naw, I ain't lettered, nohow."

John Sevier's blunt, brown fingers began to unfold the crumpled rain-and-perspiration-stained broadside. "How many fighting men would you say Colonel Cleveland's got with him?"

"Search me," the messenger grunted, then got up on badly patched cowhide boots to tramp over and help himself from a bucket of drinking water. "Four to five hundret 'twould be my guess — but I ain't nowise knowledgeable."

The Colonel of Washington County slowly smoothed the sheet of paper; then, as he read, a rich red flush appeared above his neck band and shot to the roots of his hair. "Now, by God! This really tears it!"

"How?" Colcord queried.

"Read this!" He passed over the proclamation.

To see more easily the Carolinian moved to the nearest of three small windows imperfectly illuminating the commandant's office and read in poorly set type:

> To all Rebels Lurking beyond ye Mountains:
>
> Herewith you are summoned to lay down your Arms and Disperse at once. You will then return peaceably to your Allegiance to His Britannic Majesty, King George the Third.
>
> Should you fail in this I will march my Forces over ye Mountains, Hang your Leaders and so Waste your Country with Fire and Sword that a Buzzard flying over it will find Naught on which to Feed excepting the Bodies of Dead Rebels.
>
> Patrick Ferguson
>
> Major, Commanding His Majesty's American
> Volunteers in North Carolina.

"Well, and what d'you make of *that?*" snorted Sevier. "Ain't those the words of a true monster?"

"These threats are in no way surprising, sir," Barry remarked. "They're all of a piece with what he's been doing for a long time; Ferguson's been rabid against us from the start."

Watched by the grimy messenger, the commandant for several moments strode back and forth before his desk. Finally, he halted before Colcord, growled, "Well, at least one thing's plain. We'd better fight his army to the east of the Smokies — so, if we get licked, as well we may — we still can retire through the gaps and defy those bastards to follow."

Striding to the door, Sevier roared for aides and orderlies and dispatched an especially swift courier in search of Colonel Shelby. Then he instructed clerks to start making copies of the proclamation.

"The first one's to be nailed to the gate of this Fort and next to the

Red Bull's notice board. And you," he beckoned an orderly, "bear a copy of this to Fort Pat Henry and ride like hell!"

"What about the rest?" Colcord queried.

"I'll decide that after I've consulted with Colonel Shelby."

Finally, the commandant turned to the stocky messenger. "Sorry I've neglected you, my friend, for you've our eternal gratitude. Suppose you go down to the Red Bull and eat and drink all you can hold — on me, of course. You and your mount had better get well rested. Tomorrow I want you to seek out Colonel Cleveland, wherever he is, and hand him dispatches I'll have ready by sunup."

Once the courier had clumped out, grinning like a horse collar, John Sevier returned his attention to the cavalryman. "And now, sir, will you tell me how the war goes beyond the Alleghenies?"

Seating himself, the commandant listened intently to Barry's description of disasters occurring the past few weeks.

Only when the handsome young Carolinian mentioned Colonel Armand's visit to Tranquility did the neatly uniformed figure straighten and speak. "Thank you, Captain. I feel well informed." He paused, then lowered his voice. "Before we go any further, did Colonel Armand and his friend give you words by which you and I can positively identify ourselves?"

Colcord went over to close the door, which had been left slightly ajar, then bent over the commandant's desk and in a low voice said, "Xenophon."

Sevier nodded and in equal gravity gave the countersign, "Cincinnatus."

At once, Sevier sent a runner to fetch Dr. Mason who, with Major Valentine and his daughter, were lodging in a rough little inn called the Sachem's Head.

With truly surprising speed the physician appeared and repeated the Council's words of identification. At once Barry Colcord became deeply impressed by this gray-eyed stranger's bearing and mode of speech. He took Samuel Mason, M.D., to be some seven years his senior — around thirty-four years of age. They were about of a height — five foot nine — but the newcomer was heavier built and his small, round eyes were dark brown while his own were dark blue.

Without seeming to, Barry took in the other's thin, hawklike nose, longish jaw and straight slash of a mouth marred by hard lines that somehow didn't seem to belong there. He noted also that the doctor's ruddy-brown complexion at one time had suffered what must have been a light case of smallpox.

Although the man from Eaton's Station was wearing a musty-black and often-mended long-skirted cloth coat of Eastern cut, he also had on a buckskin hunting shirt, Indian moccasins and leggings in place of boots and breeches. Before the physician had uttered a dozen words there was no mistaking the fact that he was of considerable intelligence and superior education.

"Before we go any further with this business," Sevier announced, "I believe we'd best repair to my hut. The walls around us are leaky and the floors so thin that if a mouse scratches its whiskers in here it can be heard in the guardroom below."

The doctor picked up the large and awkward leather-covered case he'd brought in and kept between his feet. Silently he prepared to follow his host.

Following a prolonged conference Sam Mason said, "Well, sir, I hope what I've said lends you a truer impression of our situation in Middle Tennessee."

"You've done that, sir," Sevier admitted, "but I would you could have rendered a more encouraging statement. Obviously, a great deal remains to be done if the stations are to hold out."

He got up and offered his guests raw whisky and branch water. Next, he said, "I trust you'll understand and excuse me if I return to Headquarters."

When the three went out into a flood of golden, late afternoon sunlight, Dr. Mason cast Barry a quiet smile. "I would be pleased, sir, if you'd join Major Valentine and me for supper. The fare at the Sachem's Head is rough, to say the best, but it seems clean and reasonably well cooked; also, there will be what you might consider an added attraction in the person of my sister-in-law, Mistress Choice Valentine."

8. *Sycamore Shoals, III*

By the means of judicious bribery Major Virginius Valentine had secured a temporarily vacated bedroom for a private dining room but retained small hopes that the meal would in any way prove cheerful. Major

Ferguson's proclamation had fanned sentiments, already bitter, into blazing resentment.

All along the settlement's haphazard streets refugees who'd been hurt or who'd been forced to witness the burning of their property or the hanging of friends and relatives listened to semi-drunken orators proclaim that a day of reckoning was drawing near.

Virginius Valentine, busily polishing a brass spur buckle, cast a quizzical glance at his son-in-law washing hands over a wooden bucket. "This Captain Colcord seems to have impressed even an impassive fellow like yourself."

"He did. So far this Carolinian has given me only a rough idea of what he's been through recently, but it must have been bad, very bad. Accounts of the Whigs' and Tories' fighting sound horrible; I've always heard that a war between brothers is the worst of all."

He considered his sister-in-law when she came in. *Certes!* Choice was a vision of loveliness; somehow she'd managed to bring along an Eastern-made dress. Further, during the afternoon, she'd found opportunity to wash and comb her honey-colored hair and even had tucked little bows of faded blue ribbon above her ears.

The two men smiled when Choice lamented because she'd no real slippers left and had been forced to wear Indian moccasins; this she hated because a lack of heels made her appear even shorter than she was.

Choice's large dark eyes glistened and her red lips formed a teasing smile. "This offers to be the event I've dreamt of so long! A real gentleman actually is coming to dine!"

While drying his hands, Samuel Mason wondered just how his wife might appear at present. Certainly Rosemary's waist would be nowhere near so slender nor her hair half so lustrous as her twin's.

Choice pleaded, "Sam, please be sweet and tell me more about this dashing Southerner. Has he a pleasing manner?"

"Yes, and without being affected about it," the doctor assured her. "To my mind he's the first thoroughly well-bred individual I've encountered in many a blue moon." He winked at Valentine. "Aside from my father-in-law, of course."

Choice went over to straighten the wick on a tallow dip. "What color are his eyes? Does he have a big nose? Is he dark or fair?"

Sam laughed. "Whoa! One at a time! First off, his hair, for better or for worse, is about the shade of mine; he's got dark blue eyes and he's almost slender in a muscular sort of a way."

"— And his voice? Does he have a nice voice?"

"Sounded pleasant enough to me."

Choice drew a quick breath. "Is — is Captain Colcord married?"

"No. I believe recently he has lost his wife and a child under tragic circumstances."

"Oh, what a dreadful pity," Choice murmured, then fluffed her hair and went to peer out of the window. "I do hope he won't be late. I vow I'm fairly perishing to —"

She broke off, hearing footsteps mounting the inn's stairway of half-logs. Came a knock and then Barry Colcord appeared in the improvised dining room's entrance; he blinked through rank-smelling fumes given off by the beef-tallow dips.

It chanced that at the moment Choice was standing opposite the entrance, so Barry's first impression of her was most effective. He caught his breath and was gripped by a reaction very similar to the one he'd experienced when first he'd beheld Laura MacDonald dancing a Scottish reel at a ball in Georgetown.

Choice's bright, brown-black eyes rounded to their limits; never before had she experienced a sensation like this — so powerful and so deliciously unique.

The electric moment ended when Dr. Mason performed introductions, but its impact lingered.

A coarse but nourishing meal of pork chitlings, applesauce, boiled turnips and sweet potatoes was consumed with ever-decreasing diffidence. Before long, Choice found herself describing with considerable vivacity and humor young Jonathan Robertson's running feud with Old Scratch, who'd survived the midwinter journey to beget a goodly number of lambs whose dispositions, happily, seemed at variance with that of their cantankerous sire.

"— And what's become of the lad?" Barry inquired, gaze riveted on the raconteuse.

"He's growing like the proverbial weed," Major Valentine interrupted. "During the troubles last summer he took after his father and assumed a man's stature — especially after his brother, James, got murdered by the savages."

"Come, come!" Sam Mason broke in. "Let us not burden Captain Colcord with our woes. I'm sure he's had plenty of his own."

Colcord held up a hand. "That's most considerate, sir, but, if you don't mind, I'd like to hear more about what happened after your expedition reached the Frenchman's Bluff."

Major Valentine stroked his large and less colorful nose a moment then described how, shortly after the overland column's fast-moving division had crossed the frozen Cumberland and had reached their goal on a particularly frigid New Year's Day, the construction of Bluff Station had been commenced right away.

Rains's and Todd Phillips's slow division, which had tarried at Mansker's, had arrived some weeks later. After that, several weak or badly sited stations had been thrown up along the river close by Bluff Station, which had been planned and constructed by Colonel Robertson himself.

About a mile and a half downstream from the Frenchman's Bluff, Amos Eaton, who had come West with a small party of his own, had raised a cluster of unfortified but fairly comfortable cabins. Dr. Mason had elected to settle there with his bride, chiefly because Eaton's Station was so centrally located.

Then, explained the Squire, Asher's Station had gone up on a buffalo road running between Mansker's and Bledsoe's Lick; after that, an immigrant named Kilgore had established himself on the Red River. Also lying within a dozen miles of the Bluff was Freeland's Station, across the river from Eaton's. One by one more clumps of cabins had come into being: for example, Renfroe's and Rogan's Stations near the Red River's mouth.

It was there that, early in the summer, the Indians had struck first, swiftly, mercilessly, slaying no less than twelve unwary immigrants.

"After that," continued the red-faced Pennsylvanian, sucking on a new clay pipe, "all our stations, excepting the Bluff, came under attack."

In fact, the Indian danger had grown so serious later on that Colonel Donelson — whose waterborne expedition had finally arrived in the early spring after an incredibly hazardous and miserable voyage — had been forced to abandon uncompleted buildings on Clover Bottom to distribute his followers among Mansker's, Eaton's and the Bluff.

"In fact," concluded Virginius Valentine, "when the doctor, my daughter and I set out for here a great many people had taken fright and were flocking to stronger forts. At the moment I fear only three or four stations are holding out in all of Middle Tennessee."

"The worst of it is," Sam Mason commented, "when spring comes we must expect even worse onslaughts — which is another reason we are here. We *must* have reinforcements, and soon, if we are to provide for the flood of immigrants we've been told to expect next year." He glanced across the rough, wood table at Barry Colcord. "In short that, Captain, is the situation out West."

When no one spoke for a moment angry voices downstairs became disturbingly noticeable.

Thanks to some tolerable Monongahela whisky absorbed by the men and Choice's determined efforts to be gay, the occasion ended in an atmosphere of something approaching cheerfulness.

Finally, Barry got to his feet and bent over Choice's hard little hand. "Ma'am, I hesitate to desert such pleasant companionship but I fear I must return to the Fort. Colonel Sevier has offered me accommodations there. Thank you, Major, and you, Doctor, for your courteous hospitality."

He bowed to the men, then brushed the girl's hand with his lips. When he straightened, their glances met and clung so long that Valentine and the doctor exchanged amused glances.

Choice murmured in soft and urgent undertones which Tim Murphy might have recognized. "For me, sir, this has been a — a — the most delightful evening. I — I trust — we, that is, will see you again?"

To his considerable surprise Barry Colcord, while riding Eclipse out to witness the hanging of the surviving Shell Towner, sensed no consuming hatred for the man — rather, he felt more like a legal representative obligated to witness an execution.

Not so Parthenia Bryant. She rode up with pale eyes dilated and bright as those of a night-hunting house cat. "Hope to God they don't break his neck when they swing him. Hope the villain strangles real slow an' kicks an' struggles the longest while! Hangin's a heap too good for the likes of him!"

At least half a thousand people must have assembled to watch an ox-cart convey the condemned man, sobbing and shivering with fear, to the base of a stunted oak. Around the prisoner's neck already dangled the rope which, pretty soon, would choke the life from his body. As the cart creaked forward, curses and primordial sounds arose — very similar to noises which once had arisen at Cobb's Mill.

Parthenia grated, "Look at him, Mister Cap'n. Only hope the Devil's pitchfork is good and hot and ready to catch his soul!"

In something like astonishment at her vindictiveness, Barry considered this lithe young creature beside him, then realized that she'd attempted to improve her appearance. Parthenia actually had washed her face and neck; her short hair looked considerably less untidy. Excitement, moreover, had heightened her color. In fact, at the moment, Parthenia Bryant, because of her buckskin skirt and a clean cloth shirtwaist, appeared more attractive, more feminine than he'd ever seen her.

When the oxcart halted under a thick limb a minister, the Reverend Samuel Doak, tried to climb up to speak with the condemned man, but the crowd pulled him back yelling, "Let the murderin' whoreson die uncomforted!"

As a barefooted youth shinnied out on the limb and quickly secured the rope, the doomed man screamed in a shrill, inhuman voice, "Spare me! For God's love, spare me! Oh, no! Don't! Please, friends, please don't kill me. I ain't fit to die!"

Parthenia jumped off her tackey and raced over to the cart, shaking her fist and squalling, "Damn yer black soul! Ye're as fit to die now as ye'll ever be! Swing him! Swing him!"

Barry dismounted, caught Parthenia by her wrist and dragged her back. "That'll do! Does you no good to sink to that poor devil's level."

To his amazement the girl all at once broke into tears, flung arms about him and clung, sobbing, "Hang onto me! I don't know how to think no more! What if *'twasn't* him shot Billy?"

A curious semi-groan rose from the crowd when the ox driver used his goad, yelled, "Hup! Git! Git!"

Even Parthenia was satisfied with the length of time the attentuated figure kicked and writhed before, gradually, its motions slowed and a fine trickle of urine began to drip proving that the man was dead.

Only because Lieutenant-Colonel Isaac Shelby, originally from Maryland, already had started back from the race meeting at Jonesborough did he appear in Sycamore Shoals so early the next morning. With him came his brothers, Evan and Moses; a third brother, James, would arrive later and bring along as many recruits as could be mustered in that part of the country.

Since Shelby already had heard about Ferguson's threat his naturally hot blood had cooled somewhat, but he still was mad clear through and in his deep-set blue eyes lurked dangerous lights.

It didn't take long for Shelby and Sevier to assemble a council of war which included citizens representing various settlements scattered about the Watauga country. Right away a rider was sent to hurry up those riflemen who'd left Bluff Station after Dr. Mason had set out.

Once the council convened there wasn't much oratory or discussion; everybody agreed with the co-commanders it was wiser to fight the Tories east of the Great Smokies than wait for them to invade and ravage the settlements.

This course also would preclude the possibility of an outbreak by pro-British tribes already stirred up by Crown agents; these would be only too eager to pounce and exterminate defeated Americans and nullify, in torrents of blood, the one-sided Treaty of Sycamore Shoals by which many hundreds of square miles had been ceded to the whites by Creek and Cherokee chiefs through dubious negotiations.

A decision also was taken to dispatch messengers to leaders of Patriot irregulars thought to be operating east of the mountains urging them to come as fast as they could to Sycamore Shoals or, if unable, to join the Western Volunteer Army just east of Jonesborough; failing that, they must appear somewhere on the Wilderness Road between the mountains and Morgantown.

"Now that that's settled," drawled the Colonel of Sullivan County, "all we need do is to find out how many troops Major Ferguson has along and how good they are."

Everybody began to talk at once but it soon appeared that no one knew anything for sure. Estimates varied that anywhere from eight hundred to two thousand Tories were in the field.

"Of course," Shelby's brother Evan pointed out, "those bastards will be getting reinforcements all along the line."

Sevier's neat bob wig inclined. "Well, there's nothing we can do about that, but maybe we'll get increased as fast or faster then the enemy, so let's try to get some idea how many men we can count on come a week's time."

He turned to Major Valentine, standing stern and important-looking across the hot and crowded room. "I believe, sir, you've encountered volunteers on the road from Fort Pat Henry. How many d'you think we can expect to arrive here?"

Choice's father raised an eyebrow in Mason's direction. "What's your guess, Sam?"

"Not more than thirty," the doctor replied. "Being well-mounted, they ought to show up in a couple of days."

Isaac Shelby and John Sevier then stated that each of them expected to furnish about two hundred and forty mounted expert shots to serve as the improvised little army's backbone.

"That's close on five hundred men," remarked Major Evan Shelby, "which ain't bad for a starter."

Next, it was decided that an immediate appeal should be hurried to Colonel William Campbell of Virginia, whose militia from time to time had been opposing Ferguson's advance. Campbell, someone volunteered, was supposed to be leading four hundred weary and hungry men.

Also to be located were other Patriot commanders: that elusive North Carolinian, Colonel Cleveland, as well as Colonel James Williams and Colonel William Graham from the same state.

Aside from these was mentioned Colonel Ben Williams and an aged General McDowell, also from North Carolina, but no one knew how many followers these officers were leading or where they could be found.

Nevertheless, riders were sent in search, hurrying along the Wilderness Road towards Morgantown Gap.

Captain Barry Colcord, sitting quietly to one side, was both amazed and stimulated by the meeting's grimly determined manner.

An important question then arose: who would assume overall command once the scattered forces became united? For this responsibility Sevier and Shelby, both lieutenant-colonels, favored hard-faced William Campbell of Virginia — a redoubtable frontier fighter who held the commission of full colonel.

Once the couriers had departed, Sycamore Shoals fairly hummed with activity. Horses were shod, doctored and fed till they could eat no more. Leather equipment was gone over, repaired or replaced. Most of all, the volunteers were anxious to get their firearms in repair, so, to help satisfy this demand, Dan Maddox ranged about the town until he found a well-equipped armorer-blacksmith who, having recently suffered a broken arm, was only too pleased to have the big, soft-spoken Pennsylvanian's undeniable skill keep a growing mob of customers satisfied after a fashion.

The first thing Maddox did was to repair the cock spring on Ilsa, and then with infinite care forged a true-tempered pan cover. Sleeves rolled up and rejoicing at the familiar tug of a leather apron at his hips, he toiled long hours, yet never seemed to catch up with the work.

Tim Murphy, who knew considerable about the simpler aspects of the gunsmith's art, worked just as hard, so it wasn't long before Kitty — the

Golcher double-barreled rifle which had killed General Fraser — had had to be re-bored to a slightly larger caliber. Tim was worried, but Dan vowed his famous piece would shoot as true as ever.

By the dozen whiskery, hatchet-faced characters came sidling up to the smithy. Sometimes the weapons brought in were magnificent examples of the gunsmith's art, the work of experts like Richard Folley, Ike Harris and Joel Feree. One was a curious, breech-loading rifle which, its owner claimed, had been invented by that same Major Ferguson they were getting ready to fight.

"Blamed if I c'n understand," the fellow grunted, "why this here gun ain't been copied by the hundred. Believe it or not, Mister, I c'n fire *three shots a minute* till she gets powder-fouled whilst you fellers are damn' lucky can you fire your danged muzzle-loaders once in fifteen minutes!"

Dan was filing a lock's side piece when he heard a stir among the inevitable throng of onlookers — who didn't like to watch a gunsmith at work? He looked up and saw a lean, sharp-featured young female pushing her way towards the smithy.

"I tell ye, that's her!" someone cried.

"Who's her?"

"The gal what kilt three men all by herself."

"Aw, yer funnin'. No skinny little female the likes of her could slay three grown men."

" 'Tis so! She's Parthy Bryant all right. I was over to Jennings' camp and saw her there. It's gospel true she kilt 'em singlehanded."

Maddox wiped the back of a blackened hand over his forehead and flicked aside a heavy beading of sweat. "Heyo, Sis, what's your need?"

The girl held out a short, brass-bound British cavalry carbine. "Mister," said she, pale, almond-shaped eyes intent, "the trigger sear on this here weapon is out o' kilter; needs stiffenin'. Reckon ye can fix it fer me?"

Dan took in this apparition from shapeless and dusty squaw boots to fringed buckskin skirt and coarse linen blouse to pointed face; then, with interest, he noted the cropped condition of her hair but somehow found her appealing. Yonder stood the alert, self-sufficient kind of female he'd always admired — and seldom had met up with.

"Well, Sis, I'd admire to oblige, but just look over there." He pointed towards a double row of guns awaiting attention. "I don't know when I can get to yer piece but I'll do it provided ye're willing to wait yer turn."

Parthenia stepped closer and disclosed good but faintly yellowed teeth in a shy, coaxing smile. "I kin pay real good, Mister." Colcord had turned over to her money found on the corpse of Jasper Skelton and those of the other dead men. "I want this gun back real quick."

"Maybe you do, Sis, but so do plenty of others. It's still a case of first come, first served."

"Look!" On a slender but none-too-clean palm she exposed a gleaming gold piece. "I'll give ye this."

In mounting interest Parthenia watched this husky, smart-looking fellow's expression change. "You really did kill those three men?"

"Sure did, and glad of it. They was thieves and Tories."

"In that case, reckon I'll fix your gun next and, since they were Tories, 'twon't cost you a penny."

Parthenia dropped her gaze and scraped the ground with the toe of a boot, then confessed, "Well, Mister, I ain't *sure* what them fellows was; maybe they weren't out-and-out Tories, but they sure weren't no Patriots, either. What really counts is they shot my brother down 'thout grantin' him the least chance for his life."

Ringed in by curious onlookers, they steadily considered one another until finally Maddox said, "Reckon since ye've been reared along the frontier ye're used to few comforts and hard livin', eh?"

"Ain't never slept in a featherbed in my whole life," Parthenia admitted, "and I bin hungry more often than not. Anyhow, I'm a damn' sight handier about the woods than most of these loons standin' about and gawkin' at us."

Dan grinned and patted her shoulder. "All right, Parthy, you can leave yer carbine over there and come back tomorrow morning. If 'tain't past repair, it'll be fixed."

Thoughtfully, Dan Maddox watched the girl's slight figure shove through the crowd and disappear.

9. *Jollification*

FOR the next few days Colonels Sevier and Shelby's Over-mountain Boys began to arrive at the Shoals; usually they came in alone or by twos and threes but sometimes even a dozen would report to the Fort at the same time. Most were reasonably well mounted and all carried long rifles, shiny tomahawks and scalping knives slung to their belts.

Hunting shirts of various sorts and colors from white to dark brown or black were so usual that these came to constitute a sort of rough and practical uniform. For baggage the new arrivals carried only a blanket, a kettle and a fodder sack in addition to an ammunition bag and a greasy haversack containing a scant supply of food.

Loud and generally obscene greetings were exchanged whenever new arrivals rode into town. Often these hard-bitten characters were accompanied by favorite bear dogs so some mighty noisy and often bloody fights took place when they tried conclusions with local canines.

Everyone felt vastly encouraged when the first elements of Colonel William Campbell's thin and footsore Virginia Volunteers appeared and went into camp near the Fort. With them they brought fresh tidings of disaster; Major Ferguson, it seemed, had chased these Virginians for several days with a well-trained and equipped army supposed to number nearly two thousand.

Later, reports came in that the Tories had halted on the other side of the mountains close to Gilbert Town and were in a position to block the retreat of Colonel Elijah Clark, who was attempting to guard a motley column of defeated Patriots and their families trying to escape westward from Georgia and South Carolina. Also it was rumored that Ferguson had appealed to Lord Cornwallis for quick reinforcements — by Tarleton's British Legion if possible.

When, on the twentieth of September, Colonel James Williams of North Carolina came in leading another hundred rangy and hard-eyed riflemen, a decision was taken to wait no longer. On the morrow the little army would set out along the well-traveled Wilderness Road towards Morgantown Gap.

To his mild astonishment Dan Maddox actually found himself anticipating another sight of that girl who'd so tickled his interest when first she'd appeared at the smithy. When finally she did appear, Parthenia examined his work with an experienced and critical eye. At last she smiled and her smooth brown face lit and softened.

"Say, Mr. Maddox, there's a real first-rate mendin' job. Thanks a heap!" She fumbled in a small leather pouch slung to her belt and offered a handful of coins. "Just take out what you figger's comin' to you."

The ex-ranger laughed and was glad that for the moment no one was within hearing distance. "All right, Sis, I'll just do that!" Before she suspected what Dan intended he'd grabbed her close and planted a resounding smack full on her mouth.

Parthenia's reaction wasn't what he expected; the girl just stood there looking as if someone had clubbed her on the head; her eyes gradually rounded and her thin brown lips parted until she raised a hand to rub its back across her lips.

"What's wrong, Parthy? Was that so bad?"

She felt blood rush up to heat her features. "— N-no, Mr. Maddox, but this is the very firstest time I ever got bussed by anybody 'ceptin' Ma."

Hands on hips, the leather-aproned gunsmith surveyed his client, a foolish half-grin decking his features. "Well, and how do you feel?"

"Don't know," came her surprising reply. "Like Ma said once upon a time, 'One robin don't make a spring.' "

Suddenly Parthenia whirled and dashed off towards Jennings's camp, where men were attempting to learn the rudiments of how to maneuver on horseback — really quite an unnecessary drill because these volunteers were supposed to fight only on foot. In other words, they weren't intended to act like real cavalry, only as fast-moving mounted infantry which, adopting Indian tactics, would drift from tree to tree and fire as they advanced.

That night began a spontaneous jollification. An enormous bonfire was kindled in a harvested cornfield near the river. Liquor flowed freely from various sources. Drums, fiddles, flutes and even a trumpet or two assembled into what might be misnamed a band of music.

By the hundreds residents and transients flocked to the scene while taverns reluctantly disgorged happily inebriated customers attracted by all that singing, shouting and stamping down by the water.

Along with a few other officers Barry Colcord handed Choice to a small rise from which the party viewed the frolics without risk of getting jostled or assaulted in drunken comraderie. He'd seen Major Valentine's daughter several times, having become attracted not only by her piquant good looks but also by her seemingly genuine desire to be near him whenever possible. Only the night before he'd been surprised to find himself describing, for the first time since it had taken place, the destruction of Ricelands and the murder of his wife and child.

"I don't see how you can ever get over it."

"Maybe I never will; not altogether, that is, but, as wiseacres say, 'Time is the great healer.' All the same, right now I doubt whether I wish ever to return to Georgetown County."

"Are you certain?" Choice asked almost too readily.

"Of course I don't know, but somehow I feel that when this confounded war ends — if it ever does — I'll send for my son and take up land somewhere around here."

Choice had caught her breath, said hurriedly, "Whatever you decide, Captain, for heaven's sake don't even dream of going so far west as the Tennessee stations."

"Don't think I will," said he seriously. "I'm far too green on the frontier to last long, but perhaps I may settle somewhere around Watauga. Think that's a sound idea?"

She did.

Faces tinted red-gold by the bonfire's glow, they listened to gaunt, hairy men sing tunes which had crossed the Atlantic long, long ago, many of them during the reign of Elizabeth, the Virgin Queen. There were wild, warlike ballads from the Scottish Highlands and many softertoned songs from Wales, home of the sweetest singers in all the British Isles.

Now flames were soaring, leaping, propelling multitudes of sparks high into the starlit sky. The bonfire's heat soon drove the onlookers into a respectful retreat.

When Barry frowned, Choice noticed, said, "What's wrong, Captain?"

"Why, I was only wondering how many of those men singing and dancing down there will be alive after we've met the Tories. A stupid, morbid thought, is it not?" Before he knew what he was doing he'd slipped a hand around her waist.

She made no effort to move aside. "I presume a good many women and children are wondering the same thing."

"No doubt. At least their men are lucky enough to have someone worry over what may happen."

Choice turned, reached up and kissed him on the cheek. "Oh, Barry, you'll have someone, too; with all my heart I'll pray for you. Should you — if you ever could want me I'll wait for you here."

"You'd really wait?"

"Oh, my dear, forever, if you tell me to."

Soon after he'd returned the gunsmith's shop to its owner, Maddox hunted up Tim Murphy and, together with some men who claimed they'd served under "The Old Wagoner," sought the nearest tavern, not unaware that the former sergeant's pockets were bulging. So many old soldiers appeared that, shortly before the bonfire began to blaze, the Pennsylvanian had become host to a mob of thirsty veterans.

Said Maddox to Tim, "What in hell ails you, Murphy? Damn' if you ain't grinnin' like an old tomcat locked in a creamery. Suppose you've got yerself a wench?"

"Hell! I've enjoyed half a dozen such since we got here, near enough to make up for that damn' starvation diet I been on lately. Come on, Dan'l, let's traipse to them doin's down by the river and find out what's goin' on."

But Dan never joined the jollification. Recalling the Bryant girl, he shook off his companions and sought the Jennings camping place. Only two or three women were sitting in semi-darkness, gossiping and vainly attempting to disguise their dread of the morrow.

Dan wasn't overly surprised to find Parthenia sitting in front of her tent chipping sharper edges onto some fine-looking gun flints.

"Heyo, Sis."

She looked up half-smiling. "Heyo yerself, Mr. Maddox. Why ain't ye whoopin' and prancin' with the rest of them drunken ijits?"

He squatted on his heels beside her. "Why ain't you?"

"Because I ain't a ijit and I don't fancy crowds nohow."

"No more do I," he said, then helped her to her feet. "Suppose you and me walk along the shore a piece and watch the goin's-on from a distance?"

Before she put away her instruments she held out a handful of dully glistening red-brown flints. "Here, these are fine French stones. I want you should have 'em."

"Why for?"

"Likely you'll have need of such 'fore you kin tack that devil Ferguson's hide to a barn door."

When she started to leave her ragged little tent she realized Mr. Maddox was blocking its exit, also that he seemed to be having trouble with his breathing. She guessed it must be the liquor he'd guzzled; his breath fairly reeked of rum.

"Parthy," he began thickly. "Parthy, I — I —" He stepped inside the tent, which stood at considerable distance from the rest. "Parthy, I don't know what's come over me, but — but Ilsa's been a long time dead now. Since she died I ain't touched never a female woman. I — I, well, I want —"

Parthy retreated a couple of steps, said softly, "I know. I know and I'd sure be pleased to oblige you and I will, but —" through the dim light her eyes bored intently into his — "I don't aim to become no man's leman. Ma, she taught me better, God rest her soul."

"Amen. But, Parthy, I ain't drunk and I — I've just *got* to have you. You're the only one I've ever wanted since Ilsa died." He put his arms around her slowly, gently. "*You* know what the frontier's like, *you* understand the meaning of fear, hunger and hardship."

She didn't resist when he drew her close enough to feel again the wondrous, delicate softness of a woman's breasts.

"Oh, Parthy, I've seen how good you work and heard how you, you 'venged yerself on those murderers all by yerself and, by God, that shines!" He tightened his arms about her, felt his blood heating past endurance and hungrily crushed her mouth.

At first Parthenia didn't resist; in fact, she pressed lips and body so hard against him he figured that, sure enough, he was home and dry with her.

But when Dan tried to slip a hand inside her shirt she suddenly twisted out of his grip and ran out of the tent. "I'm meanin' it when I say, Dan'l, I'd sure admire to live with you and bear you a lot of children — but I don't aim to, lest we visit a preacher first."

As, trembling a little, Dan hesitated before the slim, resolute figure, an overwhelming need seized him. He muttered, "Perhaps we'll do that — but why're you so confounded dead-set?"

"The reason I'm so dead-set," she explained seriously, "is 'count of I'm what some folks would call a 'woods colt' — same's a bastard in the frontier country. You see, Pa already had a wife when he married my Ma. Me, I don't want none of my get to suffer like I have."

Dan Maddox gave in with a readiness which surprised him. "All right, Parthy, we'll have it yer way. But who is there to tie the knot?"

The girl's teeth glimmered in the dark oval of her face as she laughed softly, "Why, dearie, I *just* happened to hear they's a minister up to the Fort — the Rev'rend Doak, I think."

When he held out his hand towards her Parthenia grabbed it and hugged it to her breast. "Well, come along, girl," he said. "Let's go and try to find this Bible-pounder. Ain't likely a man of God would be triflin' around a jollification."

When, not much later, they found their way back to Parthenia's tent they made awkward, violent love — as man and wife.

10. *"The Sword of the Lord and of Gideon"*

Nor long before sunup a milling swarm of horsemen began to try to form in eight columns of twos on a big, vacant tobacco field lying on the southeast side of Sycamore Shoals, for when dawn had begun to glimmer, soldiers in the Fort had fired a cannon as a warning for volunteers to assemble.

When various units more or less collected themselves and halted facing the Fort's main gate, hundreds of people who weren't going along gathered outside the palisade and, almighty somber of mien, watched the commanding officers — it hadn't yet been decided who was to be supreme commander — come trotting through the main gate.

In the lead, as commanding officer for that day, rode Lieutenant-Colonel John Sevier. He no longer was clad in neat, immaculate regimentals but wore a knee-length hunting shirt of butternut-dyed canvas such as he always used when in the field. The only indication of his rank was a pair of silver lace epaulets that flopped, awkwardly pinned to his shoulders.

On arriving in the open the staff reined in to allow the lanky, somber figure of the Reverend Samuel Doak to come before them, Bible in hand.

Hats whispered off when the chaplain bent a balding gray head and implored Almighty God to grant safety and victory to these men fighting in the cause of Liberty, men who were risking their lives in the de-

fense of all they held dear. The Reverend Doak concluded by raising his
already ringing voice to an almost thunderous pitch, "So, dear brethern,
let us earnestly pray that the Philistines shall be laid low by the sword of
the Lord and of Gideon! Grant, we beseech Thee, strength as of ten to
each of these, Thy unworthy servants and for Christ's sake preserve
them from harm. Amen."

Once the prayer ended, Sevier and Shelby rode out, first at a walk,
then at a trot and finally they took up a canter. Raggedly, the motley,
attenuated columns fell in behind their leaders. So, to the snuffle and
stamp of over eight hundred horses, the rough little army set out for
Morgantown Gap and the fate awaiting them beyond the mountains.

Soon the expedition began to disappear around a sharp bend in the
Wilderness Road. Swelling clouds of yellowish dust mounted into the
bright late September sky.

In the interests of security, Dr. Samuel Mason rode with a rear guard
composed of Over-mountain men he knew and trusted, because he was
carrying his original drawings, maps and notes describing Robertson's
route to the Frenchman's Bluff. Captain Colcord, entrusted with a set
of copies made during the past week, traveled in the van with the headquarters staff.

More through force of habit than anything else, Dr. Mason was
prompted every evening to scribble in his journal a brief summation of
the day's happenings.

> 26, Sept. 1780. This Day passed through Morgan-Town Gap
> and soon were joined by a very old North Carolina Gen'l who
> had with him about a Hundred-and-Sixty mounted Riflemen.
> Cols. Shelby, Sevier and Campbell wished Gen'l McDowell,
> because of his Superior Rank to assume Chief Command, but,
> he being Aged and Feeble, he declined the Honour in favour of
> Col. Wm. Campbell.

His next entry read:

> Colonel Shelby today is Furious and Distracted because two
> previously Trusted Men belonging to his Headquarters Co.
> have Deserted and are Presumed to be riding straight to Major
> Ferguson to apprise him of our Strength and Intention.
> Yesterday, we passed a Place called The Cowpens where it
> was learned that the Enemy, hearing of our Presence, has com-
> menced a Retreat from Gilbert Town. It is Generally felt that
> the Tories will fall back upon the British Outpost called

Ninety-six where Considerable Reinforcements and Supplies are said to be awaiting him.

A night or so later Mason wrote:

> There is much Jubilation amongst us for at last we have met the elusive Col. Cleveland. He and his Troops entered on the Wilderness Road and met us purely by Chance. For us this is a most Fortunate Occurrence since he Commands near Four hundred Men as Tough and Bitter as any I have Beheld all during this War. They are Burning with Outrage over the Barbarous conduct of the King's Followers since our Defeat at Camden. Frankly, I would not Wish to be taken Prisoner by any of them were I a Loyalist.

When the little army halted for the night of October fifth, an escaped prisoner was brought to the headquarters tent before which Colonels Campbell, Sevier, Shelby and Cleveland were wolfing half-cooked suppers.

It appeared that this ragged fellow had got away only two days earlier, and when he began to recite his observations more and more high-ranking officers came to listen. The ex-prisoner satisfactorily answered all manner of questions designed to determine his honesty. His most valuable single piece of intelligence was that the American commanders were mistaken in believing the Tory forces to be falling back on Fort 96. Major Ferguson, instead, had turned away in a southeasterly direction, apparently with intention of joining Lord Cornwallis, the security of whose left flank had been entrusted to him and his corps of Tories.

"You're positive about this?" demanded florid-faced Colonel Campbell.

"Yep. I'm sure as a feller can be about anything in this crazy war. For a fact, I overheard some Tories from New Jersey laugh because they figgered to have sure 'nough fooled you fellers into believin' they was headed for 96."

Colonel Shelby, sucking on his pipe, made little watery noises. "All right, we'll credit that. Now, tell us, friend, does Ferguson have any regular British troops along?"

"Naw! Not a single goddam one! All he's got with him is a lot of damn' tough Tories."

"What regiments are with him?" Colonel Williams wanted to know.

"Ain't exactly sure, but he's got some from a Noo Jersey volunteer regiment, some from the King's American Rangers and the Queen's Loyal Rangers. Both of 'em are from Noo York, but the heft of his people come from Georgia and the Carolinas — and a meaner lot I never want to see!"

Colonel Cleveland inquired, "About how many men would you say Major Ferguson has brought together?"

"Somewheres 'twixt a thousand or fifteen hundred of the murderin' bastards; most of 'em carry rifles and look like they know how to use 'em. Make no mistake about it, gents, if, and when, you come up with Ferguson, ye'll be tanglin' with first-class fighters."

Later on, Samuel Mason knuckled tired eyes and wrote:

> Once the former former Prisoner had been Excused it was decided to chase the Enemy with all Speed so Tomorrow Morning around 900 of our best Mounted Men are to start in Pursuit cutting across-country in the Direction of King's Mountain, which is no mountain at all, only a high Ridge which rises sixty or seventy Feet above the Plain. This Ridge, we are told, has steep, tree-covered sides and, being bald on Top, offers a First-class defensive Position for a Determined Enemy.

The physician paused long enough to take a long pull of water from his canteen; October, this year, had remained so unseasonably hot and dry that during a day plenty of dust and grit got sucked down a man's windpipe.

> At Present I can hear Men being picked for the Party which will attempt to prevent Major Ferguson from uniting with Lord Cornwallis' great Army. God send they can find our Enemies in Time.
> Have just consulted with Captain Colcord and we are Agreed that because of our Responsibilities we must remain as *Widely* Separated as is Consistent with Prudence.

Yawning, Samuel Mason, M.D., stoppered his ink bottle and restored a well-worn quill to its case, then lingered for a while staring into the coals and wondering how Rosemary Mason might be faring at this very moment.

11. *King's Mountain*

A SMALL flock of passenger pigeons flying over King's Mountain in pursuit of the main migration which had followed this route the day before flared on sighting a low, club-shaped ridge which was about half a mile long and rose only about sixty feet high on the average. At its widest point this eminence was only a hundred yards wide and ran in a generally northeast-southwest direction. Near the club's head a few canvas-covered wagons were visible, surrounded by a sprinkling of tents.

Had they been interested, the birds also would have noticed a long and very thin column of mounted men traveling towards the base of that ridge known to mere humans as King's Mountain. It being still early in the day, the horses below, refreshed after a night's rest, were moving at a brisk trot.

Flying smoothly at an arrow-like speed of ninety miles an hour, the migrants soon sighted another line of humans who, half a mile beneath them, were following a rough brown track which meandered lazily through the autumn-bright woods. These figures were advancing much more slowly than the others sighted only a few moments ago; most of them traveled on foot, accompanied by horses which limped or walked sluggishly because of sickness.

Only a strong sense of duty prevented Dr. Samuel Mason from entrusting his portfolio to some reliable officer and then pushing ahead to join the hand-picked vanguard along with Tim Murphy, Dan Maddox and other volunteers from Middle Tennessee.

Had Major Valentine been along, Mason probably would have entrusted the documents to his father-in-law, but that worthy, perhaps fortuitously, but more possibly by design, had complained of pains in his bowels severe enough to prevent his leaving Sycamore Shoals with the army of volunteers. Ostensibly, he would bring along men arriving belatedly at the rendezvous. Understanding the Squire as well as he did, Sam Mason reasoned that that astute politician probably would continue to find sufficient and plausible excuses for lingering on in the Watauga settlements long enough to play politics while awaiting the campaign's outcome.

Now Mason was riding with those unlucky volunteers who'd come in on foot or whose mounts had broken down; altogether these numbered about four hundred — all of them spitting-mad for fear the battle might be fought before they could join in and exact payment for their losses and sufferings.

Since he was a medical man, it appeared only his duty to remain with the wagons and be prepared to receive wounded men as soon as they appeared.

This, the morning of October 7, 1780, dawned without anybody's forseeing that, on this day, the greatest battle of the first American Civil War soon would be joined. Only much later would it be appreciated that the *only* professional British soldier to serve in the impending conflict was Major Patrick Ferguson himself. On both sides, all combatants were Americans.

About two hours after daybreak a galloper came racing through the unlit woods to bring the electrifying news that the advanced contingent had succeeded in their mission! The Tory Army had been found. It had camped and had taken up a defensive position on the summit of the long, low hill locally know as King's Mountain. The galloper couldn't say just how many men the Tory leader now was commanding, but it was thought that there were plenty of them.

Just as soon as the welcome news got about, younger and more athletic foot soldiers shouldered weapons and, at a space-eating dogtrot, set off along the road. Most of them would be able to maintain such a pace for hours on end.

Wagon drivers swore, cracked whips and lashed heavy-footed teams into a lumbering trot which rattled the wagons along unmercifully for a while, but, of course, such a pace couldn't be kept up for long.

What everyone urgently wanted to find out was how far away this mountain lay; optimists guessed it must be only four or five miles ahead — but maybe it was farther.

Early in the morning, scouts reported to the advanced division's commanders that the enemy apparently had elected to decide the issue on or around King's Mountain. Later, it was reported that when Patrick Ferguson had learned of the enemy's approach he'd shouted, "I defy God Almighty and all the Rebels out of Hell to overcome me here!"

His point was well taken, since that redoubtable and very able officer had under his command some eleven hundred troops. Of these around a hundred were expert riflemen selected from New York and New Jersey Loyalist regiments; the bulk of his forces, however, were battle-hardened Southern Tory militia. Most of these, in place of nonexistent bayonets, had been equipped with long steel blades which, driven down the bore of a piece, converted a gun into a spear which could prove useful at infighting when no time was left for reloading. Such weapons, of course, couldn't be fired once these improvised bayonets had been inserted.

Once Senior Commander William Campbell was satisfied that the enemy really intended to remain where they were and weren't getting set to come pouring down from the heights, he and his staff arrived at an almost childishly simple plan of battle.

Observed Colonel William Campbell, "Reckon we've got just about sufficient men with us to surround yonder pesky ridge."

A local volunteer stepped forward and, employing a twig, traced the outline of a blunt, long-handled club on ground whitened by splotches of passenger pigeon droppings.

Intently, Colonel Campbell's staff followed the movements of the twig now being manipulated by the commanding officer himself.

"Now, I want you all to look close. This is about where we're standing. See? Right below the head of this here club head. Now, I want you, Lacey, Winston, Cleveland and Hambright to stay put right here under General McDowell's direction.

"Meanwhile, Ike Shelby and you, Jim Williams, will lead your fellows along the ridge's north side till you reach the handle's end. Me and Johnny Sevier will do the same thing; only we'll advance around the south slope."

His gaze circled the intent brown faces about him. "Now, you fellows wait till you hear my men raise the war whoop Johnny Sevier's taught us. When you hear it, yell like hell, then we'll all swarm up that ridge the fastest we're able."

He spat and fingered a long knife at his belt. "Best of it is, I don't believe Ferguson's got any real notion of how many men we've brought along so he's apt to start shootin' at whichever crowd gets to the top first; probably he'll hurry his reserves to drive 'em back, which should grant us a fine chance of reachin' the summit without gettin' hurt too bad."

Colonel Campbell squinted up the hardwood-covered slope. "I want you all to remember this: if the enemy charges like he means it, just you fall back down the slope, drifting from tree to tree and killing every enemy you can. Now, I figure, and I think you'll agree, that when Ferguson hears the whooping from another direction on the hill he'll most likely order his men back to the top to meet the new threat; that's when you start back up the slope — screeching all the while."

Barry Colcord found it utterly exasperating to be forced to linger thus with the headquarters detail clutching Dr. Mason's confounded papers and enviously watching long files of volunteers go riding off through sun-dappled woods bright with gay colors. Despite their obvious impatience, he wanted to keep Black Buck and Tom Calloway close by — just in case things went wrong up on the mountain. But he wondered about how long the precious pair would linger once the war whoop was raised and shots began to ring out.

Colcord found out soon enough. The moment his attention was momentarily distracted by directing a party of late arrivals to McDowell's sector the young Georgian suddenly lashed his horse and dashed off in pursuit of Colonel Cleveland's troops and, ignoring the Carolinian's furious shouts, vanished among the beechnuts and maplewoods. The mustee, however, stayed with him for a while longer.

It was only natural that Maddox and Tim Murphy should elect to serve under John Sevier, most of whose three hundred riflemen had lived beyond the Alleghenies. So they joined up with a party of hard-eyed men from Western Virginia because they looked as if they really could handle themselves in a hot fight. Many of them had pinned up floppy-brimmed hats on one side, then had tucked a piece of paper into the fold to avoid being mistaken for Loyalists in civilian garb. A lot of Patriots were taking that precaution.

Steadily, the mounted riflemen picked a route westwards through hardwoods growing along the sides and base of King's Mountain. Already men began to fidget and check their gear against the moment they'd be told to dismount.

Now and again Dan Maddox sighted the gleam of Colonel Sevier's bleached buckskin hunting shirt between tree trunks; the width of the veteran's shoulders somehow lent him an air of competence and assurance. What a shame that that fine soldier and leader, James Robertson, couldn't be here! He'd be right in his element.

Briefly, Dan thought back to other battles he'd been in and came to the conclusion that this fight would be different and possibly more deadly than any he'd known. For one thing, this time the enemy wasn't a lot of ramrod-stiff, drill-yard-trained Redcoats who'd been taught the only way to fight a battle was to point, not aim, their muskets and deliver as many devastating volleys as they could at an enemy who should, according to the rules, be advancing in obligingly solid ranks. After that, it would be a "fix bayonets," charge and drive survivors into panic-stricken retreat. No. This time the men on top of the little ridge were no wooden-headed Europeans but a lot of fellow Americans, all too often the fathers, brothers or cousins of men beginning to take position along the base of the heights.

Tim expressed a general opinion. "Know somethin', Dan? Them fellers up there are apt to act like so many cornered wildcats. They ain't fightin' for pay like Burgoyne's Lobsterbacks and them ox-dumb Dutch hirelings. They know damn' well after that they've done, what will happen to 'em, their people and property if they get licked."

"Guess you're right, Tim, and if we get whipped they'll be no more merciful to us."

Lovingly, Tim stroked his double-barrel's satin-smooth stock. Pretty soon he aimed to stow a few rifle balls in his cheek to be spat down Kitty's muzzle when it came time to reload — a fellow could save precious instants like that.

Other riders were tightening the wrapping on paper cartridges they'd fashioned; each one contained a premeasured charge of powder which, when the cartridge's end was bitten off, could be poured down the rifle's bore a damned sight quicker than even a clever man could use his powder horn, guessing at the amount of his load.

Gradually the forward movement of the troops ahead slowed, then an order was passed back for everyone to dismount and tie their horses to trees rather than turn the animals over to horse holders — apparently every last man was going to be used once the climbing and shooting began.

Grimly silent all at once, the riflemen got off, then tied coats and unnecessary gear to their saddles; with them, aside from their firearms, they would carry only ammunition bags, knives and war hatchets. Dan noticed that not a single bayonet was anywhere in sight.

Obedient to arm signals from their officers, the volunteers began to drift forward in a long, loose line abreast, but when they reached the foot of the wooded slope they were ordered to halt and wait for that whooping from Colonel Campbell's direction which would start them climbing and screeching like scalp-hungry redskins.

As Dan had anticipated, here was a novel experience. To tell the truth, until now he'd never been altogether sure about just *what* he was fighting for. He held nothing personal against those red-faced, often strange-talking Englishmen — they hadn't cost him property nor had they murdered people he knew, but these fellows up on the ridge were different, except that they were fighting for King George III, same as the Lobsterbacks he and Tim had been battling over all these years.

A rail-thin fellow to his right reckoned this must be about noontime, account of the sun shone almost directly overhead and all shadows were short.

Crouched behind a big, gray-barked beech Tim, his small body taut and compact, fiddled with the Golcher's rear sight, adjusted it for close range. As near as he could foresee this tussle was going to develop into a nearly hand-to-hand affair offering a sharpshooter little chance to prove his skill.

Finally, from the left where Colonel Campbell had led his men someone raised a clear, blood-chilling yell: "*Whoo! Whoo-whoop!*"

Even from a distance of eighty yards Colonel Sevier's men heard Billy Campbell shouting, "There they are, boys! Now shout like hell and fight like devils!"

Along with his companions Maddox strained his throat in a series of Shawnee yells; soon the racket swelled so loud he couldn't even hear himself. But pretty soon it got quieter and Tom could hear a lot of drums beating high above him. Now, off to the right, old man McDowell's men began to whoop, and then on the far side from the club's handle more war cries arose in answer. Those should be Shelby's Over-mountain Boys, who must have skinned up the ridge in a big hurry, for the first shots to be heard broke out along their front.

Tom Calloway had kept his mount moving forward among the trees and underbrush until he found himself among Isaac Shelby's already dismounted riflemen, so he hurriedly swung down, not even bothering to secure his horse, and started to scramble after those leather-covered men who'd begun clawing at bushes and were zigzagging towards an uninterrupted expanse of glimmering bright blue sky.

Tom soon realized it was fine that the summit of this ridge was treeless; when he reached the top he'd know it. While he was jumping from behind one tree to the next he recalled how he'd begun this war as a red-hot Patriot; then, because the Sons of Liberty kept getting whipped and most of his neighbors called themselves Loyalists, he'd signed up in Capt'n Catlin's troop of Georgia Tories and even had fought in a few skirmishes. But after a party of drunken King-lovers had murdered Pa and raped his young sister, he'd switched sides again — this time for keeps even though it had seemed like a mistake after what happened at Charles Town. Even now, Tom still felt right hot over Pa and Sis.

Gritting strong yellow teeth, he squinted up through the pattern of branches; God send he'd find some of the villains who'd slain his folks!

The men above stopped climbing and opened fire at something he couldn't see. He cocked his rifle — a tired old piece the barrel of which was worn kind of thin. All around him sounded panted curses along with a continuous snapping and crackling of broken bushes. Layers of sharp-smelling burnt powder smoke began to roll downhill and hung low to the ground because there wasn't even a fart's worth of wind blowing.

Over an increasing rattle of shots he heard whooping and shouting from above and the shrill screaming of a badly hit man. A moment later Tom sighted a broad-chested fellow slipping and sliding downhill; a bayonet gleamed at the end of his gun. Checking his descent the Tory squatted behind a mossy log and was looking about for a target when Tom threw up his rifle and fired a quick shot. Whether he hit or not, the Georgian had no time to find out. Suddenly where one bayonet had caught the sunlight now there were a dozen. There was something heart-stopping about the deadly shine of them.

Tom snatched a powder cartridge from his bag, then his big teeth clamped down on the cylinder of greasy paper. Biting off its end, he spilled the contents down his rifle's bore, prayed fervently that no hot spark lingered inside — a man could get his hand blown off like that. Next, he spat out a bullet, dropped it into the muzzle, then poised a patch over the opening and gave a couple of vigorous thrusts with his ramrod to seat the ball.

He was still priming his pan when somebody shouted, "Fall back boys! Them Loyalist bastards have got bayonets and it's too soon for knives and hatchets!"

When the men nearest him began to back down the slope Tom Calloway followed their example, though it burned him to have to retreat. Still, it seemed a smart idea; one hell of a lot of Tories were appearing above. While falling back the Volunteers paused to shoot whenever opportunity offered. One after another green-coated men crumpled and rolled downhill until they were stopped by underbrush. Tom saw a Tory, yelling like a banshee, drive his bayonet all the way into the back of a fallen Patriot.

"Son of a bitch!" snarled Tom. He took a quick sight and fired and knew he'd hit this time; the fellow's black-bearded face miraculously became transformed into a scarlet, shapeless pulp.

Only dimly did the Georgian become aware that a deal of shooting was going on both to his right and left. Not only that but on the mountain's far side.

Bullet-cut twigs and leaves began to rain down; balls *thocked* into tree trunks. Through swirling, baffling, disorienting smoke Tom could hear Colonel Shelby shouting, "That's right, boys! Come along, and this time let's reach the top and whip the Tory sons of bitches!"

After climbing a while Calloway was gasping as hard as if he'd run a mile with the Devil at his heels, so was glad to pause and reload before starting on after his companions. To his right he glimpsed a young fellow who couldn't yet have reached his majority stoop over a wounded Tory who wasn't able to walk any more and could only crawl.

"Oh-h! No! Quarter! I ain't never harmed no one!"

Quite calmly, the youth jerked his tomahawk out of its sling and took deliberate aim before splitting his enemy's skull.

"And that's fer you, ye damn' whoreson," he panted, then slipped his dripping weapon back into its support before resuming his climb.

Although a fearful racket was exploding on the top of King's Mountain, the Tories attempted a second bayonet charge, but it seemed considerably less forceful then their first. Shelby's men fell back again, but in doing so exacted a stiff price. Quite a few bodies came tumbling downhill. As before, the enemy's advance was checked less than halfway down the slope, and again the men in green or brown went laboring back to the summit.

On the far side of the club's handle Dan Maddox, Tim Murphy and the rest of John Sevier's men were adopting much the same tactics. As they did so Dan became aware of murderous impulses sweeping through him as they had not since that frozen fight with the Indians after the crossing of Mad Bear Creek. Bayonets he'd seen in plenty before, but most of his companions had not, so felt less confident.

All the same, it would have been reassuring had these enemies been clad in scarlet rather than green or brown tunics or in civilian clothes.

While reloading the Golcher Tim grinned at the gunsmith. "By God, ain't this a *real* turkey shoot? Wish to God —" He didn't get any further; the man next to him went down with a ball between his eyes and thrashed spasmodically about in the underbrush until he rolled over and lay still.

Unconcernedly, Tim scrambled past him. He'd seen plenty of men die, but of course *he* wasn't going to get hit — he never did.

Twenty minutes after the first shots had crackled, the battle roared towards a crescendo because volunteers, climbing up the club's head, were nearing its summit. A fierce, ear-piercing clamor arose as, successively, Cleveland's, Hambright's and Winston's men emerged panting and sweat-soaked on the plateau.

Black Buck found a peculiar satisfaction in dropping a white who was wearing a single epaulet. Too bad he'd been forbidden to take that particular scalp; it, plus the epaulet, would have counted for plenty money after the battle. Unfortunately, Colonel Campbell had been most emphatic that no scalps were to be taken under any circumstances.

Everywhere sounded yelling and whooping and men crashing about, so the old mustee cunningly stayed where he was and took time to tighten the set-screw holding his flint in place. No use, at this late date, in getting knocked over by a stray bullet. Once he'd reloaded, he started up again, wishing his bony, bowed legs were stronger, like when he'd been a young buck full of piss and vinegar.

Wagh! By far this promised to be the biggest battle he'd ever been in; why, even Monck's Corner had been as nothing compared to this.

Once the ancient mustee gained the top it was to witness an astonishing sight; masses of white men were running, milling about senselessly, like chickens while a hawk hovers overhead.

Dan Maddox, on emerging onto open and fairly level ground, quickly perceived what was taking place; the main fight now had become centered near the ridge's head where the wagons and tents were.

In quick succession, Campbell's and Shelby's breathless followers appeared and formed a line across the center of the club's handle. Effectively, their leader cursed, forcing them to wait for reinforcements from below. Nevertheless the raging riflemen didn't waste time, they kept on shooting point-blank into the disorganized mass of Tories, who were paying no attention to a handful of brave mounted officers who were riding back and forth and using the flat of their swords trying to form the now completely surrounded men into some sort of order.

Conspicuous on horseback, these officers were shot from their saddles in quick succession; soon only two remained visible.

A South Carolinian Maddox had eaten with the night before sang out, "See that busy bastard on the tall black horse? That there's *Ferguson himself!*"

Hearing him, Tim made a quick estimate of the range. Jesus! Ferguson wasn't riding above a hundred yards away!

Continually bumped and jostled, Tim tried to take a decent sight but simply couldn't, so, angrily, he used his left barrel to kill a big officer who, amid clouds of rolling dust, seemed to be rallying some men. Next, he debated whether or not to stop and reload Kitty's empty barrel. Hell no! He'd still a charge left so why not work his way ahead, get closer and wait for an opportunity to get a clear shot?

To any experienced officer the Tory situation had become desperate, if not hopeless; Major Ferguson, who certainly was one, nevertheless continued to rage back and forth, shouting and waving his sword. Because he'd long since lost his hat, his white wig shone bright in the hot sunlight and a silver gorget slung about his neck kept winking like a bright star.

Driven into the open the Tories milled about like deer herded into a hunter's corral but a lot of them kept right on shooting. The air around Maddox's head was full of vicious humming, whining noises.

The men who'd scaled the club's handle then began to advance along the plateau but paused when a glimmer of white cloth fluttered above the struggling throng. Tim watched Ferguson's sword flash as he cut down the surrender flag, then he did the same to a second. Ferocious, animal-like noises rose from the Volunteers along with growls and infuriated shouts of, "Remember the Waxhaws!" "Remember Monck's Corner!" "Give 'em Tarleton's quarter!" "Shoot 'em, hew the bastards down!" "Kill, kill 'em!"

By some freak of battle the clumps of men in front of Tim suddenly separated long enough to afford him a brief, unimpeded view of that raging figure on the black horse. This time, by God, Tim told himself, it wouldn't be skill but the purest kind of luck if I succeed in killing Patrick Ferguson? Shouldering his beloved Kitty he sighted as quickly as if shooting at a leaping buck, then pulled evenly on the Golcher's front trigger. Ha! Fierce delight flooded him when he saw Ferguson suddenly stiffen and then crumple over his pommel. The Tory commander clutched at his side, then sagged off his horse and disappeared among men milling desperately about him.

"By God!" Tim whooped. "Now don't that shine? Got him! Fraser with the left barrel, Ferguson with the right! Now I reckon I can die happy!"

Just an instant later he did just that, for an uncommonly brave Tory

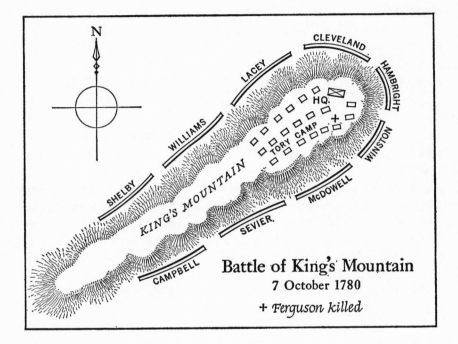

N

CLEVELAND
HAMBRIGHT
LACEY
WILLIAMS
SHELBY
KING'S MOUNTAIN
HQ.
TORY CAMP
WINSTON
McDOWELL
SEVIER.
CAMPBELL

Battle of King's Mountain
7 October 1780

+ *Ferguson killed*

who had remained in the lee of a wagon well outside the swarming mass shot Tim Murphy through the heart.

Everybody was too busy closing in on the enemy to notice the rifleman's death, and Dan Maddox by now was away off to one side leading a band of berserk Volunteers who were brandishing knives and tomahawks and ululating, "Kill the butchers!" "Slay the King-lovers!" "Tarleton's quarter!"

The battle ended shortly afterwards but not before a pair of Tories carrying white flags had been shot and killed by frontiersmen who didn't realize what they meant. Here and there, Americans kept on shooting and cutting down their fellow countrymen.

Ferguson's second-in-command, Major de Peyster of New York, forced forward his terrified mount, shrieking hoarsely, "For God's sake, stop! Stop!"

"Sure we'll stop!" shouted a big, distinguished-appearing officer. "Same way you stopped killing us at Monck's Corner and the Waxhaws!" The infuriated Volunteers continued firing into the huddled mass of humanity they were ringing until Colonel Campbell risked his life by running out into the open, holding up empty hands and yelling, "For God's sake quit! 'Tis murder to kill any more!"

Although some shooting continued on the club head's far side the staccato *crack!* of rifles gradually died out. Finally, Major de Peyster, hatless, powder-blackened and wild-eyed, emerged uncertainly from the press and advanced holding his hands high above him. "For God's sake, sir," he called to Major Evan Shelby, "what can be done to stop this slaughter?"

"Order yer officers to come out into the open straightaway, unarmed and bareheaded. Make 'em sit on the ground yonder — near that dead horse — and keep 'em quiet if they value their worthless lives."

12. Aftermath

As usual with undisciplined troops the effects of a victory proved almost as disorganizing and confusing as a defeat. For a while the victorious Volunteers remained where they were as if they couldn't comprehend that they'd won and, better yet, that most of them still were alive and unhurt. Once the initial shock wore off the victors began to look about and then move dazedly over the battlefield. Soon basic instincts asserted themselves. B'God, wasn't this just the right time to come by a good pair of boots, a fine or at least a sound rifle, a warm coat, or a bit of jewelry?

Most Volunteers began to rove about in search of dead bodies and among the bushes and weed-grown little gullies they found and stripped around one hundred and fifty-seven. Most of the enemy wounded also were plundered; if these protested, they died and not pleasantly, either. Wildly excited and vengeful riflemen continued to prowl everywhere along the crest and sides of King's Mountain, often quarreling as they found the fallen. They stuffed their pouches and carefully examined ownerless weapons.

Nobody paid the least attention to enemy wounded, no matter how a man moaned and pleaded — what had happened at Monck's Corner and the Waxhaws was still too fresh in their memories.

Dr. Mason and a few self-proclaimed medical men, working at the foot of the club's head, had an unexpectedly easy time, since only sixty-three Patriot wounded were brought in, often dripping and gritting their teeth but without exception attempting to be cheerful now that the shadow of death and destruction seemed to have been removed from their homes and loved ones.

Once the sullen and generally terrified prisoners had been placed under a guard from Colonel Cleveland's hard-bitten North Carolina Militia Regiment — which was about the only unit to preserve even a semblance of discipline — the bodies of twenty-eight Patriots were collected for burial.

Some time before this happened Dan Maddox had come to realize he hadn't sighted Tim Murphy since Sevier's men had started sweeping along the plateau towards the club's head.

Anxious, he yelled at an Over-mountain Boy he recognized, "Say, you seen anything of Murphy?"

The fellow's coonskin cap inclined as he swung by carrying a fine English saddle. "Sorry, friend, I guess he's got himself kilt."

"What!" Dan swayed as if struck by a strong wind. "You *sure?*"

"Yep, the little feller got knocked off towards the very last. It he ain't been carried off already you oughter find his corpse in a little hollow beyond the farthest wagon."

Successive ripples of icy water seemed to flow down Maddox's back to penetrate his heart. Oh hell! What was he getting so upset about? This fellow could hardly have known Tim at all; he must be mistaken! Nothing could ever happen to Tim Murphy — wasn't he as tough and durable as shoe leather?

Dan was wrong. He found Tim's small body lying all huddled up in a little gully as if he had been sleeping and had got cold. But this wasn't so; on the bottom of this depression his blood had created a glistening little pool.

For a long minute Dan Maddox stood frozen, trying to face this incredible fact. At the same time he recalled a flood of scenes: those campaigns they'd fought together up in New York State; that time an Irish bawd near had bitten his tongue through; the time Tim got carried about on his fellows' shoulders because he'd killed Burgoyne's general the way he had.

Quivering, he stood with head bent and eyes flooding until he realized only dimly that a hairy, hangdog-looking Virginia militiaman had appeared on the hollow's edge and was peering down.

The apparition then asked in obvious disappointment, "He one of ours?"

"Yes, goddam it — and one of the very best."

"You get his rifle?"

Only then did the gunsmith become aware that the famous double-barrel was missing. What kind of hellions would rob one of their own? A furious rage flooded him until he realized there was nothing to distinguish Tim's body from those of un-uniformed Tories dotting the plateau.

Once the would-be plunderer had departed Dan straightened out the body and closed the lids over Tim's small, black eyes.

Finally the gunsmith scooped the still-limp form into his arms and with a face harsh as a granite cliff carried it to a spot where silent men were beginning to dig graves.

Not far away a burial of another sort was taking place. Embittered Patriots, after having stripped Patrick Ferguson's body, divided his personal belongings — and not without considerable bickering over who should get what. More than one hollow-faced, bitter-eyed man stared on the dead commander's naked, blood-smeared corpse, then spat upon it. Presently a couple of riflemen appeared lugging the raw, red-and-yellow hide of a steer slaughtered by the Tories for breakfast. Making plenty of obscene remarks they wrapped the Englishman's body in it, then lashed the corpse tight in its grisly shroud with a length of rein from one of the wagons.

Someone grunted, "Say, fellers, just now I spied a gre't big 'chuck hole over yander; with only a little spadework 'twill do fine to hide this dog's body."

By the time twilight had set in, a comparative quiet descended upon the vicinity of King's Mountain. The prisoners, no matter how hungry and thirsty, were almighty glad to find themselves still alive although many of them foresaw that when they reached Hillsboro they likely were to get drumhead court-martials and very probably be hanged; they'd heard too many threats to expect any other fate.

Typically, most of the Volunteers wanted to go home as fast as they could; nobody felt sure that the Indians, always restless, might not have taken advantage of their absence to pounce on lonely cabins and unfortified settlements.

After supper Sam Mason, having helped to treat the last of the wounded, departed in search of Colonel Campbell's headquarters and, to his delight, came across Captain Colcord sorting captured documents by the light of a pine-knot flare. The Carolinian jumped up beaming to pump hands. "By God, Doctor, I'm mighty happy you got through all right." He hesitated, then his glad expression faded. "It's too bad about Tim Murphy."

"What about him?"

"He was killed."

"Oh God! How dreadful. He was a great friend and a wonderful man — there'll never be another like him." The physician bit his lip. "You're sure he's dead?"

"Yes, and I wish I weren't," Barry sighed, thought of his brothers and so many other good men gone. "His friend Maddox came and reported his death. The poor fellow seemed to be taking it very hard, to say the least."

Colcord folded away a sheaf of papers, then looked up. "By the way, Maddox says he is setting out for home in the morning. I presume you'd like to go with him?"

"Yes, I, too, need to get back to my wife even more than Maddox, but —"

"But what — ?"

"Well, I feel I ought to carry my report to Hillsboro personally." He smiled thinly. "Or do I appear quixotic?"

Without hesitating a second the Carolinian replied, "You do not. I see no need for you to go there — unless you want to."

"You're sure about that?"

"Absolutely! Your portfolio will be safe with me and well guarded all the way."

Samuel Mason, M.D., drew a long, slow breath. "Perhaps you're right."

"Of course I am. There's no reason why we both should go and meet that dreadful fellow Gates." Barry closed a field desk with unnecessary vigor. "Hope I arrive in time to see his replacement, General Greene, become commander-in-chief. All of us down South will feel a lot better the minute he does!"

"This is very handsome of you," the physician observed softly. "I — I hope I'm not being derelict in my duty, Barry."

Barry Colcord smiled. "You've also a duty to your wife — and my future sister-in-law — haven't you, Sam?"

"True enough, I suppose. Well, good night." He started to turn away but checked himself.

"Have you any special message for Choice?"

"Yes," smiled Barry. "Pray say that I'll come for her the very first moment I can."

"Then you'll not be going back to Carolina?"

Slowly Frederick Colcord's remaining son shook his head. "No, Sam, I don't think I'll do that. Of late I've come to believe that a better future for us all lies across the mountains."

Next morning, a band of lean, leather-clad riflemen broke camp early with the new sun warming their backs and again turned their faces toward the wild horizon.

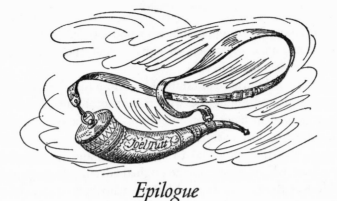

Epilogue

A T the Battle of King's Mountain the Loyalist forces were com
pletely defeated with an appalling loss of life and with all survivors captured. Through the total destruction of Major Patrick
Ferguson's force the entire left flank of Cornwallis's great army became
exposed. Consequently he was forced to abandon his advance into North
Carolina and Virginia and instead retire to winter quarters in Wilming-
ton, N. C.

Thus, the gifted fighting Quaker, General Nathanael Greene, and the
redoubtable Daniel Morgan were granted time to rally and assemble
some of the finest combat troops ever to wage war in North America. As
a result, when Lord Cornwallis resumed his northward march next
spring he continually was assailed along both flanks as well as in his front
and rear.

After the notorious Colonel Banastre Tarleton was decisively defeated
at the Cowpens, in January 1781, it was the beginning of the end for the
British forces in the South. Imaginative and crafty Patriot leaders such
as Generals Francis Marion, Daniel Morgan, "Light-Horse" Harry Lee
and others began to harry the British lines of communication with such
effectiveness that before long Lord Cornwallis was cut off from his base
at Charles Town and forced to undertake a long and difficult advance —
in reality it was a retreat — which ended disastrously at Yorktown.

When Cornwallis surrendered to Washington and Rochambeau even
the most confirmed diehard Tories in England became aware that Britain
had lost her American Colonies — but only for the time being, they
hoped.

With American and French arms triumphant and peace in sight, there
was now no need for a great retreat across the Alleghenies such as had
appeared inevitable only a short while earlier, so now the sacrifices and

sufferings of those hardy emigrants who had elected to follow Robertson, Donelson and later leaders of equal intelligence and courage appeared to have been made in vain.

Soon the original purpose of establishing those tiny, almost defenseless settlements scattered about the wildernesses of Kentucky and Middle Tennessee seemed to have been forgotten. Nevertheless, trickles of immigrants who had lost everything back East and wanted to start life anew began to arrive, prepared to settle down and gamble their lives alongside those who remained of the original adventurers.

Terrible was the fate of many of those who took part in the winter expeditions of 1779-1780. One after another isolated stations were wiped out, all too often, alas, through crass negligence and ignorance of the fact that the Indians were desperate and prepared to kill and kill and kill in order to keep their Great Hunting Ground free from white intrusion.

The bloody massacres of entire communities and the murder of countless individuals continued from 1781 until 1794, when the Battle of Fallen Timbers once and for all broke the power of tribes inhabiting what is now termed the Middle West.

John Donelson, Thomas Sharp Spencer, Mark Robertson, Isaac Bledsoe and many of their sons together with other famous frontiersmen eventually fell before the fury of the Indians. On one occasion Jonathan Robertson and his famous father were severely wounded and barely escaped with their lives; others, including John Rains, were not so fortunate. Their sacrifices, however, were not in vain; soon streams of immigrants crossed the mountains until what had once been sprawling hamlets and lonely stations developed into growing towns. Bluff Station came to be called Nashborough after General Francis Nash, a North Carolinian who had been killed in battle during the War for Independence. In 1784 it was renamed Nashville.

One of John Donelson's daughters, Rachel, became famous as the beloved wife of Andrew Jackson, while that fort which figured so importantly during the Second Civil War was named after him.

Once Tennessee had been granted statehood in 1796 the real rush began and hordes of would-be settlers poured over the Alleghenies eager to make homes in this hard-conquered promised land.

One wonders how many of these folk granted even a passing thought, let alone paid conscious tribute, to the courage and endurance of those who first had penetrated the wild horizon.